VALLEY OF LIES

A British Murder Mystery

MICHAEL CAMPLING

Shadowstone
Books

Published by Shadowstone Books
ISBN: 978-1-915507-02-0

GET THE PREQUEL FOR FREE

WHEN YOU JOIN THE AWKWARD SQUAD
- THE HOME OF PICKY READERS

Visit: michaelcampling.com / freebooks

This book is dedicated to my mum, Sheila Campling (who always knew whodunnit).

Only lying makes the difference; add that to cunning, and it is knavery.
    -Ovid

PROLOGUE

MOONLIGHT ON STILL water. A clear summer's night. The sky a pale powder blue, a hint of the solstice yet to come. But the coppice is as dark as a demon's heart, the tall switches of willow and hazel standing stiff like bones emerging from the earth, thin fingers reaching for life.

And someone is coming.

Shadows stir. Soft footsteps on grass.

A ripple dimples the water; a hand dipping below the surface, something glinting in the light. On the reservoir's bank, the dark figure stoops low, intent on a task. Silent.

Again, the water's surface is broken, but this time, the figure freezes, head turned to one side. Listening.

A sudden crack splits the silence. There's something out there, something moving through the undergrowth. But the sound is low, fast. A harmless hedgerow creature scurrying through the bracken: a badger, a fox, a rat. Nothing that need cause concern.

A soft sigh whispers across the water. The reservoir's surface is stirred once more, and then the figure rises, walks toward the coppice, and is quickly lost among the shadows.

Silence returns.
A clear summer's night.
Moonlight on still water.

FRIDAY

CHAPTER 1

"TWO POUNDS OF liver!"

Standing at the bar in The Wild Boar, a full pint glass in each hand, Dan recoiled as the plastic packet of soft meat was thrust in front of his face. But despite his revulsion, he was unable to take his eyes from the grisly parcel of shrink-wrapped offal. Kevin, the landlord of Embervale's only pub, flexed his fingers, and the livid meat squirmed inside its transparent packet as if alive.

"What's the matter?" Kevin said. "Aren't you going to check your ticket? That's prime lambs' liver, that is. Tender. You might have the winning number. Three-nine-one."

"No, I didn't buy a ticket for the meat raffle." Dan was aware of the sidelong glances he was getting from the other customers, but he wasn't going to be intimidated. "I don't eat meat."

Kevin blinked slowly. Tall and heavily built, his rugged features and thick black beard giving him the look of a lumberjack, the man seemed too large to be constrained behind the small bar. His eyes glittered darkly, and Dan fought the urge to step back. But then Kevin's features split in a wide smile, his strong teeth impossibly white against the raven black of his full beard. "Never mind. Perhaps we'll have a nut roast raffle one day, eh?"

There were murmurs of humourless laughter, enjoyment of an outsider's discomfort, and Dan turned to see a middle-aged man eyeing him with amused disdain. The man was of average height, but he had the build of an athlete: an athlete gone to seed, perhaps, but an imposing figure nevertheless. Dressed in a white T-shirt and faded denims, there was something predatory in the way the man leaned carelessly on the bar, his dark eyes locked on Dan in a calculated display of understated menace.

Dan bridled. In London, he'd go out of his way to avoid conflict, but here, in the sanctity of a small English pub in a quiet rural village, he shouldn't have to put up with this bullshit. Pulling himself up to his full height, he said, "Can I help you with something?"

The man held his gaze, unblinking, then he chuckled. When he spoke, his voice was hard, his flat vowels placing his origins firmly in the north of England. "Don't mind me. I wasn't laughing at you." He inclined his head toward the landlord. "Friendly bunch, aren't they? I've lived here for six years and they still treat me like the new boy." He straightened his back, offering his hand for a shake. "Name's Jay. Embervale's official Yorkshireman-in-exile."

Dan set down a glass and shook Jay's hand. "I'm Dan. Nice to meet you. You must know my neighbour, Alan. He's from the north somewhere, I think."

Jay's smile tightened. "I know Alan Hargreaves, all right. But he's a scouser, isn't he? We don't call that north where I come from."

"And that would be Leeds."

"How did you know that?" Jay asked. "The lads back home reckon my accent went south when I did."

"You have it tattooed on your arm," Dan replied. "I

suppose LUFC could stand for something other than Leeds United, but the white rose gives it away."

Jay laughed, his hand going to his bicep to touch the small tattoo peeking out from his sleeve. "Fair play. I forget about the tats. It's been so long since I had them done."

Dan picked up his pint. "Well, I'd better get back with these drinks. Alan will be getting thirsty."

"That's right," Kevin said. "Don't waste good drinking time." He'd followed Dan's conversation with rapt interest, and now he grinned in approval. "You and Alan have been in here a few times. Friend, is it? Visiting like?"

"Neighbour, actually. I'm at The Old Shop. It's my sister's place. I'm staying there for a while."

"Local then. As good as, anyway." The change in Kevin's attitude was instant, his features growing more animated, and he spoke quickly, his words blurring into each other in a rush. "Any time you feel like a drink, you come along. We're having a quiz tomorrow. Usually a good crowd for that. Starts around eight, but you'll want to get here before then, to get organised with your team and all that. We've a nice guest ale, should be ready for tomorrow night. Gun Dog. Brewed local. Just the job for these summer nights. Drinks lovely, it does."

Dan frowned, his mind racing to catch up with the rapid ebb and flow of Kevin's speech. Dan had assumed he'd have no difficulty with the Devon accent, imagining it was normal English only spoken a little slower. But he'd been in Embervale for a few weeks now, and it was clear that the locals had other ideas. They changed some words, invented new ones and missed others out entirely. Dan found himself cast in the role of the slow-minded idiot who couldn't keep up, and he didn't like it at all. So instead of asking Kevin to repeat himself, he simply said, "Right. Thanks. Maybe. We'll see."

Kevin's smile seemed fixed, and he stared at Dan, expecting more.

"Hey, Kev!" someone called out. "Are you doing this raffle or what?"

Kevin looked away and, the spell broken, Dan made a beeline for his seat by the window. From behind him, Kevin called out, "And the winner of this beautiful liver is pink ticket number three hundred and ninety-one!"

"Got it!" someone replied. Amid a barrage of murmured moans, an elderly man bustled through the crowd, holding a pink paper ticket aloft as though it were a communiqué from the Queen.

Dan set the pints on the table, retaking his seat on the red velour chair, and Alan looked up expectantly, his expression brightening. "At last. I was about to send out a search party." He took an experimental sip then sat back, watching as Dan tried his drink. "What did you have? Looks like IPA."

Dan took a long draught before replying. "Yes. It's not bad."

"IPA's all right, I suppose. It's the trendy drink at the moment, isn't it? Everybody keeps trying to invent some new variety of the stuff. Still, at least we've managed to wean you off the bottled beer."

"Nothing wrong with bottled craft beer. Each to his own." Dan took another long drink, then let out a murmur of content. "I'll give you one thing, though. This place is a damned sight cheaper than London. Whenever I get a round in, I keep thinking they've got the price wrong."

"You should try the Jail Ale, like me. It's that bit stronger, so you get even more bang for your buck." Alan cast a sideways look at the bar. "I see you've been making friends with the locals. What did Jay have to say for himself?"

"Not much. The man has a chip on both shoulders. He seemed to know you, but not, I'd guess, in a good way. Which is odd, because you seem to be on good terms with everyone."

Alan shrugged. "Jay's all right, I suppose. But I've never

been quite sure what he does for a living. People say he's an ex-copper, but he doesn't seem to have a regular job. He's in here most nights, flashing the cash, buying drinks for people. I reckon he keeps this place afloat single-handed. But there's always an ulterior motive with him, always something he wants in return. Do you know what I mean?"

"Oh yes. I know the type." Dan looked around the room. The raffle was still in full swing, and a young woman was proudly showing her friends her prize: an oddly shaped hunk of shrink-wrapped meat big enough to feed a family of six. "This raffle, do they really do it every week?"

"Yes. It's surprisingly popular. I don't usually take part, though. I don't have much use for big lumps of meat when I'm on my own."

"Thank goodness for small mercies. If I had to spend the evening with a chunk of raw meat sitting on the table, I might be tempted to make my excuses and leave. Especially on a warm night like this. It can't be hygienic."

Alan shrugged. "It's all vacuum-packed, and it's never done the locals any harm. At any rate, no one's died yet."

A yell from across the room made them both sit up with a start. A small knot of customers surrounded some kind of scuffle, and Kevin was already striding out from behind the bar, his broad shoulders back. "Enough of that," he boomed. "I'll have none of that behaviour in here."

A man in his early twenties stepped back from the crowd, his face pale, his hair tousled and his rat-like features twisted into an evil sneer. "He started it, Kev. Mouthing off, as per bloody usual. Ask anyone." He pointed, and Dan recognised the accused as the elderly man who'd won the liver.

"I've done nothing," the old man protested. "You bloody people are all the same. Nothing but a bunch of lazy bastards. Nothing better to do than gossip behind a man's back. Following me around, poking your noses in, making your snide little threats. Well, I won't stand for it, do you hear me? I won't bloody stand for it!"

Kevin folded his arms, then he fixed the old man with a stern look. "I reckon you've had enough for one night, Morty. Come back another day when you've cooled down. But you'll mind your manners or you'll not be served, understand?"

"It's Mr Gamble to you," the old man snapped. "And I don't have to stand here listening to all this rubbish. I won't waste another minute of my time on you bloody people. I'm going, all right, and to hell with the lot of you." Turning on his heel, he marched away, and pausing only to nod to a grey-haired woman sitting alone at a table beside the door, he swept outside.

Kevin cast a warning glance at the group of young men, then he strode back to his position behind the bar, his expression unreadable. The background buzz of conversation resumed, but now there was an undercurrent of snickering derision and the young man's friends were slapping him on the back, laughing. They were pleased with themselves and already retelling the story, no doubt building the petty argument into a confrontation on a much grander scale.

But Dan found his attention going back to the grey-haired woman beside the door. Despite Morty's obvious rage, he'd taken the time to nod to her; he'd made a point of it. And yet the woman hadn't met his eye. Instead, she'd sat erect, almost regal, her sombre gaze focused on no one in particular. It must've taken some effort to assume such an air of cool indifference when the peace of the quiet pub had been disturbed right in front of her. But nevertheless, she'd managed it.

And there was something else: a tiny gesture that had almost gone unnoticed. But it had piqued Dan's interest, and he watched the woman for a minute before turning to Alan. "Do you know that lady? The one by the door."

Alan nodded. "That's Marge. At least, that's what most

people call her, though it had better be *Mrs Treave* or *Marjorie* if you speak to her. Why?"

"I'm not sure. Does she know the man who stormed out just now? Are they friends?"

"I don't know. They're of the same vintage, you might say, and they're both local. She lives in The Old Buttery. It's a lovely old cottage, or it could be with a bit of work to modernise the plumbing and such. She must be acquainted with Mortimer, but that's probably as far as it goes. Marge keeps herself to herself, as you can probably see." He took a drink. "Why do you ask?"

Dan wrinkled his nose. "Probably nothing."

"Oh, no it isn't." Alan leaned forward, lowering his voice. "What is it? What did you see this time?"

"It's not a party trick," Dan said. "I can't help it if I'm more observant than most people. It's just the way my mind works."

"I disagree. You're an inveterate people-watcher. You work at it. I've seen you do it." Alan clicked his fingers. "That woman in John Lewis. You were dead right about her. I didn't believe you for a second. She looked like such a nice, middle-class lady, but you had her number. Half an hour later, there she was, being led out in handcuffs. Caught shoplifting, just like you predicted."

Dan chuckled under his breath. "Oh please. One look at her shoulder bag was enough for me. It's one thing to sport a Mulberry calf's leather bag on a trip to the West End, but for an afternoon trudging around Exeter? And anyway, it had been repaired, very badly. Then there were the stains on her skirt. Anyone could see the woman had fallen on hard times, but she still craved luxury. Do you see?"

"So she visited an upmarket shop, knowing she couldn't afford to buy," Alan said. "The poor woman."

"A thief. And I wouldn't call John Lewis upmarket. I suppose for Exeter it's high-end, but…"

"Here we go," Alan said. "Nothing around here quite matches up to London. We're all just peasants with no clue about anything."

"Oh, come on. I've never said anything like that."

"You've implied it often enough."

"Well, if I've offended you, I'm sorry," Dan said. "But that's never been my intention."

The two men eyed each other warily until Alan broke the silence. "I fancy some crisps." He stood. "Do you want anything? I don't know which ones are vegan, I'm afraid. Presumably not the cheese and onion."

"That's right, but funnily enough, the meat-flavoured ones are usually fine. No meat in them at all." Dan smiled. "If they have them, I like the chilli flavour. That would be great, thanks."

"No problem." Alan headed to the bar, and Dan sat quietly, sipping his pint. But his gaze wandered back to Marjorie Treave. She was watching the group of young men, following their conversation. And in such a small way that almost no one would notice, she was smiling to herself.

Alan was right, Dan thought. *I do have a tendency to watch people, looking for clues*. It wasn't a habit he'd consciously acquired—it was more of a natural ability—but in his old job in the City, his flair for perceptive observation had stood him in good stead.

He'd been involved in scores of high-stakes negotiations, and unlike the showdowns between heroic individuals depicted by Hollywood, clashes in the boardroom were always crowded and messy affairs: competing groups vying for some advantage, jockeying for position, constantly probing the boundaries of the debate to see what they could get away with. In these situations, a fleeting glance, a twitch at the corner of a lip or a tightening of the muscles around the eye could speak volumes. Dan had grown adept at noticing such things.

Like now, for instance, as he watched the carefree way Alan sauntered back from the bar, he knew that the storm clouds of disagreement had passed. Alan was an open book: slow to anger and quick to forgive and forget. Sure enough, Alan grinned as he tossed a packet of crisps onto the table. "Thai chilli. I asked Kev to check the ingredients very thoroughly, just to see his face. Priceless."

"Thanks. How much do I owe you?"

Alan waved his words away as he sat down. "Don't worry about it. You can get the snacks next time."

"Deal."

They sat in companionable silence for a while, crunching on crisps and sipping their drinks, until Alan said, "Okay, it's driving me mad and I have to know. What did Marge do that was worth noticing? Because I didn't see a thing, and I have to admit, if it was anything outlandish, I'd be surprised. Very surprised indeed."

"On the face of it, it wasn't anything shocking. But when the old man nodded to her, she didn't make eye contact with him. She shook her head ever so slightly. Just enough to mean *no*."

"No? Well, that makes sense. She probably thought Morty was making a fool of himself, and I expect she didn't approve. Marge is a quiet sort of person. Polite but very reserved."

"No, it wasn't disapproval," Dan said. "It was more definite than that. A signal, or an instruction, perhaps even an order."

"Good luck to her if she's trying to take Morty in hand. He doesn't take a blind bit of notice of anyone, and he doesn't care who he rubs up the wrong way. He shouted at me in the street once, apparently under the impression I'd pinched something from his front garden."

"And had you?"

"No. Of course I hadn't. I stopped to admire his roses for a

13

second, that was all. The next thing I knew, the old fool was yelling at me through the window." He laughed under his breath. "I just gave him a smile and a friendly wave. There was no way I was going to give him the satisfaction of spoiling my day."

"Always forgive your enemies; nothing annoys them so much," Dan said. "Oscar Wilde."

"Yes, I've always liked that one. But seriously, do you really think mousy little Marge can boss a man like Morty around? I can't see it myself."

"But I *did* see it. I'm sure of it. The question is, what was she saying no to?"

Alan tilted his head to one side. "Unless… No. You don't think she meant *not tonight*, do you? As if she was turning him down, fending off his passionate advances."

"These things happen. It's a small village. People get lonely."

"Yes, but those two? I'm not being ageist, but I can't see them as the Romeo and Juliet of Embervale." Alan glanced over at Marjorie. "She's a nice lady. A gentle soul really. You often see her out walking across the fields. She goes for miles. I think she picks wild flowers because she always seems to have a trug on her arm. That's a kind of wide basket."

"I know what a trug is," Dan said. "My mother had one. But you're not helping your argument. It sounds to me as though she's a romantic character, so why shouldn't she fall in love?"

"No reason at all. She lives alone, and so does Morty, but honestly, you saw what he's like. Obnoxious. Maybe he has a grudging respect for Marge, but I'm willing to bet that's all there is to it."

"Don't look now," Dan said. "She's leaving." He watched Marjorie Treave straighten her tweed skirt as she stood, then she picked up her empty sherry glass and headed for the bar.

"Wrong again," Alan said in a stage whisper. "She's going for a refill. She has a taste for dry sherry."

But Dan didn't reply. He was taking in the stately way she crossed the room, her posture proudly upright. Instead of making a detour around the gaggle of young men gathered beside the pub's only fruit machine, she marched into their midst. If she was intimidated by their open-mouthed stares, it didn't show in her haughty expression. But before any of the young men could speak, she fixed her eyes on the individual who'd badgered Morty.

"Steven Holder, you ought to be ashamed of yourself, boy," Marge snapped, her voice edged with steel. "I knew your mother, God rest her soul, knew her like she was my own daughter. I can tell you, she'd be sore disappointed in you, boy. Carrying on like that, tormenting poor old Mr Gamble. It's a disgrace. Pure and simple."

Every head in the room turned to watch Marjorie's speech, but no one said a word.

One of Steven's friends started to laugh, and Dan held his breath, his whole body tensing. The mood of the young men was already shifting, an ugly hatred in their eyes. Dan was no barroom brawler, but he could handle himself well enough, and there was no way he'd stand back and let an elderly woman go unprotected. Thankfully, he wouldn't be alone in stepping forward: Alan was already pushing back his chair, ready to move.

"Shut up!" Steven barked. But his anger was not directed at Marjorie. He was glaring at his snickering friend, his hands forming into fists. "Shut your gob, you stupid bastard!"

All the young men took half a step back from each other, eyes flicking around the group as they weighed the odds, chose sides.

Dan started to stand, but Alan laid a restraining hand on his arm. "It's all right," Alan muttered. And when a loud voice boomed across the bar, Dan understood.

"Now, now, children," Kevin called out, shouldering his way into the throng. "Behave yourselves, boys and girls. Don't make me knock some sense into your thick heads." He bared his teeth in the parody of a smile, the fierce glint in his eyes saying he'd like nothing better than to be provoked.

Steven scowled, shaking his head, but his friends had seen enough. "Come on, Steve," one of them said. "Let's get out of here. We can go around mine. I've got plenty of lagers in."

Steven fixed Kevin with a look, then he nodded to his friend. "Yeah, all right. I'm sick of this place, anyway. The beer tastes like rat piss." He threw a scowl around the room, then he made for the door, his friends following behind.

Kevin held out his hand to Marjorie, indicating her glass. "Can I take that for you, m'dear? Refill? On the house."

Marjorie thought for a moment. "No, I don't think so. I've had enough sherry. But since you're paying, I'll have a G and T. And just for taking such a casual tone with me, you'd better make it a double."

Kevin's bellowed laughter broke the tension, and as others joined in, more than one person gave a cheer. Kevin returned to his position, and Marjorie hoisted herself onto a bar stool, perching on its edge as she waited for her drink.

In seconds, the scene had returned to normal, and Dan shared a look with Alan. "Is it always like this on a Friday night?"

"Certainly not," Alan replied. "It's usually much more exciting and dramatic."

"Really?"

"No. Don't be silly. It was a joke."

"Thank God for that," Dan said. "I don't want to go through that again in a hurry. I thought we were about to have a murder on our hands."

"Yes. Marge is a tough old girl, but I wouldn't have given much for her chances against that lot. Still, it would never have come to that. We'd have stepped in, and I dare say a few more would've helped."

Dan took a gulp of his drink. Then another. He was thinking about the way Steven Holder had hung his head when Marge had scolded him, turning on his own friend for laughing at her. Dan looked at Marjorie with fresh eyes. Here was a formidable lady: not some frail senior citizen, but a woman with authority. A woman with power. And she was very careful and very calculating in the way she chose to wield her influence.

Fascinating, he thought. *There's something going on here. Something below the surface, something I can't quite see.*

And when he took his eyes from Marjorie, he saw that she was the focus of someone else's attention. Jay was staring at her from his place along the bar. There was a cold darkness in his glare: a gleam of... what? Resentment? Suppressed anger?

The man was holding back a deeply felt emotion, but what lay at its heart, Dan couldn't decide. He only knew that whatever it was, it sent a shiver to run down his spine.

CHAPTER 2

THE NIGHT WAS still warm as Dan walked back from the pub with Alan. There'd been no further incidents or upsets, and together they'd spent a pleasant few hours talking about nothing in particular and sharing a joke or two.

They left Fore Street, turning into the lane that led down to their houses, and Dan stopped, looking up at the night sky and breathing deeply. "I can't get used to the stars. So many."

"It's the lack of light pollution." Alan joined him in admiring the heavens. "You should see it in winter. On a clear frosty night, the Milky Way is fantastic."

Dan didn't reply. *I'll be long gone before winter*, he thought. *Back to London and night skies obliterated by a dull orange glow.* But he didn't want to linger on thoughts of his real home, and anyway, it would be churlish to spoil the moment. So he stood, gazing upward, and listened patiently while Alan pointed out a few constellations, old memories stirring in the back of his mind.

"I used to do this when I was little," Dan said. "My dad used to show me the planets and constellations. Sometimes, we'd go out in the garden and, if there was a bit of mist in the air, he'd shine a torch up into the sky, tracing out the shapes, over and over again until I could see them."

"Ah, that's a nice memory. Is he…?"

Dan looked down. "Yes, he's still alive, but Mum and Dad are separated."

"I'm sorry to hear that. I didn't mean to pry."

"It's all right. They split up six years ago. Mum went to live in Brighton and Dad moved to the Lake District. I think they were trying to get as far away from each other as possible without actually leaving the country. They parted amicably enough, but it makes it hard to see them as often as I'd like. I must visit them both soon. Especially Dad; it's been ages."

"It's a long and tortuous drive to the Lake District from this part of the world," Alan replied. "Beautiful when you get there, though. He'll be pleased to see you."

"Yes. But you know how it is. He'll want to know what I'm doing with my life. And since I left my job…"

"It's more like your job left you," Alan said. "If you ask me, you're well out of it."

"Maybe." Dan hesitated. "How about you? Are your parents still alive?"

"Mum and Dad are down in Cornwall. A cottage by the sea."

"Sounds idyllic," Dan said, and a slight pang of envy drew tight in his stomach. Although they were about the same age, Alan's life was so much more ordered than his. Alan lived in a cosy little house, everything neat and in its proper place. Although he never boasted, Alan was doing well. Dan had looked online, and Alan's adventure stories for children were popular, selling all around the world. They were a big hit with parents and teachers too. There was talk of prizes and awards. And now this: the perfect set of proud parents living in the neighbouring county in a cottage by the sea. *Still, there's no sense in being jealous*, Dan told himself. *Good luck to him.*

Breaking in on his thoughts, Alan said, "What did you think to that last pint?"

"I think," Dan said, laying his hand on his stomach, "I think I probably shouldn't have had it."

Alan chuckled. "But the Jail Ale, what did you think of it?"

"It was good. Better than I expected. I see what you mean about it being stronger, but it was nice."

"Say what you like about Kev, but he keeps a good cellar."

"In that case, I'll say that for a big man, Kevin has very small feet. And very fancy shoes."

"You and your shoes. What are they, running shoes or something? I must say, I can't see Kev pounding the streets in Lycra."

"Nobody runs in Lycra anymore. Anyway, that's not what I meant." Dan scratched his chin. "I've lost my thread. Where was I?"

"Kevin's fashion sense, or lack of it."

Dan clicked his fingers. "Ah! I've just remembered. I was supposed to tell you something. When I got the last round in, Kevin said you'd left your hiking stick behind. The last time we were in, after that walk on Wednesday, you left it on the floor."

"Damn. I'm always leaving it somewhere or other. I suppose it's too late to go back for it now."

"I wouldn't bother. He's put it behind the bar for you." Dan offered an apologetic smile. "I meant to tell you, but then you got on to that joke about the camels, and for some reason it slipped my mind."

"That's my standby joke," Alan said. "I keep it in reserve for emergencies."

"I'm not sure how to take that. I'm flattered you've shared

one of your limited supply of jokes with me, but on the other hand, I'm slightly offended that an evening in my company represents some form of emergency."

"Well, if I'm honest, you were getting a bit maudlin, banging on about some girl or other."

"*Some girl?*" Dan puffed out his chest. "Frankie Herringway has been described as many things, but no one, not since she cast aside her knee-high hockey socks in favour of a Beverly Hills haute couture business suit, has ever referred to her as *a girl*."

"And *that* is why I broke out the camel joke. No sense in moping over a woman you broke up with months ago. Move on; I'll bet she has."

"Easy for you to say."

"Meaning what?" Alan asked. "I haven't always been single, you know. I do have some idea about women."

"It's hardly the same. The height of sophistication in this village is wearing wellies that match your thorn-proof waxed jacket."

"And what's wrong with that? Personally, I prefer to spend my time with someone who has their feet on the ground: someone who understands what's really important in life. It's all very well knowing one pair of shoes from another, but what good are your Johnny Choos when your car breaks down in the middle of Dartmoor and it's a twenty-mile hike before even the fanciest new phone can get a signal?"

The two men locked eyes, but it wasn't long before a burst of laughter escaped from Dan's lips. "You're right. It's Jimmy Choo, by the way, not Johnny, but your point still stands. Not everyone in London is posh, far from it, but in the company I kept... Let's just say that when I lost my job, the silence was deafening."

"You'll get back on your feet soon enough, you'll see. A few more nights in the pub and you'll be rehabilitated entirely." Alan laughed under his breath. "We had a good night, didn't we? The threat of a punch-up notwithstanding."

"Yes." Dan smiled, looking back along the street toward the pub, and a movement caught his eye: a solitary figure marching along the side of the road, the person casting a long shadow as they marched away from the lonely beam of the only working street light. "Speaking of which, that looks like Marjorie."

"Yes. On her way home." Alan raised a hand in greeting, but Marjorie Treave was intent on her purpose, looking neither to the left or the right, and she passed them by, oblivious to their presence.

They watched her as she turned from the main street, making her way into a quiet lane that led away from Embervale. The lane's pitted tarmac was just wide enough to admit a car, and Marjorie quickly disappeared into the deep shadows that lingered beneath the tall hedgerows.

"Should we let her go down there alone?" Dan asked. "She doesn't even have a torch."

"She's all right. She lives right on the edge of the village. Her place stands on its own. A little way down that lane, there's a public footpath to one side. You'd miss it unless you knew it was there. It leads across a couple of fields, then it goes past Marjorie's cottage. It's not far, and she's made that journey many times over the years. She could probably walk it with her eyes closed."

"Even so, it doesn't seem right. Anything could happen."

Alan held out his hands. "Like what? How many cars have passed while we've been standing here?"

"None. But anyone could be wandering about down there. Those lads from the pub; they'd know that she'd come this way."

"Steve isn't that bad," Alan said. "I know he looks a bit rough around the edges, but it's all talk: a show of bravado. I don't think he'd hurt anybody. He'll be round at a mate's house drinking warm lager and watching football."

Dan grunted under his breath. "I suppose you're right. Anyway, Marjorie wouldn't thank me if I offered to walk her home."

"Definitely not. And you wouldn't want to go bumbling about near her house at this time of night. Her geese would probably attack you."

"She has geese?" Dan asked. "Strange."

"Not really. Quite a few people keep them. The eggs are wonderful. She has chickens too, and a goat. She grows all her own veg. They say she's pretty much self-sufficient. She even keeps bees."

"A menagerie. She looks after all that on her own?"

Alan nodded. "Sure. Well, it's about time I turned—"

Alan's words were cut short by a guttural yell: a man's voice, strained to breaking point, a furious full-throated roar echoing along the empty street.

"Marge!" Alan said, his face pale. "That came from the field she goes through."

"I'm not sure," Dan said, turning, listening hard. Waiting. "The echoes... it's hard to tell."

Another shout: "Get out of here! Go!" And this time, he knew Alan was right. The yells were definitely coming from the direction where Marjorie had headed.

"Come on." Dan set off, running into the lane's dark mouth, Alan hard on his heels.

Another burst of outraged hollering rolled through the still night air, the words lost in a babble of incoherent rage. Dan ran faster, spurred on as the cries of anger gave way to howls of anguish. He couldn't see where he was going, and he almost turned his ankle as his feet found a pothole. But he ran on, his breath thick and fast in his throat, his heart hammering. He'd missed his regular runs for the last few days, and now he cursed his own laziness. His head spun, his legs unsteady as he raced over the uneven surface. The beer he'd so enjoyed now churned in his stomach, his gut cramping, but he pushed the sensation aside and ran on. A thin branch whipped across his face, narrowly missing his eye, but he didn't slow his pace.

A blue-white light glimmered on the tarmac: Alan using his phone as a flashlight. *Good idea.* But Dan didn't stop to take out his own phone. "Where's the footpath?"

"Wait," Alan called out from behind him. "I'll have to show you."

"There's no time!" But Dan had no choice; he'd never find the path on his own. He staggered to a halt, breathing hard. "Quickly. It's gone quiet." He turned around, but the only sound was Alan's footsteps as he hurried to catch up.

"Wait a minute." Alan gasped for air. "Whoever it is, they could be anywhere. Once you stray from the path, there's nothing but fields for miles."

"We have to start somewhere. Show me the path." Dan fumbled for his phone and switched on the flashlight, playing its white beam along the hedgerow.

Alan strode past him. "Here! It's here." He clambered up the bank as if climbing into the hedgerow, but when Dan joined him, he saw a narrow wooden gate set back from the lane, and an algae-streaked sign pointing to the open space beyond.

Alan barged through the gate, Dan right behind him. "Which way?" Dan shone his phone's flashlight across the expanse of tall bracken that stretched out on either side, but its pale beam was swallowed up by the darkness.

"It's right in front of us." Alan urged him onward, indicating a faint path with his flashlight: a thin cleft in the towering bracken. Dan crept forward, unnerved by the oppressive darkness beyond his flashlight's meagre beam. The bracken's soft fingers dragged against his legs as he passed, and flying insects, attracted by the light, fluttered in front of him, danced erratically from side to side, then flitted away. A sudden breeze stirred the bracken, the fronds shushing gently against their neighbours, and brigades of crickets chirred in a demented whispering symphony. Something whined in Dan's ear and, startled, he flapped it away then immediately felt foolish.

"Can you see anything?" Alan asked.

Dan stopped. "No. What's happened to Marjorie? She's nowhere in sight."

"It's not far to her house. She might've made it home before all that shouting started."

"I hope so." Dan started forward, but a soft sound rose over the crackling rhythm of their footsteps, and he stopped in his tracks. From somewhere in the expanse of swaying bracken, a low cry was carried on the breeze, and the murmured moan was heavy with despair.

"This way!" Dan struck out across the bracken, taking great strides. The vegetation was taller here, as high as his chest, but he pushed the stems aside and moved on.

"We're headed toward the spoil heaps," Alan said. "Whoever it is, they must be up there."

"What kind of spoil heaps? Are they dangerous?"

"There were mines out here. Silver and lead. They say the spoil heaps are safe, but nothing grows on them. It's not a place I'd want to hang around, especially after dark. Maybe I should call an ambulance. If someone's fallen…"

Dan took a breath. "Give it a minute. It might be nothing: kids mucking about, a drunk."

Another moan, quieter this time, and though the breeze made it hard to pinpoint the source of the sound, Dan broke into a jog, Alan following close behind.

Soon, the bracken gave way to gravel, the stones crunching underfoot. In front of them, rising sharply from the landscape, ridged banks of stony grey earth climbed into the night, the rugged slopes bleak and naked. Against the backdrop of lush vegetation, the spoil heaps' sterile surface seemed otherworldly, as if a chunk of the lunar landscape had been smuggled back to Earth in the dead of night.

"Hello?" Alan called out at the top of his voice. "Is anyone up there? We're here to help."

There was no reply.

"They must've heard that," Dan said. "Either they're unconscious, or they don't want to be found."

"So what do we do? Do we climb up?" Alan shone his light along the spoil heaps. "These things are huge. I don't know where to start."

"Look for footprints. A track. Anything. You go that way, and I'll head in the opposite direction. If you see anything, shout."

"Will do," Alan said, and moving slowly, they separated to skirt the lower edge of the heaps, the gravel rasping beneath their shoes with every step.

Dan had rarely felt so alone, so exposed. But at the same time, he was exhilarated, a savage sense of excitement thrilling through him. This was real. It meant something. He'd faced physical challenges before, but nothing could compare to this. For the first time in his life, the fate of another human being hung in the balance. If he failed now, a man may die.

"Hey!" It was Alan, his voice sharp. "Over here! Quick!"

Dan sprang into action, haring along the slope's edge, arms pumping. Ahead, Alan's phone bobbed in the darkness, loose stones skittering down the slope as he clambered up the unforgiving terrain. Dan dashed toward him, covering the distance in seconds. And there, on the slope, a dark shape lay immobile. A figure. A man.

Alan reached him first and crouched at his side. "Mr Gamble," Alan said, then again, raising his voice: "Mr Gamble! Mortimer, can you hear me? Are you all right?"

Dan slowed as he reached them, squatting next to the

stricken figure and shining his light along the man's body. He wasn't sure what he was looking for, but he saw no obvious signs of injury. Mortimer Gamble's face was pale, streaked with dust, but he seemed placid, his eyes closed, and Dan felt a flood of relief; it could've been so much worse.

"He's alive," Alan said. "I'm calling an ambulance. Don't try to move him. His head…" He stepped away, lifting his phone to make the call.

There's nothing wrong with his head, Dan told himself. *He must be stunned, that's all.* But when he stood and walked carefully around the unconscious figure, Dan's breath caught in his chest.

Mortimer Gamble had suffered a terrible wound to the side of his head, and a thin trail of dark blood still trickled from a deep gash above his ear. The bleeding had almost stopped, but he'd lost enough blood to form a broad stain on the ground, and Dan was forced to accept the facts that his mind had tried to reject. Mortimer's body was limp, his features robbed of their natural expression, his face ashen. Dan could hear Mortimer's shallow, halting breath, but the old man seemed unbearably frail, as though he was already slipping into death.

"We're getting someone to help you," Dan said, hoping Mortimer would hear him. When he shone his light on the man's face, Mortimer's eyelids twitched. "Don't try to move," Dan went on. "Stay very still. You've hurt your head, but help is on its way. It's very important that you don't move."

A wheezing whisper escaped from Mortimer's lips, and Dan leaned close. "Mr Gamble, don't try to talk. Save your strength."

But Mortimer's eyes fluttered open, just a slit, squinting into the light, and Dan moved his flashlight away.

"Stop them," Mortimer whispered.

"Stay calm," Dan began, but it seemed as though Mortimer couldn't hear him.

"Don't let them get away with it," Mortimer said, his face pinched in pain. "I'm begging you. Stop them. Whatever it takes. Stop them."

"All right," Dan said. "Whatever it is, don't worry about it. Just lie still."

And with a long, rattling sigh, Mortimer Gamble closed his eyes.

MONDAY

CHAPTER 3

A T HOME IN the kitchen, Dan was halfway through his
second coffee of the morning when someone knocked
at his front door. But he didn't answer. He stood, bleary eyed,
leaning against the kitchen counter as he drained his mug
dry. *Let them wait.* He hadn't slept much the night before, nor
the night before that. And Friday night had been a write-off:
answering questions, repeating himself to faceless people in
uniforms, and yet receiving no answers himself. It wasn't
until Saturday that Alan had come around to tell him the
news: Mortimer Gamble had made it to the hospital, but he'd
died from his injuries. An elderly man, and not in the best of
health, the blow to his head had caused swelling and internal
bleeding. He'd been made comfortable, but he hadn't
regained consciousness, and in the early hours of Saturday,
he'd passed away.

Alan had done his best to soften the blow, but from the
moment he'd heard the grim tidings, Dan had been swamped
with guilt and confusion. How could this have happened?
And why hadn't he found the old man sooner? Perhaps he
could've done more to help, perhaps he could've done
something.

But try as he might, he couldn't rewrite the past, and now the future seemed more uncertain than ever. Dan only knew that he couldn't go on as before, living from one moment to the next, squandering his days. A man was dead. Dan had been the last to hear him speak.

He put the empty mug in the sink where it sat alongside a solitary side plate, the toast crumbs still on it. At least he'd had some breakfast today, his appetite returning. Maybe he'd take a long walk, get some air, clear his head. But he'd have to take the car and get well clear of the village. In one weekend, Dan had gone from anonymous outsider to minor celebrity, and now everyone in Embervale knew his name. Over the last two days, it felt as though half of the village's residents had asked him how he was, while the other half had peered at him with open curiosity. Only Alan remained the same, having the good sense to remain quiet and offer no sympathies. Could it be him knocking at the front door? No. Alan always came through the back garden, usually tapping at the kitchen window.

Another knock, more insistent. *This had better not be some busybody*, Dan thought, and he went to find out who'd come calling.

The man on the doorstep was in his late fifties and smartly dressed, though there was an air of shabbiness to his blazer: the bold tartan check faded, the sleeves frayed at the cuffs. The jacket, perhaps, was an old favourite, bought at a time when the man's shoulders had been squarer, his back straighter. His waistcoat had certainly last been adjusted when his stomach had been flatter.

But the man's gaze was sharp and he studied Dan for a second, sizing him up. Only then did he offer an identity card. "Detective Sergeant Spiller, Devon and Cornwall Constabulary. It's Mr Corrigan, isn't it?" His smile was businesslike but not unfriendly, his tone authoritative but edged with sincerity, the hint of a Midlands accent lingering in the cadence of his voice. His eyebrows lowered in concern. "I do have the right house, don't I?"

Dan nodded. "Yes, I'm Dan Corrigan. Sorry, what was your name again?"

The smile was back. "DS Spiller. I called earlier, and you said this would be a good time."

"Yes, of course. I'm not quite with it this morning. Come in." Dan stood back to allow DS Spiller to enter, and with the door closed, the narrow hallway seemed cramped. "We can talk in the kitchen," Dan said, leading the way. "Tea? Coffee?"

"No thanks. I'm fine." Spiller cast an appraising glance around the room. "Just you, is it? No one else home?"

"Just me. This is my sister's place. I'm staying here while she's abroad. San Francisco."

"Very nice." Spiller laid his hand on a chair. "All right if I take a seat?"

"Please. Go ahead."

They sat, facing each other across the pine table, Dan leaning forward, but Spiller taking his ease, smiling as he produced a pocket notebook and pen, flipping the pages with a practised ease. "Thanks for seeing me this morning, Mr Corrigan. I know this must've been a trying time for you, so I'll try to keep this short, okay?"

"Sure. But I don't know what else I can tell you. I've already said what happened, and I haven't really got anything else to add."

Spiller nodded slowly. "That's fine. I've read your statement, but there are a few things I want to check. It never hurts to be thorough, in my experience."

"Okay. What do you want to know?"

"How long had you known Mr Gamble?" Spiller asked.

"Oh, I didn't know him at all."

"Really? It's a small village, but you'd never passed the time of day, talked about the weather?"

Dan took a breath. *He doesn't believe me*, he thought. *Why would I lie?* But he already knew the answer: he'd lie if he had something to hide. He'd lie if he'd been involved in the attack.

"It's a straightforward question," Spiller insisted with an amiable smile. "I'm not trying to trip you up, Mr Corrigan."

"As far as I know, I'd never laid eyes on Mr Gamble until Friday night. I saw him in the pub, but we didn't speak to each other. Not until we found him."

"So, when you heard him call out, you had no idea who it was, but you went to help, running out into the dark field to help a complete stranger."

Dan shrugged. "Yes. It's just what anyone would do, isn't it?"

Spiller chortled softly. "You'd be surprised. Very few people would do what you did. Almost everyone looks the other way, walks on by. They hear a noise and they hurry home, draw the curtains."

"I suppose so. It's certainly like that back home, but I thought that out here it would be different."

"And where's home, Mr Corrigan?"

"London. I gave my address before. Do you want it again?"

Spiller glanced at his notebook. "No, that won't be necessary. How long do you intend to stay in Embervale?"

"I haven't decided. I'm helping my sister to refurbish this place, and I'm between jobs, so I have no reason to hurry back."

"No commitments, then. That must be nice."

Dan made a noncommittal noise in his throat, but Spiller watched him as if expecting more, so Dan asked, "Is there anything else I can help you with? Only, I was going to go out later."

"Somewhere interesting?"

"Not really. I need to buy some paint. For the house."

"In that case, we'll press on. On the night of the incident, you mentioned that Mrs Marjorie Treave entered the lane before you heard someone shouting. How long was the gap between the two?"

"A matter of minutes," Dan replied. "But hang on a second. You said, 'Mrs'. Is she married?"

Spiller nodded. "Widowed. But let's concentrate on the sequence of events. In your opinion, was it definitely the victim who shouted?"

"I can't be sure. As I said in my statement, I'd heard the man arguing in the pub, but I didn't know him, so I didn't recognise his voice."

"Fair enough." Spiller made a note before continuing. "So, you didn't know who was calling out, but you were pretty clear on what was said. He shouted, 'Get out of here.' Yes?"

"That's right. And I think he might've said, 'Go.' Then later, he said, 'Stop them.' So whoever attacked him, there must've been more than one of them."

"Mm. Can we be sure he was attacked?"

"Yes. Surely, he must've..." Dan left his sentence unfinished. "Wait a second. Do you think he was on his own? Shouting at no one?"

"It's a possibility. We've seen no evidence to the contrary. The only potential witnesses saw no one in the vicinity."

"But... his head wound. It didn't look like an accident."

Spiller pursed his lips. "I'm sure you'll understand, sir, that I can't discuss details of an ongoing inquiry. But we don't want the rumour mill going into overdrive, so let's just say that we're keeping an open mind. Mr Gamble was not entirely steady on his pins, it was dark and the ground was treacherous. Falls can be very unpredictable. I've known people slip from a twenty-foot ladder and get away with a few bruises. Someone else can slip on their own kitchen floor, but if they land in the wrong way, it's all over."

"I can see how that might be the case," Dan admitted.

"And it's true that we saw no one else out there. It was very quiet, but we didn't hear anyone running away."

"Exactly. Now, let's go back to that night. Remember, it's very important that we don't allow ourselves to be influenced by preconceived ideas. For the sake of the victim and his family, we need to concentrate on the facts."

Dan nodded slowly. "I didn't know he had a family. They must be very distressed."

"Yes. So, according to my notes, when you found Mr Gamble, he managed to say a few words to you. Would you mind trying to recall them for me now?"

"I'm not likely to forget them," Dan replied. "He said, 'Don't let them get away with it. I'm begging you to stop them.'"

"Definitely *them?*" Spiller asked. "Plural. Not *him?*"

"I'm sure. His voice was weak, but I was right next to him. I heard every word."

Spiller studied Dan for a moment. "And what did you take those words to mean?"

"That someone, presumably a group of people, had attacked him, and he was asking us to go after them. But, of course, we didn't. We waited until the paramedics came. He was still breathing, so we thought it was best not to move him." Dan hesitated. "Were we right, do you think?"

"Definitely. Mr Gamble was an elderly man, and wounds to the head are always tricky." Spiller leaned forward. "You found him, then you called for help. You did everything you could, sir. There's no doubt about that. None whatsoever."

"Thanks," Dan said. "It's been preying on my mind."

"These things take their toll. It's only human to be affected. But if you don't mind, I have a few more questions."

"Okay."

"Earlier that evening, you saw Mr Gamble in the pub, yes?"

Dan nodded. "Briefly. He left quite soon after we arrived."

"*We*, being you and your neighbour, Mr Hargreaves."

"That's right. Are you speaking to him as well? I think he's at home."

"Next on the list," Spiller replied. "About what time did Mr Gamble leave the pub?"

"We got there around eight," Dan said. "I think Mr Gamble left about half an hour later. I didn't check the time."

"And how did Mr Gamble strike you? Was he in good spirits, or did he seem worried or upset about anything?"

Dan hunted for the right turn of phrase. "He was agitated. I'd guess he'd been drinking."

"Guess? Did you *see* him drinking?"

"No. I suppose I'm putting two and two together. Sorry."

Spiller waved his apology aside. "Don't worry. If I need something qualifying, I'll ask. So, what made you think he may have been under the influence, so to speak?"

"He was loud, and he looked flushed. He seemed to get very excited when he won a prize in the meat raffle." Dan broke off suddenly. "What happened to that? He was carrying a packet of meat. Liver. I saw him take it out the door, but he didn't have it when we found him. We stood over him for ages while we waited for the ambulance. If he'd still had the meat, we would've seen it."

Spiller was listening carefully. "This is the first I've heard of this. Thank you. I'll follow it up." He scribbled something in his notebook. "And what about this argument he had in the pub? Did you witness that?"

"Oh yes. I didn't see what started it, but he was shouting at a mob of young men, and they didn't like it."

"*Mob?* That's a very emotive word," Spiller said. "Were they being rowdy? Making a nuisance of themselves?"

"Not as far as I could see. I assumed they'd walked into each other or something. Mr Gamble was very angry. He said something about people being nosey, making snide remarks.

It looked as though something might happen, but then Kevin, that's the landlord, he told Mr Gamble to leave."

"He threw the old man out? Not the lads?"

"Yes. Later on, he told the young men to leave, but only after Marjorie Treave had given them a piece of her mind."

Spiller shifted in his seat. "Yes. I saw that in your statement, and I have to say, it struck me as odd. An elderly lady taking on a gang of lads?"

"Have you met Marjorie?"

"Not yet."

Dan smiled. "You'll understand once you've met her in the flesh. From what Alan tells me, she's a formidable character. She's like royalty in this village, so when she scolded those lads, they backed down."

"So, she stood up for Mr Gamble. Was there some sort of relationship between them, do you think?"

Dan looked down at the table, his lips pressed tight as he wondered whether to explain his theory about a connection between Marjorie and Mortimer. Spiller clearly wanted to concentrate on verifiable facts, and that was only right. *So where do my observations fit in?* Dan asked himself. *What if my ideas affect the investigation? Can I take that risk?* Dan shook his head. "I really couldn't say."

"You know, sometimes an impression can be valuable," Spiller said. "Was there something you picked up? Some sense that something wasn't right?"

"Nothing concrete. But I did get the idea that Mr Gamble and Marjorie had some sort of shared understanding. It was in the way they looked at each other."

Spiller nodded slowly. "Anything else?"

"Not really. My only other impression was that Mr Gamble wasn't well liked in the community. This may sound silly, but when he won a prize in the raffle, people muttered and grumbled. I didn't think much of it at the time, but now, I wonder why. People cheered for the other winners, but not him."

Spiller pursed his lips. "Envy, perhaps. Did you hear anything specific said against Mr Gamble?"

"Only what I said earlier. It sounded like a general grumble. Steven, the lad he was arguing with, said something about Mortimer mouthing off as usual, or something like that." Dan paused. "Why do you say *envy*? What was there to be envious of?"

"Didn't you know? I'd have thought it was common knowledge." Spiller sniffed. "Mr Gamble owned land. Lots of it. Mainly around here, but some stretches along the valley. In fact, he owned the field in which you found him, spoil heaps and all."

"And that explains what he was doing there," Dan said. "It was his land, so he could walk around it whenever he wanted."

"Perhaps."

Dan tried to read Spiller's expression. The man gave little away, but there was a hint of resignation in his eyes, as though he'd reached the limit of his interest. "Can I ask something?" Dan began. "Do you really think this could've been an accident, or are you treating it as an assault?"

"It's a fair question. As things stand, Mr Gamble's death is suspicious, and we're running an inquiry on that basis. Where we go from there depends very much on what we find."

"I suppose there'll have to be an autopsy and so on."

"That's not a term we use," Spiller said, "but yes, there was a post-mortem examination."

"Oh, then you must know whether it could've been an accident or not."

"This isn't *CSI*, Mr Corrigan. These things are not always as conclusive as we'd like, and the forensic tests take time."

Dan nodded thoughtfully. "The spoil heaps, are they still a crime scene?"

"Why do you ask?"

"Curiosity. I was wondering if I could take a walk over there; see the place in daylight. I thought something might come back to me."

"We should be finished with the field soon, but in the meantime you can walk along the footpath, by all means." Spiller lifted his chin. "Keep away from the spoil heaps though; we may want to come back and search them again, so some poor devil will be stuck out there to guard the scene. Otherwise, any subsequent evidence wouldn't count for much. You see, any decent defence barrister would claim that the scene had been contaminated."

"Ah, so anything like footprints or fibres or anything—"

"Could've been left at the scene after the event," Spiller said. "But, to be perfectly honest with you, I'm not expecting any earth-shattering revelations at this stage. Quite rightly, the first people to arrive were trying to preserve life, so there was you and Mr Hargreaves, and then a couple of paramedics and a pair of local constables, all trampling over the place. The initial investigating officer did a good job of looking after the scene, but out here, it's difficult. Something has been out there, digging around, making holes in the ground. We think it was a badger, but who knows?" He raised his hands then let them fall to the table. "Give me city streets any day. Crowds of witnesses, CCTV, dash-cams, ANPR: it all makes things easier."

"I couldn't agree more. I've always felt safe in London. So long as you keep your wits about you and mind where you go, you're fine. But people around here seem to think that city-dwellers will stab you in the back as soon as look at you."

Spiller's smile was as careworn as his blazer. "People are pretty much the same wherever you go. That's something you soon realise in this job."

"Every street tells a story? A murder on every corner?"

"Nothing quite so dramatic. We get called out to a lot of

everyday, run-of-the-mill events I'm afraid. We often see people at their worst. But every now and then, we see people at their best too. Like you and Mr Hargreaves. You didn't have to help, but you did."

Dan looked away, his gaze fixed on the middle distance. He could think of nothing more to add, and Spiller seemed to take his cue. He rose to his feet, pocketing his notebook. "Right, I'll leave you in peace. If there's anything else that comes to mind, give me a call." He produced a business card and handed it to Dan. "All my numbers are on there, so feel free to call anytime. But please, if you do go anywhere near the spoil heaps, keep well away from the cordoned-off area, all right?"

Dan stood, glancing at the card. "Definitely. I wouldn't want to interfere with your investigation.

"I'm off to see your next-door neighbour. Friend of yours, is he?"

"Yes. I haven't known him long, but..." He shrugged. It was hard to explain his friendship with Alan. On the face of it, they had nothing whatsoever in common, but they got along. Spiller looked as though he expected more, but what else was there to say?

"Okay," Spiller said slowly, extending his hand for a shake. "Nice to meet you, Mr Corrigan. We'll be in touch at some point, and in the meantime, you know how to reach me."

"What happens next? I've never been involved in anything like this before."

"That depends. It's early days. If it comes to a trial, you might be called as a witness. You'll be able to contribute to the moments leading up to the incident."

"I see."

Dan's expression must've given him away because Spiller sent him a reassuring smile. "It's nothing to worry about. We'll take you through it, make it painless. It's what we do."

"Right. Well, I'll let you out the back door. Alan's house is just over the alley." He led Spiller outside, but the moment they stepped out into the garden, a shrill tone chirruped, and the policeman paused to pluck a phone from his pocket. "Ah, a signal. At last." He checked the screen, his brow furrowing. "Just hold on a moment, will you, Mr Corrigan? I need to make a quick call."

"Yes, of course."

Spiller turned away, speaking quickly into his phone, his voice low. There was an urgency in his tone, and when he ended the call, he spun around on his heel, his eyes locked on Dan. "Your friend, Alan Hargreaves, does he own a walking stick?"

"Yes. A kind of long staff, with—"

"A staghorn handle?" Spiller asked.

Dan nodded.

"And was Mr Hargreaves carrying his stick on the night Mr Gamble was attacked?"

"No, he…" Dan broke off, his thoughts in a whirl, and a dizzying sensation swept through his mind as if his world had been abruptly kicked out of kilter. He stared at Spiller as though the policeman had just materialised in front of him. "Are you saying that Alan's stick was used to attack Mortimer?"

"I'm saying nothing, Mr Corrigan. Not yet."

Dan took a quick breath. "But, you must've found it. Otherwise, why would you bring it up?"

"Please, answer the question properly," Spiller said. "Can you categorically state whether Mr Hargreaves was carrying his stick when you left the pub?"

"Alan didn't have his stick at all that evening. In fact, Kevin mentioned it. He said Alan had left it behind. He asked me to tell him he'd put it somewhere safe, but somehow, I… I forgot."

"So, you're saying that you *knew* Mr Hargreaves had lost

his stick, and you knew where it was, but you didn't tell him."

Dan paused before replying, gathering his wits. "No. I *did* tell him where it was, but not until we were almost home, and we didn't go back for it. Alan definitely didn't have his stick with him when we found Mr Gamble, so if it was used in the attack, it had nothing to do with us."

"Let's not be too hasty. I didn't say the stick was used as a weapon, did I? Let's not jump to conclusions, but I have to ask you a couple of simple questions. Firstly, are there any identifying marks on the walking stick belonging to Mr Hargreaves?"

"Not marks," Dan said. "It's not carved or anything, but it does have a leather tag: a fob, I guess you'd call it. It's attached with a short leather strap, and his initials are stamped on the fob. AH."

Spiller nodded. "And you last saw this walking stick, when?"

"Last week. On Wednesday, in the afternoon, we took a walk down to the river and along the valley, and afterwards we went to the pub for a quick drink. That must be when Alan left his stick behind."

"And on the night of the attack, when you left the pub, how many other customers were still in the room?"

Dan shrugged. "A handful. I can recall four others: a man called Jay, Mrs Treave, and a couple I didn't recognise."

"And apart from the landlord, was anyone else working in the pub?"

"Not as far as I know. I think Kevin was the only one behind the bar, but he wasn't there the whole time. He must've been clearing up, collecting glasses, that kind of thing, but I don't remember."

"So at times, the bar was unattended," Spiller said. "And during the evening, was Mr Hargreaves out of your sight at any time?"

"Yes. We don't follow each other around. I must've gone to the gents a couple of times."

Spiller stared at him levelly. "And remind me, Mr Corrigan, when did you decide to go haring after Mr Gamble?"

"*After* we heard him crying out," Dan stated. "We were on our way home when we heard him. If we'd left just two minutes earlier, we wouldn't have heard a thing. But we stopped to... to talk."

"Talk? About what?"

Dan shifted his weight from one foot to the other. "Just a chat. You know. We looked at the stars. It was a clear night."

"So it was." Spiller took a breath, flaring his nostrils. "Right. Thanks for your help, Mr Corrigan. We'll be in touch. Sooner rather than later. Now, I must get on." He turned away, making for Alan's house.

"Wait a minute," Dan called out. "Alan didn't have anything to do with this." But Spiller didn't slow his pace, and Dan could only watch as Spiller knocked on Alan's door.

Alan answered the policeman's knock, greeting the new arrival with a genial smile. But when he saw Dan watching from his step, he must've read the concern in Dan's expression, because his smile quickly faded.

Spiller frowned at Dan, then turning to Alan, he said, "We'd better go inside, Mr Hargreaves. I have a few questions for you, and we need to talk in private."

"All right. That's fine," Alan replied, but Dan could see that his friend was rattled by the policeman's stern tone. Alan stepped back to allow Spiller to enter, and the door closed.

Dan went back inside, standing by the kitchen window to stare morosely into the back garden. *What have I done?* he wondered. *How did I manage to make myself sound so shifty?* It was ridiculous. They'd done nothing wrong. Nothing. But if Alan's stick had been used to attack Mortimer Gamble, there'd be more questions to answer. *Spiller didn't confirm that*

43

the stick was the weapon, he reminded himself. But he and Alan were the only two people who could be placed at the spoil heaps. Perhaps Spiller thought they'd got into a drunken argument with Mr Gamble and lashed out, only calling for help when they realised what they'd done, the cover story cooked up afterwards. As an explanation of the events, it was staggeringly simple. If Alan owned the weapon, the situation did not look good. After all, Alan could've retrieved his walking stick from the pub easily enough without being seen. There was no one who could prove they were innocent.

No one except for the real murderer, Dan thought, and his expression hardened. There was one way to clear this mess up for certain. He had to find the killer himself. There was no doubt about it.

CHAPTER 4

D AN PACED THE length of the kitchen, keeping an eye on
the view from his window. When the gate that led to
Alan's garden swung open, Dan halted, watching with bated
breath. Would Alan be dragged outside and bundled into a
car? Would he be taken to the station to help the police with
their inquiries?

But DS Spiller left alone, marching away without a
backward glance, and twenty seconds later Dan was rapping
his knuckles on his neighbour's door.

There was a pause before Alan opened the door, his
expression clearly troubled, and he glanced nervously along
the alley. "Has he gone?"

"Yes. Can I come in? We need to talk."

Alan nodded. "I'll put the kettle on."

In the kitchen, Dan sat at the long table while Alan
watched the kettle in silence, his head down, his hands
gripping the edge of the counter.

"What did he say?" Dan asked, but Alan simply grunted
and started hunting through a cupboard. "I need a strong
coffee. Want one?"

"No, thanks. I'm fine."

"That's a first," Alan said. "In that case, I'll settle for instant." He pulled a jar from the cupboard and spooned coffee into a mug, adding water as soon as the kettle boiled. Turning to face Dan, he took a sip, wrinkling his nose. "Ugh. I used to be quite happy with this stuff until you came along with your freshly roasted Colombian and your organic Costa Rican."

"Sorry about that," Dan said with a wry grin. "Once you've converted to the real thing, there's no going back. But sit down and tell me what Spiller said. Did he say anything about your walking stick?"

Alan nodded, then he sat down, his shoulders slumped. "They found my hiking stick. It had been thrown into a ditch alongside the lane, not far from Marjorie's house."

"The path we walked along on Friday night?"

"No. The footpath we used is a shortcut. You can get to Marjorie's house by road, but it's a less direct route. Anyway, someone must've taken that way because that's where they found my stick." Alan paused, his lips pressed in a tight line. "It had blood on it. Mortimer Gamble's blood."

"Damn! That's what I was afraid of," Dan said. "I knew something was up when Spiller started asking about it."

"Did you tell him? Did you explain that I didn't have the damned thing?"

"Of course I did. I spelt it out as clearly as I could. But I'm not sure if he believed me."

Alan took a gulp of coffee. "I got the impression DS Spiller doesn't believe a word anyone says about anything. For a minute, I thought he was going to read me my rights."

"That's an American thing. We say *interviewed under caution*." Dan smiled hopefully. "I did some research while you were talking to Spiller, and if he didn't caution you, that's a good thing. It means you're not really a suspect."

"I should bloody well think not. Why would I hurt the poor old man? We tried to help him, for God's sake."

"I know. It's not fair, but we have to face up to the reality of this thing." Dan hesitated. "Now that they've got a weapon, they'll start a murder inquiry."

Alan's face, already pale, now turned to the colour of ashes. "Do you really think so? Only, when I tried to ask Spiller about that, he dodged the question. He said that decision was up to a senior officer. Apparently, there's some doubt over the head injury. When Morty arrived at the hospital, the doctors cleaned him up and dealt with the wound, and now the pathologists can't decide whether he was hit first, or if he fell down and cracked his head on the rocky ground."

"Can't they tell from the crime scene?" Dan asked.

"They're running tests. That's all I know."

"But now that they have a potential weapon, they'll be trying to match it to the wound," Dan said thoughtfully. "I read about this. They call it Locard's exchange principle: whenever people come into direct contact, tiny traces of physical material are passed from one to the other. As well as examining the blood on the stick, they'll be looking for traces of the stick on Mortimer's skin or his clothing. If they can find a tiny splinter of wood or a fragment of staghorn from the handle, they can show that your stick was used to attack him."

Alan stared at him. "Don't think I'm ungrateful for the research you've been doing on my behalf, but if you're trying to make me feel better, you're doing a rotten job. Don't forget, you can't prove a negative, so I have no way of showing that I *didn't* take my stick from the pub."

"In that case, we'll have to find the person who *did* take it."

"I don't see how," Alan said. "We could ask around, but we have no authority."

Dan grunted in disapproval. "We can't sit back and do nothing. The way things stand, it will be all too easy for the police to build a case against us. We have no alibi. No one else can get us off the hook; we'll have to do it ourselves."

Alan sat back, pushing his half-drunk mug of coffee away. Lowering his voice, he said, "I have to go to the police station later. Spiller said it was a formality, a quick interview, but…" Alan's voice faltered. "Do you think I need a solicitor?"

"It couldn't hurt. A solicitor might keep you from digging yourself into a hole. And they might be able to prevent the police from pressuring you. Unless you've been arrested, you can leave an interview whenever you want, and a good solicitor will stand up for you."

"It won't come to that, will it?"

"I doubt it. If Spiller had wanted to arrest you, he'd have done it already."

"He said the interview is purely so that I can confirm the stick is mine. He asked me how much it had cost, and when I told him, he seemed to think it was a bit suspicious that I hadn't gone back to the pub to look for it. I explained that, with all this drama going on, I forgot all about the stupid stick. Suspicious deaths are hardly everyday occurrences around here. I had no way of knowing it had been used as a weapon, so I had no reason to mention it until he asked."

Dan nodded slowly. "On the plus side, an official interview will give you a chance to set the record straight."

"Yes, it's just as well to get my side of the story down in black and white," Alan said, though he didn't sound convinced. "At any rate, I have to go over to Exeter for the interview, so you'll have to go shopping for paint on your own."

"Don't worry about that. Your interview is much more important. I could come with you if you like."

"Thanks, but there's no need to drag you over there. Anyway, it might look suspicious if you tag along, as if we're in cahoots."

"What are cahoots, do you think?" Dan asked. "It's always struck me as an odd word."

"I'll be sure to look it up later. I'll probably have plenty of time to kill when I'm hanging around, waiting to be grilled." Alan stood stiffly. "I'd better go and make some calls. The only time I've needed a solicitor was when I bought this place. I used a local firm, but I'm not sure if they handle this kind of work very often. I'd better see if I can find someone more experienced, someone who can come at such short notice."

"Okay, but remember, the ball's in your court." Dan pushed back his chair and stood. "They can't force you to attend, so make sure you get a solicitor organised before you go for the interview."

"I will."

Dan headed for the door. "Let me know how you get on. If you can pick up any details about the case from Spiller, that would be great."

Alan gazed at him levelly. "I hate to break it to you, but I think DS Spiller is imagining a one-way exchange of information."

"That's his problem," Dan said, opening the door but pausing on the threshold. "He's blinkered by institutional thinking, tied up in red tape, but we don't have to be. We can look around and see what we can piece together. We've got time, and we have ample motivation."

"To clear our names? Isn't that a bit melodramatic?"

"No. Anyway, there's more to it than that. Somewhere in this village, there's a killer, and we can't let them get away with it."

"But the police—"

"Won't act fast enough," Dan interrupted. "It's taken them all weekend to figure out what we knew all along. Mortimer Gamble was attacked and left for dead, and the police are wasting their time on the wrong people. We can do better."

"All right," Alan said. "You're on."

"That's the spirit. I'll see you later, and we'll make a plan of action. Good luck with your interview, and remember, find out as much as you can."

"I'll try." Alan managed a brave smile. "See you later."

"Good man." Dan closed the door, but not before he caught a glimpse of Alan's expression. The smile had been for show, and it had vanished as soon as he'd thought Dan wasn't watching. Alan was worried. He'd done his best to hide it, but Dan knew the signs of strain all too well, and in that split second, he'd seen it in the sudden slump of Alan's shoulders, the set of his jaw and the tight creases in the skin around his eyes.

Don't worry, Dan thought. *I'll get to the bottom of this.* Then with his head held high, he strode back toward his house.

CHAPTER 5

I N THE DAYLIGHT, Dan found the entrance to the public footpath easily. He wasted no time in hurrying through the gate and making his way along the path. But then he slowed down, determined to pay attention to his surroundings.

The day was warm, the birds were singing and the faint suggestion of a breeze crept over the expanse of bracken that stretched out on either side, the tall fronds stirring in a stately dance. The place still seemed alien to him: a million miles from the carefully tended parks of London. This place was wild, but even so, it seemed too peaceful, too serene to be associated with violence. But as he walked on, the spoil heaps came into view, their grey peaks protruding from the lush vegetation to look scornfully on the verdant landscape below.

There was a flash of high-vis yellow: a police officer patrolling the spoil heaps' perimeter, stretching his legs. No doubt it was a dull posting for the constable, so perhaps he'd welcome the opportunity for a chat. But as Dan grew nearer, the policeman must've heard him coming, because he turned around sharply, folding his arms across his chest and delivering a stern glare.

Dan raised a hand in acknowledgement, but the constable's only response was to call out, "Keep to the path, please, sir. There's nothing to see here."

I'll bet he's always wanted to say that, Dan thought, but he wasn't about to argue. The policeman was probably tired of the locals wandering around to poke their noses in, and it wouldn't do any good to arouse suspicion, so Dan kept walking, looking around him as he went. But what was he hoping to find? Something the police may have missed? That seemed unlikely, but it was possible: they didn't know the area, so there was always a chance they wouldn't notice if something was out of the ordinary.

But it wasn't long before Dan reached the end of the path, a rickety wooden gate leading to a narrow lane beyond. On the other side of the lane, a sturdy fence of railings and chicken wire cordoned off a vegetable plot. Behind the neat rows of beans and peas, a whitewashed cottage kept its sleepy vigil, its small windows glittering in the sunlight, and its thatched roof giving it an air of shabby permanence. The scene was down-to-earth rural rather than chocolate-box chic, and Dan was sure this was Marjorie Treave's hideaway. He glanced nervously at the fence, wondering whether it was high enough to contain Marjorie's livestock, but it looked as though there was no immediate danger of being chased by a flock of enraged geese, so turning away from the garden, he made his way to the end of the lane. The roadway terminated in a curved turning area, the surface pitted with potholes, and beyond a rickety fence, an unkempt field sloped downhill and stretched back toward the spoil heaps. There was little to see: a few stunted trees poked up through the bracken, and a little way off, a broad clump of tall shrubs looked out of place, their deep green leaves and vivid mauve flowers seeming more suited to the gardens of a stately home.

But what was that sound? Something within the shrubbery rustled the leaves as if an animal were trapped or tangled in the branches. A deer perhaps? Alan had told him that muntjac deer were common in the fields, warning that they sometimes strayed onto the lanes and panicked when cars approached.

Have I ever seen a deer in the wild? Dan wondered. *Probably not.* At the edge of the clump of shrubs, a patch of leaves shook, and Dan kept his eyes on the place. Yes. There was definitely some kind of creature disturbing the foliage.

But as Dan watched, it was not a deer that emerged from behind the tall shrubs, but a person. A person he recognised instantly. Marjorie. Dressed immaculately in a long skirt and a tweed jacket that must've been uncomfortable in the heat, she was intent on studying the shrubs, and Dan was certain she hadn't seen him. He stood still, waiting, though for what, he couldn't say. Then Marjorie went into action.

She was carrying a long-handled gardening implement, something like a scythe, and as Dan watched, she swung it vigorously, setting about the bush, hacking at the branches with all her might. Leaves flew, blossoms tumbled to the ground, but Marjorie struck again and again, slicing through stems and branches with brutal efficiency.

She's lost it, Dan decided. But there was method in her furious activity, and she moved steadily along the shrub, cutting the low-growing foliage first, and then working upwards to hack at the highest branches she could reach with her long-handled tool.

That blade would make a ferocious weapon, Dan thought. *You could kill a man with a thing like that.* Keeping his movements quiet, he pulled his phone from his pocket and activated the camera. A few seconds of footage would be enough. But the recording had hardly begun when Marjorie stopped her work, tilting her head. There was no way she could've heard him, but she turned to stare directly at Dan.

Busted. Dan ended the recording, pocketing his phone, then he raised his hand in a friendly wave. But Marjorie was already storming toward him. "You can't come in here. This is private land."

Dan armed himself against her anger with his warmest smile. "Hello, Mrs Treave. I'm Dan Corrigan. I saw you the other day, in the pub."

She stopped short, peering at him intently. "What of it? What do you want?"

"Nothing. I'm just out for a walk, getting to know the area. I live in the village." It wasn't a lie exactly, but he guessed that, as far as Marjorie was concerned, newcomers were bad enough but tourists were even worse. So he added, "I moved into The Old Shop. I'm a friend of Alan's."

"Oh, yes." Marjorie lifted her chin as realisation dawned. "You're the one who found poor old Morty, God rest his soul."

"That's right. We did what we could, but sadly, we were too late," Dan said. "I don't suppose you can spare a few minutes to talk about that night, can you?"

Marjorie grunted. "No. Why should I? I've had the police pestering me from morning till night, and I don't know any more than what I told them. So if it's all the same to you, I'll be getting back to work." She indicated the lane. "The road's that way. Follow it around and you'll get back to the village. Eventually." She sniffed. "Quicker to go back by the path, though. Goodbye."

She made to leave, but Dan said, "We saw you walking home on Friday night. We know which route *you* used."

Marjorie froze, her gaze growing cold as she studied him.

"You passed us by, but we saw you head this way just minutes before Mortimer was attacked," Dan went on. "You must've seen something, heard something."

"No. Not a thing. I don't hang about, you know. When I'm going somewhere, I get on with it. It takes me but a few minutes to get from one end of the path to the other. By the time Mortimer met his end, I was safe at home, thank the

Lord. Otherwise, who knows what might have happened."
She shook her head sadly. "'Tis a sorry business, and you
were good to try and help the old man, but what's done is
done, and there's no good can come of talking about it now. I
should keep quiet if I were you. There's plenty of folks
around here that won't thank you for poking your nose in, so
let's leave it at that. Move on, as they say. Now, I don't know
about you, but I have work to do."

"Yes, I saw that you were busy," Dan said before she had a
chance to turn away. "You said this is private land. Is it
yours?"

"No. All this belonged to Mortimer. Been in his family for
a long time, but I don't know what'll happen to it now.
Maybe they'll farm it, although 'tisn't much good for
anything. Too boggy to grow good grass, even at this time of
year. A few sheep maybe; they'll live most anywhere. Mind
you, whoever takes it on will have to do something about all
that bracken before they can farm it. If it was up to me, they'd
leave it well alone, but it's not."

Dan's attention had wandered as she'd started talking
about sheep, but now there was something in Marjorie's
expression that reawakened his curiosity. When she looked
over the land, her gaze grew sharp, as though she was seeing
something he could not. There was something in her tone too:
a hint of bitterness. Was she holding something back?

Sensing a loose thread that he could tug, Dan said, "So, if
this isn't your land, why are you cutting back the plants?"

"Rhododendrons," Marjorie stated as though that made
everything clear. "They go wild. They didn't ought to be here,
not really. Foreign plants. Invaders. If you don't keep them
under control, they get everywhere. They don't mind the
boggy ground, see, and like I said, it's boggy all year round,
on account of the reservoir."

"I didn't know there was a reservoir. I've never seen it. It
can't be very big."

"'Tisn't." Marjorie pointed into the distance beyond the clump of rhododendrons. "'Tis yonder. No more than a big pond, but 'tis deep, and always full; the spring sees to that."

"And did Mortimer own the reservoir too?"

"Oh yes. And the land beyond, right down to the river and for miles along the valley."

"I see." Dan sensed his smile was earning nothing but distrust, and he changed tack, bowing his head slightly and summoning up every ounce of sincerity he could muster. "Mrs Treave, I know this is an imposition, but you see, I really do need your help. At least, Alan does."

Marjorie paused before replying. "Oh yes?"

"Definitely. I don't know if you've heard this, but the police found a hiking stick belonging to Alan, and they think it was used to attack Mortimer. They think it was the murder weapon."

Marjorie snorted in contempt. "Nonsense. It's got nothing to do with Mr Hargreaves. Nothing at all. I dare say the police will realise that soon enough. They can't be that stupid."

"I wouldn't bank on it. I'm afraid they found blood on the stick, and they're saying it's Mortimer's blood. They have some very precise tests these days, and—"

"I know about blood types and such," Marjorie interrupted. "I'm not stupid." Marjorie pursed her lips. "Where was this stick, then?"

"They found it in a ditch, quite near to your house as it happens." Dan pointed along the lane. "I was going to have a look and see if I can spot where it was left."

Marjorie stared at him. "I don't understand. What was his stick doing down here?"

"I presume the attacker threw it into the ditch as they made their getaway. Alan had left his stick in the pub a few days earlier, and we know it was still in the pub on Friday, but we don't know who took it."

"I don't know about any of this," Marjorie said, "but it's

all a load of nonsense. It wasn't anything to do with Mr Hargreaves, I can tell you that for nothing."

"How can you be so sure?" Dan asked. "Is there something you're not telling me, Mrs Treave? Something about the attack?" He watched her reaction very carefully, taking in the tiny muscles twitching around her lips. She was trying to hide it, forcing herself to bite back her words, but she knew something. Something important. "It really would be a good idea to talk to me," Dan went on. "I'm not a policeman, and I have no axe to grind. I'm just trying to help a friend. Alan is with the police right now. He had to go to Exeter to answer their questions. I know he did nothing wrong, but the police have other ideas. He could be in trouble."

Marjorie closed her eyes for a moment, and when she looked up at him, her expression had softened. "You'd best come in for a minute. I'll make a pot of tea."

"Thank you."

"This way." Marjorie marched toward her garden, pushing a low gate open. "Shut it behind you."

Dan did as he was told, then he followed her along the path of mismatched stone slabs until they reached the cottage. Marjorie propped her long-handled tool against the wall then pushed the door open, marching inside. *Not locked*, Dan thought, then he took a long, hard look at the vicious blade of the scythe-like implement. The tool was old, its wooden handle worn smooth from many years of use, its thick blade blackened from age, gleaming dully as if coated in oil. But its edge caught the light, glinting brightly in the sunshine. It had been sharpened from haft to tip, and recently, too. Could it be the murder weapon?

"Hurry up," Marjorie called out. "Shut the door, or you'll let the flies in."

"Okay." Dan stepped inside, shutting the door carefully, and he took a deep breath. Since he'd arrived in Embervale, he'd spent much more time outdoors than he ever had in London, and on the whole, he'd been enjoying the warm weather. But to enter Marjorie's kitchen was to step into an oasis of cool air, the soft scents of home baking mingling with a delicate aroma he couldn't quite identify. It was instantly soothing to the soul, and Dan found himself smiling. "It's lovely and cool in here," he said. "And what's that delicious smell?"

Marjorie hooked her thumb at the low ceiling, and Dan looked up to see bunches of herbs and flowers hanging upside down from a wooden rack. "Rosemary, bay, marjoram, thyme and sage. If it'll thrive, I'll grow it. I've coriander and parsley outside, and plenty of others besides. It's enough to last me all year." She pointed to a chair beside a waxed pine kitchen table. "Sit down. I'll get the tea. I've got PG Tips, and that's all, so don't ask for anything else."

"Any chance of a coffee?"

"Don't be daft. Not in this heat." Marjorie filled a kettle at the sink and fussed over a teapot while Dan sat down. *Two chairs*, he thought. *Two coasters on the table. And that teapot is too big for one.*

"Won't be long," she said. "Milk? It's from my own goats."

"Black," Dan said quickly. "I don't drink milk."

She looked down her nose at him. "Allergy, is it? Intolerance? Because goats' milk is all right for most people. My goats don't get shot full of antibiotics and all that rubbish. They're the healthiest creatures you'll ever see. Nothing wrong with their milk."

"All the same, I take it black," Dan said. "I'm more or less a vegan."

"Oh well, no accounting for taste." She went back to the counter, and while she swirled hot water around the large brown teapot to warm it, Dan noticed a row of gleaming glass jars on the draining board. "Are those jars for your honey?"

he asked. "Alan told me you keep bees. Are you preparing a new batch?"

Marjorie didn't turn around to answer him. She simply said, "Something like that."

"If it's for sale, I wouldn't mind trying some. Some vegans object to honey, but I'm not that strict, and I don't see the harm when it's from a smallholder like yourself." Marjorie seemed intent on making the tea, so Dan said, "Is it for sale? I've got some cash on me, so it depends—"

"'Tisn't ready," Marjorie said before he could ask about the price. "I've none for sale. You might try the shops in Bovey Tracey. I expect there's someone over there selling local honey."

She set a mug down on the coaster in front of Dan, taking her own drink to the opposite end of the table before sitting down herself. She slurped her tea, then she sighed and said, "All right, young man. If you really think it will help, we'll go through the whole business about Mr Gamble one more time."

"Thank you. That would be great. To start with, what do you think Mortimer was doing down here on that night? I know it's his land, but why would he climb onto the spoil heaps after dark?"

Marjorie looked down as she took another drink of tea. "That's not a bad drop of tea. I needed it. Can I offer you a biscuit? Or I've a date and walnut loaf that needs eating."

"No thanks. I'm not hungry, but I am keen to hear your opinion on why Mr Gamble was out there when he was attacked. Perhaps he'd arranged to meet someone."

"No. Not him."

"What makes you so certain?" Dan asked.

"Well, he wasn't one for socialising," Marjorie said. "He kept himself to himself. No friends to speak of. And nothing in the romantic line, if you know what I mean."

"Could it have been something to do with the mines?

Perhaps Mortimer had some ideas he wanted to discuss in secret."

"You're barking up the wrong tree, there," Marjorie said. "Mortimer had no sense for business. Head full of dreams. What do you know about the old mines?"

"Only what Alan told me. Lead and silver, I believe."

"That's right. Poor old Mortimer got it into his head they weren't all worked out. Reckoned the price of precious metals was going up so fast that, one day soon, he'd be able to open up the old mines, make them work and turn a tidy profit." She put her mug down so hard that a drop of tea splashed onto the table. "Nonsense. Pipe dreams. The old fool had no idea what he was talking about."

"Maybe." Dan sat back, letting his gaze wander around the tidy kitchen as he considered this bombshell. He hadn't heard of anyone opening up old mines in England, but that didn't mean it couldn't happen in the future. New technologies were being introduced all the time. Take fracking; who could've predicted such a thing twenty years ago?

"I know what you're thinking," Marjorie said. "You're wondering if maybe there was something else. Oil maybe or gas. Well, you can dream if you want to, but I reckon that if there was anything like that around here, we'd have heard about it by now." She chuckled to herself. "No, we've got china clay and granite in Devon, and that's it."

A sudden thought struck Dan. "Do you happen to know if the old mines are inside the Dartmoor National Park?"

"They certainly are. And the authority wouldn't stand by while some fool started digging holes in the countryside. Lord knows, I said the exact same thing to Morty often enough."

That's the first time she's called him Morty, Dan thought, and he said, "So, you spoke together often? Was he in the habit of calling in to see you, by any chance?"

Marjorie jutted her chin. "Sometimes. Why wouldn't he? He was my landlord, after all. Came regular to collect the rent."

"He owned your house?"

"Oh yes. Do I look like I can afford to buy a cottage like this? And there's the garden too. Have you seen the property prices around here? With my little bit of savings, I could scarcely afford a broom cupboard, and even then, it would have to be in Newton Abbot or somewhere like that." She grimaced. "I suppose it might come to that. I'll end up in a council house or a dingy little flat. Damp on the walls, no garden, noisy neighbours. It doesn't bear thinking about."

Dan leaned forward. "Marjorie, I'm not an expert on this, but whoever inherits the land, I honestly don't think they can just throw you out. You have rights. If you have a rent agreement or some kind of tenancy or lease—"

"Don't make me laugh. My Archie sorted all that out, bless him. He shook hands with Morty more than twenty-five years ago, and that's always been good enough for us."

"That's nice, but it's hard to prove." Dan took a sip of his tea. It was bitter and far too strong, the tannin shrivelling his tongue. "Is there anyone who can help you with this? A family member, perhaps, or a friend."

Marjorie looked at him, unblinking. "What do *you* think? Do you reckon it's a mad social whirl in this house? Maybe Viscount Exmouth will drop in later; I'd better whip up a batch of scones."

"What I think is that you're being a little too defensive," Dan said slowly. "I'd say that you've been on your own for a long time, and perfectly naturally, you formed a friendship or some kind of bond with Mortimer Gamble."

"Rubbish! We didn't get along at all. We barely passed the time of day."

"But that's not true, is it?" Dan smiled. "You see, I noticed the way Mortimer looked at you when we were in the pub that night. He clearly felt affectionate toward you. You tried to conceal your reaction, but you were pleased. He admired you, and you liked that. Who wouldn't? And that's why you stood up for him against those lads."

Marjorie shook her head firmly, her lips clamped tightly together.

"I'm right, aren't I?" Dan went on. "You were friends. Go on, admit it. Honour his memory. Where's the harm in it?"

"You have no idea what you're talking about." She stood stiffly. "Go. Get out of my house. Bugger off."

"All right. If that's the way you want to play it. Thank you for the tea." Dan placed his mug carefully on the coaster, then he stood. "There's just one more thing, Mrs Treave. I have to ask you this. As far as you know, was Mortimer coming here to visit you on the night he was killed?"

"I've got nothing to say to you. Go."

"Fine. It wasn't my intention to upset you." Dan made to leave, crossing the room quickly. But as he pulled the door open and sunlight streamed into the cool kitchen, his gaze went to a small ceramic bowl on the terracotta tiled floor, glistening chunks of meat piled neatly in its centre. "You have a dog? I didn't see it in the garden."

"A cat. She comes and goes as she pleases. What about it?"

Dan studied the small bowl before answering. "I don't know much about cats, and I haven't eaten meat for a long time, but unless I'm much mistaken, your cat doesn't seem too fond of that liver."

"She eats what she's given."

"But you don't, do you, Mrs Treave?"

Marjorie bridled. "I beg your pardon. How dare you talk to me like that?"

"Just making an observation," Dan said. "I'd say that when you got home on Friday night, you found a packet of liver on your table or in your fridge. A gift from Mortimer. You didn't want him to bring it, but he left it for you, anyway. Perhaps he thought you'd appreciate it, and either your door was left unlocked, or Mortimer had a key; he was your landlord, after all. But you really didn't want that liver, so you've been feeding it to your cat ever since. You've given the poor creature so much of the stuff that it's grown sick of it. I hear they can be fussy eaters."

Marjorie's face fell. "How did you know all that?"

"When Mortimer left the pub on Friday, I saw something pass between you. He had his back to me, but I think he was showing you his prize from the meat raffle. You shook your head, and I can't say I blame you. But Mortimer wasn't going to discuss the matter with you in public. He respected your wish to keep your arrangement private."

"And what *arrangement* is that?" Marjorie demanded. "Just what do you think you know?"

Dan held out his hands, his palms outward. "I'm not suggesting anything sinister. Maybe you just kept each other company from time to time, but the fact that he brought the meat to your house, despite your expression of distaste, suggests that he expected you to cook it for him. Mortimer probably wasn't much of a cook, was he?"

Marjorie's stern expression crumbled, and she smiled sadly as if recalling a fond memory. "The man could boil an egg, but that was his limit. My Archie was the same. Worse, come to think of it. We used to say he could burn water."

"Were they similar, your husband and Mortimer?"

"No. Chalk and cheese. My Archie never raised his voice to me in forty-nine years of marriage, but Morty had a temper. He was always the same. Lose his rag at the drop of a hat, raging over nothing."

An unbidden image came to Dan's mind, a scene playing out in his imagination: Mortimer alone with Marjorie, a confrontation in the dark. She meets him on the path, and he demands to know why she stayed in the pub for so long, wants to know why his hot meal isn't ready. He squares up to her, towering over her, and then... what?

It's no good, Dan told himself. There was no reason for them to meet on the spoil heaps. And what weapon would she have used? She'd been carrying nothing when she'd entered the lane.

"Mrs Treave," Dan began, keeping his voice calm, "did Mortimer ever turn his temper against you? Did you argue?"

"Don't be stupid." Marjorie sent him a look of pure pity. "Your generation, you don't understand. Morty was an old mule, and he didn't take kindly to fools, but he knew how to behave. As far as I was concerned, he was always a proper gentleman. That's why..."

She looked down, shaking her head.

"Why what?" Dan asked gently. "What is it that you're not telling me?"

"Nothing."

"Did you see Mortimer on the night he was killed? Was he here when you got home?"

"No. You were right about what you said. He'd been here that night, but I didn't know about it until the next day when I found that bloody meat in the fridge. Oh, I heard an ambulance on Friday because I had the windows open, but I didn't know what was going on. How could I? I didn't find out what had happened until it was too late."

"Did you tell the police he'd been here?"

"What would be the point?"

"You have to tell them. It could be important. It explains why he was out on the path, and you never know, he might've left some clue." Dan stopped himself short, catching his breath. "Did he leave anything? A note? A message of some kind?"

"No. Like I said, I didn't even know he'd been here until the next day. He *left* nothing apart from that liver."

Her emphasis struck Dan as odd, but before he could say

another word, she shooed him out of the door, advancing on him so that he had no choice but to step outside. "I've told you all I can, so goodbye. I have work to do. I hope Mr Hargreaves can sort things out with the police. I expect it'll be all right. These things have a way of working out in the end. It'll all come out in the wash, as my Archie used to say. Goodbye."

Dan found himself staring at a closed door. He could hammer on it with his fist, but it would serve no purpose. For a few short minutes, he'd got through to her, broken down her protective shield of haughty indifference. But Marjorie Treave was no fool, and she hadn't given much away. *She's still hiding something*, Dan thought, but at that moment, there wasn't anything he could do about it. It was time to move on.

Looking around the garden as he made for the gate, Dan saw nothing unusual apart from the pens and sheds where her livestock were housed, and he fared no better in the lane. There was no sign to show where the police had found Alan's hiking stick. The hedges along the lane were dense and impenetrable, sitting as they did atop the banks of rock and earth that bordered most of the lanes in this part of the world. He found the ditch that ran alongside the road, but it was overgrown with nettles and some kind of tall weed that bore clusters of dainty white flowers. There were broken stems throughout the tangled undergrowth, but there was no clear pattern, or at least, none that Dan could see. The police searchers had probably poked into the weeds for a considerable distance along the lane, and Dan's heart sank. What had he expected: a mysterious clue visible only to him? Life just didn't work like that.

Turning around and heading back toward the footpath, he approached Marjorie's house from a different angle, and he slowed to cast his eye over the yard that housed her livestock. A trio of goats watched him from behind a wire fence, their keen eyes following his progress with interest while they chewed as if deep in thought. Half a dozen hens pecked and scratched their way around the concrete yard's perimeter, while a pair of geese held centre stage, craning their necks to survey their dominion. Suddenly, one of the geese hissed and stalked forward, flapping its wings. Dan flinched, but the target of the bird's anger was a plump tabby cat that had strayed too close. The cat marched away, its tail in the air, head held high, and Dan paused for a moment to take in the scene. The yard was clean and tidy, the troughs of water topped up, and the sheds were pristine, perhaps given a fresh coat of wood stain in recent months. The animals were all bright eyed and full of life, as pampered as pets. Whatever else you could say about Marjorie, she certainly looked after her livestock.

But where does she keep her bees? he wondered. There were no hives in her garden or around the yard, and judging by the number of empty jars he'd seen in Marjorie's kitchen, there would have to be several hives, wouldn't there? *I have no idea,* Dan thought. *For all I know, she might be making jam.* But the thought stirred a memory. When he'd asked Marjorie about the honey, she'd been evasive, fobbing him off with vague answers. He'd have expected her to be proud, extolling the virtues of her produce, but she'd been just the opposite. *Why?*

Dan headed back to the footpath, looking out across the fields as he walked. But if Marjorie had resumed her attack on the rhododendron bushes, he couldn't see her. All seemed quiet and still. There were no answers to be gleaned here, so Dan slipped quietly through the gate and took the footpath back toward the village. With any luck, Alan would be back soon, and they could compare notes. Because one thing was certain: on his own, Dan was making no progress at all.

CHAPTER 6

I T WAS ALMOST midday when Dan arrived home, his mind
teeming with questions for Alan. But his neighbour's car
wasn't in its usual parking spot. Dan knocked on Alan's door,
but there was no reply, so he stomped back home, slamming
the door shut and kicking off his shoes.

The day had grown hot, and the walk home had left him
light headed and thirsty, his shirt clinging to his back. In the
kitchen, he leaned over the sink and ran the cold tap,
collecting handfuls of water and splashing his face, dousing
his hair and the back of his neck. *That feels so good*, he thought
as the cold water tingled his scalp, letting him know he'd
caught the sun. He ought to be more careful. Alan had
already told him to get a baseball cap or something similar,
but he'd resisted. He'd always shied away from any item of
clothing that might brand him in some way, and to his mind,
all variants of the baseball cap were unacceptable. He
preferred to wear clothes that didn't advertise a
manufacturer: the kind of clothes that were only recognisable
to those in the know. Unfortunately, exclusive garments came
with eye-watering price tags, and until he found a new source
of income, they were out of his reach. He had some savings,

and he owned shares in a few well-chosen start-up businesses, so he'd manage for a while, but not forever. The mortgage payments on his London flat ate up almost all of his income. It was only a matter of time before he'd have to find a new job, and he wasn't looking forward to it.

He splashed more cold water on his face, closing his eyes and rinsing his skin until the chill made him gasp for air. Then he grabbed the hand towel from its hook, and pressing the cool cotton against his face, he rubbed the life back into his skin. But when he lowered the towel and looked up, his heart leapt in his chest.

The woman peering in through his kitchen window had an austere beauty. Her cheekbones were high and yet delicately defined, emphasised by the sophisticated sweep of her casually jagged pixie hairstyle. The rich chestnut sheen of her hair set off the steely deep blue of her eyes.

To Dan's chagrin, as the woman studied his dishevelled appearance, her perfectly shaped eyebrows slid upwards in an expression of bemused superiority. But then she smiled.

Dan didn't have a type, but if he did, this woman would set the standard by which all others would be judged. Her poise and posture, her artfully applied make-up and the dazzling whiteness of her perfect teeth: these were enough to turn his head. But the warmth of her smile seemed calculated to steal his heart. Here, in this rural village, was a vision from another world: a world of catwalks and red carpets, vintage champagne and chauffeur-driven limousines. It was as if this woman had stepped out from his dreams, and Dan had no idea what to do next.

"Hello," the woman called out, raising her hand to deliver a refined wave. "Mr Corrigan? Can we talk? Would that be all right?"

"Yes," Dan whispered, then again, louder, "Yes. Of course. Just… give me a minute." He dashed out into the hall and stood in front of the wall-mounted mirror, smoothing down his bedraggled hair and straightening his shirt. He looked a mess. He hadn't shaved that morning, and really he needed to go and grab a clean shirt, but that would be weird, wouldn't it? The woman outside would notice that he'd changed, and right from the outset, she'd think him odd. He really didn't want that. He didn't want that at all.

You'll have to do, he told himself, and taking a breath, he marched to the back door, presenting himself with as much nonchalance as he could muster. "Hello. I'm Dan Corrigan. What can I do for you?"

The woman held his gaze, one eyebrow raised. "Have I come at a bad moment? Only you seem rather flustered."

"No, not at all. I've just been out for a walk, and it's a hot day, so..." He gestured unnecessarily at nothing in particular. "You know how it is."

"Not really. I drove down to the village, and the climate control in the Jag is first rate. I hardly notice the weather these days." She stepped closer, placing her feet as though taking up position for a formal dance, then she extended her hand, her wrist gracefully limp. "Kristen Ellington. Perhaps you were expecting me."

Dan took her hand for a brief shake, and unlike his own sweaty palm, her skin was cool and dry. "Expecting? No. Should I have?"

Kristen's smile became a shade less dazzling. "Oh, I'd have thought you knew my life story by now. In this village, everybody knows everyone else's business. Since poor Uncle Morty died, the jungle drums must've been beating night and day."

It was Dan's turn to exercise his eyebrows. "Oh, I knew he had a family, but I didn't know... I mean, I wasn't expecting anyone like you." Dan closed his mouth before he could make even more of a fool of himself. *Get a grip, man*, he thought, and recovering quickly, he searched for the right words. "I'm sorry for your loss. Mortimer was quite a character."

"Oh yes, you can say that all right." Kristen lifted her gaze to look past Dan. "Shall we go in? I hate to stand on the doorstep; it gives the gossips too much ammunition."

"Certainly. Come in, please." He held the door open for her, gesturing toward the front room. "Would you like to go through?"

But Kristen stood in the kitchen, turning to inspect every surface and cabinet. "In here is fine. It's rather charming. Do you mind if I sit down?"

"No, please, go ahead. Can I offer you anything? I make a mean espresso."

She smiled, crinkling the corner of her eyes. "Wonderful. I haven't had a decent coffee since we arrived. We're staying at the Dower House, and Morty let the place get run down. It's been empty for months and everything's in a shocking state. Shocking." She sat at the table, smoothing her skirt, and Dan tried very hard not to stare as she crossed her long legs.

"Right," he said, heading to the counter and snatching up his stovetop espresso maker. He'd retired his cafetiere after a few frustrating days, returning to Exeter to purchase a traditional espresso maker. Thankfully, he'd bought a pot that was big enough for two. Measuring coffee into the compartment, he said, "When you say *we*, is that you and your husband?" He almost winced at the impudence of his question, but he had to know, and anyway, Kristen didn't seem to mind.

"No, I'm not married. I'm here with my brother, Craig. We're here to sort out Morty's affairs. You see, we were all the family he had. Our mother was his only sister, but they were never close. Morty could be... difficult. And truth be told, Mum was every bit as stubborn. They were much too alike to get on."

Dan added water to the espresso maker and assembled it, setting it on the electric stove and turning the ring on to its highest setting. "The coffee won't be long. This stove is a bit antiquated, but it does the job." He hunted for the only cups small enough for espresso, finding them on the draining board and checking they were clean. "Is your mother still alive?"

Kristen shook her head. "There's just Craig and me. We visited Morty when we could. Sometimes he came across as a real grump, but he wasn't a bad sort. Deep down, I think he was lonely. After his wife died, he was never the same again. I don't think he ever got over it. Aunt Caroline was lovely. A real sweetie."

"When did she pass away? Was it a long time ago?"

"It must be seven years." Kristen smiled sadly. "They lived in the Dower House in those days. That house was Aunt Caroline's pride and joy, but when she passed, it was far too big for Morty. He moved into a little cottage in the village. They say he never set foot in the Dower House again, and judging by the state of the place, I can believe it."

"What is a dower house, exactly? I've never been sure."

"Traditionally, when the owner of a great estate died, the main house passed to his eldest son, so the bereft widow was packed off to a dower house."

"Interesting," Dan said. "So your family are titled gentry, are they? Should I bow?"

Kristen laughed. "Good lord, no. We're new money. Well, since Victorian times. Our family made their fortune moving stone from place to place. Granite mainly. There was a string of quarries once, a fleet of lorries, even a tramline. It was all very industrious."

"Past tense?"

A barely perceptible twitch of Kristen's lips betrayed her distaste. "Yes. Those days are gone." She brightened, shaking her head as if dismissing the past. "But I didn't come here to talk about me. I came here to thank you for everything you did for Morty. I heard all about it, and it was very noble of you. You were very brave."

Dan shrugged off the compliment. "It was nothing. I was only sorry that we didn't get to him in time."

"At least you tried. Listen, we'd like to say thank you properly. Perhaps we could go for a drink later. You must know the village pub. We could meet there if you like."

"Definitely," Dan said. "That would be nice."

"Good. Shall we say around eight? Craig will be there. He's dying to meet you, but he's tied up all day in meetings. There's so much to sort out. Morty left his affairs in a dreadful mess. The poor man wasn't equipped to deal with the modern world. Everything was scribbled down on scraps of paper. Can you imagine? It's a nightmare."

"It must be very trying," Dan said, tending to the coffee. He poured carefully, setting a cup before Kristen, and then joining her at the table, taking the seat next to her.

Kristen lifted the cup, pausing to savour the aroma. "Heavenly. Just what I needed."

"You're very welcome. While you're staying in the village, if there's anything you need, I'm happy to help."

"My, you're a perfect gentleman, aren't you. A knight in shining armour."

"I don't know about that," Dan said, and despite himself, he sat a little straighter, puffing out his chest. "I know what it's like when you come into the village unprepared. You find yourself missing all kinds of things, and it's not like you can nip out to the local shop to fetch supplies. I've trekked over to Exeter more times than I care to admit."

"I live not far from Exeter. Woodbury. Do you know it?"

Dan shook his head. "No, but I think Alan mentioned it."

"Ah, would that be Alan Hargreaves. He was with you when you found Morty, wasn't he?"

"Yes. He lives next door."

"Right, well he must come along this evening, too. I'd better go and see him." She drank the last of her coffee then made to rise.

"He's not in," Dan said quickly. "But I'll pass on the invitation. There's no need for you to rush off."

"Thanks, but I really must be going, anyway." She stood, extending her hand as before. "It really was lovely to meet you, Mr Corrigan, and I look forward to seeing you later."

"Yes, me too. But please, call me Dan." He took her hand for a brief moment, and she bestowed a knowing smile on him, apparently all too aware of the effect she was having.

"I'll see you at eight, Dan. Craig will be thrilled to meet you, I'm sure."

"It's a date. Well, not a *date* date, obviously, but I'll be there."

"And bring your neighbour," Kristen reminded him. "We can't leave him out, can we?"

If only, Dan thought. If three was a crowd, four was even worse. It wasn't a charitable sentiment, but he didn't want to share his time with Kristen. *We've only just met*, he reminded himself, but there was no logic to the way he felt. Kristen had tilted the Earth on its axis, and he was going to spend the evening in her company. That was all that mattered, and he maintained a cheerful smile as he showed her to the door.

She gave him a little wave, waggling her fingers in the air, a flirtatious glint in her eye, and then she was gone, striding toward the road and disappearing around the corner.

My God, Dan thought. *She is amazing.*

CHAPTER 7

D AN AND ALAN arrived at the pub early, and the place was deserted. They took a table in the back room, and Alan set about downing his first pint with more than his usual enthusiasm.

"Steady on," Dan said. "At this rate, you'll be half cut before our visitors arrive."

"You haven't had the day I've had," Alan replied. "I've never been so mortified in my entire life."

"It sounds awful. You shouldn't have been subjected to that. Your solicitor should've got you out of there."

"I know, but he was out of his depth. He did his best, the poor chap, but the police ran rings around him." Alan took another long draught of his beer. "It wasn't so much the questions that got to me; it was the constant repetition. They kept harping on the same things, over and over, the insinuation being that I'd lied the first time around. Oh, they dressed it up nicely enough, always calling me *sir*, and throwing in polite phrases like *if you wouldn't mind*, and *it would really help us if you could just go through it one more time*. But there was always another *one more time*. It was enough to drive you to distraction."

"It sounds hideous." Dan sat quietly for a minute, giving Alan a chance to relax, then he said, "Did you manage to get any information out of Spiller?"

Alan swirled the beer around his glass before taking another drink. "There was one snippet that I thought you might like."

Dan sat forward. "Yes?"

"Get me another pint and I'll tell you."

"But you haven't finished that one yet."

Alan grinned. "But I will have done by the time you've been to the bar and back."

"All right. Same again?"

"Oh yes."

Slouched behind the bar, Kevin looked up hopefully as Dan approached. "What can I get you? Did you change your mind about having a look at the menu?"

"No thanks. Another pint of Jail Ale for Alan, and I'll have a half of the same."

"Jail for Alan, eh? Very appropriate from what I've heard." Kevin chortled as he pulled the pint. "Police knocking at his door, dragging him off to Exeter. Who'd have thought it?"

"Hopefully, no one, because it didn't happen like that," Dan said. "Alan went to see the police voluntarily. He's done nothing wrong, as you well know."

Kevin rocked on his heels. "Maybe, but how do you explain about his stick? I heard they found it in a ditch with the old man's blood all over it."

"For God's sake," Dan muttered, then he fixed Kevin with a look. "You were the one who told me Alan's stick was behind the bar, and you saw us leave without it."

"Except, I didn't. I was clearing up in the back room, and when I came back, you'd gone and so had the stick."

"Are you sure about that?" Dan asked. "Could you swear that the stick was there until we left? When did you last see it?"

Kevin finished pouring the drinks before he replied. "It was there when I went into the back room. I know that because I was going to remind Alan to take it. So I'm sure it disappeared around the same time you did."

"Dammit."

"But you weren't the only ones to leave around then," Kevin went on. "The place was a good deal quieter when I came back with the empties."

"I know Marjorie was still here when we left, and I think I saw a few people leave just before us. They were together: a little group of four or five middle-aged men, but I can't remember if they were carrying anything."

Kevin nodded. "They were here for the snooker. I've a full-sized table upstairs if you're interested. Those blokes come regular."

"Yes. I remember now. They had those long thin cases with them. I presume they're for carrying snooker cues, but I wonder…"

"Those cases aren't long enough for a hiking stick." Kevin placed the drinks on the bar. "The cues come apart so they're easier to carry. You're barking up the wrong tree, there."

"We'll see about that. Who else left at the same time as us? What about Jay?"

Kevin's eyes beetled from side to side. "Yep. He was gone when I came back. I remember thinking it was a bit peculiar. He's usually the last to leave; I can't get him out, most nights." Kevin's lips formed an O. "You don't think it was him, do you? Hell's teeth, that would be something. And him an ex-copper."

"Let's not jump the gun. There was a couple in here. Alan said he didn't recognise them."

"Tourists," Kevin replied darkly. "They're in one of the holiday cottages. Married, I'd say. They didn't talk to the locals. Hardly spoke to each other. But they sat there most of the night, taking their time. I said to the bloke, 'Are you drinking that pint or waiting for it to evaporate?', but he didn't take it kindly. Miserable sod. They left just after you, dragging their heels. None too keen to be left on their own, if you ask me."

Dan looked at Kevin with fresh eyes. "I suppose you get plenty of practice in people-watching."

"I don't know about that. We get all kinds of people in here, and I can usually spot a troublemaker."

"And what about that night? Was anyone behaving oddly? Did you see anything that struck you as strange?"

"No. You were here when young Steve tried to throw his weight about, but that's nothing new. The lad's harmless. The youngsters get bored; there's not much for them to do. They get a bit rowdy now and then, blowing off steam, but then they go home and drink themselves stupid on supermarket lager. It does nothing for my profit margin, but what can you do?"

"I've no idea, but here's my contribution." Dan held out his debit card, but Kevin scarcely glanced at it.

"Forget it. On the house. You tried to help the old man, and most wouldn't. That's got to be worth something."

"Thanks. I appreciate that." Dan pocketed his card and picked up the drinks. "By the way, we're meeting Mortimer's niece and nephew later. Craig and Kristen. When they come in, can you send them into the back?"

"Yeah, I know them. No problem." Kevin busied himself, wiping down the bar, and Dan headed back with his prizes.

"What took you so long?" Alan waggled his empty glass meaningfully. "I was about to send a search party."

"You said that on Friday." Dan sat down, pushing the pint toward Alan.

"Did I? I must be losing my grip."

"And you said *that* on Wednesday." Dan grinned. "You should see your face. But don't worry; I just made that up. I can't remember much about what we said on Wednesday, but I don't think you've got anything to worry about."

"Apart from the dark cloud of suspicion hanging over my head. Is that what you were talking to Kevin about?"

"Yes. I was doing my best to quell the rumours. But never mind about that. Tell me what you found out at the police station."

Alan raised a finger. "You'll like this. Spiller kept banging on about the blood on my hiking stick, and in the end, my solicitor finally spoke up and demanded to know the details. He wanted chapter and verse, sight of the lab report and all that kind of thing. Now, most of it didn't mean much to me, but there's a whole branch of forensics devoted to bloodstains. They can tell a lot from the patterns, and apparently the blood on my stick isn't necessarily from an impact. They called it a 'wipe pattern'. It could've been from someone attempting to clean the handle, or it could've been transferred by someone with blood on their hands."

Dan sat back. "So, someone, whether by accident or design, smeared the blood onto the stick sometime *after* the attack."

"Could be. They said it was still fresh when it was smeared on the handle, but even so, it introduces an element of doubt, and that was music to my ears." Alan raised his glass. "Cheers."

Dan took a distracted swig from his unfinished pint. "I see. So your stick might not be the murder weapon after all."

"That's right, and without the weapon, they can't even be certain they've got a murder on their hands. All they really have is an unexplained death. But that hasn't stopped Spiller from clinging to his theory. He kept insisting that someone had simply tried to wipe the blood away and failed, but he didn't look happy. My solicitor thinks Spiller's case might not stand up in court. He reckons a good defence barrister would tear it to shreds. We can cast doubt on whether my stick was even at the scene when it came into contact with the blood."

"Which is good for us," Dan said. "Good for *you*, I mean."

"It's a start, but it doesn't put me in the clear, not by a country mile."

"What we need is someone else to place in the frame," Dan said. "If we can give Spiller a few credible leads to follow, he might take his beady eyes off you."

"Perhaps," Alan replied, but he didn't look convinced.

"Trust me. Spiller isn't going to go out of his way to look for suspects if he thinks he can pin this on you. If you ask me, he's a washout: passed over for promotion and cruising toward retirement. I can see it in his eyes."

Alan grunted. "I saw a different side to him in that interview room. He was like a dog with a bone."

"Two can play at that game," Dan said. "I'm nothing if not persistent. We just need to do a bit of digging: talk to the right people, ask the right questions."

"And who are the right people? We can't go around interrogating everyone and making accusations. This is a small village. People talk, and personally, I don't want to stir up any more trouble for myself. I've had more than enough aggravation from DS Spiller."

"You can't have it both ways," Dan argued. "Either you sit back and take the flak from Spiller, or you stand up for yourself, even if it means opening a can of worms."

Alan opened his mouth to protest, but Dan didn't give him the chance. "We can sort this mess out," he went on, "but we can't afford to pussyfoot around the edges of this thing. It's no use worrying about what the neighbours might think. We'll have to get stuck in, even if it makes us unpopular."

"You know what? If you'd said that to me yesterday, I'd have told you we should leave it to the police, but now…" Alan regarded his glass thoughtfully before taking a swig.

"Now, I'd say that it has to be worth a shot." He raised his glass. "Count me in."

They clinked glasses and Dan drained his pint before sitting back and flexing his fingers. "Okay, I think our main suspects are Marjorie Treave—"

"Seriously?" Alan interrupted, chortling under his breath. "I can't see Marge bludgeoning a man to death. She's tough, but her heart's in the right place."

"I told you about the liver and the late-night visits," Dan said. "On the night he was killed, Mortimer let himself into her house and left the meat in her fridge. It proves a link."

"It proves she's a decent person." Alan held out his hands. "So she cooked the old man a hot meal once in a while. So what? Why would she attack him? Do you think he made a rude remark about her mashed potatoes? Did he complain there were lumps in the gravy?"

"Perhaps this will change your opinion of dear sweet Marjorie." Dan pulled his phone from his pocket and selected the short video of Marjorie hacking at the rhododendrons.

Alan watched in silence. "She really doesn't like those blossoms, does she?"

"What do you mean? This isn't a bit of light gardening, it's a frenzied attack. If you ask me, she's lost the plot entirely. Mad as a hatter."

"Play it again."

Dan pressed play, and Alan pointed at the screen. "Look, she's just cutting away the flowers. She's not pruning the longer branches unless they have blossoms on them."

"Oh yes. I never noticed that before. Even so, it proves that she has the strength and the ability to wield a long-handled weapon."

"Okay, so theoretically, she could've attacked Mortimer, but what's her motivation?"

"He owned her house and the land it sits on," Dan replied. "Maybe he'd threatened to evict her."

"So, she kills him, the land is sold off, and she ends up evicted anyway," Alan said. "Marjorie would've been able to figure that out. She isn't stupid."

"I don't know, maybe she lost her temper. They could easily have fallen out over some little thing."

Alan looked doubtful. "Moving on from Marjorie, who else can we look at?"

"Jay," Dan said. "He was in the pub, and according to Kevin, Jay left without being asked, which was out of character. Plus, we know that he left at around the time the stick went missing."

"Motive?"

Dan shrugged. "The other night, you hinted that he's a dodgy character. He flashes money around, but as far as we know, he has no job. An ex-cop turned to crime, perhaps?"

"What kind of crime?"

"No idea," Dan admitted. "I wonder if there are any records we can access? You know, crime reports from the local press. If he's been in trouble before, it might give us a lead."

Alan nodded. "He's too young to have retired, isn't he? Perhaps he was kicked off the force."

"Now, we're talking. I'll do some research online later."

"Any other suspects?" Alan asked.

Dan thought for a moment. "There was a couple in the pub that night, remember? You didn't recognise them, but Kev says they're in a holiday cottage. They shouldn't be too hard to track down, should they?"

"I could ask around, but there are a lot more holiday cottages in the village than you might realise. It's a bone of contention around here. When houses are turned into holiday homes, it drives the price of property up. The locals get priced out of the market, especially the younger folk. They can't afford to live here, so they have to move away, and that takes the life out of the community. We end up with an ageing population plus a load of houses standing empty for large chunks of the year."

"That could be relevant," Dan said. "A young guy like Steve might harbour a grudge against a man who owns property."

"I've heard that Mortimer owned a few houses in the village, but I'm not sure which ones or what they were used for." Alan peered over Dan's shoulder, looking back toward the bar. "Perhaps your friends will be able to fill us in. I think this must be them."

Dan swivelled in his seat. Yes. Kristen was making her way toward him, and behind her, a man in his early forties trailed in her wake. Dan jumped to his feet, smoothing down the creases in his shirt as he stepped forward to meet the new arrivals. And he smiled. In the room's soft light, Kristen Ellington was even more dazzling than before, and she sashayed across the threadbare carpet as though making a grand entrance at an elite social gathering.

"Dan," Kristen said, taking his hand. "Lovely to see you again. And this must be Alan, the famous writer. Nice to meet you."

"Oh, I'm not famous," Alan said sheepishly. But he couldn't hide his delight when Kristen turned her thousand-watt smile on him.

"Don't be so modest," Kristen admonished. "This is my brother Craig. Craig, these are the fine chaps who did their best for dear Uncle Morty."

Craig beamed as he shook their hands. "Great to finally meet you chaps. That was a great thing you did for the old boy. It means a lot, it really does. We can't thank you enough."

"I'm only sorry we weren't able to do more," Dan said, and despite the occasion, he found himself casting a critical eye over Craig. In his striped shirt and understated grey suit, Craig would fit perfectly into the offices of any financial institution in a provincial city. The suit was by no means in its first flush of youth, and it was definitely off the peg rather than bespoke, but it was well made, and it did a reasonable job of sharpening Craig's slightly stooped shoulders. Unfortunately, the jacket didn't fare quite so well around the man's midriff, and the buttons pulled the fabric a little too tight: evidence of a burgeoning paunch. Add in the man's Mediterranean tan and neatly trimmed hair, and Dan felt he knew Craig already.

As if anxious to conform to type, Craig rubbed his hands together and said, "Right, introductions over. Who's ready for a drink?"

"I'm fine, thanks." Dan indicated his untouched half, but Craig waved his words aside.

"Nonsense. I'll get you a pint. If memory serves, they have a decent ale or two. How about you, Alan? You look like a man in need of a pint. Same again?"

"Thanks, I'll have a pint of Jail Ale," Alan said. "I can recommend it."

"Okay, same for me," Dan said. "Thanks."

Craig smiled. "Sis, I know what you want. I'll be back in a tick. Oh God, I do hope they accept cards in this place. I never carry cash around these days. Who does, eh?" Craig made a show of patting his pockets.

"They take cards," Alan chipped in. "Contactless. You can even pay with your phone."

"All mod cons, eh? Thank God for that." Craig flapped his hands at Dan and Kristen. "Sit down, make yourselves at home. This isn't a funeral." He grimaced in mock horror. "Oops. Bad choice of words. Still, you know what I mean. Relax, and I'll get the drinks."

He seemed intent on waiting until his instructions had been carried out, so forcing a smile, Dan sat down and Kristen followed suit. Only then, apparently satisfied, did Craig bustle to the bar.

"Sorry about Craig," Kristen said. "He's good as gold really, but he's always been a bit of a control freak."

"Imagine that," Alan said, casting a meaningful glance at Dan before swiftly changing the subject. "But you know, I remember Craig. We met once at some occasion in the village. I think it was the summer fair."

"Quite possibly," Kristen replied. "My dear brother enjoys all that kind of thing: the country life, shooting pheasants, yomping about in waxed cotton and wellies." She rolled her eyes upward. "Give him a time machine, and he'd zoom back to the thirties in a flash, wearing a monocle and tormenting the parlour maids." She laughed gently. "Sorry, that makes me sound positively bitchy, but it's just our little joke. You know how it is with families. We're at each other's throats over the tiniest things, but we stick together through thick and thin."

"I've always got on pretty well with my sister," Dan said. "I'm sure we had plenty of arguments in our teens, but once we grew up, it was all fine. I'm living in her house while she's abroad."

Kristen nodded. "Good idea. Best not to leave the place empty. These old houses need looking after. The Dower House is in a terrible mess. It really is a shame."

"You should see the Dower House, Dan," Alan said. "I think you'll be impressed."

"That would be nice," Dan replied. "Although I must confess, I don't have much of an appreciation for architecture. One old house looks very much like another to me, I'm afraid."

"Oh, you'll like this one," Alan insisted with a twinkle in his eye. "I guarantee it."

"Yes, you simply must call on us," Kristen said. "I'm busy tomorrow, but you can pop around the day after if you like. We'll have afternoon tea. Alan, you must come too. Three o'clock?"

Dan and Alan shared a look, then Alan said, "Certainly we'll come. Thank you. We'll look forward to it."

Judging by the roguish gleam in Alan's eyes, Dan knew there was something going on here, but before he could ask, Craig returned with the drinks.

"Here's your large G and T." Craig pushed a glass toward Kristen. "They didn't have that fancy one you like, but this is local stuff. It's made on Dartmoor, apparently."

"It gives the prisoners something to do," Alan said.

Kristen stared at him, her drink halfway to her lips. "No. Seriously?"

"Oh, yes. They brew it in the kitchens. From potato peelings mainly. Dartmoor is the only one of Her Majesty's prisons to turn a profit."

Craig let out a bellow of laughter, slapping his hands against his thighs. "Nice one, Alan. You really had her, there."

Alan chortled. "Sorry, I couldn't resist. There are two things that most people know about Dartmoor: the Hound of the Baskervilles and the prison. You can usually work one or the other into a little joke."

Kristen sat upright. "I'm not a tourist, you know. I do live in Devon."

"Ah, you only frequent the posh parts," Craig said. "You live in a world of chocolate-box thatched cottages and old mansions with ivy on the walls. You don't mix with the salt-of-the-Earth types in places like this." He looked around the room appreciatively. "I mean, just look at those beams in the ceiling. Hundreds of years old. And that fireplace with its great stone hearth. Solid slate. Fantastic."

Kristen sent her brother a tight smile. "On the other hand, some of us think the South-West needs to be dragged kicking and screaming into the twenty-first century." She turned to Dan. "This area could be so much more than it is. With a bit of investment in infrastructure, it could be a hub for all kinds of enterprise."

"So long as no one needs to get anywhere in a hurry," Craig said. "The transport links are shocking. Have you seen how long it takes the trains to crawl toward London? It's hopeless."

Kristen groaned as if she'd heard it all before. "That's old-school thinking, Craig. With decent broadband, people can work remotely. Tech start-ups don't need freight trains."

"If you want to know about start-ups, ask Dan," Alan said. "He's the expert."

Kristen's gaze grew sharper. "Really? Is that your field?"

"It was until recently," Dan replied. "I was a consultant on a number of start-ups, and most of them did pretty well."

Alan nudged him with his elbow. "Don't be so modest. Dan was a top troubleshooter, brought in to get things moving."

"I helped to oil the wheels," Dan said modestly. "You sound very interested in business, Kristen? Is that what you do?"

Craig let out a guffaw. "Oh, Saint Kristen doesn't soil her hands with anything so tawdry. She's an angel of mercy."

"You're a nurse?" Alan asked.

"I work in health care," Kristen replied. "I'm a therapeutic facilities coordinator."

Dan nodded wisely. He had no idea what such a job might entail, and judging by the silence around the table, no one wanted to be the first to ask.

"NHS?" Alan ventured.

"Good God, no," Craig blurted. "Where Kristen works, it's not so much hospital food and bed baths, but personal chefs and Jacuzzis with gold-plated taps."

Kristen maintained her smile, but it looked as though it cost her a considerable effort to do so. "Our company provides first-class health care for a select clientele. We cater for a range of therapeutic needs, but there's certainly nothing as vulgar as gold-plated taps."

"And the personal chefs?" Alan asked. "Is that an exaggeration?"

Kristen turned her smile on Alan. "Our clients tend to come from a background of exclusivity. They don't feel the need to share."

"And no doubt they have deep pockets," Alan said.

"You bet," Craig chipped in. "How the other half live, eh?"

Alan shook his head in disapproval. "More like the other one percent."

"Oh, like that is it?" Craig said. "Bit of a lefty, are you?"

Alan lifted his jaw. "Not necessarily, but I worked as a teacher for several years, in the state sector, and it gives you a certain perspective on the distribution of wealth. I've never seen the gap between rich and poor as something to be celebrated."

"But I hear that you're our resident writer," Craig protested. "Presumably, you abandoned education to write, simply because the money is better. So where are your principles now?" He let out a bark of laughter. "Admit it, old man. When the chips are down, you're a sink-or-swim, devil-take-the-hindmost capitalist."

Dan watched Craig carefully. The man's smile was good natured enough, but his voice had taken on a gruff, bullying tone. Here was a man who was used to getting his own way; a man who enjoyed confrontation. And there was something else. As he'd warmed to his theme, perhaps sensing a soft target in Alan, Craig's eyes had lit with a cold glint of determination: the greed of a predator closing in on its prey.

But Craig didn't know Alan.

"I don't accept your assertion," Alan stated firmly. "It just doesn't stand up."

"Come on," Craig began, but Alan didn't give him the chance to continue.

"I'd be much better off if I'd stayed in teaching," Alan

said. "With my qualifications and my years of experience, I'd have been promoted by now. I'd have been working toward a leadership role, training to be a headteacher. You see, there's a very clear career structure in education, and a pension at the end of it. Sure, it's hard work, but very worthwhile, and reasonably secure. Whereas now, I get by, but I'm not exactly raking it in."

"So why did you leave?" Craig demanded. "Were you straining against all the red tape and bureaucracy of the public sector?"

Alan shook his head. "It's simple. I found my vocation."

Craig stared at him for a moment, but then his stern expression collapsed into a boyish grin. "Ah, then you're a lucky man, my friend. I found my vocation years ago, but sadly, there's precious little call for sailing boat captains in this day and age, so I work at the day job to fund my sailing habit."

"See what I mean about the thirties?" Kristen asked Dan.

Craig eyed her suspiciously. "What was that, sis? Having a dig are we?"

"And what is your day job, Craig?" Dan asked quickly, earning a grateful smile from Kristen.

"I'm an asset manager for a transport firm in Exmouth," Craig said. "We deal in logistics solutions, moving all kinds of gear from one place to another. It's a tricky business unless you know the ropes, but I came up through the army, so there's not much that can throw me off my stride. I don't mind a challenge. Once you've been in a combat situation, anything else is easy."

"I'd have thought you'd have opted for the Royal Navy," Alan said.

Craig seemed to find this amusing. "It's an odd thing, isn't it? Here's me, a water rat to the bone, and I wind up in some godawful desert getting eaten alive by the flies." He laughed darkly. "The thing is, I didn't get the sailing bug until after I left the army. Still, the training set me up for later life, so it was all for the best. I was an officer in the Royal Logistics Corps. Second lieutenant. *Movers*: that's what they used to call us, and by God, we shifted some kit. Happy days."

"Anyway," Kristen said brightly, "we mustn't monopolise the conversation." She turned her inquisitive gaze on Dan. "Tell me, how are you finding Embervale? It takes some getting used to, doesn't it?"

"I'm quite enjoying it," Dan found himself saying, aware that Alan was watching him carefully. "It's good to have a change of scene, and it's certainly very different to London."

"You can say that again," Kristen said. "It's not exactly a hive of activity. No bright lights and nightlife. No hordes of eager young people striving to get on."

Dan bowed his head slightly, conceding the point. "No, but it does have a certain bucolic charm. I can see the attraction of living in a place like this. On the whole, the people are friendly, and they have a way of life that's simpler, more authentic."

"Oh, the folks around here are authentic, all right." Kristen raised her glass in a mock toast, and a sneering tone crept into her voice. "They're the real deal: sons and daughters of the soil." She leaned forward, lowering her voice to a stage whisper. "And what do you think about this place, the pub?"

"We quite like it," Alan said. "It's a hub for the community, a place for people to get together and keep in touch with their neighbours."

"You mean gossip and spread rumours." Kristen grimaced. "And do they still do that awful thing with the raw meat?"

Alan nodded. "The raffle. Yes."

"Ugh!" Kristen took another sip of her drink. "You know, I rarely eat meat these days. Where I work, we have chefs who can make the simplest salad into a feast."

"Good for you," Dan said. "I totally agree. We don't need meat to stay healthy, and we can make food that's just as tasty without it. It's all about respecting the ingredients."

"Dan's almost a vegan," Alan explained.

"Oh God, not another one," Craig moaned. "I get tired of the food police telling us what to eat and drink all the time. What's wrong with a bit of meat? It's only natural."

Dan's smile tightened. "Do you really want me to answer that question? It could take some time."

"I'm game." Craig folded his arms. "Give it your best shot."

"Leave him alone, Craig," Kristen said. "I admire anyone who sticks to their guns. It's good for a person to be anchored by their ideals." She eyed Dan appreciatively. "Besides, it's easy to see who's in better shape. Perhaps, dear brother, you'd do well to lay off the roast beef for a while."

Craig grunted. "He's younger than me, that's all."

"Yes, I'm sure that's all it is," Dan said with an innocent smile. "I expect you were accustomed to regular exercise in the army. Perhaps you'd like to come out for a run. There's a nice little 5K route I've worked out. You might enjoy it. I'm heading up there tomorrow. Alan's coming."

Alan nodded uncertainly. "Looking forward to it. Almost."

"I'll think about it," Craig said, eyeing Dan as if trying to decide whether he was being genuine or poking fun at him. "Anyway, who's for another drink?"

Dan patted his stomach. "I don't know. If we're running tomorrow…"

"Another one won't hurt you," Alan said. "I'll get them in. Same again?" Receiving their murmurs of agreement, he headed to the bar.

Looks like I'll be running alone tomorrow, Dan thought. But that was okay. He needed some time to clear his mind, to whip himself back into shape.

As if reading his mind, Kristen said, "Is it boys only, or are you going to invite me for a run as well?"

"Sorry, I didn't mean to leave you out," Dan replied. "Of course, you can come along if you'd like. I should warn you though, it might be different from what you're used to."

Kristen regarded him coolly. "Meaning what, exactly? Do you imagine that I spend all my spare time in the gym, trundling away on a treadmill?"

"Not at all. It's just that, when I came here, it took time for me to adjust. In London, I was mainly running over flat ground and the paths were smooth. But around here, it's more like cross-country running, with dips and hills, and muddy paths or rocky trails. It's set me back. My time for 5K is nowhere near my personal best, but I'm improving, little by little, day by day. I'll get there in the end."

"Yes, I'm sure you will," Kristen said. "I'm not sure I'd be able to keep up with you. You're a very determined man, I can see that."

Dan held her gaze. "I know a good thing when I see it, and I've never been afraid to pursue my goals."

"Same here," Craig said, seemingly unaware he was spoiling the moment. "When you see what you want, you've got to get in quick and snap it up. That's how you win."

Kristen arched an eyebrow. "So you never tire of reminding me. But things didn't go your way with the solicitor, did they?"

"The man's a fool," Craig stated. "But I'm not done with him yet. I'll sort this mess out if it's the last thing I do."

"Legal troubles?" Dan asked. "Nothing too serious I hope."

"It's Morty's will that's causing all the problems," Kristen replied. "He was quite savvy in some ways, but in others he was a law unto himself. You'll never guess what he's done. He's left that wonderful little cottage to Marjorie Treave. I don't know what he was thinking, but he must've had a brainstorm, because while he was at it, he left her the land adjoining the property. It's maddening, it really is."

Dan ran his hand along his jaw, deep in thought. "This changes everything."

"You're damned right, it does," Craig said. "For one thing, we'll have to work out how to contest the will. The old crone must've got her claws into Morty somehow. I'm convinced she's up to no good."

"What makes you say that?" Dan asked.

"Well, for one thing, she won't talk to me," Craig replied. "We've been trying to get hold of her, so we can have a proper discussion with the solicitor, but she won't hear of it. I even went around there this afternoon, but she slammed the door in my face, and she used a few words she shouldn't have."

"I don't think she could've known about the will," Dan said, thinking aloud. "I talked to her earlier today, and she thought she'd have to move out. She seemed very certain."

"It's all a front," Craig growled. "The damned woman knows how to put on an act. She can play the part of the sweet old lady when it suits her, but by God, when she turns, you see a very different side to her. She's a viper, a harridan. I wouldn't trust her as far as I could throw her."

Dan studied Craig's expression, and there it was again: the glare of bitter anger in the man's eyes. It was one thing to be irritated by Mortimer's arrangements, but this was something else. This was hatred.

"Listen," Dan said, keeping his voice calm. "I don't know if this helps, but from what I understand, Mortimer and Marjorie were friends. She cooked meals for him and kept him company. I'm sure that's all there is to it. He wanted to repay her by making sure she wouldn't end up homeless after his death."

Craig didn't reply. Kristen looked uncomfortable, and she cleared her throat quietly. But before she could say anything, Alan returned with the drinks, carrying all four with a practised ease. "Here we are." He slid the glasses onto the table, glancing around the group as they muttered their thanks. "What's happened? I've only been gone a few minutes, and you three are looking like you've lost a pound and found a penny."

"It's all right, Alan," Kristen said smoothly. "Nothing to worry about. Craig and I were just telling Dan about the house and land that Morty left to Mrs Treave."

Alan sat down quickly, reaching for his pint. "You don't think…"

Kristen sent him a puzzled look, then her eyes went wide in horror as she realised what he was implying. "No. I'm not suggesting she was involved in the attack. Not at all. It hadn't even crossed my mind."

"Hadn't it?" Craig demanded. "It crossed mine. About half a second after I heard about the will."

"That night," Alan began, his voice faint, "she was out there, just before Mortimer was attacked. We saw her go past, didn't we, Dan?"

"Yes," Dan admitted. "But I talked to her today, and I really don't think she had anything to do with it."

"Maybe not directly, but that doesn't mean she wasn't involved," Craig said. "*Cui bono*. Who benefits?"

Alan thought for a moment. "But if she didn't know about the will, then surely she had no motive."

"We can't say for certain whether she knew or not," Craig insisted. "But it stands to reason that he told her. Why wouldn't he? Hell, he probably enjoyed himself: playing the great benefactor, lording over her, making promises. I'll bet she enjoyed the prospect. That land could be—" He broke off suddenly, shaking his head.

"I think you're getting carried away," Kristen said, though not unkindly. "It's the grief talking. A delayed reaction. That's all." Craig had gripped the edge of the table with both hands, and Kristen laid her hands on his. "We'll sort it out, Craig.

Don't worry. There's always a way around any problem. Leave it to me."

Craig nodded dumbly. The fight had gone out of him, so perhaps Kristen had been right about his state of mind.

Grief affects people in odd ways, Dan thought. *Craig needed to blow off some steam*. But one thing niggled at Dan as he took a sip of his pint. Craig had been about to say something when he'd stopped himself, and from his tone, he was clearly angry about the value of Marjorie's inheritance. But it wasn't the cottage that was vexing him, even though the house would fetch a good price; it was the land.

According to Marjorie, Mortimer had claimed he could reopen the mines and make a fortune. Could there be something in the idea? It seemed ridiculous, but Dan knew nothing about minerals and mining. Perhaps it wasn't a coincidence that they'd found Mortimer on the spoil heaps.

Then the image of Mortimer lying on the ground came back to him, and he recalled the old man's pained entreaty, perhaps the last words he ever spoke: *Stop them. Whatever it takes. Stop them.*

TUESDAY

CHAPTER 8

D OZING ON THE couch, Alan sat up with a start.
Something had woken him, though he wasn't sure
what.

Rubbing his eyes, he checked the time on his phone. It was
already eleven o'clock in the morning, and a twinge of guilt
made Alan wince. He'd cried off the planned run with Dan,
citing a headache, though they both knew the beer was to
blame. After Kristen and Craig had gone back to the Dower
House, Dan and Alan had stayed in the pub to discuss the
implications of Marjorie's inheritance. Had she known about
it beforehand? And if she had, was it really motivation
enough to kill Mortimer? After all, she already lived in the
house and apparently had free run of the land. But Dan had
been sure there was something in Mortimer's last words: *Stop
them*. Who were they to stop, and from what? What did it all
mean?

A series of thuds echoed down the entrance hall. Someone
was knocking on the front door, and that's what must've
woken him. Grunting as he climbed to his feet, Alan yawned
and then padded to the door. Perhaps Dan had come back
from his run already, in which case, a fresh pot of coffee

would be in order. *That'll wake me up*, Alan thought, but as the hammering on the door intensified, another, less welcome possibility crossed his mind. *Oh no, not the police again.*

But when he opened the door, Marjorie Treave stood on the step, studying him with a jaundiced eye, a wicker basket gripped tight in the crook of her elbow.

"Mrs Treave, how can I help you?"

She sniffed. "A few weeks back, you had a jar of honey off me. Bought it at the gate."

"Yes, that's right. Very nice it was too."

The corners of her lips turned even further downward. "You ate some? When?"

"Erm, a couple of days ago. I had it on toast. Why do you ask?"

"'Tis a bad batch," Marjorie said. "No good at all." She craned her neck to peer up at him. "Are you all right? You don't look well."

Alan scraped his hand down his face. "Marjorie, I'm fine. What's this about?"

"Like I said, 'tis a bad batch of honey. Something wrong with it." She held out her hand, a collection of coins on her palm. "I'll take it back. Here's your money. It's the right amount, but you'd better count it, just to be sure."

"But, that's not necessary. The honey's fine. I—"

"I won't hear a word of argument," Marjorie interrupted. "Just take your money, give me back that jar of honey, and I'll be on my way. That's an end to it."

Alan didn't reply.

"I'll be glad if you'd help me, Mr Hargreaves," Marjorie went on. "I'm sorry to put you out like this, but there's no sense in making a fuss. It really can't be helped, so if you could be quick and fetch the jar, I can get on. I've a few houses to visit, and I want to catch people before they sit down for their dinner."

"Well, if you're sure, I'll just go and find it. Do you want to step inside while I look?"

"Thank you." With a glance over her shoulder, Marjorie stepped inside, and Alan led her to the kitchen where she stood, casting her eye over the work surfaces while Alan began rummaging through the cupboards.

"It's here somewhere," he muttered. "Ah, here it is." He emerged from the cupboard victorious, offering the jar of honey for Marjorie's inspection.

"That's it. Thank you very much." She took it from him, depositing the coins in his hand before stowing the jar in her basket and covering it with a tea cloth. "And before you argue, I insist on you taking the money, Mr Hargreaves. Full refund. 'Tis only right."

"Okay, if that's how you feel." Alan laid the coins on the table, keeping his gaze on Marjorie. She seemed agitated, and if Dan were there, no doubt he'd make a good guess at the state of her mind from her body language. Alan only knew that something was wrong. "Listen, Marjorie," he went on, "can I offer you a cup of tea or coffee? I was about to have one myself, and you seem… troubled."

"Well, I usually have a mug of coffee in the morning, but I had too much to do today. I suppose it can't do no harm. I like fresh ground if you have it."

Alan smiled. "You'd get along with my neighbour. He's a fan of the roasted bean."

"I don't know about that." Marjorie looked distinctly put out. "That Dan Corrigan came round my house yesterday, asking questions, poking his nose in. I don't know who he thinks he is. He's only been in the village for five minutes."

"We're both very concerned about what happened to Mortimer. We're trying to help, trying to see if we can get to the bottom of it."

Marjorie tutted, unimpressed. "That may be so, but you'd be better off not bothering. Morty's past helping, so there's no use stirring up trouble now. No good will come of it."

"But I thought you'd be keen to see the perpetrator brought to justice. He's still out there, somewhere. And with you living on your own—"

"There's nothing to be afraid of," Marjorie interrupted. "That's one thing I can tell you, sure as I'm standing here. So like I say, you'd best let the whole thing alone. Tell your nosey neighbour to do the same." She looked around the kitchen airily as if dismissing Alan from her thoughts. "Right. I don't reckon I've got time for that coffee after all. Thanks for the offer, but I'd best be off. I'll see myself out. No need to trouble yourself on my account." She bustled toward the hallway, but before she could leave the house, Alan called out to her: "Marjorie, wait a second."

She marched as far as the front door, but then she paused, her hand on the doorknob, and she half turned to look back at him. "What is it? I've no time to stand here talking."

"Marjorie, there's nothing wrong with that honey, is there? That was just a pretext to come around here and say your piece. You just wanted to tell Dan and me to mind our own business. Am I right?"

She matched his stare, and then, without saying a word, she shifted her arm to bring the basket forward, pulling the tea cloth from it. The basket was half full, at least half a dozen jars of honey crowded side by side at one end.

Alan's face fell. "You're really trying to retrieve every jar of honey you've sold?"

Marjorie nodded. "Well, just this batch. I told you, it's bad. I don't want to make anyone ill."

"I'm sorry, it just didn't sound right. I've never heard of honey going bad before. What's wrong with it?"

"I don't know the technical name for it. I just know it's bad, and now you know it too, so there you go. You learn something every day." She pulled the door open. "Goodbye,

Mr Hargreaves," she said as she marched out. Then the door closed, and Alan stood for a moment, staring into space. *What was all that about?* he asked himself. Something about Marjorie's sudden visit didn't add up, but on the face of it, it all made perfect sense.

What would Dan make of it? They'd discuss it later, no doubt. In the meantime, Alan needed something to recover his spirits. The insistent fingers of his nascent hangover pressed firmly against his skull, and he headed back to the kitchen to hunt out the coffee.

As he passed the table, he spread out the coins Marjorie had given him. He recalled how much he'd paid for the honey, and the amount was correct. To the penny. The accuracy of the amount made the transaction seem all the stranger. Marjorie had come equipped with exactly the right coins in her hand. It was a curiously precise piece of preparation, especially if she was really expecting to repeat the process at a number of houses. But she'd obviously been certain that the exchange would happen exactly as she'd planned it; she hadn't expected anyone or anything to stand in her way. *She's old fashioned*, Alan told himself. Marjorie came from a generation where every penny mattered, and fair dealing and honesty were paramount. But even so, Alan's mind was unquiet. As he waited for the kettle to boil, he decided to fetch his laptop. His inquisitive streak had been prodded into wakefulness, and now it wouldn't let him rest until he had some answers. The best way to find them was through careful research.

Fortunately, Alan was good at research.

CHAPTER 9

I T'S A PITY *Kristen didn't come for a run with me*, Dan thought as he wiped the sweat from his brow and climbed into the old Toyota RAV4. But like Alan, Kristen had declined the offer of a swift 5K across Dartmoor.

He grabbed his water bottle and took a few contemplative sips, staring out through the windscreen at the tangled mass of undergrowth that nestled beneath the trees. He'd found this quiet car park on the edge of the moor and quickly adopted it as the base for his runs. It had taken him a while to work out the best route, and most of his early experiments had left him stymied, the promising paths leading only to impenetrable jungles of bramble and blackthorn. But he'd figured it out on his own, and crucially, he hadn't fallen back on the GPS on his watch, nor had he used the running apps on his phone. He'd wanted to prove something to himself. He could take on this wild landscape and win, beating it on its own terms: man against the wilderness. He had to admit, it had given him a tremendous sense of satisfaction.

I ought to look for some more routes, he told himself. *Mix things up a bit*. But he'd only need to do that if he was staying in Embervale. And that was by no means certain.

Still, he'd be here for a little while at least; he'd promised his sister he'd help with redecorating the cottage, and so far he'd got no further than the preparatory work, cleaning everything down, washing the paintwork with sugar soap, and filling a few cracks in the ceiling. He didn't even have all the gear he'd need: dust sheets and brushes, rollers and paint trays. Alan had said he'd help with buying all the equipment, but Dan could manage quite happily on his own.

He checked the time on his watch. It was just after half past eleven. Instead of heading home for a shower, he could take a detour toward Newton Abbot and drop in at one of the DIY stores. He could have everything he needed by lunchtime.

Sure, he was probably a bit dishevelled, but so what? It was not like he'd run into anyone he knew, and nobody really cared what anyone looked like in a DIY shop. They wouldn't look twice at him if he wore old overalls spattered in paint from head to toe, so his running gear would hardly be a problem.

Taking a last drink of water, Dan fastened his seatbelt and started the engine. An old habit made him reach out to switch on the radio, but he changed his mind. Recently, he'd taken to driving in silence, using the time to think, living in the moment.

And people pay good money for mindfulness classes, he thought. *It couldn't be much simpler*. Then, smiling to himself, he sent the Toyota bumping gently over the potholes and out onto the lane.

IN THE CAR park at B&Q, Dan found a spot opposite the store's entrance and parked, but as he bent to retrieve his rucksack from the passenger footwell, a large pickup truck swept past, so close that Dan's car swayed in its wake.

"Idiot," Dan muttered, staring after the pickup as it swerved into a disabled parking bay and ground to a halt, its tyres grating on the tarmac.

Guilt prickled Dan's conscience. Perhaps the disabled driver was in trouble and in need of assistance. But the figure who leapt down from the driving seat seemed to be in no hurry. The man pulled the brim of his baseball cap down to shade his face then, slamming the door, he stalked toward the store, his shoulders hunched and his head low.

The man's athletic build was familiar, and when he turned to glance back across the car park, Dan found himself ducking down to hide behind the steering wheel. But he'd seen enough. The man's face may have been partially hidden by his cap, but there was no mistaking the piercing glint of his stare nor the hard line of his mouth. If those features hadn't been enough, the distinctive blue and yellow logo emblazoned on his black T-shirt gave the game away: Leeds United.

Jay. Dan lifted his head, but Jay had disappeared, presumably entering the store. *Why did I hide?* Dan asked himself, but he knew the answer. There'd been something about the way Jay had moved, every step surreptitious, his body language calculated to attract no attention, while his gaze had been the opposite: aggressively suspicious, searching for any sign of trouble. *A policeman's stare*, Dan thought, thanking whatever instinct had made him duck out of sight in time. He didn't want to be spotted, because he was sure of one thing: Jay was up to no good.

He wasn't in the pub last night, Dan thought. From what he knew, it was not often that Jay missed an evening in the pub, so perhaps the man was keeping a low profile. Changes in patterns of behaviour could be very telling. Plus, there was the fact that Jay had left the pub early on the night of the attack on Mortimer.

Moving quickly, Dan slid from his car, throwing his

rucksack over his shoulder and locking the door. He jogged across the car park, slowing as he approached Jay's pickup. The back of the vehicle was a flatbed, open to the elements, and Dan peered inside. It was empty apart from an oddly shaped bundle near the tailgate, a long shape concealed beneath a plastic tarpaulin.

Glancing toward the shop and seeing no one near the glass-doored exit, Dan leaned over the vehicle's side and tugged at the tarpaulin's edge. Whatever was in the bundle, it was heavy, its weight trapping the tarpaulin tightly. *Come on*, Dan thought, pulling the plastic sheet harder. One corner of the bundle came free, and Dan worked at it, teasing the folds apart. There. He'd created an opening, but he couldn't make out what was hidden inside. Leaning further over the edge, he yanked at the tarpaulin's edge one more time, and now he could see exactly what Jay had concealed in his pickup. "Hell's teeth," Dan murmured.

The tarpaulin held a collection of heavy-duty tools, and on the top lay a long steel rod, one end crowned by a rounded handle, the other hidden within the tarpaulin. And smeared on the handle was a broad daub of what could only be dried blood.

It was him! Dan almost staggered back, but on impulse, he tucked the tarpaulin back into place.

"Oi! Get away from my truck!"

Dan swivelled on his heel to see Jay striding from the shop, his glare fixed on Dan, his shoulders back. Jay held a long roll of chicken wire in his arms, but he tossed it aside and dashed toward Dan, powering across the car park.

"It's all right." Dan stepped back, raising his hands. "I was just looking."

Jay halted at the last second, squaring up to Dan, his face a mask of cold fury. "Is that right? Looking at what?"

"Jay, it's Dan. We met the other night, in the pub."

A flicker of recognition dulled Jay's glare, but only for a

second. "What the hell do you think you're doing, messing about with my truck?" He glanced into the back. "Did you touch anything? If you did, I'll smack you one, pal."

"No. Like I said, I was just looking at the truck," Dan protested. "I've been thinking of getting something like it." He gestured toward his own car. "The RAV4 isn't really big enough."

"*You?*" Jay's lip curled in disbelief. "You want a truck? Are you taking the piss?"

"No. I'm serious. I need to shift some stuff, and anyway, the Toyota belongs to my sister. I need to get my own vehicle."

Jay's stare was unflinching. "That's bullshit and you know it. Come on, out with it. What were you doing nosing around my truck?"

"I wasn't," Dan began, but his attention went to Jay's right fist. A neat dressing had been taped around Jay's hand, and as another piece of the puzzle clicked into place, Dan's expression hardened. "So, what happened to your hand, Jay? Get into a fight?"

Jay lowered his hand, pressing it against his side. "Nothing. Cut myself opening a can."

"That's a big dressing and properly applied," Dan said. "I'd say it was done in a hospital, or at the very least in a doctor's surgery. You wouldn't go to all that trouble for a little cut. So why lie about it? Why try to cover it up?" He stepped a little closer to Jay. "What are you trying to hide?"

"Mind your own damned business. It was an accident. End of. So what if I had to go down to A & E? That's where you'll end up in a minute, pal."

"I don't think so, Jay. But it looks as though you might be heading to the police station." Dan took a breath, summoning the courage to venture a bluff. "That's a nasty-looking metal tool you've got covered up in the back. I don't know what it's for, but I just took a few photos of the blood all over the handle. Considering that Mr Gamble was hit on the head, that blood looks suspicious, wouldn't you say?"

"Are you having a laugh?" Jay demanded. "Why the hell would I do anything to old Morty? And what's it got to do with you, come to that?"

"DS Spiller seems to think the attack was something to do with Alan and me. But now it looks like I can put him straight and send him after the real culprit."

Jay shook his head in disbelief. "You're off your head, mate."

"Maybe, maybe not. Either way, I might have sent those photos to DS Spiller already, in which case, you've got some explaining to do."

"You stupid sod!" Jay hissed. "What the bloody hell have you done?"

"The question is, what have *you* done? It might be better if you came clean, turned yourself in. Come on, Jay. You were a cop, you know how it works."

"Oh, you're a bloody-minded little bastard," Jay muttered, but the aggression had gone from his voice, the hard edges of his anger replaced by the bitter rumbling of sullen defeat. He shook his head. "Just tell me one thing: did you send those photos or not?"

"I'm not going to tell you that. I might have sent them to someone else as an insurance policy. But if I have sent them, I can always get in touch with Spiller and tell him I made a mistake. I'd guess we have a window of around ten minutes before the trouble starts. To me, you look guilty, but I'm a reasonable man. Change my mind. It's up to you. Talk and I'll listen."

Jay studied him carefully, then he grunted under his breath. "Do you play poker?"

"No. I've never been much of a gambler."

"Pity. You'd be pretty good. I can't tell if you're bluffing, and I was a copper." He exhaled, puffing out his cheeks. "All right. We'll talk, but not out here. Get in the cab while I go and get my wire." He unlocked his pickup, but Dan shook his head firmly.

"I'm not getting in the vehicle with you, Jay. It's not going to happen."

Jay's gaze flicked upward. "No need to get dramatic, pal. This isn't the bloody *Godfather*. I'm not going to take you for a ride."

"Nevertheless, I'd prefer an alternative. You know the town better than me. There must be somewhere we can talk."

"There's a cafe down the road. Nothing fancy, but it'll do at a pinch."

"Fine," Dan said, regretting it already.

"Let me get my wire. They charge a fortune for it in this place, thieving bastards. They want locking up." Jay marched off to retrieve his wire, and Dan took out his phone, composing a quick text message to Alan: *Going for coffee with Jay. Newton Abbot.* His thumb hovered over the screen. What else should he add? Could Jay really have been the one to attack Mortimer? He wasn't behaving like a murderer. *But then, he knows the ropes*, Dan thought. *He knows how to play the innocent.*

He added the phrase: *I'll call soon*, then he pressed send.

Jay returned with the wire, placing it inside his truck's cab before locking the door. "Come on. Time's pressing. We'd better get this straight before a squad car appears, all blues and twos and overenthusiasm."

"Blues and twos?"

"Blue lights and two-tone sirens. That's what we call it." Jay paused, then said, "Right, I need a coffee." He started walking, his hands in his pockets. "You're paying, by the way," he called over his shoulder. "And I hope you've got cash. They don't like cards."

"I think so." Dan hurried to catch up.

It took them only a couple of minutes to reach the

Paradise Cafe, both men marching with grim determination in every step. They didn't speak until they found a table inside, and Jay asked Dan what he wanted.

"Americano. Black," Dan said, and Jay headed for the counter.

Dan took a seat by the window and looked around, feeling as though he'd stepped into a coffee house from the fifties. The bare brick walls, chipped paintwork and scuffed floorboards might've been the work of an interior designer with a passion for retro-chic, or simply the result of decades of neglect, he couldn't be sure.

Outside, a stream of shoppers bustled along the pavement: that curious crowd of customers who emerged only when most people were in work. Mums pushed strollers or held hands with toddlers, pensioners strode gamely or took it slowly with the aid of aluminium walking sticks. Here and there, a few youths skulked aimlessly, disaffected, their gaze on the ground, disinterested in all that surrounded them.

Where does Jay fit into this scene? he wondered. *Come to that, where do I fit in?* Dan glanced around the cafe's sparse clientele, deciding he was easily the youngest person in the room. If that wasn't enough to make him feel out of place, his running gear completed the task. But Jay seemed at home, chatting to the young woman behind the counter, and exchanging greetings with a few of the customers.

Dan watched him for a second, noticing the ease with which Jay could switch roles. Acquaintances received a sincere smile and a restrained wave, but closer contacts were favoured with a joke or a few respectful questions. Loved ones were asked after, children's names were remembered. And though Dan couldn't quite hear the remarks Jay murmured to the young woman taking his order, he'd clearly made her day, and she beamed a smile as she promised to bring their drinks to the table.

Dan knew a player when he saw one in action, and when

it came to dealing with people, Jay clearly had a few tricks up his sleeve. *I mustn't let him pull the wool over my eyes,* Dan told himself. *He has something to hide, I'm sure of it.*

But Jay's display of bonhomie vanished as he sat down opposite Dan, and he leaned forward, his elbows on the table and an earnest expression on his face. "Let me get one thing straight," Jay began. "I had nothing to do with what happened to Mortimer Gamble. Nothing. Understand?"

"We'll see," Dan replied. "For a start, whose blood is on the tool in your pickup?"

"Mine." Jay turned his hand to show the dressing. "I caught the back of my hand on a nail. The damned thing was sticking out of a fence post, and it got me. It went deep, so I had to go to A & E, get it cleaned up. Five stitches." He winced. "At the time, there was blood all over the place. I never got around to cleaning up my tools. To be honest, I haven't touched them since Saturday."

"That's when you hurt yourself?"

Jay nodded. "In the afternoon. I couldn't have picked a worse time. A & E was heaving. It's like the sunshine sends people stupid; they burn themselves on a barbecue or fall off a ladder. Then there were all the amateur sportsmen, hobbling about on sprained ankles or moaning about their broken collarbones. Nightmare."

"And what were you doing when you cut your hand?" Dan asked. "The average DIY enthusiast doesn't usually have a heap of heavy-duty tools at home."

Jay pursed his lips, and then he looked up as the young woman appeared beside their table with their drinks on a tray. "Here we are," she said, placing each cup in front of the right person without being told. "One large, black Americano, and one flat white."

"Thank you, Maddy," Jay said. "That was quick. You remembered my sweetener, too. You're a star."

"That's all right," Maddy said with a grin. "I ought to know what you like by now. Anyhow, enjoy your coffees."

"Yes, thank you," Dan chipped in, though his words seemed inadequate.

Maddy sent him a smile, and although there was a questioning look in her eye, she didn't say anything more, but waltzed away, tucking the empty tray under her arm.

"You know the problem with you?" Jay said, his gaze fixed on Dan. "You're cold."

"Sorry? What on earth are you talking about?" Dan held up his hand. "Don't answer that. I make it a rule to never take advice from anyone suspected of a serious crime."

"You see. There you go again." Jay pointed at Dan, his finger jabbing the air. "You've no feeling for ordinary folk. No empathy. We're all just a bunch of bloody peasants as far as you're concerned."

"That's nonsense," Dan protested. "I'm not some aristocrat. I've worked hard all my life."

"Not now, though, eh? You can afford not to go out to work. Most of us will never know what that's like."

"I don't have to defend myself to you, Jay, but if you must know, I'm not well off. I'm taking a break, but I'll have to go back to work soon."

Jay looked him up and down. "Nice running gear. How much were them trainers?"

"That's got nothing to do with it."

"Ah, touched a nerve. Go on. How much were they? Tell me, or I'll look it up myself." Jay pulled a phone from his pocket, glancing under the table at Dan's shoes before he began tapping on the screen.

"They were three hundred pounds," Dan snapped. "But I bought them when I still had a good job. I run a lot, so I need a decent pair of shoes." Dan drummed his fingers on the table, irritated that he'd let Jay goad him so easily. "I'm not going to let you off the hook, Jay. What are all those tools doing in your truck? And this had better be good because they can tell all kinds of stuff from a bloodstain. If it's not your blood—"

"It *is* my blood," Jay interrupted. "And I've got those tools because I was doing a job for someone. We were replacing some old fence posts. That's what that tool is: it's for digging holes for fence posts, breaking up the rocks. I was hacking away at the ground around this post, really going for it, but I didn't see the nail sticking out of the old timber. It was a bloody four-inch nail, bent upward, and the head had snapped off, so it was just a spike, sharp as a blade. It stabbed right into my hand, practically came out the other side, and it bled like hell. They say I must've nicked a blood vessel. To tell you the truth, I'm still taking the painkillers, otherwise, I wouldn't be able to do a damned thing. That's why I'm off the booze. I can't drink with the painkillers, so I haven't been to the pub for days."

"And who can verify your story? Who was your employer?"

Jay pursed his lips. "I can't tell you that, old son. No way."

"Come on, you can't expect me to buy that. I need the details."

"Tough. You'll just have to take my word for it. That's that." Jay took a drink from his cup, smiling as if their business had concluded satisfactorily.

It was Dan's turn to produce his phone. "I'd better go outside to make this call. I have a lot to tell DS Spiller. He'll want your pickup impounded and taken apart. They'll need to check it for fibres and fluids and all that kind of thing."

"For God's sake," Jay moaned. "Don't be such a bloody idiot. You can't go around making accusations. They'll have you for wasting police time. Believe me, if you go on like this, you'll end up looking very stupid, *and* you'll be in deep shit."

"That's a chance I'll have to take," Dan said slowly. "You said you'd explain, but you've given me nothing concrete.

You've reneged on our deal, so I have to go down this path. You've given me no choice."

"Bloody hell," Jay muttered. "All right. Listen." He leaned forward, lowering his voice. "You know I was a copper, right?"

Dan nodded, leaning closer, drawn in by the conspiratorial gleam in Jay's eye. "Yes. Retired or kicked out?"

"Retired due to ill health." Jay's hand went to the side of his neck. "I was involved in a car chase. We were after this kid, barely fifteen years old, jacked up on God knows what. He took a BMW and wound up on the M5. A hundred miles an hour on the wrong bloody side of the road. It was three in the morning or there'd have been dozens killed. As it was, he put nine in the hospital before we stopped him. There was a woman on her way home from a late shift. A nurse. She never walked again."

Dan felt the blood drain from his face. "That's awful."

"You can say that again. We moved in to stop him, but he wasn't having it, and he sent us off the road. It might have been all right if I'd been driving; I always kept my skills up to date. I've done every advanced driving course there is, and I can handle any kind of car. But I was riding shotgun to a sergeant who didn't know his arse from his elbow, and he sent us straight into a signpost and totalled the car. I got an injury. Whiplash. I wore a neck brace for months."

"I'm sorry to hear that," Dan said, "but I don't see how—"

"Do I have to spell it out for you? I was injured in the line of duty, and it wasn't my fault. I got compensation, early retirement, the whole package. So what's it going to look like if they find out I'm fit enough to do manual work? They'll hang me out to dry."

Dan leaned back. "Seriously?"

"Yes. When I started my claim for compensation, they sent

investigators to follow me around. There were blokes with long lenses hiding in the hedgerows."

"So, what are you saying? Your claim was false?"

"No, of course it wasn't. I was in agony back then. But what can I say? I got better. I went to the gym, built myself back up."

"But if you have all this compensation money, why are you going around pulling up fences?"

"The compo only went so far. Anyway, I got bored. There's this guy in the village: Derek. Do you know Derek?"

Dan shook his head. "I don't think so."

"Best to keep it that way." Jay shrugged. "Derek's all right, really, but let's just say that he's not a feller to trouble himself with paperwork and the like. He gives me a few jobs, he pays cash in hand, and he's a bit on the forgetful side when it comes to filling in his tax return, know what I mean?"

"I'm getting the picture. This is all very interesting, but there's one thing you haven't explained."

"Only one?" Jay let out a bark of laughter. "Tell me, Dan, what've I left out? What priceless nugget of information will make your day? Want to know my inside leg measurement? Like that is it?" He sent Dan a salacious wink. "Can't say I blame you. I'm not that way inclined myself, but whatever floats your boat."

Dan stared at him levelly. *Classic distraction technique*, he thought. But he wouldn't allow himself to be derailed. "On the night Mortimer was attacked, you left the pub early. Where did you go?"

"Easy. I went around to Derek's. He owed me a few quid, and I went to collect." Jay chuckled to himself. "The bastard still owes me. But don't even think about asking him to give me an alibi. He'll swear he's never laid eyes on me in his life. Deny everything, that's his motto."

"So, I'll have to take your word for your whereabouts."

Dan almost smiled. "Very neat. I don't know whether to be annoyed or impressed."

Jay spread his hands wide. "I aim to please. Are we done?"

"You'll have to hand over that bloodstained tool," Dan said, his voice edged with determination. "I can't let you leave with it."

This time, Jay's laughter was full-throated but heavy with contempt. "I don't know where you think you are, pal, but this isn't like on TV. There are rules to say how these things are done. Procedures. I hate to rain on your parade, but you can't just make these things up as you go along. Anyway, I'm willing to bet you never took any photos of that bloodstain. I've figured you out. It took me a while, but I can see right through you, pal. I've had enough of your bullshit." He drained the last of his coffee, then stood. "Sit tight. You usually pay when you order, but they know me here, so they did me a favour." He sent a cheery wave to Maddy behind the counter. "Can we have the bill please, love? Mr Corrigan will pay."

He marched away before Dan could protest, and Maddy came toward Dan, a bill in her hand and an expectant smile on her lips. "Jay, wait," Dan called out, but Jay was already exiting onto the street.

"Dammit!" Dan reached beneath the table for his rucksack, and that was when he realised it was missing. He pushed his chair back to search the floor, but there was nothing there except crumbs and a crumpled serviette. Someone tapped on the cafe's window, and Dan looked up, a cold sense of dread twisting in his stomach. Sure enough, Jay was outside, peering in through the window, Dan's rucksack dangling from his hand. He grinned evilly, then he hurled Dan's rucksack into the air. The bag landed in the middle of the road, and a white van swerved to avoid it, the driver honking the horn. But Jay just walked away, his hands deep in his pockets.

Maddy watched the proceedings open mouthed. "What was that about?"

"Just a joke." Dan stood stiffly. "Listen, I have to go and get my money and things from my bag."

Maddy held out the bill. "You need to pay for your drinks."

"I know, but I can't pay until I get my bag. Listen, I'll only be a second." Dan edged toward the door. "Don't worry. I'll be right back."

"You'd better," Maddy said, her hands on her hips.

"Thanks." Dan made his retreat while he had the chance, dashing outside and dodging between bemused shoppers as he headed into the road. Years of honing his reflexes on London's streets meant that he had nothing to fear from Newton Abbot's relatively tame drivers, and a second later he'd retrieved his bag and was heading back to the cafe. *God, I screwed that up*, he thought bitterly. *I must be going out of my mind.*

Jay had beaten him with nothing more sophisticated than the tactics of the playground bully. But Dan wasn't about to give up. He might be down, but he'd come up fighting. *You'd better watch out, Jay*, Dan thought. *You're not in the playground now. I'll find out what you've done, whether you like it or not.*

CHAPTER 10

O N THE DRIVE back to the village, Dan turned all kinds of possibilities over in his mind. But by the time he arrived home, he hadn't decided whether he could believe Jay or not. He was still cursing himself for the way he'd handled their encounter; it had been a mess from start to finish.

At least I bought some paint, he thought. He climbed down from the driver's seat and went to unload his purchases.

"Do you need a hand?"

Dan turned with a start; he hadn't heard Alan approaching. "Thanks, Alan, that would be great. I think I might've bought more than I need."

"You'll be surprised what it takes." Alan grabbed hold of a couple of large tubs of emulsion. "You'll need a fair amount, especially if you're changing the colour. I presume this white is for the ceilings."

"Yes. I bought half a dozen variations of off-white for the walls. But don't ask me which one is going where, because I haven't a clue." Dan picked up some tins and inspected their labels. "I can't for the life of me remember whether I wanted Vanilla Mist for the lounge or the bedroom. As for Natural Calico, I have no idea."

Alan chuckled. "Let's get them inside. You can always daub a few patches on the wall and see what they look like."

"I guess so."

They trudged back and forth until the car was unloaded and the kitchen floor was cluttered with paint pots, roller trays and a selection of brushes and rollers.

"You're going to be busy," Alan said. "But is something up? You seem a bit subdued."

"I'm just hungry. I haven't had any lunch yet."

"Ah, I see. I had mine ages ago. I'd better leave you to it."

"No, it's okay," Dan said quickly. "Stay and have a cup of tea. I'll grab a sandwich."

"Sure. I need a break. I've actually been getting on with some writing this morning."

"Good." Dan switched on the kettle then hunted through his fridge in search of anything he could slap between two slices of bread. A few minutes later, he'd assembled a concoction of dairy-free cheese, salad and vegan mayonnaise. He added a few olives to the plate and grabbed an apple before tending to the hot drinks.

"That doesn't look too bad." Alan peered at Dan's plate. "Is that some kind of cheese substitute? I always wonder what goes into that stuff."

"And yet, you think so little about how dairy cheese is made," Dan replied, taking a large bite of sandwich. "This one is made from coconut oil, but there are all kinds of alternatives. To be fair, some of them taste like sweaty socks, so you have to shop around until you find one you like. Do you want to try some?"

"Not right now, thanks." Alan took a sip of tea. "And there's oat milk in this, isn't there."

"You're learning fast."

"I've had to," Alan intoned, then he grinned. "I want to run an idea past you. It might help us work out what happened to Mortimer."

"That sounds intriguing. As it happens, I have something to tell you, but you start."

"While you were out, I had a visit from Marjorie," Alan began, and he recounted the events in detail, ending by saying, "What do you make of it?"

"It's interesting. When I went around to her house, I asked about the honey, and she snapped at me. She had all these empty jars, but when I asked her about them, she was evasive." Dan thought for a moment. "If there's something wrong with the honey, I suppose it stung her pride. She's a strange character, perhaps a bit eccentric, but I don't see what any of this has got to do with Mortimer."

"I'm getting to that," Alan said. "You see, Marjorie's visit got me thinking. Do you remember what I said about that video you took? The one where Marjorie was attacking the rhododendrons?"

Dan nodded. "You said she was only removing the flowers."

"That's right. So I did some research, putting the two things together. Rhododendrons and honey. You'll never guess what I came up with."

"Surprise me."

Alan held out his hands, his fingers spread wide. "Mad honey."

"What?"

"Mad honey," Alan said. "It's rare, especially in this country, but sometimes, honey can contain toxins that bees gather from certain plants, particularly..."

"Rhododendrons."

"Exactly. Rhododendrons are very attractive to bees, and with some varieties, the nectar contains toxins that are hallucinogenic."

Dan shook his head. "I've never heard of anything like it. Are you sure this isn't some nonsense invented by cranks on the internet?"

"No, it's true. I double-checked everything. The toxins are part of the plant's defence mechanism, and in humans the toxin can have quite severe effects, including hallucinations and loss of coordination, even difficulty breathing. It depends on the dose. It doesn't happen much with commercial honey, partly because of the scale. If a few bees went to the wrong sort of rhododendron, the toxin would be incredibly diluted, so it wouldn't have any effect in a large batch. Anyway, most honey is heat-treated and that would break the toxin down. But Marjorie's honey is different. There aren't that many flowers near her house; it's mainly grassland. The rhododendrons are growing right next to her garden."

"Mortimer was in Marjorie's kitchen on the night he died," Dan said. "Maybe he ate some honey while he was there. When I asked her if Mortimer had left a note or anything, she denied it, but there was something odd in the way she said it. I thought she was just being cagey, but she said Mortimer hadn't *left* anything. Maybe she was thinking about the fact that he'd *taken* something while he was there. Perhaps he'd helped himself to some bread and honey."

"That, we don't know. But it might explain why he was wandering about on the spoil heaps in the dark. Think about all that shouting we heard. The man was raving."

"*Stop them,*" Dan murmured. "But there was no trace of anyone else having been there."

Alan nodded. "It might be something we can take to the police. I assume the post-mortem will have looked for toxins, but this is a fairly obscure one, and from what I gather, it's short lived. People usually get better after twenty-four hours, and Mortimer didn't pass away until he'd been in the hospital for a while. There's a chance the toxin could've left his system."

"If she did poison him, the question is, did she do it on purpose?" Dan asked. "It wouldn't have been difficult to leave a honey-laced treat for Mortimer to eat."

Alan shook his head firmly. "If she poisoned him, and that's a big *if*, it must've been an accident. Otherwise, she'd have risked poisoning half the village."

"Unless, having done the deed, she was struck by the fear of being found out, so she set about removing all trace of her honey from the neighbourhood, just in case a connection could be made."

"I still don't think it adds up as a deliberate act," Alan insisted. "It's an unreliable method of murder. The chances of the toxin being fatal are quite remote."

"I suppose you're right. Anyway, I found a much more likely suspect. Guess who I ran into earlier."

Dan explained the events of his run-in with Jay, and tempted though he was to gloss over the more embarrassing parts, he left nothing out.

"I always thought there was something dodgy about him," Alan said. "I bet he faked his injuries for the compensation. That gives him a motive."

"I thought of that. If Mortimer had threatened to expose Jay, saying he'd tell the police about Jay's little sideline in manual labour, there'd have been a good reason to shut him up. But somehow I don't like it as a motive for murder."

"I'd guess he only meant to wound him," Alan suggested. "Let's piece together the chain of events. Having been threatened with exposure, Jay bears a grudge. So when he's worked up enough Dutch courage in the pub, Jay goes out to find Mortimer."

"How would he know where to find him?" Dan asked.

"He knows the old man's habit of visiting Marjorie, so Jay takes a tool from his truck and waits on the footpath. He intercepts Mortimer, luring him onto the spoil heaps where they won't be seen or heard. He threatens Mortimer, telling him to back off. But the old man is stubborn, and he won't give in. They argue, and Jay loses his temper, lashing out. Then, when he realises what he's done, he scarpers."

"And how does your stick come to be covered in Mortimer's blood?" Dan asked.

"He must've taken it with him when he left the pub. Being an ex-policeman, he knew how important the weapon would be, so he used it to lay a false trail."

"And what about Mortimer's last words? *Stop them.* He was very insistent, very clear, but who did he mean? Did Jay have an accomplice?"

Alan shook his head. "I don't know. Maybe our two theories go together. The toxins in the honey made Mortimer confused. On the one hand, it left him vulnerable, but on the other, he might've been unpredictable, like someone who's had too much to drink. Perhaps he struck the first blow, cutting Jay's hand, and that's why Jay retaliated."

"It fits together fairly neatly," Dan admitted. "The question is, what do we do about it? We have no evidence. Jay will have ditched the bloodstained tool by now, and he'll be busy arranging an alibi, probably from this Derek character. He'll be in the clear."

"I know Derek," Alan said. "He's some kind of contractor. He works for various farms in the area, and as far as I know, he's legit. I don't think he'd perjure himself to save Jay."

"Even so, we don't have anything to give to the police. If we start talking to Spiller about mad honey, he'll laugh in our faces." Dan ran his hands through his hair. "There has to be something we can do. Maybe we could try following Jay, see where he goes, who he meets."

"In a village of this size? He'd see us a mile off." Alan offered a wry smile. "Anyway, I'm not sure we're up to the task. I don't know about you, but I'm not really au fait with modern methods of surveillance."

Dan returned Alan's smile. "You were a teacher, and in my day, the staff all had eyes in the backs of their heads. Isn't that a skill they give you at college?"

"Surprisingly, intelligence gathering was hardly

mentioned in the curriculum," Alan said, "which was a shame because it would've come in handy when I wanted to know where all the felt-tip pens kept disappearing to. But that is a mystery for another time."

"Definitely," Dan replied. "Right now, we need to decide on a plan of action. We can't just sit on our hands."

"We don't have much choice. On the plus side, if Jay is guilty, you've probably rattled him. He might do something stupid and give himself away. In the meantime, we can keep digging gently around the edges to see what we can turn up." Alan paused. "Tomorrow, for instance, we've been invited to tea with Kristen and Craig. If there was a history of disagreement between Jay and Mortimer, they might know about it. Plus, they'll be able to shed some light on the whole business of Marjorie and the inheritance. I still think there could be something suspicious in all that."

"Possibly," Dan admitted. "We still don't know *when* Mortimer changed his will. What if it was just before he met his untimely end? That would paint a very different picture of Marjorie's poisonous honey."

Alan rubbed his hands together. "You know what? I wasn't looking forward to tea at the Dower House, but now I'm starting to think it could be interesting."

"Me too," Dan said. "I can't wait."

WEDNESDAY

CHAPTER 11

A LAN GUIDED THE VW Golf into yet another narrow lane, and in the passenger seat, Dan checked his watch for the third time. "We're going to be late. It's almost three."

"We're nearly there," Alan replied. "You'll see the gatehouse in a minute."

"The Dower House has its own gatehouse? What kind of place is it?"

Alan sent him a smile. "You'll see."

A minute later, the car rounded a bend in the lane, and Dan understood. The gatehouse was not a large building, but solidly built of mellow stone, each feature small, neat and in perfect proportion, like a child's idea of a fairy-tale cottage. But the gatehouse was made to seem even smaller by the grand frontage of the vast country house that sat behind it. Each corner of the Dower House boasted a broad angular tower, crowned with crenellations. The main entrance was framed by an impressive portico supported by columns of smooth stone, and row upon row of tall windows glittered in the afternoon sun.

"*That* is the Dower House?" Dan asked. "Why didn't you warn me?"

"What? And spoil the surprise?"

Dan looked down at his white shirt and blue cotton trousers. "If I'd known the place was a mansion, I'd have worn a jacket. And a tie."

"Relax. You're not being presented at court. It's just afternoon tea, and we've already met our hosts." Alan glanced at Dan as the Golf trundled over the broad gravel driveway. "You're fine. I don't know what you're worried about. Unless… Oh, I see. Kristen caught your eye, has she? I can't say I'm surprised. She's your type."

"What do you mean?"

"High maintenance," Alan replied. "Charming but highly strung. Bright but finicky."

"Rubbish," Dan muttered, although truth be told, Alan had just described his last three girlfriends to a tee. "Anyway, what if I am interested in her? She's single, I'm single. I haven't really had the chance to get to know her, but it would be nice to have some female company."

"True," Alan said. "And it might stop you moping over Frankie what's-her-name."

"I don't mope. I've never moped in my life."

Alan cleared his throat meaningfully. "Anyway, here we are. Three o'clock, on the dot."

"Thanks. A lift *and* relationship advice. It must be my lucky day."

"All part of the service." Alan parked the car, the tyres biting into the gravel with an oddly satisfying crunch, then he led the way to the imposing wooden door and pressed the doorbell.

"Maybe we should've used a side entrance or something." Dan straightened his shirt. "It seems a bit presumptuous to march up to the front door."

"Nonsense. We're invited guests." Alan smirked. "I wonder if we'll be met by a white-haired old retainer." He hunched his shoulders, twisting his features into a comic scowl. "You rang, milord?"

"Stop it," Dan said, but he had to laugh. "You should be on the stage. I bet you go down a storm in the village pantomime."

"There isn't one, not anymore. Hard to put on a production of Puss in Boots when there's always a new boxset for people to binge-watch in the comfort of their own homes." Alan raised a finger. "I think I hear someone coming."

The door creaked open slowly, and Dan found himself holding his breath. But they were greeted by Craig, his smile wide and his cheeks flushed. "Right on time, chaps. Come in." He gestured for them to step inside, and they made their way into a wide hallway. "We're using the front drawing room," Craig went on. "Sis is fussing over the scones and Darjeeling, but we can always rustle up something stronger if you know what I mean."

"Later, maybe," Dan said, trying not to look too awestruck as he glanced around the oak-panelled hallway. Oil paintings hung in heavy gilt frames, a crystal chandelier hung from the high ceiling, and to one side, a grand stairway swept upwards in a majestic curve. "Tea is fine for now."

"Same for me," Alan said. "Thanks, but I'll stick with the tea."

"Ah well. Please yourselves." Craig's smile lost some of its warmth. "It's this way. Follow me." He set off down the hallway, leaving Dan and Alan to trail after him, their footsteps echoing from the polished parquet flooring.

"This is *not* what I was expecting," Dan murmured to Alan. "I thought Kristen said the place was rundown."

"These things are relative," Alan replied. "It depends what you're used to."

Dan nodded thoughtfully. What standard of living did Kristen expect? And when she'd visited his temporary home, what had she made of The Old Shop's tired decor and its down-at-heel furniture?

But he didn't have time to brood. Craig was already taking them into a spacious lounge, the room's effortless air of timeless elegance dispelling the image of Dan's humble cottage from his mind. The sofas and armchairs were upholstered in leather worn smooth from years of careful polishing. The afternoon sunlight poured in through the tall windows, bathing the room in a warm glow, and holding court from the centre of the Turkish carpet, Kristen stepped forward to meet them. Her long dress, cut from a silky fabric the colour of cornflowers, shimmered with each step, lending a fluid movement to her body so that she seemed to float across the room. She lowered her chin, her short fringe tumbling a little over her forehead, and when she looked up at Dan, a flash of mischief made her blue eyes even more arresting than before. "You came. How delightful." She shook hands with both of them, and Dan realised he hadn't spoken since he'd entered the room.

"Yes, of course," he murmured. "We wouldn't dream of missing this. Thank you for inviting us."

"That goes for me too," Alan added. "Thank you."

"It's my pleasure," Kristen said. "Now, take a seat, and let me introduce you to everybody."

She placed her hand on Dan's arm, and in a daze, he let himself be guided to the centre of the room. He hadn't registered that there were other people present, but now he took stock of the other two guests as they rose to greet him.

"Dan, this gorgeous creature is Jess, and her charming companion is Martin. Everybody, this is Dan and Alan, the brave chaps I was telling you about."

"Hello," Martin said gruffly, shaking hands with Dan and Alan in turn. He seemed anything but charming, and his expression made it obvious that he was far from pleased to meet them.

In contrast, Jess's demure smile seemed genuine, and there was a warmth in her eyes when she said, "It's so nice to meet you. We've heard all about what you did for that poor man, and I must say, it was incredibly brave of you."

"Oh, it was not so extraordinary as everybody makes out," Dan replied. "Really, I wish everyone wouldn't keep making such a fuss of us."

"Speak for yourself," Alan put in with a smile. "Please feel free to shower me with praise as often as you like. I really don't mind."

A brief silence hung in the air as the guests tried to decide if Alan was joking, so Dan laughed, giving the others permission to join in.

"Please, everyone have a seat," Kristen said. "Make yourselves at home."

Two large leather sofas and an armchair were arranged around a coffee table. Craig took the armchair, and the others performed an unnecessarily complex dance as they took their places on the sofas. Somehow, Dan found himself sitting next to Jess; a bitter blow until Kristen took the seat directly opposite him so that they were facing each other.

Kristen poured the tea from a white porcelain pot decorated with fine lines of gold, and Dan took his cup very carefully, the delicate china handle seeming foolishly small between his fingers. Thankfully, the tea was Darjeeling and Kristen took hers black as well, so there was no need for an awkward discussion over milk.

"What do you think of the Dower House?" Kristen asked. "I'm afraid it's seen better days."

Dan floundered, unable to think of a reply that wouldn't make him sound foolish, but Alan came to his rescue.

"It's fascinating," Alan said. "I've often seen the house, but only from a distance. I've always wondered what it was like inside."

Kristen sighed. "Oh, you should've seen it twenty years

ago. It's not a patch on what it used to be. It needs a ton of work doing on it. The roof leaks, the windows are rotten and the wiring is an absolute mess."

"It needs some money spending on it, that's for sure," Martin said. "It's Grade I listed, so everything has to be done just right."

"Is that your area of expertise?" Dan asked.

Martin and Jess exchanged a look. "I am a surveyor," Martin said, "but not the architectural kind."

"We work on mapping and so on," Jess added. "It's all very dull."

"You work together," Alan said. "Are you here for some special project?"

Martin shook his head. "Holiday. Taking a break."

"Kristen offered us the use of a holiday cottage in the village," Jess chipped in, "and we jumped at the chance. We don't get away often."

Dan looked from Martin to Jess, taking in the stiffness of their body language, the coldness in their expressions when they deigned to look at each other. If they were a couple, they were the product of a spectacularly unsuccessful pairing. He turned to Kristen. "I didn't know you owned property in the village."

Craig let out a humourless chuckle. "She doesn't. They're Morty's cottages, or they were anyway. They mainly belong to me now. Funny how things turn out." He sent Kristen a patronising smile. "All the years of hard work you put in, labouring away for the old man, and he reaches out from the grave to stab you in the back."

The only visible sign of Kristen's anger was a slight flaring of her nostrils. "You're being ridiculous, Craig. You really shouldn't drink in the daytime, it doesn't agree with you."

Craig grimaced, but he didn't argue. He simply made a show of picking up his cup of tea, sipping it with exaggerated care.

Kristen smiled bravely as though overcoming a private struggle. "I used to run the holiday lets for Morty. He owned so many houses, and he couldn't manage them on his own. If it had been left to him, everything would've been done on the back of an envelope. But these days, you need a website, you need a system to handle the bookings, and you have to be so careful with all the paperwork."

"I'm sure he appreciated your help," Alan said. "It was kind of you to take it on."

Craig chuckled to himself, but he said nothing, concentrating on his tea.

Kristen made a point of ignoring her brother. "Well, it was the least I could do. I even formed a company on his behalf. It was so much better from a taxation point of view, and—"

"And you made sure you had a stake in the business," Craig interrupted. "Twenty-five percent. I bet you thought the old bugger would leave you the rest when he snuffed it. You should've seen your face when we found out the truth. I wish I'd taken a photo. I could've had it framed."

"I think it's time we changed the subject," Alan said. "I'm sure it's been a difficult time for both of you."

Kristen nodded gratefully. "Yes. Thank you, Alan."

Alan turned to Martin. "Have you seen much of the local area while you've been here?"

"A little," Martin replied.

"We've been for some lovely walks in the evenings," Jess said. "It gets too hot in the afternoons, but the nights are perfect for walking, and the starlight makes the landscape seem magical. You should see the moonlight on the water; it's beautiful."

Alan raised his eyebrows. "Oh. Have you been down to the river? Which way did you take?"

"It was just a narrow lane," Martin said quickly. "We drove. I didn't see any signposts. None at all."

"Did you park near the stone bridge?" Alan asked.

"There's a path along the river from there, just before you get to Trusham."

"Yes," Martin replied. "I think that was it. I didn't notice the name of the village. It was dark, and we didn't stay long. We're not really interested in long walks. A quick stroll and then home to put our feet up, that's right, isn't it, Jess?"

Jess smiled sadly. "We don't stray far."

"But you must explore the area while you're here," Alan insisted. "The moors are fantastic at this time of year. There's the coast too, of course. I can tell you some good places if you'd like."

Jess's cheeks coloured, and when she stole a glance at Alan, her smile was unguarded. "That would be very kind of you."

"Thanks for the offer," Martin said, "but I don't think we'll have time. We're not here much longer. We're almost finished."

Dan raised an eyebrow. *Not a couple*, he thought. *And not on holiday.*

As if sensing his thoughts, Kristen said, "Martin and Jess are old college friends of mine. This has been one of our regular reunions. We like to get the gang back together once in a while, don't we?"

Martin nodded distractedly as though utterly bored, but a flicker of confusion passed across Jess's expression. Sensing she had something to say, Dan fixed her with an inquisitive stare, but before he could ask her a question, Alan clicked his fingers. "Oh, how silly of me," he said. "I didn't recognise you at first, but you were in the pub the other night. Friday."

Dan's eyes widened. Yes. The change in setting had thrown him completely, and of course, they'd been wearing different clothes, sitting quietly in the pub and blending into the background, but he could see it now. Martin and Jess were the mysterious couple: the pair they'd all thought were tourists. And Kevin had said they'd left the pub shortly after Dan and

Alan had called it a night. "If you don't mind me asking, did either of you see anything odd on that Friday night?" Dan said.

Martin turned his disinterested stare on Dan. "Like what?"

"Anything out of the ordinary," Dan replied. "Was anyone hanging around outside? Anyone behaving in a suspicious way?"

"No." Martin seemed content to leave it at that, but Jess added, "We went straight back to the cottage. We didn't see anybody on the way."

Alan leaned forward in his seat. "Before you left the pub, did you see anyone take anything from behind the bar?"

Martin shook his head, a bemused smile on his lips. "What is this? Twenty questions?"

"Someone stole my hiking stick," Alan explained. "It's a long walking stick, topped with a staghorn handle. It's quite distinctive."

Martin shrugged. "Sorry, but I didn't see anyone with a stick. I'm not sure I would've noticed though. A hiking stick: it's the kind of thing people have around here, isn't it. Like Labradors."

Alan's smile tightened. "And where do you two hail from?"

"Liverpool," Martin replied, at exactly the same time as Jess said, "Chester."

Martin flashed an annoyed glance at his companion. "We live in Chester now, but I'm from Liverpool originally."

"Me too," Alan said. "Which part are you from?"

"I'm from The Wirral rather than Liverpool, but if I say that, I get blank looks." Martin studied Alan. "You've lost your accent."

Alan nodded. "Yes. I've moved around a lot, and it's faded over the years. I could say the same about yours. I didn't notice your accent at first, but now that you mention it, it seems obvious." He turned to Jess. "But you're not from Liverpool, are you?"

She laid her hand on her chest. "No. I'm from Chester. That's where we met."

She's playing a part, Dan decided. *They're trying to pass themselves off as a couple, but I'd swear they're not together*. He wore his most disarming smile and said, "So, how are you enjoying your holiday in Embervale, Jess? When did you arrive?"

Jess licked her lips. "We arrived on Friday. We were supposed to be meeting for a drink, weren't we, Craig? But you didn't make it."

Craig looked up. "That's right. Tailback on the A38, as bloody usual."

"You were in the village on Friday?" Dan asked Craig. "The day Mortimer was killed?"

Craig bowed his head. "Yes. We didn't know about poor old Morty, but Kristen and I were both here. I didn't arrive until very late, and by the time I'd unloaded the car, I didn't much feel like going for a drink, so I downed a whisky and called it a day."

"We were both tired that evening," Kristen explained. "It's a shame. Looking back, I wonder if things might have been different if you'd gone to the pub as planned, Craig. You could've looked after Uncle Morty and made sure he was okay. Then everything would've been fine. He'd still be alive."

Dan stared at Kristen. "Why didn't you mention this before? I can't believe you were here all along, and you never said a word."

"It didn't seem relevant," Kristen replied. "It was a coincidence, nothing more. Just one of those things. I didn't set out to conceal the fact that I was here. It never came up in our conversation, that's all."

"I see." Dan looked to Alan, but his friend simply shrugged, and an awkward silence made itself at home.

"Would anyone like more tea?" Kristen asked. "And do dig into the cakes. I bought far too many."

"I'll have a top-up." Alan offered his cup. "And these scones look delicious."

Kristen relaxed, her smile regaining its cordiality. "Help yourself, Alan. I like a man with an appetite. I can't stand all the fuss people make about every little thing we eat. It's becoming quite—" She broke off, looking at Dan in alarm. "I'm sorry, I forgot you were a vegan. I didn't mean…"

"It's all right," Dan said. "Don't worry about it."

"I could go and check the ingredients," Kristen said. "They put everything on the labels these days, don't they. I'm sure I could find something for you."

"Please, don't bother. I don't want to put you to any trouble, and anyway, I'm really not hungry." Dan took a drink of his tea while he marshalled his thoughts. It was time to turn the conversation back to Mortimer's estate.

Martin saved him the trouble. Clearing his throat as if to make a speech, he said, "I hear that when you found Craig's uncle, he said something to you. Was it anything significant?"

"Just a few words, though we're not sure what he meant," Dan replied. "Why do you ask?"

"Passing interest." Martin affected a shrug. "There are all kinds of rumours flying around. It's like Chinese whispers. So I thought I'd get the facts, straight from the horse's mouth."

Dan glanced at Kristen. She'd cast her gaze downward to the Turkish carpet, and it may have been a trick of the light, but it looked as though her eyes were filling with tears.

"I'm not sure that the events of that night are a fit topic for a summer afternoon," Dan said. "It was a terrible thing that happened, but I don't want to add to the speculation."

"Least said, soonest mended," Craig chipped in. "It was a damned shame. The way it happened was dreadful. It should never have…" Craig cut his sentence short, pressing his lips together tight.

"What do you mean?" Dan asked. "What were you about to say?"

But Craig shook his head, looking away. When he spoke, his voice had grown distant, as though he was talking to someone who wasn't there. "It really was a damned shame."

"Craig feels," Kristen began, "that is, we *both* feel that there are plenty of people in the village who really aren't all that upset by what happened to Morty. They seem to think he got what he deserved."

"No," Alan protested. "Surely not. I know he could be a bit short with people, but I don't think—"

"He didn't have time for fools," Craig interrupted, his attention back on the group, a fierce determination in his eyes. "He had an awkward streak a mile wide, but he did a lot for this place. He wasn't one to boast, but he helped this community in more ways than most people imagine."

"That's very true," Kristen said. "Once you got past his gruff exterior, you realised that Morty had a soft streak for this place. The village, I mean. He kept quiet about it, but whenever people were trying to raise funds, he'd support them. Without his help, the church's bell tower would never have been rebuilt. When the village hall needed renovating, he paid for the materials. The primary school were given land for a football pitch. Then there were the little things: harvest festivals, summer fairs, shelves for the community library. He gave generously, without being asked, and he made sure his gifts were anonymous."

"You helped him with all that," Dan suggested, and Kristen nodded, wiping the corner of her eye with the back of her hand.

"Maybe it's time to let the village know what he did," Alan said. "It seems a shame to let his generosity go unrecognised."

"He wouldn't want that," Craig stated. "We'll keep it quiet and respect his wishes. All the old man wanted was to preserve the village, to keep it alive for future generations. Quite right."

"Perhaps that's why he left the cottage to Marjorie," Alan said. "After all, she's been there so long it's like she's part of the landscape."

Craig raised his eyebrows as if giving the matter serious thought, but his downturned mouth betrayed his displeasure.

"I expect the lawyers will sort all that out," Kristen said brightly. "It'll probably take ages and cost an absolute fortune, but we'll get there in the end."

"Do you know when your uncle changed his will?" Dan asked as casually as he could.

"Recently," Kristen replied. "Very recently. We think there's a chance that he wasn't quite with it at the time."

"Difficult to prove," Martin said. "He had it all drawn up properly, so—"

"We're not saying he'd lost the plot completely," Kristen argued. "But when you look at it logically, it was such an odd thing for Morty to have done. He left almost all the land to Craig and me, but that one little patch, he made over to *her*. It makes no sense to split the land up."

"If the land isn't to be split, how can you share it between you?" Alan asked.

"Simple," Craig replied. "On paper, the land belongs to a company. Me and sis already had small shares in the company, and now we're partners."

"I'm only a minor partner," Kristen said. "But that's fine by me."

"I hope you don't mind me asking," Dan began, "but is there anything in these rumours about the old mines? Is there anything of value down there?"

"I thought you didn't want to add to the speculation,"

Martin shot back. "There's nothing worth having in those mines. As far as minerals go, they're worthless."

Dan focused his attention on Martin. "You sound very sure of your facts."

"It's common sense." Martin met Dan's stare, unblinking. "If there was anything of value down there, it would've been exploited by now. Anyone can see that."

"Yes, I'm sure you're right," Dan admitted, noticing the way Martin relaxed once he thought he was off the hook, his shoulders sagging slightly, and the lines on his brow softening. Martin clearly knew more than he was telling, and it had cost him some effort to conceal the fact.

Jess made a show of checking her wristwatch. "Oh, we were going to go for a stroll this afternoon. It's about time we headed off or we won't make it in time."

"Where are you headed?" Alan asked. "I can give you some ideas if you like."

"No, thanks, we're fine. We've got it all worked out." Jess placed her cup on the table.

"But I thought you didn't know the area," Alan said. "And it can be quite confusing until you know your way around. Not all the lanes are signposted."

Jess dithered for a second, but Martin stood, puffing out his chest. "We're fine thanks. We've got a map."

"Okay. If you're sure." Alan sat back. "Only trying to help."

Jess sent Alan a grateful smile. "Thank you. You're very kind." Again, her cheeks coloured a little, and she bowed her head as she stood, raising a hand to straighten her hair.

"Thanks for the tea," Martin said. "Sorry we couldn't stay longer. Another time, perhaps." He nodded to Alan and Dan. "Nice to have met you. Goodbye. I don't expect we'll see you before we head back, so all the best."

Kristen rose smoothly to her feet. "Well, if you really must go, I'll see you out." She led her guests from the room, and the lounge suddenly seemed unnaturally quiet.

Craig beamed at them in turn. "Ready for that drink yet?"

"It's a bit early for me," Dan replied. "Maybe we should be going too. I don't want to outstay our welcome."

But Craig waved the idea aside. "Can't have you leaving just yet, old boy. Sis will be most put out until we've made a dent in the cakes and whatnot. Dig in, Alan. Dan, maybe you could force down a bite of something. Or failing that, shove a scone in your pocket—" He broke off abruptly. "Sh! Mum's the word." Tapping the side of his nose, he tipped them a wink before standing and shambling across the room.

He returned with a crystal tumbler of amber liquid just as Kristen strode back into the room. Her eyes flicked toward the ceiling, but her expression said that she'd long ago given up any effort to modify her brother's behaviour. Instead, she sat down, studiously ignoring her brother and focusing her gaze on Dan. "Have you decided how long you're staying in Embervale?"

"I'll be here for a few weeks," Dan said. "I've started redecorating the cottage, so that'll keep me out of mischief for some considerable time."

"Oh, I do hope not," Kristen replied with a smile. "You've got to have some fun once in a while."

Dan, rendered dumb by the subtly suggestive curl of her lips, could only nod. He made to take a drink, but finding his cup empty, he replaced it, clattering it against the saucer.

"You should have a word with Jay," Craig said. "He's the man for decorating. Any odd jobs you want doing, he'll take care of it."

"I know Jay," Dan intoned. "But I'd rather do the work myself."

"You really are an awkward bugger, aren't you," Craig said. "Why work hard when you can work easy? I'm telling you, Jay does a good job, and he doesn't charge the earth, which is more than you can say for most of the tradesmen around here. Half the lazy sods never turn up when they're meant to. But Jay's as solid as a rock. And if you pay him in cash, there's no need for the taxman to take a cut. Better all around."

Dan studied Craig's expression for a moment, wondering whether he knew that Jay's sideline was supposed to be under the radar. "I take it that Jay's done some work for you. Was it on this place?"

"No," Kristen said firmly. "A house like this requires specialists. You have to use all the right materials, and you need to know precisely what you're doing."

Craig grunted in disapproval, but Kristen silenced him with a look. "You can't let some bloke you met in the pub come around to slosh cut-price paint on the walls. Everything has to be in keeping with the period." She lifted her chin in a defiant gesture, settling the argument before turning back to Dan. "Anyway, if you've met Jay, you can probably guess why I wouldn't want him in the house."

"Jay's all right," Craig muttered. "He's a bit of a rough diamond, but he does what he's told and he keeps it off the books. What's wrong with that?"

"I'm with Kristen on this," Dan said. "I'm not sure I trust the man."

Dan's reward was a gracious smile from Kristen. "Thank you. It's so nice to talk to someone who understands."

"So I imagine," Craig said. "Time for a refill." He jumped to his feet and strode to the back of the room, his step sprightlier than before.

After that, Craig took little part in the proceedings, preferring to sit in silence, nursing his whisky and staring morosely into space. Kristen made a point of ignoring him, but though she kept up the flow of pleasant conversation, Dan grew increasingly uncomfortable. Alan looked as though he felt the same, his smile becoming strained as time wore on.

Time to go, Dan decided, and he exchanged a look with Alan, hoping his thoughts would be clear.

Alan nodded. "Well, I ought to be getting back to work. It's been lovely, it really has. Thank you so much, but I should be heading back."

"Oh, really?" Kristen asked. "Are you sure?"

"I'm afraid so." Alan stood, turning to Dan. "You could always walk back later if you like."

Dan jumped to his feet. "No, I'll come back with you."

"Well, it's up to you, of course," Kristen said. "I'll see you out." Kristen accompanied them to the front door, pausing on the threshold, a faintly desperate look in her eye as though she didn't want them to leave. "Thank you for coming over. I hope it wasn't too much of a bore for you."

"Not at all," Alan replied. "It was very kind of you to invite us. I enjoyed seeing your lovely home."

Kristen brightened, but there was a sadness in her eyes. "It's a wonderful old house, but I wonder whether we'll be able to keep it. The way things are going, we may have to sell."

"I'm sorry to hear that," Dan said. "Are the renovations too expensive?"

"Astronomical." Kristen shook her head. "But never mind about that. We must enjoy it while we can, and who knows, something might turn up."

"Perhaps you could sell off some of the other properties and use the money for this place," Alan said. "I expect the holiday cottages would go for a fair price, and then there's the land."

"The property is all tied up in the company, and let's just say that Craig and I have very different ideas about the way the estate should be managed."

"I'm sure you'll work something out," Dan said. "You're a highly experienced facilities coordinator."

"A *therapeutic* facilities coordinator," Kristen corrected

him. "It's very sweet of you to remember; most people forget instantly. But not you. You're different."

Alan cleared his throat. "Well, thank you again for everything. I must go and open the car windows to let the heat out. It'll be like an oven in there." He waved cheerfully to Kristen then marched across the driveway with an air of deliberate nonchalance.

Kristen leaned closer to Dan, lowering her voice. "Oh dear, I think your friend felt like a gooseberry."

"I don't know. Maybe he just really wants to let the car cool down."

"It's not a long drive back to the village," Kristen said. "You could've walked. I've done it myself. It only takes twenty minutes or so."

"Maybe next time." Dan smiled. "Assuming we're invited back, that is."

Kristen laughed. "Oh please. Come as often as you like. Best to call first, in case I'm not here. In fact..." She ducked back inside for a minute, and when she returned, she offered a business card to Dan. "Here. It's got all my numbers. I've scribbled down the landline for this place. The mobile reception here is terrible."

Dan glanced at the card before pocketing it. "Thanks. I'll give you a call. Maybe, if you're free one evening, we could go into Exeter. I know a nice little Moroccan place."

"Definitely. I'll look forward to it." Kristen nodded toward Alan's car. "I think you'd better go before Alan suffers from heatstroke."

"Yes, he does seem to have turned a delicate shade of scarlet." Dan moved slightly closer to take Kristen's hand, and she held his grip for just a moment longer than necessary. "I'll call. Soon."

She studied him with an amused gleam in her eye, and Dan's confidence faltered. Was he supposed to kiss her on the cheek? And if so, would a chaste peck be correct, or would that be too formal?

Kristen settled the matter by saying, "Goodbye, Dan. It was lovely to see you."

"Right. Yes. You too. I mean, it was good to see you as well. I'd better..." He hooked his thumb toward the car, then finding he had nothing useful to add, turned and started walking, trying to look calm and unflustered. And failing miserably.

CHAPTER 12

J AY MARKHAM PEERED over his shoulder, taking a long
look along the dark street. He was alone. Everyone else
was safely inside, tucked up in their beds most likely.
He'd spent a miserable evening at home, slumped in front of
the TV, flipping channels and munching toast, washing the
painkillers down with mugs of tea. The pain in his hand had
receded to a dull ache, but his skin itched, and when he
looked in the mirror, his pupils were the size of pinpricks. He
needed a drink; he hadn't had one for days. He'd tried a can
of beer, and it hadn't agreed with the painkillers at all. A few
mouthfuls from a can of IPA and a rush of dizziness had sent
him staggering to the sofa. His stomach had squirmed, his
chest muscles clamping so tight he could scarcely breathe,
and his heart had shuddered violently against his ribs. He'd
dropped the can on the floor, the beer soaking into the carpet,
and he'd vowed not to drink until he was off the medication.
The problem was, the more he took the damned pills, the less
effective they seemed to be.

Bloody doctor, he thought bitterly. *I'll have to find another
way, get something else for the pain.* One thing was for sure: he
couldn't go cold turkey. He'd been through this before, after

the whiplash injury to his neck. He was sensitive to opiates, that was the problem. Back then, the doctors had said they'd done everything they could, then they'd delivered a diagnosis of chronic pain and sent him home. It was a question of managing his pain, they'd said, living with it, accommodating it, putting up with a new set of limitations.

But he'd shown them. He'd proved them wrong, using most of his compensation to pay for a private physiotherapist: a specialist in spinal injuries. She'd put him through the mill, but he'd persisted, pushing himself to improve, retraining his body, building himself up until he was just as strong as before. It hadn't been easy, and it had cleaned out his bank account, but it had been worth it to feel like himself again, to be a man.

Look at me now, he thought, hunching his shoulders, his hands in his pockets as he dawdled along the uneven pavement. All that work, all that effort, and now it was lost, ruined by a stupid accident and a cut on his hand.

When he'd gone in for his stitches, he'd tried to tell them he didn't want any strong painkillers, but they hadn't listened, hadn't understood. So here he was, hooked on the damned things all over again. He'd phoned the doctors' surgery, but when they'd told him there was a week-long wait for an appointment, he'd slammed the phone down. *A week!* He couldn't stand a week of this. No way. There were private hospitals he could call if he had the money, and maybe they could help. He just needed the cash to pay for the consultation, and he had nowhere near enough.

But maybe he could do something about that, sooner rather than later. *If this works out*, he thought, *I could get myself sorted out*.

He halted beside a wrought-iron gate, then taking a last glance at the empty street, he pushed the gate open and walked silently over the brick-paved driveway toward the semi-detached house.

There was a doorbell beside the double-glazed door, but Jay raised his left hand and rapped on the frosted glass. Inside, a light glowed and a dark shape loomed as the resident approached.

Jay stepped back, squaring his shoulders, and when the door was yanked wide, the imposing figure of a middle-aged man filled the opening.

"All right, Derek," Jay said. "You know why I'm here."

Derek's humourless grin pinched his flabby cheeks into a clownish expression, but his eyes burned with resentment and mistrust. "Jay, we've been through this a hundred times. You get paid when I get paid, all right?"

"So bloody well get off your arse and go and get my money. It's been weeks."

"Tell me about it," Derek said. "I laid out for the materials. I'm out of pocket on this job."

"So what are you mucking around at?"

"You know what she's like. Ah, she can look like butter wouldn't melt when she puts her mind to it, but she's hard as nails. I've argued with her until I was blue in the face, and she always swears blind she'll pay. But I've not had a penny from her. Nothing."

Jay shook his head slowly, his gaze fixed on Derek. "Not good enough. I need that money, Derek. I need it now. Not tomorrow, not next week, *now*."

"I can't help you, mate. What can I do about it?"

Jay lunged forward, grabbing the front of Derek's T-shirt with his left hand. He leaned in, pressing his face close to Derek's. "Give me my money, Derek. I won't ask again."

Recovering fast, Derek planted his meaty hands on Jay's chest and shoved him away. "Watch yourself, Jay. You don't come around here, to *my* house, making demands. Now piss off home before I teach you some respect."

"You'll be the one learning a lesson," Jay growled. "If my hand wasn't buggered, I'd—"

"You'd what?" Derek demanded, folding his arms. "I could wipe the floor with you. You're all talk, Jay. You're a joke. You make out like you're big news, but guess what. You're not a copper anymore. One word from me, and your old pals will come looking for you. And they might just want their money back."

Jay took a breath, letting it out slowly, staving off the red mist before it made him do something he'd regret. "Listen, Derek, I earned that money. I didn't spend five days wading through the shit for nothing."

"I know, and you'll get—"

"Bollocks! I completely rebuilt those bloody sheds, *and* I had to replace all the fences. Marjorie Treave never so much as offered me a mug of tea. She *owes* me. So tell her to pay up, or I swear I'll go around there and knock the whole bloody lot down."

"All right, all right," Derek said. "I'll tell you what I'll do. I'll give you something to tide you over, and I'll get the rest as soon as I can." He rummaged in his pocket and produced a roll of banknotes, peeling off five of them with a practised ease and holding them out to Jay. "Here's a ton. Don't complain or you'll get nothing. Take it or leave it."

Jay eyed the money. He should tell Derek what he could do with his hundred quid, but the temptation to take the money was too great, and he snatched it from the man's hand, pocketing the notes.

"Everything all right, Dad?"

Jay looked up to see a young man appear in the hallway, and Derek turned to acknowledge his son. "No problem. Just doing a bit of business with Jay, but we're done now. He's just leaving."

"Now then, Steve," Jay said, looking past Derek. "All right?"

Steven Holder stood at his father's side. "Yeah, I'm all right. What do *you* want?"

"Like your dad said, we had business to discuss," Jay stated. "Going out somewhere, Steve? At this time of night?"

Steve bridled. "What if I am? What's it got to do with you?"

"Just asking," Jay replied.

"It's what they do these days," Derek said. "They don't go out until late, then they finally crawl home at four in the morning."

"I blame the parents," Jay said. "No discipline."

"Ha-ha," Derek mocked. "Very funny."

"Ignore him, Dad." Steve pushed past his father. "See you later. I'm off round Billy's house." He marched past Jay without looking back, and a moment later they heard the garden gate click shut.

"Has he not got work in the morning?" Jay asked.

"He's no need to worry about that. That's the benefit of having your dad as the boss." Derek smiled. "Right, I'm off to bed, and if you've got any sense, you'll do the same. Goodnight."

Derek closed the door, and though Jay was tempted to deliver a swift kick to the PVC panels, he turned on his heel and walked away. In the street, he stopped to take a breath of night air, and in the distance, he spotted Steve marching away, his hands hanging loose at his sides. *I only know one bloke called Billy*, Jay thought. *And you don't go that way to get to his house.* Jay paused for a split second, watching the way Steve moved, then he set off after him, keeping his footsteps light and sticking to the shadows.

Within minutes, Steve reached a quiet cul-de-sac, and Jay hung back, pressing himself against a tall hedge. Watching.

Steve marched toward a cottage that stood on its own. The windows were dark, but without hesitation, Steve slipped down the side of the house and disappeared from view.

Jay moved closer, placing his feet carefully so as not to

make a sound. From behind the cottage, a sharp crack rang out, like the snapping of a bolt. Then there was silence.

Dear, oh dear, Jay thought. *What are we up to, young Steven?*

He moved into the deeper shadow beneath an old horse chestnut tree, and leaned his back against the trunk, taking out his phone and settling in for a patient vigil. But he didn't have to wait long.

Steve emerged from the front door, closing it quietly before setting off into the street, sauntering along as though he didn't have a care in the world. And slung over his shoulder, a large black holdall bulged ominously.

Jay waited until Steve was right in front of him, then he stepped from the shadows. "Nice night for it, Steve."

"Bloody hell! What do you want now?"

Jay waggled his phone in the air. Just doing a little late-night photography. He aimed his phone at Steve to take a picture, and since he'd activated the flash while he'd been waiting, the white light bathed Steve's scowl in an unflattering glare.

"Stupid bastard!" Steve snarled. "That doesn't prove anything." He made to walk away, but Jay darted forward, his hand closing tight on Steve's arm. Steve struggled, but Jay was ready and he held firm, spinning the younger man around, shaking him.

"Does your old man know you've been robbing the holiday cottages? I doubt it. Even Derek's not stupid enough to crap on his own doorstep."

"Don't know what you're talking about. Let go of my arm, or you'll get a slap."

"What, like this?" Releasing his grip on the young man's arm, Jay lashed out with his fist, his swiping blow catching Steve on the side of his face.

Steve grunted in pain, raising his hands to his head, but before he could do anything else, Jay set about yanking the holdall from his shoulder, pulling it free. Steve resisted, but he was no match for the older man.

"Let's see what we have here." Jay peered into the holdall. "What the hell's this? Power tools or something?" He pulled out a large carrying case, its sides made from sturdy black plastic. "What have you nicked, Stevie boy?"

"It's a drone," Steve muttered. "We saw them using it." He sniffed. "You're not going to tell my dad, are you?"

Jay stared at him. "That depends. Tell me about this drone, and I might keep quiet."

"What do you mean?"

Jay curled his finger. "Step this way. My truck's parked down the road. We'll talk in there."

"I'm going home."

"No, you're not." Jay held on to the plastic case then hefted the holdall onto his shoulder. "Bloody hell. What else have you got in here?"

Steve shrugged. "Dunno. Electronic stuff. Looked valuable."

"I'll have a look. Follow me." Jay led the way, Steve traipsing meekly at his side.

But when they arrived at Jay's truck, Steve kept his distance. "I'm not getting in."

"For God's sake, what do you think is going to happen? I have zero interest in driving off with a snivelling little pillock like you in the passenger seat, so shut up, get in and stay quiet."

Reluctantly, Steve complied, and sitting in the driver's seat, Jay rummaged through the holdall. "I don't know what half this stuff is, so I'm willing to bet you have no idea what you've got here. You really are a complete amateur, aren't you? A total no-hoper. What were you expecting to do with all this stuff?"

Steve regarded him sullenly. "Flog it. Got to be worth something."

"I'll tell you exactly what you'd get for this little lot," Jay said. "About five years."

"You're not going to shop me, or you'd have done it by now." Steve tried to make his face hard, but Jay had seen it all before. The kid was scared, out of his depth. Like almost all thieves, Steve was lazy to the core, unwilling to work for the things he wanted. And like all lazy people, he'd take the easy way out as soon as it was offered.

Jay smiled. "Here's what we're going to do. You're going to tell me all about the people in that cottage, and you're going to tell me exactly where they've been flying this drone. Then you're going to leave this bag with me, and you're going to bugger off home."

"I don't know," Steve said, but his stony expression was already giving way. "What are you going to do with the gear?"

"I'm going to take it back. In the morning, I'll pop in and tell them I found this bag lying around outside. I'll say a thief must've been disturbed and decided to ditch the lot. If you're a good lad, Stevie boy, I'll keep you out of it."

Steve considered for a second, then he nodded.

"Right," Jay said. "If you're sitting comfortably, we'll begin."

THURSDAY

CHAPTER 13

DAN WOKE UP early after a fitful night. His bedroom had been too hot and far too airless to allow for proper sleep. And anyway, his tired mind had refused to rest. Recent events had replayed in a muddle of half-dreams, disjointed sequences running over and over like some angst-ridden experimental film. He'd tried to push the thoughts away, to focus on pleasant memories. But a devilish part of his subconscious had needled him all night, urging him to untangle the mystery of Mortimer Gamble's death, to solve the problem, to help his friend.

And Dan recognised the signs: the broken night, the restlessness, the sense of impending failure. This was how he'd felt in the long weeks before he'd lost his job in the City. Back then, he'd spent his days wired on caffeine but unable to concentrate, his wits stretched tight like wires pulled to breaking point. His nights had been lost to dark imaginings, scattered dreams shot through with fragments of unspoken fear. Eventually, day and night had merged into perpetual gloom, and he'd frittered the minutes away until they'd turned into hours, hamstrung by indecision, uncertain at every turn.

He couldn't go down that path. Not again. He had to break free from anxiety's oppressive gravity before it took him spiralling down. Before it was too late.

I need to go for a run, he told himself. *I need to go right now.* He climbed out of bed, but somehow he didn't want to run on his own, didn't want to be alone with his demons. If he waited just a little while, he might be able to persuade Alan to come with him.

By seven o'clock, Dan's patience had reached its limit. He made his way across the alley, letting himself into the garden at the rear of Alan's house and taking the short path to the back door. But he didn't knock.

Perhaps Alan wouldn't be awake, perhaps he'd be annoyed at being disturbed at this hour. There was only one way to find out. Dan rapped his knuckles on the wooden door, and a minute later, Alan appeared, wearing a dressing gown and slippers, a mug of tea in his hand. "Dan, what's up? Everything all right?"

"Fine. Have you eaten yet?"

"No, I was just about to."

"Don't," Dan said. "We're going for a run."

"Are we?"

"Yes. Can I come in? I'll wait while you get ready."

"You can come in," Alan replied. "But I don't know about going for a run. I've hardly had time to wake up." Alan shambled back into his kitchen, calling out, "I'm making toast. Would you like some?"

Dan followed. "No thanks. Wait. Yes, maybe just one piece. I shouldn't really, but if you're having some…"

"All right. Coming up." Alan busied himself at the counter, sawing at a large loaf with a bread knife then posting the thick slices into his cheerfully red toaster. He stowed the loaf in a wooden bread bin, brushed the crumbs from the breadboard into the palm of his hand, and once he'd stood the board neatly on its edge, he headed for the door.

"Where are you going now?" Dan asked.

Alan stopped in his tracks, turning to study Dan. "If it's all the same to you, I'm going to put these crumbs out for the birds. I think you'd better sit down and take a minute. Otherwise, no toast, and definitely no run."

Alan continued with his task and, chastened, Dan did as he was told, sitting down and watching as Alan shuffled outside. *He looks even more tired than me*, Dan thought. *This business with Mortimer must be playing on his mind.* When Alan came back in, Dan said, "Sorry. I didn't mean to be so..." He waved his hand in the air.

"So *you?*" Alan smiled. "No worries. It's these hot nights; they make everyone fractious. I hardly slept a wink."

"It wasn't just me then."

"No." Alan placed a jar of honey and a plastic tub of spread on the table. "Don't worry, the spread is dairy free. And that's not Marjorie's honey. I found it at the back of the cupboard, and if memory serves, I bought it from the village shop."

"Ah, the legendary shop. I haven't sampled its hidden treasures."

"Oh, but you must go," Alan said. "If we don't support it, we'll lose it."

"I have tried, several times, but whenever I get there, it seems to be closed."

Alan nodded wisely as he placed a plate of toast in front of Dan. "The opening hours are somewhat erratic. It's best to try it early in the mornings. There's a young woman who keeps the place running almost single-handedly, and she's there most mornings. In the afternoons, Gary is supposed to take over. He owns the shop, but he's also a keen fisherman. As the day wears on, he loses interest in cans of beans and pots of instant noodles, so he heads for the coast and his boat. Still, if you get to know him, he might offer you a few mackerel. You won't find fresher."

"Good to know." Taking a knife from the cutlery holder on the table, Dan applied some spread to his toast and took a bite, chewing enthusiastically. "I skipped the honey, but this bread is good. Is that from the shop too?"

Alan looked quietly pleased. "I made it myself. It's not difficult once you know how, and living out here, it's easier than going to the supermarket."

"What about supporting the village shop?"

"You've got me there," Alan admitted. "They do sell bread, although they have a tendency to run out of the good stuff. But to be honest, I really enjoy making bread. It's very therapeutic. You should try it. I can give you the recipe."

"Thanks. I might give it a try." Dan munched the last of his toast, then brushing his hands together, he said, "About this run. I've figured out a new loop."

"Oh good," Alan said, his voice heavy with reluctance.

"It's an easy route," Dan went on. "We take the public footpath past the spoil heaps, pass Marjorie's house, then we take the lane that leads back to the village. The whole route is roughly five K, and according to my app, it's mainly level, so no problem."

Alan scratched his jaw. "*Mainly* is the operative word. There's a steep hill along that lane."

"Then we'll take that part a bit slower. Come on, it'll do you good."

Alan grunted under his breath. "Define *good*." He held up his hand. "I take that back. Whatever you do, please don't start a lecture on the benefits of cardiovascular exercise. I give in."

"You'll come?"

"Yes. You'll have to give me a few minutes. My running gear is… well, to tell the truth, I've no idea where I left it. I think it might still be in the wash."

Dan smiled. "Is that what your pupils used to say when

they wanted to get out of PE lessons? I bet it didn't work when they tried it. Am I right?"

"No comment." Alan marched from the room, and a moment later, Dan heard him trudging up the stairs.

∿

THEY ALMOST MADE it to the end of the public footpath before Alan jogged to a halt, his hand pressed against his side. "Hold on a sec," he said between gasps. "Stitch."

Dan nodded. "We'll walk for a bit. Try touching your toes. Remember what I said about the—"

"Yes, I know all about the blood supply to my diaphragm, thank you." Alan threw his head back, gasping for air, and he staggered toward the gate that marked the end of the path.

Dan followed at a respectful distance. Alan's prickly moments never lasted long, he was too good natured for that, but at times, he needed to be given some room. *That's what happens when you live in a place like this*, Dan thought. *Will I end up the same way if I stay here long enough?*

In London, Dan had grown used to the idea of space as a luxury: something to be enjoyed on a walk through the park on a Sunday. Yes, he loved the excitement of bustling streets, the sense of energy, the idea that there was always something happening. But he'd rarely stopped to consider what it meant to live in proximity to so many people. He'd accepted that he must travel pressed shoulder to shoulder with his fellow city-dwellers, breathing the same stale air in the underground, squeezing past each other in the rush to gain a prime position on the platform, dodging through crowds to catch a connection, hail a taxi or leap aboard a bus.

Here, surrounded by acres of empty countryside, it was the other way around. Space was a given, but the company of others was a luxury to be savoured from time to time, and best taken in small doses. Dan took a deep breath of sweet air and smiled to himself as he followed Alan through the gate. Perhaps it wouldn't be so bad to grow accustomed to this way of life. It wouldn't be so bad at all.

Alan cast an appraising glance in Dan's direction. "I know why you're smiling."

"I very much doubt it."

"You were thinking I shouldn't have had that second piece of toast." Alan stifled a belch. "And to be honest, I'm starting to think you were right."

"I wasn't going to lecture you. We can walk for a minute if you like."

"Fair enough." They ambled across the road, passing the entrance to Marjorie's garden. "That reminds me," Alan said, nodding toward a pair of plastic crates at the roadside. "I must put my recycling out. They'll be coming for it this afternoon."

Dan halted, staring. "Look at that."

"What?" Alan moved closer to the crates, peering inside. "Oh yes. She must've had a clear out."

Dan stooped to pluck a glass jar from the crate, holding it up to the light. "There must be thirty jars in here and all completely clean. She washed them out then threw them away."

"Yes. You're meant to rinse them out. It helps with the recycling."

"Alan, this jar wasn't just rinsed out; it's been scrubbed clean. Does Marjorie strike you as the kind of woman to throw away so many perfectly good jars?"

"No," Alan admitted. "If anything, I'd have her down as a hoarder of bottles and jars and the like. But she must've had a good reason." His lips formed an O. "You think she's getting rid of the evidence. The toxin from the honey."

Dan nodded, then he gave the jar an experimental sniff. "Bleach. If she wanted to hide her tracks, she's done a good job. I doubt whether a forensic expert could glean much from these."

"You're not still thinking she might've poisoned the old man deliberately, are you?"

"It's unlikely, I know, but I wish there was some way we could be sure." Dan looked across Marjorie's yard. "I wonder where she keeps the hives."

"Stop right there," Alan said. "You can try raiding a hive if you really want to, but there's no way I'm doing battle with a swarm of angry bees."

"But if we just had some honey to test, it would make it easier to see if we're barking up the wrong tree."

"You mean, we could eliminate Marjorie from our inquiries," Alan intoned. "Honestly, Dan, you're going too far. We're not the police. There's only so much we can do."

"But that's the frustrating thing. We have to do more. Spiller is never going to get very far. He was here for an hour at most, then off he went to type up his reports. I wouldn't be surprised if the whole investigation has been rubber-stamped already. *No further action*, that's what they'll say. No admissible evidence, no witnesses, no real motive. Nothing."

"Even so," Alan began, but Dan didn't let him finish.

"And anyway, I want to *help*," Dan said. "I know this is serious, and ordinarily I wouldn't get involved. But as long as this remains unsolved, you'll have a cloud of suspicion hanging over you, and you're putting a brave face on it, but I can see what it's doing to you."

Alan's expression fell. "Really?"

"Yes." Dan took a breath, exhaling slowly. "I didn't want to say anything before, but you're not just tired, Alan; you're all in. You look defeated, ready to give up. So let me help you. Between us, if we keep trying, I'm sure we can piece this together."

Alan held his gaze for a second. "All right. I must admit, it was starting to get to me. I was thinking it over last night, and it all felt a bit hopeless. We don't seem to be getting anywhere, but we'll give it another shot." A brief smile lit his features. "After all, who better to get me out of a tight spot than a troubleshooter? I just hope you're not intending to send me a bill."

Dan laughed. "Believe me, if I did, you couldn't afford it."

"Well, shall we head back to the village?" Alan asked. "My stitch has gone, and I reckon I'm ready to run the rest of the way."

"All right. Let's go."

~

ON THE WAY back into the village, Alan halted by a crossroads, breathing hard. "Which way?"

"We turn right here. It's an easy stretch, then we'll be home."

"I can't believe I'm saying this, but I'd like to make a detour. If we go down here and then take a left, it makes the run a bit longer, but we can go past the shop."

Dan shrugged. "Yeah. It's no problem for me, but are you sure you're up for it?"

"Definitely. I've got my second wind." Alan grinned. "Plus, if we call in at the shop, I can stock up on supplies. All this pounding the tarmac has given me an appetite. I'm famished."

"Okay, but if you follow up a run with a full English breakfast, you'll cancel out all that exercise."

"Exactly," Alan shot back. "I've earned it, so I'll enjoy it all the more. Come on. Catch up." He set off at a brisk pace, and Dan matched his speed easily.

"You're doing well," Dan said. "We'll make a runner of you yet."

Alan didn't reply; he simply jogged on, determined. The rest of the run passed quickly, and before long they were slowing outside the squat stone building that advertised itself as Embervale's General Store.

"Time for your initiation," Alan said with a wink as he pulled open the door, and Dan stepped inside.

The shop was surprisingly large, the impression of space conjured by the tightly packed rows of shelves, all crammed with a curious assortment of colourful packets and cans. Scotch broth sat alongside shoe polish; dishcloths flopped lazily against plastic bottles of shampoo; and boxes of washing powder vied for space among a crowd of gleaming jars, instant coffee rubbing shoulders with jams, chutneys and pickled beetroot.

The word *cornucopia* sprang into Dan's mind, and he found himself wandering between the shelves, gazing in wonder at the profusion of mismatched items. Only one display seemed to be thoroughly organised, and he stopped in front of it, running his hands over the neat rows of cardboard boxes. "Why are there so many candles? Who buys their candles in boxes of twenty or more?"

"Stay here until winter and you'll find out," Alan replied. "How many power lines do you think there are between this village and the nearest substation?"

"I don't know. A dozen?"

Alan chuckled. "One." The expression on Dan's face made him laugh even more, and still chortling to himself, Alan strolled away between the shelving units and disappeared from view.

"Can I help you with something?"

Dan turned to see a young woman staring at him with frank curiosity. Her deep brown eyes lent her an open expression, but when she smiled, her cheeks dimpled in a way that hinted at hidden depths of impish charm.

"Thanks, but I'm fine," Dan replied. "Just browsing."

"Oh right, I'll leave you in peace then." The woman folded her arms, but she showed no sign of moving away.

As far as he knew, Dan had no need of candles, but since the woman was still following his every move with rapt interest, he picked out a box of white candles and examined the label, hoping to be seen as a serious customer who just wanted to be left alone.

"Dinner party, is it?" the woman asked.

"No. I was thinking about stocking up. You know, just in case."

The woman narrowed her eyes, then she smiled. "Oh, it's you, isn't it? I didn't recognise you at first, what with all your multicoloured Lycra and that."

"It's not Lycra," Dan stated as carefully as he could. "It's textured polyester, actually."

The woman waved his objections aside. "Whatever. You're in your running kit. You know what I mean." She thrust out her hand. "I'm Sam. I work at the pub."

"Oh." Dan shook her hand briefly. He had no recollection of the young woman, but he could hardly admit to that. "Of course. Right. The pub. Silly of me."

"You probably never noticed me. I'm always stuck in the kitchen, slaving away over the fryer, or washing up, cleaning the glasses: all the mucky jobs. But I've seen you lots of times. You're from London, aren't you? You come in with Alan." Her lips curled slowly into a knowing smile. "And you found old Morty, didn't you? Tried to save him."

"Yes. We tried."

Sam watched him, expecting more, and when he didn't elaborate, she said, "I suppose you'll be going back soon. To London." She grinned. "I love it down there. I haven't been for years. But it's better than this dump, that's for sure."

Dan looked at her more closely and realised that she was nearer his own age than he'd first thought. She had the artlessness of youth, but her eyes betrayed a hint of weariness with the world. She was like an unfinished painting: a portrait of a young woman denied the chance to fulfil her potential. Dan pictured her strolling along Oxford Street in the sunshine, her crumpled overall swapped for a summer dress, and her hair shaken free from its ponytail.

Meeting his gaze, she smiled. "Well, are you?"

"Am I what?"

"Going back to London." She watched him carefully as if everything depended on his answer.

"Eventually," Dan said. "I'm not sure when. I'm here for a while yet. So I'd better get these." He held up the box of candles. "Do you take cards?"

"Yeah, but you need to come over to the machine." Sam headed back toward the counter, installing herself by the till and tapping the buttons rapidly. She pushed the card reader across the counter. "This might not be London, but we're not quite in the Stone Age."

"I know." Biting back a number of smart remarks, Dan offered his card to the machine and was rewarded with a beep. "Oh, I forgot. I was going to have a look around, but I don't suppose you have any oat milk, do you? Or soy. Anything like that."

She eyed him levelly before pointing across the shop. "Soy or almond. Over there, next to the bran flakes. There's quite a lot of demand, as it happens. Lactose intolerant, are you?"

"No, but I don't eat dairy products." Dan smiled. "Anyway, it's great that you have them. I'll be able to pop in more often."

She returned his smile but there was no warmth in it, and Dan had the impression she'd already dismissed him from her mind. "Right, well, I'd better go and see what's taking Alan so long."

"I'm here," Alan said, bustling into view with a plastic basket in his hands. "It turned out I needed more than I bargained for." He flashed Sam a smile. "Morning, Sam. How are you?"

"Fine, thank you, Mr Hargreaves," she said brightly.

"Here, let me take that for you." Reaching over the counter, she lifted Alan's basket easily, setting it down and beginning to unload it, entering the prices into the till. "Shall I put all this in a bag for you?"

"If you wouldn't mind," Alan replied. "Thank you."

"No trouble." Cheerfully, Sam packed the groceries into a carrier bag, and Dan watched their exchange with interest. Sam had become more animated, the twinkle returning to her eye. For his part, Alan seemed absorbed, his gaze lingering on Sam's face.

"There we go." Sam handed the carrier bag to Alan. "Anything else I can get you?"

"No thanks," Alan replied. "Dan, are you finished?"

"Er, I was going to get some soy milk, but I only have my card and…" Dan indicated a notice attached to the till, the bold capitals forbidding card payments for any amount less than five pounds.

"Add it to my shopping," Alan said. "You can settle up later. Problem solved."

"Okay. Thanks. I'll go and get it." He set off for the promised shelf, and found it easily, pleasantly surprised that there were several dairy-free products, and all brands he'd tried before. Grabbing a litre of soy milk, he added a small carton of custard, then he headed back to the till where Sam and Dan were deep in conversation.

"I'll take these, please," Dan said, placing his items on the counter.

"Right." Sam quickly added Dan's shopping to Alan's bill. "When you're ready, Alan. It's gone over the limit, I'm afraid, so you'll have to enter your PIN." She smiled sweetly, and Alan inserted his card into the reader and tapped the keys.

"All done." Ignoring Dan, Sam said, "Are you going to the pub later?"

Alan tilted his head to one side. "I'm not sure. Maybe."

"We could pop in for a pint," Dan suggested. "Perhaps we'll see you there, Sam."

She rolled her eyes. "Not much chance of that. There's a darts match on, so I'll be stuck in the back making sandwiches all night." She shook her head. "It's always the same. Kev's not much help. He'll pull the pints, all right, but he leaves everything else up to me. And you know what? Every night, as soon as he's called time, he clears off and goes out the back for a smoke. He leaves me to collect all the glasses and wipe down the tables, when by rights my shift should've finished."

"It's a long day for you," Alan said. "And hot work in the kitchen at this time of year."

"Tell me about it." Sam wiped her brow. "Anyway, if there's nothing else I can do for you, I'd better get on. Gary's gone fishing, and I've got a delivery to unpack."

"Anything exciting?" Dan asked.

She stared at him wearily. "Instant barbecues. Gary reckons we'll need them if we get a good weekend. But on the radio, they're giving rain. Non-stop." She eyed Dan as if somehow, he bore the blame for the gloomy weather. "Typical. Just when I've got the weekend off for once."

"Ah, well, maybe the rain will miss us," Alan said. "It has been known to happen." He turned to Dan. "It's the microclimate in the valley. Sometimes, the weather patterns skirt around us. You'd be surprised how often it happens."

"And sometimes the rain gets stuck here for days on end," Sam put in. "So if it rains all weekend, it wouldn't surprise me at all."

"Yes, there's a reason it's so green around here." Alan picked up his bag of shopping. "Right, I'd better get going. Bye, Sam. We might see you later."

"Bye," Dan added. "Thanks for your help."

"No problem."

Sam watched them leave, but when Dan paused at the

door and glanced back, she'd already disappeared from behind the counter. He pictured her surrounded by towering crates of instant barbecues, then he let the door swing shut.

"Nice girl," Alan said breezily as they walked away. "You've got to feel for young people, though. There aren't a lot of opportunities for them."

"I guess not," Dan said. "But she's not that much younger than you, is she? I'd say there's only five or six years between you. That's nothing."

Alan pursed his lips. "I'm hopeless at guessing how old people are, but you're probably right. I always think of her as younger, but I suppose I've grown used to seeing her in the shop. She's worked there for as long as I've lived in the village, so I suppose I'm remembering her as she was back then."

"Right. Does she smile so warmly at all her customers?"

"I expect so. As I said, she's a nice girl. I mean, a nice young woman." He cast a questioning glance at Dan. "Why? What are you trying to say?"

"Nothing really. But it seemed as if she was keen on you, that's all."

"No." Alan chuckled at the thought. "Sam was just being friendly. It's how people get along in a small place like this. The problem with you is, you don't make time for people. You don't show an interest."

"Probably because I'm not interested in small talk. It's a waste of time."

"Honestly," Alan muttered. "Why do you have to make everything so difficult? It costs nothing to spend the time of day with people. Not every conversation is a competition, you know."

Dan could think of no suitable reply. He wanted to explain that resolving conflicts had been his stock in trade for the last few years, but although he hated to admit it, Alan's words had struck home. It wasn't easy for Dan to adapt to relaxed social interactions. His mind was a greyhound, always longing for the sprint, the headlong dash. He'd never allowed himself to stroll through life, and until recently that had worked to his advantage. But not anymore. Now, he knew where his old way of life would inevitably take him, and he wasn't at all happy with the destination.

His stay in Embervale had allowed him to break free from his old routines, but he still hadn't found new ones to replace them. Perhaps that would take longer than he'd thought. He'd just have to be patient.

Dan and Alan didn't talk much for the rest of the journey home, and when they reached The Old Shop, they went their separate ways, Alan handing over Dan's cartons of dairy-free products in a strange parody of a parting gift.

"I'll see you later," Alan said, heading for his door.

"Did you want to pop into the pub this evening?"

"I'll see. Possibly."

"Okay. Give me a shout," Dan said. "I still want to figure out what happened to Mortimer."

Alan barely paused. "Go ahead. If you need any help, give me a call." He smiled. "But do me a favour, and let me finish my breakfast, okay?"

Dan returned the smile. "Sure." He raised his hand to wave, then he headed for his own home. In his kitchen, there was a new packet of coffee beans just waiting to be opened, and he had a sudden craving for a really good espresso.

CHAPTER 14

IT WAS AROUND noon when Dan heard a knock at his kitchen window. He'd been working at the table and, looking up, he saw Alan peering in excitedly.

"Come in," Dan called out, gesturing in case he couldn't be heard, and Alan hurried in.

"I'm not disturbing you, am I?" Alan asked, his gaze going to the sheets of paper scattered across Dan's kitchen table.

Dan pushed his notepad aside. "No. I need a break. I've been working on a few ideas, trying to map out where everybody was on Friday night. I want to work out who went where, and when, but there seem to be too many unknowns."

"Perhaps this may help," Alan said, proudly placing a jar on the table.

Dan picked it up. "Honey. But this is the jar you were using this morning, isn't it? You said it was from the shop, not from Marjorie."

"Yes, but I made a mistake. This is the honey that Marjorie wanted to take back. Look at the label."

Dan examined the jar, and although, at first glance, the label resembled those found in any supermarket, there was something amateurish in its layout, and the colours were not as vibrant as they should be. The label was home made, produced on a decent colour printer perhaps, but not quite up to scratch. And anyway, there was no mistaking the address inscribed in small letters on the back: *The Old Buttery, Embervale, Devon.* "What happened? Did you give Marjorie the wrong jar? Surely she'd have noticed if you'd fobbed her off with honey from the shop."

"Yes, but that's where this comes in." Alan took his hand from behind his back, revealing another jar of honey. "This is the one from the shop." He placed the jar on the table, and the label, while similar to Marjorie's, had clearly been professionally printed.

"So originally, you had three jars at once?"

"Apparently."

"But you always have everything so neat and tidy," Dan said. "I've never seen such organised cupboards. Why would you have *three* jars of honey? Unless... wait a minute. Are you sure this is yours? Could someone have put it there? Maybe, when Marjorie was in your kitchen, she slipped a jar into your cupboard."

"Why would she do such a thing?"

"To muddy the water, to throw us off the scent."

"No, I was with her the whole time." Alan raised his hand to ward off further argument. "Listen for a minute. I think I know what happened. Whenever there's an event in the village—the summer fair, the village show, apple day— anything like that, Marjorie sets up a stall to sell her produce. I don't like to pass by without buying something. I feel sorry for her, stuck on her own out there, but there's only so much honey a man can eat."

"I have a question," Dan said.

"Go ahead."

"If it doesn't take too long to explain, what is an apple day, exactly?"

Alan's eyes flicked upward. "A traditional autumn fair on the theme of the humble apple. Apples are pressed to make cider, cake is eaten, a raffle is drawn, there are activities for the kids and a good time is had by all. Is that succinct enough for you?"

"Admirably." Dan smiled. "So, of the two jars of local honey: how do you know that this is the jar you bought recently?"

"It was at the back of the cupboard."

"So?" Dan asked.

"I have a system. I use things in date order. When I've been to the shops, I always shuffle everything forward, so that new purchases can go—"

"At the back," Dan said. He turned the jar around in his hand. "There's no *best before* date."

"Marjorie doesn't bother with that. She says honey lasts forever."

"How come you didn't think of this earlier?"

Alan shrugged. "When Marjorie came knocking on the door, she caught me on the hop. It was all so unexpected, I must've given her the first jar that came to hand without thinking about it."

"You gave her an old jar," Dan said. "One you bought at a fair."

"Right. But this morning, I knew I still had a jar I'd bought from the shop ages ago, so when I grabbed it from the cupboard, I didn't look too carefully at it. I was a bit bleary eyed, and then you came around and distracted me in the middle of making breakfast, so I didn't notice which jar I was using. It wasn't until I started tidying the kitchen that I finally saw the label and realised what had happened."

Dan nodded thoughtfully. "And you ate from this jar this morning?"

"Yes. I had two slices of toast, remember. Then I went on a run. No problem. I'm fine."

Carefully, Dan unscrewed the jar and peered inside. "It's still very clear and runny. If it was old, it probably would've started to crystallise."

"Definitely. Come to think of it, the jar I gave to Marjorie was looking a bit murky." Alan pulled out a chair and sat down. "I'm telling you, that jar in your hands is the new one. I bought it three weeks ago, and at the time Marjorie assured me it was freshly made. She sold it to me at her gate."

"Maybe I should try some," Dan said. "It could be that you've built up some kind of immunity to the toxin."

"You can try it if you really want to. But I only opened it today; I haven't had time to develop any kind of resistance."

"Even so." Dan stood, taking the honey and crossing to the counter, then he pulled a dessertspoon from a drawer. He dipped the spoon into the jar, scooping up a large dollop. "Here goes." He paused with the spoon in mid-air. "You know, I followed up your research into mad honey. There was this one case I found online. A man brushed up against a rhododendron, and he got a tiny drop of nectar on his hand. He licked his finger clean, and quite soon afterwards, he collapsed, barely able to breathe."

Alan's face fell. "Maybe you shouldn't try it. Perhaps some people are more sensitive than others."

Dan licked his lips. "The other day, it took quite a long time for the ambulance to arrive for Mortimer, didn't it? A very long time."

"I'm afraid it does take a while. For a real emergency, there's the air ambulance, but they have to land on the playing field. So you'd better stop and think for a minute. There must be another way to test this. We could send it somewhere to be checked."

"I did think of that, but I doubt we'll find a lab nearby. And if we send a sample by post, it'll take far too long."

Alan looked as though he was about to argue, so before he

could speak, Dan closed his eyes and plunged the spoon into his mouth, sucking it clean. "Agh!"

"Are you okay?" Alan jumped to his feet.

"Too sweet." Dan stuck his tongue out. "That is too much honey to eat in one mouthful. Way too much."

"But are you feeling all right? Any dizziness, shortness of breath?"

Dan laid his hand on his stomach. "I feel slightly nauseous, but that's probably psychosomatic." He mashed his lips together. "I'll sit down for a bit. Let it pass."

They sat at the table, Alan watching Dan anxiously as though expecting him to keel over at any moment.

"I'm fine," Dan said. "So whatever happened to Mortimer, it looks like the honey wasn't to blame. But where does that leave us?"

"We're back to square one. We still don't know enough about the events leading up to the attack. There are so many people with a connection to Mortimer, and all of them were in the area on Friday."

"Like the mysterious Martin and Jess. There was something fishy about them."

"She seemed nice," Alan said quickly. "I can't imagine she'd hurt anyone. She isn't the type to get involved in anything underhand."

"She certainly took a shine to you," Dan said thoughtfully. "She hung on your every word. What is it with you and the ladies?"

"I don't know what you mean."

Dan grinned. "Oh, come off it. You can turn on the old-school charm when you want to."

"I was brought up to be polite, that's all." Alan sat up straight. "I'm not going to apologise for knowing how to treat others, so if you want to stir up an argument, you can forget it."

Dan lifted his hands in surrender. "Sorry. I didn't mean to

put my foot in it. For what it's worth, I think you're right. About Jess, I mean. I'm pretty sure she wasn't hiding anything. At least, nothing serious."

"Go on. You can't just say that without explaining what you mean."

"It's just that they were trying very hard to give the impression they were a couple."

Alan nodded. "I assume they are. They're away on holiday together." He paused. "I suppose they might just be good friends, but that seems unusual."

"But if you remember, Kristen introduced Martin as Jess's *companion*. That's an odd word to use if they're partners. Then we found out that, not only do they work together, but they also went to the same college. That's all very cosy, but at no point did anyone describe them as a couple. And if I know anything about body language, they were decidedly not together. Not in *that* way, at any rate."

"Interesting." Alan raised his eyebrows. "Well, well."

"Maybe you should drop by and renew your offer to show Jess around."

"Maybe." Alan examined Dan's expression. "Are you still feeling okay?"

"I'm fine, and there's no need for you to change the subject. I won't harp on about Jess. But let's talk about Martin. He was hiding something."

"He's not the most likeable person," Alan admitted. "He's probably mean enough to thump an old man with a stick, and he left the pub at around the right time on Friday. But what was his motive? Did he even know Mortimer?"

Dan consulted his notes, tapping a diagram showing a web of interconnected circles. "My best guess is that he's in cahoots with Craig. Martin is a surveyor, and we know that Craig has inherited the bulk of his uncle's estate. But Craig isn't happy with his lot. He'd like to retire and sail boats, so perhaps he wanted to get his hands on the land and sell it off to developers. That would give him the cash to fund the lifestyle he clearly craves."

"And Craig has been hitting the bottle," Alan said. "That could be his way of dealing with the guilt. He's feeling remorse at what he's done."

"Does he strike you as the type of person to be bothered by feelings of guilt?"

"No. Maybe he's one of those middle-class alcoholics they keep talking about in the papers. He can function perfectly well, so long as he can lay his hands on a large glass of whisky at regular intervals."

"In which case, it's all the more likely that he'd get involved in a hare-brained scheme to bump off his uncle," Dan said. "Craig and Martin are mixed up in this. We just need to figure out how."

"Okay. We know that Martin left the pub after we did, so he could've waited until Kevin's back was turned, and then grabbed my hiking stick." Alan grimaced. "It's no good. Martin didn't come past us. How could he have got to the spoil heaps in time to attack Mortimer? We'd have seen him."

"He took the other way around."

"No. We ran that way today, and it would've taken him far too long. He'd never have made it in time."

"Dammit," Dan muttered. "What if he drove around? How long would that take?"

"You saw how narrow the lane is. It's not a route you can drive at any kind of high speed. He'd have ended up in a ditch."

"For the sake of argument, let's say he's a fantastic driver," Dan said. "He leaves the pub, jumps into his car and tears along the lane in record time."

"Okay. He still needs to park his car, run along the path, then cut across the field to the spoil heaps." Alan shook his head. "We're forgetting Marjorie. She was on that path. Martin would've run straight into her. Or at the very least, she'd have seen or heard his car. It's so quiet and desolate out there, and she had her windows open. If there'd been someone screeching along the lane, she'd have known about it."

"It could be worth talking to her again," Dan said. "And while we're at it, we can tell her that there's nothing wrong with her honey. I feel absolutely fine."

"Is that enough to put her in the clear?"

"Not definitively. She's inherited her house and land, so she has a good motive, and she's been behaving very strangely. We only have her word for it that she went straight home on Friday and saw no one."

"But we definitely saw *her*," Alan said, "and she wasn't carrying my stick."

Dan nodded. "Agreed. If I had to guess, I'd say that she's the victim of her own conscience. She's put two and two together and made ninety-three. Maybe Mortimer ate some honey while he was in her kitchen, and she *thinks* that she accidentally poisoned him. She's got it into her head that the honey made him confused and unsteady. Afterwards, he scrambled onto the spoil heaps, fell over and hit his head. That's why she's getting rid of the honey and cleaning out the jars."

"And she's removing the flowers from the rhododendrons so that her bees can't poison the next batch."

"That's right," Dan said. "She's got it all wrong, but she doesn't know that. In her eyes, everything she's done makes sense. There is a kind of logic to her behaviour. Plus, she's probably overwrought. I'll bet she was the closest thing Mortimer had to a friend, so she can't bear the thought that she might've contributed to his death."

"The poor woman. That's a dreadful burden for her to bear alone."

"Yes." They sat in silence for a moment, then Dan stood,

brushing his hands together. "The holiday cottages where Jess and Martin are staying: do you know where they are?"

"Well, there are holiday homes scattered throughout the village, but when people say *the* holiday cottages, they usually mean a little street near the pub. There's a row of houses that are only used as holiday rentals. It's a shame, really. The whole street is dead in winter."

"I could send Kristen a message and get their address," Dan suggested. "Thanks to your kind offer to show Jess around, we have a pretext for calling in on them."

"And then what? Are you planning to grill them for information?"

Dan chuckled. "Not directly. But we could take a look at their car, and we might pick up a snippet or two of information over the course of a friendly chat."

"Friendly is not a word that springs to mind when it comes to Martin. But it could be worth a try."

"Good. That's settled." Dan grabbed his phone from the table and began tapping the screen. "Done. I've messaged Kristen, but there's no need to wait for a reply. If you're ready, we'll take a stroll through the village, and with any luck, she'll send the address while we're on the way."

"No time like the present." Alan stood, straightening his shirt, then he paused to run his hands over his hair.

"You're presentable," Dan said with a wry grin. "But I'll wait if you want to put on a clean shirt or something."

"This *is* a clean shirt," Alan replied. "It's one of my newer ones, actually."

"As I said, presentable." Dan gestured toward the door. "Let's go. And by the way, if things look promising with the fair Jess, I promise to make myself scarce."

"I'd settle for you behaving like a normal human being for a while. Whatever happens, try not to embarrass the poor woman. Or me. Or anyone."

"I'll do my best," Dan said. "Scout's honour."

"You were a scout?"

Dan waggled his hand in the air. "Only briefly. I was thrown out. The quasi-military command structure didn't have room for my inquiring mindset."

Alan rolled his eyes. "Why am I not surprised? No, don't answer that. We haven't got all day." He headed for the door, and as the two men stepped out into the midday sun, they shared a smile.

They were back on good terms, and for Dan, it felt good to be pursuing the truth, good to be doing something to keep his mind active and his wits sharp. They had a line of inquiry to follow up, and with Alan to keep him company, they were bound to make progress. One way or another, they'd soon be on the right path to solve the mystery.

CHAPTER 15

DAN AND ALAN had just passed the pub when Alan's phone rang. Frowning at the screen, Alan accepted the call, then he stopped in his tracks.

"Who is it?" Dan asked.

Alan held the phone away from his face and lowered his voice: "Spiller."

"What does he want?"

But Alan shook his head, taking a step away from Dan and turning to one side. "Yes. I see." A pause. "Well, it's short notice. Is it really necessary?" Alan listened, then said, "I can explain that. It was all a misunderstanding." Another pause. "No. That's all right. I'd rather drive myself. Okay, I'll see you then." He pocketed his phone, turning back around, his lips drawn tight in a grim line. "They want to talk to me again. It sounds serious."

"And you agreed to go," Dan stated. "Was that a good idea?"

Alan hunched his shoulders. "I didn't have much choice. He started talking about sending a patrol car to pick me up, and I wasn't having that. I don't want to be trapped there all day, and if I take my car, I can leave whenever I want."

"In theory," Dan intoned. "I don't like this. Did he say why he wants to talk to you? Do they have any new evidence?"

Alan shook his head sadly. "Not really. He's got hold of that argument I had with Mortimer. Do you remember? I told you about it before all this happened."

"When he shouted at you in the street because you were smelling his roses." Dan tutted. "And that's why they're hauling you in? Ridiculous."

"Spiller didn't give me the chance to explain. He said we had to discuss it at the station, make it official. He wants to know why I never mentioned it before. At the first interview, he asked me if I got on well with Mortimer, and of course, I just said yes. The business with the roses was nothing. A storm in a teacup. I don't know how Spiller even heard about it."

"I wonder…" Dan mused.

"What?"

"The timing is interesting. Why now? Why didn't Spiller find out about this before?"

"I wouldn't read too much into it," Alan said. "It was probably some busybody spreading gossip. That's the problem with this village. People repeat rumours and half-truths, and before you know it, everything gets twisted beyond recognition."

"Maybe. But there is another possibility. Someone might be laying a false trail. After all, the attacker took your stick, and then they either used it as a weapon or planted it to be found by the police."

The colour drained from Alan's cheeks. "You think I've been targeted deliberately? Why me? I can see that someone might want to cover their tracks, but why am I the fall guy?"

"That's an extremely good question. I've been assuming that your stick just happened to present itself. I know it has your initials on it, but until now, it hadn't occurred to me that someone might have selected it deliberately. But the way things are shaping up, it's starting to look like someone bears a grudge against you."

"Who? I haven't offended anyone; at least, not as far as I know."

"No one at all?" Dan asked. "Not even slightly?"

"No. I can't think of anyone. I haven't had a single serious disagreement since I moved here."

"What about in your former life?"

"When I was teaching? No. There was never any question…" Alan stopped abruptly, visibly shaken.

"I didn't mean anything terrible," Dan said quickly. "It's just that these things can run deep. Parents tend to be very protective, and small things can get blown out of proportion. When I was at school, parents were always kicking off about something or other. If little Bertrand wasn't picked for the first eleven, or Tobias dropped a grade in his chemistry test, there'd be ructions in the corridors."

"That's private education for you," Alan said. "I never worked anywhere like that, and I wouldn't want to. In my schools, the playgrounds may have been a bit shabby around the edges, but there were always smiles in the classrooms. I may not have been perfect as a teacher—God knows, I could always have done better—but I did my best. And that included working with the parents to keep things positive. There was no one with a grudge. Honestly."

"What about your former pupils? They'd be older now. Maybe someone moved here and recognised you."

"And I'd be delighted to see any of them again," Alan replied. "You know me. I'm an open book. I don't even publish my stories under a pen name. I have nothing to hide."

Dan pursed his lips. "Okay. Let's backtrack a little. Say your stick was used by pure chance, why would the person who attacked Mortimer go out of their way to lead a trail to your door?"

"Perhaps they heard I'd been interviewed by the police already."

"Yes. By pulling you in the first time, Spiller created a ready-made patsy. Now the killer has seized on that advantage, digging up some gossip to use against you."

"That sounds plausible," Alan said. "But how would they get the information to Spiller? An anonymous phone call?"

"Perhaps. But we know someone who has a close link with the police. Someone, quite literally, with blood on his hands."

"Jay." Alan scowled. "He's been known to spread tittle-tattle. He spends half his time in the pub, so if there's a rumour flying around, he'd get to hear about it soon enough. He could easily have found out about my run-in with Mortimer."

"Yes. I know we can't place him on the spoil heaps at the right time, but Jay could be involved. He likes to rub people up the wrong way, so it doesn't take much to imagine a conflict brewing between him and Mortimer."

"So what now?" Alan asked. "Do we press ahead and talk to Martin?"

"Yes. I think we should follow one avenue at a time." Dan checked his phone. "Kristen hasn't sent the address yet. But we might still be able to figure out which cottage Martin is using. We should stroll past, see what we can see."

"All right, but we can't hang about. I have to be in Exeter in a couple of hours." Alan started walking. "It's not far to the cottages, and there are only about twenty or so. It won't take us long."

A few minutes later, they turned into a secluded street, the houses all smartly painted in subtle pastel shades, the front gardens neat and orderly though somehow lacking in personality.

To Dan, each house looked like a glossy photo from a holiday brochure: *Book now, no pets, towels provided*. The street had no soul, as though the life had been sucked out of it. It had become a place where people passed through, never staying long enough to leave a trace of their daily lives. Even the name plaques beside the doors seemed contrived: *Hideaway Cottage, Wild Meadow House, The Snug.*

"Here we are," Alan said. "These are the cottages. What do you think of them?"

Dan made a disapproving noise in the back of his throat. "It's strange. Once, I would've been perfectly happy to book somewhere like this for a long weekend. But now…"

"Ah, you're turning into a local. You see things in a different light when you've been here for a while. I mean look at this one. *Shangri-La.* For goodness' sake!"

"At least it's literary," Dan muttered, checking his phone. "Still no message from Kristen, so where shall we start? There are a few cars in the driveways. When we met Martin and Jess at the Dower House, I'm pretty sure they hadn't walked there, but I can't remember seeing another car. Did you see what they were driving?"

"No. They must've parked around the back." Alan indicated the nearest cottage. "I can knock on a few doors and ask, but the whole street feels deserted. With this fine weather, people will be out for the day, sitting on the beach or walking on the moors."

"But I'm sure that Martin and Jess aren't here on holiday," Dan said. "Let's give it a minute. We'll see if Kristen comes through with the address."

They turned at the sound of a car approaching. A Land Rover swept toward them, and Dan stepped back as the vehicle pulled up to the kerb right in front of him. The Land Rover's window was already wide open, and Craig looked out at them, a broad smile on his lips. "Hello, chaps. Out for a stroll?"

Dan forced a smile, peering past Craig in case Kristen was with him, but the passenger seat was empty. "Yes, we thought we might call in on Martin and Jess, show them around."

Craig's expression remained fixed, but a steely glint crept into his gaze. "So I hear. Sis let me know, and that's why I popped over."

"Have you come to give us the address in person?" Dan asked. "There was really no need. A text would've been fine."

"More to it than that, old man," Craig said. "It's hard to explain over the phone."

Alan stepped to Dan's side. "Is there a problem?"

"A smidgen of inconvenience, that's all." Craig tilted his head and screwed up one eye. "Martin's a good chap, but he doesn't like to be disturbed. He's what you might call a very private man."

"That's all right," Alan countered. "We can have a chat with Jess."

Craig didn't reply. His boyish grin remained, but he seemed stumped, as if he hadn't expected to encounter any argument.

"If you could just give us the address," Dan prompted, "that would be most helpful."

"Not today, old boy." Craig lowered his eyebrows. "Look, if you must know, they've had a bit of an upset. There was a break-in at the cottage. Nasty business."

"Oh no," Alan said. "Are they all right? Was anyone hurt?"

Craig held up a hand. "No need for alarm, I assure you. They didn't know a thing about it until they came down to breakfast and found the back door had been forced. They're fine, thank goodness, but they're a bit shaken up. Poor Jess's nerves are in tatters."

"What was taken?" Dan asked. "Nothing too valuable I hope."

"Not a thing," Craig replied. "The thief must've been disturbed, or maybe he lost his bottle. Either way, the little bugger left empty handed, but not before he'd stuffed a load of Martin's gear into a bag and dragged it outside." Craig let out a grunt. "Probably too heavy for the blighter."

"In that case, we should definitely call on them," Alan said. "They'll appreciate seeing a friendly face, and perhaps there's something we can do to help. Which cottage are they staying in?"

"They're not there," Craig stated. "They're out for the day. Working. They can't be reached."

"Working?" Dan said quickly. "They said they were here on holiday."

"Ah. Yes." Craig looked away for a second, then he nodded as if coming to a decision. "Hang on a sec." He turned off the Land Rover's engine and removed his seatbelt, then he climbed down from the cab, slamming the door.

Dan stood his ground, waiting, while Craig stood in front of them, pulling himself up to his full height as if about to make a speech. "It's like this," Craig began. "As you know, my dear sister has been more or less running the estate for a while, and truth be told, Morty had let things slide."

"In what way?" Dan asked.

"You name it," Craig said. "Basic land management. Boundaries and fences. Drains and ditches. Which bit of ground belongs with which property. Frankly, the whole thing was a bit of a shambles. And the paperwork..." He shook his head in dismay. "You don't want to know about it."

"So where do Martin and Jess come into it?" Alan asked. "I know they're surveyors, but they didn't explain exactly what they did."

"Nail on the head, old man," Craig replied. "Sis wanted the estate mapped out properly, and Martin and Jess are old friends of hers. She put me in touch with them, and I gave them the job. Simple as that."

Dan narrowed his eyes. "They said they arrived on Friday. So you must've hired them while Mortimer was still alive."

"That's right."

"Did Mortimer know you were mapping out the estate?" Dan asked.

Craig's smile was back. "Couldn't say, old chap. I expect we told him, but he wasn't much interested in the business side of things. He was content to let it all go over his head."

"I wouldn't be too sure of that," Dan countered. "From what you said the other day, Mortimer was very involved in village life. I know he liked to keep his contributions private, but when someone gives so much to a community, they're hardly likely to let things slide."

Craig laughed without any trace of humour. "The old boy wanted to keep this village just as it is, and quite right. I totally agree; the place needs preserving. But although he was always keen on handing out the cash, he didn't like to trouble himself with the nuts and bolts, if you know what I mean."

Dan nodded thoughtfully. "Okay, but why are you keeping the survey quiet? What's the big deal?"

"Think about it," Craig replied smoothly. "When we started the project, we didn't know some thug was going to bash poor old Morty on the bonce. But after it happened, well... you can see how it might look."

"Not really," Dan replied. "Maybe you should enlighten us."

"Come on, chaps," Craig said. "There's no need to be difficult. Any fool can see how it might look suspicious." He sent them a pleading look. "One minute, we're measuring the place up, the next, we're inheriting the whole lot. Some people might be tempted to put the two together and point the finger. We can't afford that kind of talk, especially with everything... everything that's been going on." He clamped his lips shut suddenly, turning to Alan. "So, are you dropping into the pub later? I reckon I still owe you a pint from the other night."

"Possibly," Alan replied. "I might need a drink by then."

"He has a busy afternoon planned," Dan put in quickly. "Lots of writing to catch up on. Deadlines looming. Isn't that right, Alan?"

The tightness of Alan's lips betrayed his irritation at Dan's condescending tone, but after a moment's awkwardness, he nodded. "Never a day's rest for us authors. Always tapping away at the keys."

"Really?" Craig said. "I thought you scriveners spent all day locked up in your poky garrets, staring into space and knocking back the whisky."

"If only," Alan shot back. "I need a clear head to get anything done. I drink industrial quantities of tea."

Craig chortled, finally growing more relaxed, and Dan sensed an opportunity. Fixing Craig with a look, he said, "Why are you really here, Craig? Why did you come here to intercept us?"

"What?" Craig spluttered. "What on earth are you talking about?"

Dan took a step closer to him. "You know perfectly well what I mean. You didn't want us to meet Martin, so you drove over here in a rush, interrupting your lunch." Dan sniffed the air. "I smell smoke and scorched grease. Having a barbecue, were you? Yes. Sausages, and possibly a little chicken."

Craig blinked. "How would you know that? I thought you were a vegan."

"That's why I can smell the meat so easily," Dan said. "It's a myth about vegetarians missing the smell of sizzling bacon. After a while, the stench of hot fat turns your stomach. And that's not the only thing around here that doesn't smell right."

"Look here," Craig began, "I don't know what your problem is, my friend, but I came here to talk to you in a civilised manner. Surely you can see that Martin's work must remain confidential. It's all above board, but I cannot have the estate embroiled in any kind of scandal." Recovering his spirits, he pointed at Dan. "There's no sense in stirring up wild rumours and allegations, and you have no business sticking your nose into my affairs."

"On the contrary," Dan said. "We've both been questioned by the police, and Alan is being hounded by the detective in charge, so we have a vested interest in finding out exactly what happened to Mortimer. There's no way either one of us will let this go, especially since we were the only people who lifted a finger to help your uncle. Remember that."

Craig looked down at the ground for a moment, and when he raised his head, his indignant anger was already fading. "I appreciate what you did for Morty. And I'm sorry the police have been bothering you. You're right. That is unfair. I'm sure they'll realise they're on the wrong track pretty quickly." He adopted a sincere tone. "It's a shame, but there's nothing I can do about your unfortunate situation."

"You can put us in touch with Martin," Alan said. "There are a couple of things we'd like to check."

Craig shook his head slowly. "As I said, they're working today. They're in the middle of nowhere, and they can't be raised on the phone. I tried, but I couldn't get through to them."

"When will they be back?" Dan asked. "I can call later."

"I don't know," Craig replied. "They're shipping out tonight and going home. The job is pretty much finished, and Martin told me they'd already packed their things. When they finish for the day, they're going straight home. They're not coming back to the village."

"Surely they'll be reporting back to you," Dan argued.

"There's such a thing as email," Craig said. "I'm expecting their report in a few days, but I don't suppose I'll see them again for months. As far as you're concerned, they're gone, and there's no point pressing me for more information, because I won't give it to you. But I will say this: Martin and

Jess can't help you. They have nothing to do with what happened to Morty. I paid them for their services, but really, they came here as a favour to Kristen. They had a job to do, and they got on with it. They had no way of knowing what was going to happen, and the whole affair has been acutely upsetting for them, especially for Jess."

Dan opened his mouth to reply, but Alan laid his hand on his arm and said, "Enough. Everyone's had a chance to say their piece, and Craig has made his position clear. There's nothing to be gained from arguing about it."

Craig inclined his head. "Thank you, Alan. I'm glad we see eye to eye."

Dan clenched his jaw, but it was time to make a tactical withdrawal. "Okay. But this isn't over, Craig. Your friends might've slipped through our fingers for now, but there are plenty of ways to track people down. We won't stop until we get to the bottom of this."

"I'm warning you, Dan," Craig spluttered, his cheeks colouring. "Keep Martin out of this. He's blameless. You can go poking around if you really want to, but keep yourself off my estate, or I'll have you arrested for trespass."

Dan smiled. "*Your* estate? I thought you shared the inheritance with your sister."

"When all the paperwork goes through, I'll be the majority shareholder, so what I say goes. I'm going to be here for a long time, so you might want to think about that before you go putting my nose out of joint." He glared at them in turn. "Goodbye, gentlemen. That concludes our discussion. I can only hope that what I've said will sink in. Perhaps, when we meet again, you'll conduct yourselves in a more appropriate manner." With that, he marched back to his Land Rover, climbing into the cab and driving rapidly away.

"This should be good," Alan said.

"Why?"

Alan smirked. "Wait and see."

A moment later, they heard the crunch of gears, and the Land Rover sped past them in the opposite direction, Craig staring straight ahead, his cheeks puce.

"Cul-de-sac," Alan said.

Dan chuckled quietly, but not for long. Craig, it seemed, wasn't the only one who'd just been confounded by a dead end.

CHAPTER 16

WATCHING WHERE HE placed his feet, Jay crept cautiously into the shade of the coppice. Despite the warm weather, the ground was damp here, the mossy surface giving way underfoot, and with each step, the scent of moist, peaty earth rose to his nostrils. At least, that's what he hoped the smell was. There was something else here. Something dank. An acrid tinge to the air that caught in the back of his throat.

Ignore it, he told himself. *You've smelt far worse than this.* And he pressed on.

Rays of sunlight filtered through the lush canopy that crowned the untidy stand of trees, and clouds of flying insects danced in the shifting sunbeams. But Jay stuck to the shadows, altering his path to avoid the worst of the boggy ground. Soon, he could make out the silvery surface of still water, and he heard the broken rhythm of ripples lapping against the bank. The old reservoir.

He was near the edge of the coppice now, and he sidled slowly between the trees, his sharp gaze seeking out a hiding place. But there were no boulders nor sturdy trees to hide behind, only the spindly stems of hazel and willow clustered together into tangled clumps.

Never mind. They would have to do. At least the ragged rows of unkempt trees would break up his outline, allowing him to stalk through the mottled shadows unseen.

There.

He'd found a good vantage point. From here, he could see over the reservoir and on into the open field beyond it. It was just as well; he could go no further without breaking cover.

Moving carefully, he lifted his hand to shade his eyes from the sun. Beyond the reservoir, the land fell away in a gentle slope, a carpet of coarse grass and dark green reeds undulating in the gentle breeze.

But Jay hadn't come to appreciate the verdant landscape.

"There you are," he whispered. "Let's see what you're up to."

He stood perfectly still, watching.

And when he'd seen enough, he retraced his steps, smiling grimly as he picked his way back through the coppice and onto open ground.

I've done a good day's work in half an hour, he told himself. *Payday, here I come.*

He'd learned something, and information could be valuable, could even be used as leverage. Yes. He'd cash in one way or another. But how would he make the best use of his new-found knowledge? Did it have direct monetary value, or could it be parlayed into influence and power?

Deep in thought, he skirted the spoil heaps, and when he arrived at the public footpath, he picked up his pace. Sweat trickled across his brow, and he ran his palm across his forehead. Dust and grit clung to his hands, and it scratched his skin, dirt smearing across his face as he wiped the sweat away. But he scarcely noticed the discomfort; an idea was forming in his mind.

Yes, he thought. *This is going to work out better than I expected. Much better.* Smiling, Jay opened the gate and strode down the lane toward the village. His destination was not far away.

CHAPTER 17

A FTER A HURRIED lunch in Dan's kitchen, Alan headed off to get ready for his drive to the police station in Exeter. Dan was left alone to brood over his increasingly untidy pile of scribbled notes.

An hour later, he crumpled his latest attempt: a complex web diagram of people and possible motives. He pulled his pad toward him to start afresh, but before he could begin, there was a knock on the back door.

Standing wearily and arching his back, Dan padded across the kitchen, half-expecting Alan to have come back early. But when he opened the door, his eyes went wide. "Jay. What are you doing here?"

"That's a nice welcome," Jay drawled. "Especially when I've come all this way to do you a favour."

"Is that so?" Dan made a show of patting his pockets. "Nope. I haven't got any cash on me, so if you've come to steal my dinner money, you're about twenty years too late."

"Very funny. Still, I suppose I had it coming." Jay hunched his shoulders then let them drop. "The other day, you caught me at a bad time. I behaved like a silly bugger, and well, you know…"

Dan folded his arms. "I know what?"

"I shouldn't have nicked your bag. It was juvenile. But you, you got me riled, know what I mean? You wound me up."

"So, it was my fault that you stole my rucksack, including my wallet and my phone, and threw it into the road. Is that right?"

"Bloody hell, you're hard work," Jay said. "No, it was not your fault. I was just being daft, and for what it's worth, I regret it."

"Something tells me that I'm wasting my time, but even so, I'd like a proper apology."

Jay stared at him. "You want me to say I'm sorry? Bloody hell, pal. You'd just accused me of cold-blooded murder! As good as, anyway. That's enough to make most folks hot under the collar, wouldn't you say? Plus, you interfered with my personal property on my truck, and I know plenty of blokes who'd have punched you in the face for that alone. You were in the wrong, mate, so let's not forget that. We had a disagreement, but it takes two to tango, and you started it when you messed with my stuff."

"All right. I shouldn't have looked through your things. I accept that, so let's draw a line under it. Satisfied? Is that what you came here for?"

"No, on both counts." Jay peered past Dan. "Are you on your own today?"

Dan nodded uncertainly. "Why do you ask?"

"Because I've already knocked on Alan's door, and he wasn't home, so I thought he might be with you."

"No. In fact, he's gone to talk with your erstwhile colleagues. But then, you already knew that, didn't you?"

"No. I had no idea. Whatever you might think about coppers, it's not all one big club where we swap secret handshakes and stitch up anyone we don't like. It's a profession like any other. Besides, I'm not on the force anymore, and when you're out, you're out. I've got no more idea about the goings-on at the Devon and Cornwall Constabulary than you have."

"Come on, I bet you still have a few old friends who owe you a favour."

"Not one," Jay said. "So what, exactly, are you accusing me of this time?"

Dan held his stare. "You told DS Spiller about Alan's argument with Mortimer Gamble. You spread that nugget of information to make Alan look guilty, and to distract attention from the real killer."

"What? I've never heard such a steaming pile of bullshit in my life."

"Is that so?" Dan said slowly, enunciating every word.

"Yes, it is," Jay replied, mocking Dan's tone. "Now, shut your trap for five seconds and listen to me, because I have some information that will put Alan in the clear. Does that sound like something you might want to hear?"

"What kind of information?"

"Certain facts that have come to my attention. Observations which can be corroborated independently, and which, in my opinion, would stand up in a court of law."

Dan stood back from the door, opening it wide. "I think you'd better come in."

"Now we're getting somewhere." Jay rubbed his hands together and marched into the kitchen, casting a professional eye around the room. "Good light, but it needs a lot of work. I can give you a quote if you like."

"Not right now, thanks." Dan indicated a chair at the kitchen table. "Take a seat."

"Right." Jay slid onto Dan's chair and made himself comfortable, picking up a sheet of paper and examining it. "Blimey. What's all this? Don't tell me you're one of them conspiracy nutters."

Dan plucked the paper from his fingers, adding it to the others and shuffling them together. "It's just something I'm working on. A few ideas I'm piecing together." Dan sat down opposite Jay, placing the papers in front of him and resting his hands on top of the pile. "Now, what can you tell me?"

"I'm just wondering what it's going to be worth." He broke eye contact to glance around the room. "You know, I figured you were loaded, but looking at this place, I'm not so sure. Maybe I should take my valuable information elsewhere."

"I can lay my hands on some funds if I have to, but it depends on what you're providing." Dan paused, locking eyes with Jay. "Alternatively, I could call DS Spiller and let him know that you're withholding evidence. I'm sure he'll be only too keen to sweat it out of you. That option will cost me precisely nothing."

Jay shook his head. "If you do that, I'll get a sudden attack of amnesia. They won't get a word out of me. Don't forget, I know the ropes. I've been in more interview rooms than you've had hot dinners."

"All right. How much money are we talking about?"

"It's got to be worth a few grand to get your mate out of trouble. Say, ten grand. You can scrape that together between you, I've no doubt about that."

Dan repressed the urge to laugh out loud. "That's ridiculous. It's far too much. We're neither of us rich. In fact, you can forget it." Dan stood. "You know, when you told me why you'd come, I thought for one second that you might actually be a decent human being after all. I honestly believed you'd come here to do the right thing, to help one of your neighbours. I can see now that I was mistaken. You'd better go."

Jay stayed exactly where he was. "It's about that couple of so-called holidaymakers. The ones who've been staying in the cottages. The ones who were in the pub the night Mortimer was attacked."

Dan tried not to display a reaction, but he couldn't keep an edge of curiosity from creeping into his tone. "Martin and Jess? What about them?"

"Ah, you know them already. Interesting." Jay smirked. "But do you know why they're really here?"

"Yes, they're carrying out a survey of the estate, drawing up a map of the land that belonged to Mortimer."

A flicker of disappointment showed in Jay's eyes, but he recovered quickly. "That sounds like a cover story to me. I've seen what they're doing, and it's more than making a map, that's for sure."

"Go on."

"What about the money? You don't get owt for nowt, not in this world."

"I'm not going to pay you for information, Jay. If you know something relevant, you should go to the police. I believe I've made my position clear."

Jay stood, anger darkening his stare. But his head was down, and when he placed his hand on the back of the chair as if to push it away, he kept hold of it, his knuckles whitening. "I won't go to the cops," he growled. "You know that, and you know why." He looked up at Dan. "I need the money. But... Ah, what's the use?" He stared into space, but he didn't make a move toward the door.

Dan waited a moment, savouring his victory. He had Jay on the ropes, and they both knew it. Keeping his tone neutral, he said, "Listen, Jay, if you have an alternative proposal, I'm willing to listen."

"Really? You're not just going to rub my nose in it?"

Dan wore his most benevolent smile. "I stick to my word. I said I'll listen, and I will."

"I don't know." Jay pressed his lips together as though

struggling to contain himself. But finally, he began speaking, his voice low, and his words tumbling over each other in a rush. "It's like this. I'm divorced, and I've got payments to make. Child support for a son I hardly ever see. The cash slips through my fingers like water. The compensation ran out years ago, and my pension disappears into my former wife's purse. So I do a bit of work for Derek, but he pays me a pittance because he's got me where he wants me. I'm still paying for my truck, but I need it or I can't work. Not that I can work much. I can't hardly do a thing, thanks to this bloody hand."

"I'm sorry to hear that," Dan began. "But—"

"All I want is a chance to get myself back on my feet," Jay blurted. "If I could just do some work, all above board, I could set myself up, see what I mean?"

"Not really. What kind of work are you talking about?"

Jay chewed on his lower lip. "Back when I was married, we bought an old house, and I did all the renovations myself. I had a knack for it, that's what everybody said. I had that place looking like a palace."

"I've heard you do some painting and decorating," Dan said. "Craig mentioned it."

"I probably told him in the pub. You see, I've been thinking about this for a long time. Instead of working for Derek, I could set up as a decorator and work for myself. It's not like it's heavy manual labour, so I reckon the cops won't come breathing down my neck and querying my compensation. I'd be in the clear. Trust me, I'd do a good job. All I need is someone to give me a start."

Dan raised his eyebrows. "And you think I'd hire you, is that what you're saying?"

Jay nodded. "I give you this information, and to return the favour, you take me on to do this place up. I mean, no offence, but you obviously haven't got a clue." He strode over to the counter and pointed at the wall. "Look at these tiles. Who put these up?"

"I think my sister did it herself," Dan replied. "I was just going to leave them."

"With that grouting? You must be joking. It'll ruin the look of the whole room. They've not been laid properly. They're all over the shop. No. They'll have to come off. Then there's the plaster."

"What about the plaster?" Dan cast an anxious glance around the room. "There are a few cracks, but I thought I'd just stick some filler in and paint over them."

Jay sucked the air over his teeth. "You've got to repair things properly. With these old houses, once you start work, you never know what you're going to find. When I take the tiles off, there'll be a lot of work to do before the new ones can go up. Mind you, in these period properties, you have to be careful with the materials." He sent Dan a wry smile. "I'll bet you just went out and bought a few cans of emulsion."

"What's wrong with that?"

Jay chuckled. "Oh dear. That's no good at all, lad. Modern paint doesn't let the walls breathe. You need to be sympathetic to the stone, or you'll be stuck with condensation and mould growing all over the place."

"There is some mould on the walls upstairs," Dan admitted reluctantly.

"I guessed as much. But you can't just paint over it. It'll always come back until the underlying problem is dealt with."

"It doesn't need to be the Ritz," Dan protested. "It's just going to be a holiday cottage."

"Is it though? From where I'm standing, you look pretty settled to me." Jay nodded toward the counter. "I see you're stocking up on candles already. You must've heard about the power cuts."

"An impulse purchase." Dan looked once more around

the room. Not for the first time, he felt a creeping sense of defeat. He could handle a brush and a roller, but he was no decorator, and if he was honest, he hated the tiles in the kitchen. He just hadn't known how to go about replacing them, so he'd deleted them from his to-do list. *Can I trust Jay?* he asked himself. *He's a chancer.* But perhaps he was right; the place would certainly benefit from a more professional touch. He looked Jay in the eye. "How much would you charge?"

Jay waved his hand in the air. "We'll settle that later. I'll put a quote together, and I'll figure out the market rate. I'll need to take a look around the rest of the property first, mind you, but I'll set it all down in black and white. I'll take care of the materials. It'll all be in the quote. I'll make sure it's fair, and if you don't believe me, you can go ahead and get some quotes from other decorators. But I won't be charging as much as them, because unlike the bigger firms, I won't be charging VAT. Not yet, anyway. What do you say?"

"So, if I agree to consider your quote, when will you give me the information?" Dan asked.

"Now."

"Seriously? What if I see your quote and back out?"

"You won't. You stick to your word, remember?"

"All right," Dan said. "I accept. I think you'd better sit back down."

They retook their places at the table, Dan feeling as though he was about to interview a prospective employee. *What's really going on here?* he asked himself. *Am I being played?*

But Jay seemed in earnest, his expression alive with boyish hope, and the situation called for a change of approach. The pressure on Alan wasn't going to go away, and as far as Dan knew, time might already be running out. Dan's attempts to solve the mystery had all floundered, so if Jay could bring a few extra facts to light, it might provide just the break they needed.

"Start at the beginning," Dan said. "Give me the details, and please, be as specific as you can."

"Right. I had reason to believe that those so-called tourists were up to something, so I decided to go and see for myself."

"Why?"

Jay tapped the side of his nose. "I had an informant."

"Hang on a minute," Dan said. "Did you have something to do with the break-in at the holiday cottage?"

"No. Well, not directly."

"And what does that mean?"

Jay lifted his shoulder in a half-shrug. "I found out about the break-in when I came across a young man with some stolen property. Rather than cause a lot of fuss, I dealt with it. I took the valuables back to their rightful owners."

"So that's what happened," Dan said thoughtfully. "I thought Craig's version of events was a bit odd. What had been taken? Laptops? Mobile phones?"

"A drone." Jay smiled as if enjoying the look on Dan's face. "But this wasn't the kind of thing kids play with. It was a professional bit of gear, and it was equipped with a very particular state-of-the-art camera. I looked it up afterwards. It's used for land surveys, and it's worth thousands."

"That confirms what I already know. They're drawing up a map."

Jay shook his head. "There's more to it than that. I found out where they've been flying their drone, and I went over to take a look." He paused.

"And?" Dan prompted. "Where were they working?"

"Do you know the old reservoir?"

"I've heard of it. Hang on. There's a map around here somewhere." Dan jumped up and hurried through to the front room. There, on the bookshelf, his sister had left a stack of information for the cottage's temporary residents: brochures, booklets and a handful of Ordnance Survey maps. Dan had studied the local area when he'd been planning his runs, and he grabbed the OS Explorer from the shelf and carried it back to the kitchen, laying it out on the table in front of Jay.

"Here's the reservoir." Jay pointed to the map then traced a path with his finger. "This is an old coppice, and this open area below it is where they were working. They had their car with them, so they must've driven around this lane here." He indicated an unclassified road. "Now, here's the interesting part. They weren't just mapping, they were taking samples from the ground. I watched them for a while. The bloke, Martin, would drive a tool into the ground, twisting it around, then he'd pull it back up and empty it out. They had these long wooden boxes, and they were packing everything in there. The woman stood by with a laptop, and it looked like she was in charge of writing it all down."

"Could it be something to do with the old mines?" Dan asked. "Apparently, Mortimer had some wild ideas about opening them up."

Jay looked doubtful. "It wasn't like they had a digger down there. They were just using hand tools, taking samples from about two metres down at most. I know nothing about mining, but surely you'd have to drill quite deep to get to the minerals and all that kind of thing."

Dan thought for a moment. "Okay, so whatever they were doing, Craig clearly hasn't been telling the truth about it. But I don't see how this will help Alan. You said you'd give me something that would stand up in court."

Jay leaned forward, tapping the map with his finger as he spoke to emphasise each point. "The cops have got two things on Alan. One, they've got what they call *means*, because they think they have the murder weapon. Two, they've got *opportunity*, because they can place both you and Alan at the scene. But what they're stuck on is motive. They're coming up empty, and that's why they're chasing down this argument that's supposed to have happened between Mortimer and

Alan. But I'm offering you a way out of this. I'm giving you a way to prove that someone else had a motive *and* a likely reason to be out on the spoil heaps at night."

"It's a bit of a stretch."

"Is it? This Martin character and his little friend were working their way downhill from the reservoir. But if you think about where they must have started..." Jay dragged his finger across the map, ending on a rounded shape enclosed by a dashed line.

"The spoil heaps." Dan clicked his fingers. "When Spiller first came around, he said something had been digging on the spoil heaps. They thought it might have been badgers."

"There we are then." Jay sat back. "Martin and Jess must have started taking samples up there, and since they're pretending to be here on holiday, they couldn't very well have done it in daylight; they'd have been seen from the path. So they worked at night. *Friday* night."

"It was a fine evening," Dan said thoughtfully. "Lots of starlight. It might have been light enough for them to work, especially if they had a flashlight or two."

"Right. So on Friday night, Mortimer sees a light on the spoil heaps, and he marches over, shouting the odds, knowing him. An argument ensues and boom! It all kicks off, and Martin just happens to have a heavy-duty steel rod in his hands."

"No," Dan said. "The timings are all wrong. Martin and Jess left the pub after Alan and me. Anyway, they couldn't have known they were going to have a run-in with Mortimer, so why would they take Alan's stick from behind the bar?"

"They didn't," Jay stated.

"How do you know?"

"Simple. They left before I did. Empty handed."

"Are you sure?" Dan asked.

Jay stared at Dan from beneath lowered eyebrows. "What do *you* think?"

"I think that when you consider the time it would've taken them to get to the spoil heaps, and without the stick, this story doesn't add up."

"Forget the damned stick," Jay said. "It was probably planted after the fact. But you're not seeing the bigger picture, lad."

"Is that so?"

"Yes. If you want to know who's really behind this, you have to think about who Martin and Jess are working for. That's the one thing that ties the whole case together."

"Craig hired them." Dan's hand went to his brow. "Oh my God. Do you think he prearranged the whole thing? Are you really suggesting that he deliberately set out to murder his own uncle?"

"Why not? I know Craig comes across like a harmless upper-class idiot, but he was an officer in the army, and he's not as daft as he makes out. After all, he has the most to gain from Mortimer's death. I hear he's inherited most of the land, and he's obviously got big plans for it."

"Ah!" Dan closed his eyes for a second. "How could I have been so slow? I see what you're saying. I'm no expert, but I'm willing to bet you don't take soil samples from two metres down just to see how the grass will grow."

Jay mimed a round of applause. "Exactly. He must want to build, and I can say from personal experience, that whole area is one giant bog. He'll need all kinds of groundwork doing before he can lay a single brick. But that's a prime area for development. It stretches all the way down to the main road, and it's right on the edge of the National Park."

Dan consulted the map. "Yes. You're right. The National Park border is just to the north of that field, and that'll probably make it easier for him to build."

Jay chuckled darkly. "You can say that again. Inside the park, you can forget about it. The Dartmoor National Park Authority control what gets built and where. I've known people who've been told their woodshed was too big. If the DNPA don't like something, they'll make you take it down."

"So Craig has a great deal at stake," Dan said. "That sounds like a motive to me. He could easily have told his uncle to be on the spoil heaps at a prearranged time. Do you know if Mortimer had a mobile phone?"

"Yes. He used to curse at it whenever he tried to send a text. It was an old Nokia. It was ancient, but even so, the police should've checked the call logs by now."

"It might not help," Dan said. "In itself, a call isn't incriminating. Why shouldn't Craig call his uncle?"

"But if he called just before the attack, the cops will be able to say where Craig was at the time," Jay said. "If they can trace his movements, it'll give them another piece of the story."

"Craig claims he didn't arrive here until later that night. He said he was held up in traffic, but that might be a lie. Now that I think about it, I wonder whether he sat through afternoon tea at the Dower House purely to plant that piece of information in my mind. He clearly found the whole thing excruciating, but he wanted to establish a cover story."

Jay shrugged. "We can speculate all day, but I reckon I've given you enough to take to Spiller. There's every chance Martin and Jess were at the scene at some point immediately prior to Mortimer getting his head bashed in."

"But they can't have actually carried out the attack, because they didn't come past us," Dan protested. "I keep going through this, and I always get stuck on the same point. Alan and I would've seen anyone heading for the public footpath. We left the pub *before* Martin and Jess. I know there's another way around, but the timing doesn't work."

Jay waved his argument aside. "They might've just knocked him out and then left him for dead. They knew he was an old man, and they figured he wouldn't wake up, so they went to the pub to give themselves an alibi."

"Oh my God," Dan murmured. "Why didn't I think of that before?"

"Because you haven't seen the worst in people. Nothing surprises me anymore." Jay grunted under his breath. "Anyway, when you give this information to Spiller, it'll be his problem to sort out."

"I suppose so."

"Let him get on with it," Jay said. "You don't solve a murder case in one fell swoop. It's a matter of teasing it apart, looking for weak spots and pushing them as far as they'll go. Spiller knows that, and if he thinks Martin and Jess were working on the spoil heaps, he'll wonder why everyone's been so keen to keep that fact under wraps. That gives him reasonable cause to pull them in for questioning. When they crack, it'll all come out. Believe me, if either of those two think they can save their own skins, they'll do it in a heartbeat. Especially the young lady. She looked like a timid little thing, and any good lawyer will tell her to cooperate and distance herself from Martin."

"Unless it happened the other way around," Dan pointed out. "Jess doesn't seem like the type to lash out, but in the heat of the moment, she might have taken a swing at Mortimer. Or it could have been an accident."

"What do you care? Either way, you and your friend will be in the clear."

"And you're prepared to go on the record and back all this up? You'll make a statement?"

"I'd rather not, but if it can't be avoided, I'll talk to Spiller," Jay said. "But remember, you need to come through for me. All I want is an honest day's pay for an honest day's work. Judging by the state of the kitchen, I reckon there's a good three or four weeks' work here. We'll swap numbers for now, and I'll call you with a quote for what needs doing inside the house. We'll talk about the outside later."

"The outside?"

"It won't paint itself. These old houses need repainting every few years. It's the only way to keep the damp out."

"I'm starting to think I should have just given you the money. It might actually have been cheaper."

Jay smiled. "Too late for that now. A deal's a deal."

"Yes," Dan said. "It certainly is."

CHAPTER 18

ON THE WAY to the pub in the early evening sunshine, Alan and Dan talked in low voices, their heads close together. Dan's eyes darted across the quiet street, his gaze lingering on every open window, every twitch of the lace curtains. But Fore Street was deserted, and they met no one.

"You've had a rough time of it," Dan said. "It's ridiculous, the way the police are pursuing you."

"Well, they're only doing their job. I'll laugh about it, one day. Probably."

"I'm not sure I'd take it so calmly."

"I *know* you wouldn't," Alan said. "Anyway, it sounds as though you've made a breakthrough. Who'd have thought Jay would be so helpful? What did he want in return?"

"Nothing much. To be honest, I think he felt bad about the way he spoke to me before. He's not so bad once you get to know him."

"I'll take your word for it," Alan replied. "But the question is, should we go to the police with what he found out?"

"Not yet. We don't have enough to put anyone in the frame. I checked Craig's alibi, and according to the traffic reports for Friday, there *was* a tailback on the A38. A lorry blew out a tyre halfway up a hill, and it ended up stuck across two lanes. They had to close the road for a while, and it took hours to get everyone moving again."

"Probably the infamous Splatford Split," Alan said. "It's a notorious spot for accidents. Hardly a week goes by without somebody getting into trouble."

"Yes, that was the place. It's not a name you easily forget. The problem is, Craig would almost certainly have taken that route, and that backs up his story."

Alan pursed his lips. "There's another way he could've come from Topsham. It's longer, and it's mainly B roads, so it's what you might call the pretty way around. But Craig's a local, and he might've wanted to avoid the main road on a Friday."

"Possibly. I've only been here for a few weeks, but I've already learned about the Friday night traffic jams. Saturday mornings are bad too."

"Holidaymakers," Alan said. "In summer, hordes of people head into Devon as soon as they finish work on Friday. The influx continues on Saturdays because that's changeover day for most holiday lets. So you're right: Craig would've known about the traffic, and he could have avoided the tailback."

Dan sent Alan a meaningful look. "If all goes to plan and Craig turns up at the pub, we might be able to winkle the truth out of him. Or at least, we can try to trip him up."

"*If* he's there. We didn't part on good terms, and I'm starting to think Craig's a much slipperier fish than we gave him credit for."

"That sounds like a phrase from one of your adventure stories," Dan said with a smile. "In real life, people are more predictable. Craig will turn up. He made a point of promising to buy us a drink, and people like Craig calculate everything they say and do. He probably regrets his little outburst, and he'll be Mr Nice Guy again, you'll see. He's putting up a front, trying to build up an image."

"The friendly country squire rather than the privileged and powerful landowner," Alan suggested. "Yes, I had the distinct impression he was trying too hard. It's as if he's playing a part: the whimsical toff from a P.G. Wodehouse novel."

"I'd say your assessment is spot on," Dan said. "I couldn't have put it better myself."

Alan smiled modestly. "My stories are known for their likeable characters, you know. They might be larger than life, but there's always a grain of truth in each fictional personality. I know the real thing when I see it, and Craig doesn't quite measure up."

"I'd better watch my step or you'll put me in a book."

"Too late," Alan said. "I've made a few notes already. The problem is, there's too much material."

Dan's smile faded. "Oh. I'm not sure how to take that."

"No offence meant." Alan chuckled. "It's just that you're a little too complex for my children's stories. My readers prefer their characters to be a little more... relatable. But if I ever publish a book for adults, you'll be perfect."

"Right. Okay. Well, we're almost there," Dan said. "Showtime."

The pub seemed quiet, and when they stepped inside, they discovered that they were the only customers.

Dan drew a deep breath, grateful for the cool air, and for the thick stone walls that kept the room chilled.

Kevin greeted them from behind the bar, a broad smile on his lips. "Evening, gents. What can I get you?"

Dan glanced along the bar, his gaze flitting to the chiller cabinet behind it. On such a warm evening, his taste for ice-cold bottled lager called out to him, but Kevin seemed to take it personally if he didn't order a pint of ale. *The customer is always right,* Dan thought. But all he actually said was, "I'm not sure. I might try something different."

"No rush," Kevin replied. "Oh, by the way, if you'll be wanting to use the Wi-Fi, you'll need the new password." He raised a finger to point to a chalked sign above the bar.

Dan and Alan whipped out their phones and began altering the settings.

"Why the change?" Dan asked.

"New router," Kevin said. "The old one was no good. That's what the new boss says."

Alan looked up from his phone. "I always thought you were the boss."

"Not likely. I'm the licensee, but I don't own the place. At least..." Kevin broke off suddenly as if distracted, his eyes darting past Dan to the open doorway.

"You were saying?" Alan prompted.

Kevin shook his head, laughing to himself. "Nothing, gents. Just daydreaming for a minute. It's the heat. I spent all afternoon in the garden out back, tidying the place up. Reckon I caught the sun. It sends you a bit mazed after a while, don't it?" He rubbed his eyes with the heels of his hands. "Mind you, it was worth the effort. I cut back that hedge and mowed the grass. I've even sorted out the flower beds. I'm telling you, it looks proper now, it does. You should take your drinks out there, make use of it."

"Maybe we will," Dan said. "But just out of interest, if you're not the owner, who is?"

Kevin blinked as though shocked at Dan's ignorance. "Kristen Ellington, of course. She was always the apple of old Morty's eye, and now she's the sole proprietor."

"Wait a minute," Dan said. "The other night, you threw Mortimer out, even though he was your employer at the time?"

"Well, I wouldn't put it quite like that," Kevin replied. "I just sent him home. It wasn't the first time. Every now and then, he'd get a bit cantankerous, and I'd tell him to call it a night. It was for his own good. It was better for business too. No one wants to drink in a pub with a nasty atmosphere. He knew that, and he generally trotted off home like a lamb." Kevin sniffed. "Poor old sod. It was shocking what happened. There was no need for it. No need at all."

Dan gave Kevin an appraising look. "Would you say that you were close to Mortimer?"

"Not especially. Why do you ask?"

"I just wondered," Dan said. "Sometimes, friends have a habit of keeping each other in line."

"Yes," Alan put in. "That's because close friends can speak more honestly to each other." He cast a glance at Dan. "They don't hold back."

Kevin's gaze went from Alan to Dan and back again. "I have no idea what you're on about, but if you want to know about Morty, I'll tell you this: he was nice enough, underneath it all, but he was a stubborn old bugger. Far too stubborn by half. There was no changing his mind. It didn't matter what anybody said. He wouldn't listen to reason." Kevin looked down for a moment, and when he looked back up, his smile was back. "Now, we've stood here all this time, and you still haven't told me what you want. How about the usual? Pint of Jail for you, Alan, and an IPA for you, Dan."

Alan studied the row of pumps. "I'm not sure. It's still early, and the Jail is quite strong."

"Ah. How about this?" Kevin patted a metal keg mounted on its side behind the bar. "Dartmoor Best. Our new guest ale." He beamed proudly. "It's an amber ale, and it's very light. Perfect for a summer's day. Want to try a taste?"

"Why not?" Alan said. "Go on, Dan. You have a taste, too."

Dan nodded. "Okay."

They waited while Kevin poured small measures of beer

into a pair of half-pint glasses, then they both drank solemnly, keenly aware of Kevin's watchful eye.

Alan smacked his lips. "Very good. I'll have a pint."

"Me too," Dan said. "And I'm paying."

"Two pints of Best coming up." Kevin grabbed a clean glass and tilted it beneath the tap, turning the handle carefully to allow a thin stream of beer to flow. "Anything else?"

"No thanks," Dan said. "By the way, you haven't seen Craig Ellington, have you? We were hoping to bump into him."

"Not today." Kevin remained intent on the beer, but his smile slipped. "A word to the wise. You want to take most of what that man says with a pinch of salt. He's going around making out like he owns half the village, but if you ask me, he's got more hot air than the Sahara."

"But Craig has inherited the bulk of the estate," Alan argued. "That's right, isn't it?"

Kevin tilted his head from side to side. "From what I hear, it's a deal more complicated than that. As far as I know, it's all tied up in one business or another. Morty owned quite a few houses in the village, and he had half a dozen farms nearby, plus all the land between here and the river. Then there's the Dower House, and the holiday lets, and the pub was always a separate concern. Morty could never be much bothered with this place, but now, with Kristen in charge, things might look up. We reckon it might be worth trying some new things to pull in the punters. Watch this space, as they say."

"It's all change then," Dan said. "I get the impression that Craig wants to put his share of the estate to work. Do you happen to know whether he has any big plans?"

Kevin grunted in disapproval, then he plonked a pint onto the bar and began pouring the second. "His idea of a plan is to treat the whole village like a museum. He wants everything to stay just as it is. Mortimer was just the same: stuck in the past."

"Hang on a minute," Dan said. "Just now, you said that the estate is divided into several businesses. Did Craig inherit them all, or were they divided up between him and Kristen?"

"I know he's got the lion's share of the properties in the village. Not counting this place, of course. And he didn't get Marjorie's cottage." Kevin paused while he lifted the second pint. "When it comes to the farms, it's another matter entirely. Very complicated, so they say. Not that he cares much about the land. Most of it is no good for anything. There's hardly a year goes by without a farm closing down, and the rest are clinging on by the skin of their teeth. But with the price you can get for a cottage around here, the houses are worth a fortune. It's no wonder Craig's cock-a-hoop."

Dan and Alan shared a look, then they picked up their glasses and sipped. The dry, hoppy ale tingled Dan's tongue, but he hardly noticed the taste. His mind was too busy replaying every conversation he'd had with Craig.

"Cash or card?" Kevin asked, and without saying a word, Dan grabbed his wallet and plucked out a debit card, holding it aloft.

"I'll get the machine." Kevin turned around to operate the till, then he returned with a careworn card reader, laying it on the bar in front of Dan. "There you go. It's a bit slow to connect, but we're getting a new machine soon. It's on order already. The latest thing in point-of-sale technology, so I'm told. I can't wait."

"I'll bet." Dan placed his card against the small screen. "It certainly seems as if Kristen has the bit between her teeth."

Kevin rubbed his hands together. "You'd better believe it. There's no stopping that woman. She knows what she wants, and she goes for it."

"I'm sure she does." Dan took another sip of beer. "Come

on, Alan. Let's go and sit outside. I'm finding it a little too cool in here."

Alan nodded. "Okay. But what about Craig?"

"If he comes in, I can send him out to you, if you like," Kevin replied. "I'll tell him you're looking for him, anyhow."

"Thanks," Dan said distractedly, and he headed for the back room and the entrance to the garden. Suddenly, he needed some space.

CHAPTER 19

T HE PUB GARDEN was as deserted as the bar, but Dan noticed that it was much smarter than when he'd last seen it. As well as the freshly mown lawn, the hedges had been trimmed, the shrubs tamed, and the old stone trough had been planted with a profusion of colourful summer flowers. It even looked as though the patio had been pressure washed, and the plastic tubs of dazzling red geraniums were brand new.

"*The Interminable* is going upmarket," Alan said. "What next? Bistro-style wrought-iron furniture and little umbrellas in every gin and tonic?"

"That was last century." Dan took a seat at a picnic bench. "Now, your gin is more likely to come with a sprig of rosemary and some sea salt, or possibly a handful of seasonal berries."

"In London, maybe," Alan said as he sat opposite Dan. "Although where would you get seasonal berries in the middle of a city?"

"Waitrose."

Alan chuckled, and Dan took a long gulp of beer, realising

how thirsty he was. The beer was worryingly good, and it took all his willpower to lower his glass and place it on the table. But for some reason, his fingers were reluctant to let go, as if deep down he feared the glass would slip away if he released it for even a second.

"Good, isn't it?" Alan said. "I feel better already."

"Well, we won't find the answers at the bottom of a glass. We need to talk the case through, look at it from a different angle."

Alan wiggled his eyebrows. "*The case?* You're not going to go all Miss Marple on me, are you?"

"No. It's just a phrase. What do you think we should call it? We can't keep saying *the attack* all the time. It makes it sound like we're discussing an epic battle."

"Fair enough. *The case* it is. Here's to it." Alan raised his glass in a toast. "So, apart from a whole heap of theories, what do we have so far?"

"We have a possible motive. Greed."

Alan nodded. "Craig, Kristen and Marjorie all gained by Mortimer's death. But which one has the strongest reason for wanting to see him dead?"

"That's hard to call. Until just now, I'd been happy to rule Marjorie out. I was pretty sure she didn't know about her inheritance, but Kevin set me thinking."

"Go on."

"Let's say that she *did* know she'd inherit. It seems clear that Craig and Kristen wouldn't be happy with the arrangement."

"With you so far," Alan said. "They were already mapping out the estate, although what their plans were, we don't know."

"Right. While Mortimer was alive, there was always a chance that Craig or Kristen would talk him out of leaving the Old Buttery to her. From Marjorie's point of view, it would be better if Mortimer were to die before he had a chance to change his will."

"And she's the only person we can place at the scene at the right time," Alan said. "But what about all that business with the honey? I thought we'd established that she was mistaken."

Dan shook his head. "We let ourselves be sidetracked by that. I should've been more critical. Think about it. She may not have poisoned him, but that doesn't mean she couldn't have lured him onto the spoil heaps and whacked him on the head."

"And when would she have taken my stick?"

"That's the part that doesn't fit," Dan admitted. "She couldn't have been carrying it when she went past. It's too big for her to conceal."

"It's a deal-breaker. Don't forget, Mortimer's blood was transferred to the stick while it was still fresh. The police report was very specific on that point. Spiller mentioned it again today."

"All right. Let's put Marjorie to one side," Dan said. "And while we're at it, we should probably rule out Martin and Jess."

"Because they don't stand to gain from the will?" Alan asked.

"It's not that. In fact, they have an extremely good motive. They were being paid to keep their work under wraps, so if Morty had cottoned on to their activities, they'd have been in trouble. As Jay suggested, they could've knocked Mortimer out cold and left him for dead, sauntering off to the pub and making sure they were seen. But there's a problem." Dan sat back. "When we met them in the Dower House, they told us that they'd gone to the pub early, hoping to meet Kristen and Craig for a drink. I'm pretty sure I saw them sitting quietly in the back room. As far as I remember, I didn't see them leave."

"I think..." Alan's voice trailed away, and his gaze grew distant. "I think you're right. They were in the back room all night. I saw them when I went to the bar." He smiled sadly. "They're off the hook. In a way, it's a damned shame, because frankly, they've been very underhand."

"I thought you'd taken a shine to Jess."

"A man can change his mind, can't he? I mean, they went out of their way to deceive us, then they hightailed it out of here." Alan tutted. "They shan't be showing their faces around the village in a hurry, you can be sure of that."

Dan paused for a gulp of beer. And another. "I hate to say this, but I think we need to seriously consider Kristen."

"Yes. Although..." Alan wrinkled his brow. "I get the impression that before Mortimer died, she was more or less running the show. She told us that Mortimer left business matters to her. Whereas now..."

"She's been sidelined by her brother," Dan said. "I agree. On the surface, Mortimer's will has left her worse off. But financially, the situation has changed completely. She's gone from running a few properties to owning a share of the estate."

"I see what you're saying. But one thing bothers me, and it all comes down to temperament."

"Go on."

"Kristen is cool and collected," Alan said. "She's a sophisticated woman, and maybe she has a taste for the finer things in life, but I believe she was genuinely fond of her uncle. Whereas Craig is a bully with a bad temper."

"Yes. We saw another side of him when he intercepted us by the holiday cottages. He can be very domineering. He acts as though the world revolves around him." Dan laid his hand flat on the table. "And do you remember when we met them in the pub? Craig was all over the place, but Kristen calmed him down. She was almost like a mother figure, soothing the tantrum of an overgrown schoolboy."

"You're right. At the time, we put it down to grief. But maybe that's the way they've always been. She reigns him in, keeps him from losing his temper."

They sat quietly for a moment, sipping their drinks until Dan broke the silence: "Unfortunately, we're going way beyond the evidence. We have no way of backing any of this up."

"Granted. So, what's our next move?"

"We can go back to our theory about Craig and the traffic jam," Dan suggested. "If we could prove that he *wasn't* stuck on the A38, we might be on to something."

"Well, we're about to get our chance." Alan nodded toward the pub, and Dan turned to see Craig strolling onto the patio, three pint glasses clamped in his hands.

Craig grinned. "Ah, there you are, chaps." He began ambling toward them, keeping his gaze fixed on the brimming glasses.

Dan leaned closer to Alan, lowering his voice. "Pretend you've left your phone at home."

"What? Why?"

"Just go along with it," Dan insisted.

"What are you two plotting?" Craig said as he made his way to the table.

"Just making plans for tomorrow," Dan replied. "Thought we might go for a walk."

"Rain tomorrow," Craig stated, setting the pint glasses on the table before taking a seat. "Hope you don't mind, but I took the liberty. Kev told me what you were drinking." He placed a pint in front of each of them. "Olive branch. My way of apologising for the other day. There was no need for me to fly off the handle like that." Craig's features formed an exaggerated wince. "Truth be told, things have been a bit fraught since old Morty passed, and I don't mind telling you, it hasn't been a walk in the park. Still, that's no excuse for my behaviour. I hold my hands up. My fault entirely." He looked at them in turn. "What do you say, water under the bridge?"

"Of course," Alan said. "We understand. A death in the family is always hard."

"All forgotten," Dan said. "There's nothing for you to worry about. Thank you for the drinks. Much appreciated on a hot day like this."

"You can say that again." Craig smiled then took an experimental sip. "Dartmoor Best. Lovely stuff. I told Kevin to get a guest ale, and fair play to him, he's picked a winner."

Dan and Alan exchanged a look, then Alan said, "I hope you managed to straighten everything out at the holiday cottage. I've always thought it must be awful to be burgled."

"All sorted," Craig said. "New locks all around. It was about time. The old latches could barely stand up to a stiff breeze. Still, it's all done now. Safe as houses, eh?" He smiled expectantly, inviting them to enjoy his play on words, and Alan, ever the diplomat, said, "Very good."

"What did the police say?" Dan asked.

"Didn't bother talking to plod," Craig replied. "Waste of time. Nothing was taken, and as I said, it's all fixed up now. I had the place cleaned from top to bottom. It's all ready for the next customers. Onward and upward."

"I'll drink to that." Dan raised his glass and took a sip.

"Cheers." Craig took a long draught, emptying half his glass in a few greedy gulps, then he wiped his mouth with the back of his hand. "Marvellous. Just what I needed. Been stuck in a sweltering office all day."

"You've been at work?" Dan said. "Exmouth, wasn't it?"

Craig pulled a face. "Yes. Nearly finished with the beastly place, but I have to work out my notice. Only fair, I suppose."

"Does that mean you'll be running the estate full time?" Alan asked.

"Definitely. There's so much to do. You wouldn't believe it." Craig paused. "The first thing is to get the Dower House up to scratch. Once that's done, I'll move in. Then I'll sell my place in Topsham."

"Interesting," Dan said. "Alan was just telling me about the area around Topsham. It sounds great. You said there was a nice restaurant, didn't you, Alan?"

Alan raised his eyebrows, and there was an awkward silence until he noticed the fierce look Dan was giving him. "Oh, yes. A nice place. Good food and not too expensive."

"What did you say it was called?" Dan wondered aloud.

"I really cannot remember," Alan said firmly. "It seems to have slipped my mind completely."

"I might know it," Craig put in. "Where is it? On the estuary?"

"Yes. I'll look it up." Dan pulled out his phone, then feigning irritation, he stuffed it back in his pocket. "The damned battery's flat. Alan, do you have yours with you?"

"No," Alan said. "I've left it at home. I'm always doing that. I've got a mind like a sieve, apparently."

Craig chuckled. "We can use mine. It's the latest Samsung. All the bells and whistles you could ever want, and then some." He produced a large phone and peered at it intently. "If you know the name of the place, I could—"

"That's no good," Dan interrupted. "We really have no idea about the name, but if you look on Google maps, we should be able to find it."

Craig's smile slipped as if he was annoyed by Dan's tone, but he dutifully tapped the screen and opened a map. "Here we are. Here's the estuary, and here are all the restaurants in the area."

"Could I have a closer look?" Dan asked. "I'm still trying to orient myself. You know how it is when you're new somewhere."

"Be my guest." Craig handed over the phone. "You probably know better than me how it all works."

"Thanks." Dan tilted the phone upright so that Craig

could only see its back, then he set to work. Opening the menu, he selected the timeline, tapping the screen to reveal the daily entries, then he chose the previous Friday.

"Wouldn't it be better if Alan looked for the restaurant?" Craig asked. "He's the one who knows where it is."

"Maybe," Dan muttered without looking up. "But I want to take a quick look to see if any of them have vegan options." When the timeline appeared, Dan found a section of the evening that was allocated to driving, and when he tapped it, a map opened, the road highlighted. Dan's mouth was dry as he expanded the map, searching along the route. He turned to Craig. "How long does it take to drive from here to Topsham?"

Craig puffed out his cheeks. "On a good day, about half an hour. That's if the lamentably misnamed Devon Expressway is all clear."

"Right. Thanks." Dan closed the timeline and returned to the map, performing a quick search and scanning the list of restaurants. "Was it called The Galleon?" he asked Alan.

"Yes, I think so." Alan tried for a smile. "That certainly sounds familiar."

Craig slapped his palm against the table. "I should've guessed. Cracking spot. I go there all the time. It's run by a chap called Brian. Great bloke. Did you meet him?"

Alan's smile failed him. "I don't think so. I forget. It was quite a while ago."

"Oh, you wouldn't forget Brian. Huge fella. Built like the side of a house." Craig leaned closer to Alan. "Mind you, he's got a temper. Used to be a chef himself, and you know what they're like."

"He sounds like quite a character," Dan said with a smile. "Are you sure you don't remember him, Alan?"

Alan shook his head firmly. "Perhaps he had the day off. I couldn't possibly say."

"You would've known if he'd been around," Craig said.

"He's got a tongue like an RSM; that's a regimental sergeant major, to you. Once old Brian gets up a head of steam, he makes Gordon Ramsay look like a choirboy."

"That's fascinating, but in my experience, if you expect people to cooperate with you, you treat them with respect," Alan said pointedly. "I think you'd better give Craig his phone back, Dan."

"Right on both counts," Dan replied, closing the map and handing the phone back. "Thanks for that Craig. Very helpful."

"Anything to oblige." Craig checked the screen. "Huh! Look at that."

Dan had been lifting his drink, but he froze with the glass halfway to his lips. "Something wrong?"

Craig scowled, turning the phone around to show them the screen. "This thing is showing sunshine all day tomorrow, but I tell you, it's going to rain. Sure as eggs is eggs."

Alan's hand twitched toward his pocket, but he remembered his subterfuge just in time. "Oh, I think it might stay dry tomorrow. It's a fine evening."

Craig pointed toward the horizon. "Look at the height of that cloud. Cumulonimbus. It's right above the valley and heading this way. We're in for a storm." Craig sat back, looking pleased with himself. "When you've sailed through as much mucky weather as I have, you never forget the signs. I'm telling you, it might be localised, but in a few hours, it will hit us." He drained his pint, slamming the empty glass on the table. "So, while we've still got the sunshine, whose round is it?"

"I haven't touched my second one yet," Alan said.

"No, me neither," Dan added. "We're taking it steady."

"Oh dear." Craig jiggled his glass. "Tell you what. I'll hop inside and grab another, give you time to catch up." He stood, grabbing his empty glass. "Anyway, it was nice talking to you chaps. See you inside later."

"I expect so," Dan replied.

Alan and Dan watched as Craig made his way back to the pub, his stride growing more purposeful as he hurried for the door.

"Well?" Alan asked. "I hope all that embarrassment was worth it."

"Oh, it was," Dan said. "Absolutely."

FRIDAY

CHAPTER 20

THE STORM RAGED through most of Thursday night, the wind rattling every door and window in The Old Shop. But Dan slept better than he had for a while, his restless mind soothed by the rain's relentless rhythm. In the morning, his dreams vanishing as abruptly as the storm, he awoke refreshed and ready for action.

Dan checked the time on his phone. He'd set the alarm for seven, and there were still five minutes remaining, so he cancelled the alarm and jumped out of bed, wrapping himself in his bathrobe before heading downstairs.

He breakfasted quickly, bolting a bowl of cereal topped with pumpkin seeds and sunflower kernels, and washing it down with an espresso. *I ought to bring my coffee machine from London*, he thought. But that was a foolish idea. It wasn't as if he was planning to stay in Embervale long term. That would be ridiculous, wouldn't it?

Dan looked around the kitchen, viewing it through the eyes of his recent visitors. What had DS Spiller seen when he'd cast his gaze over the place? And what about Jay and Kristen? Had they seen a temporary resident or a man intent on putting down roots? *Which is it?* Dan asked himself. But he really had no idea what the answer might be. Not yet.

Still, he had a schedule to keep, and if he was quick, he could squeeze in a shower and a shave before Alan arrived. He ditched his crockery in the sink and hurried upstairs, taking the stairs two at a time.

At eight o'clock sharp, Alan arrived, dressed for a hike and with a daypack on his back. Dan opened the door before he could knock.

"Morning," Alan said. "Lovely day. It's like the storm has washed the world clean." He looked Dan up and down. "Is that what you're wearing?"

Dan's smile faded as he looked down at his jeans and trainers. "Yes. It'll be fine."

"You really need to get some proper walking gear, but in the meantime, I have a pair of walking boots you could borrow. What size do you take?"

"Nine. But seriously, these shoes are waterproof. They're perfectly all right."

"You don't know the fields around here," Alan said. "After last night, they'll be treacherous, and where we're headed, it's going to be even worse. I hear it's boggy at the best of times." He paused. "You take the same size boot as me. I'll go and see what I can find, shall I?"

"No thanks. I'd rather get moving." Dan stepped outside, locking the door and pocketing the key, but he registered Alan's disapproving look. "Listen, I'll be fine. By the time we get there, the sun will have dried up all the rain."

Alan started to protest but Dan didn't give him the chance. Striding toward the garden gate, he said, "Honestly, it's only a bit of mud. What's the worst that can happen?"

∼

DAN STIFLED a groan as his foot sank ankle-deep into the mud, a fresh spurt of cold water trickling into his already sodden socks. He pulled his foot free, holding out his arms to maintain his balance, and studied the state of his expensive trainers. "Ruined. Completely bloody ruined."

"Oh dear." Alan looked like a man who was trying very hard not to chortle. "I expect you'll be able to get them clean, eventually. You can put them in the washing machine, can't you?"

"They're stained. Why is this water black?"

"I'm not sure. I'd say it was peat, but around here, the soil is usually fairly heavy and full of clay. This looks different."

"Whatever it is, it's seeping up my jeans. They're never going to be the same." Dan glanced back at the way they'd come. "Is it something to do with the spoil heaps?"

"I doubt it," Alan replied. "The heaps are quite a way behind us, so it seems unlikely that the run-off would make it this far. It's probably just stagnant water. This whole area is badly drained."

"Maybe that's why Craig had the survey carried out. He wanted to see if the ground would be solid enough to build on."

"Maybe." Alan looked around. "Whatever the cause, this bog looks like it's getting worse. Do you want to head back? We could pick up some wellies and try again. Or we could drive around to the far side of the field. There's a lane, but it takes the long way around."

"We could've taken the car? Why didn't you tell me that before?"

Alan shrugged. "It's much quicker to walk. There's nowhere to park in the lane, and even if there's an unlocked gate, you can't just drive onto the field. It's private land." He paused. "I know what you're thinking. You're going to say we're trespassing anyway, but there are limits, Dan."

"All right. I give in. We'll press on."

"Good," Alan said. "I don't think it's much further."

"And we can't get much muddier," Dan replied. "By the way, I'm impressed."

"With the mud?"

"With the fact that you've made it this far without laughing at me."

Alan grinned. "I'm saving that treat for later. Schadenfreude is a dish best savoured in bite-sized morsels."

"Very deep," Dan said. "Like this filthy quagmire. Is it really going to get worse as we go on?"

"They say it gets pretty bad around the reservoir in winter, but I think we'll be okay. You'll need to watch your step though."

"You don't say," Dan intoned. But as they trudged across the uneven ground, he began to get used to the treacherous terrain. The vegetation underfoot was sparse: spongy mounds of moss interspersed with a coarse grass-like plant. But if he avoided the moss and trod on the tough clumps, the fibrous leaves were slow to give way beneath his weight. So long as he kept moving, he could stride from one clump to the next without sinking into the surface.

"If I didn't know better, I might think you were enjoying yourself," Alan said.

"I wouldn't go that far," Dan muttered, although he found himself smiling. He'd always tested himself, pushing hard to overcome any obstacles that stood in his way. But while he'd often tackled the challenges of city life, and in his running he'd pushed at the limits of his mind and body, it was only since he'd come to Embervale that he'd gone up against nature in the raw. He was starting to get a taste for it.

"You're certainly setting a good pace," Alan went on. "We'll be there in no time." He pointed to a stand of trees. "If I'm remembering the map correctly, the old reservoir is beyond the coppice. Below that, the land runs all the way down the valley to the main road and the river beyond. If Kevin was right, Mortimer owned the whole stretch."

"And according to Jay, that's where Martin and Jess were taking soil samples," Dan said. "He thought they'd spent quite a bit of time down there. It has to be important."

They marched on in silence, and it wasn't long before they arrived at the coppice. Picking their way between the dense clusters of straggly trees, Dan's spirits rose. They were on the verge of discovering something; he could feel it. The land was almost certainly the key. Mortimer had owned enough of it to make himself rich, but he'd deliberately left it empty, preferring to live in genteel poverty. Now the old man was dead, how much would the land be worth to a developer? A million pounds? More?

Dan's scant knowledge of property prices was based on the absurdly high values of London; out here, it would be different. But whatever the sums involved, it must've been enough to drive someone to violence. It must've been enough to become the motive for murder.

Wealth is always relative, Dan thought. People like Craig and Kristen lived comfortable lives, and while their inheritance would've been a welcome windfall, it might not have been enough to turn their heads.

But what about Marjorie? Living hand to mouth, and day to day, her cottage was her kingdom; it was everything. What would she do to protect her way of life?

And there were some in the village, the disaffected young people with little in the way of prospects, for whom a thousand pounds would be a fortune, a ticket to a new life. Dan thought of the argument in the pub on the night of the attack, Steve Holder squaring up to the old man. There'd been a cold glint of repressed rage in the young man's eyes, bitter hatred in his scowl. Surely, there'd been more to that confrontation than one man jostling against another. That much anger could only come from a deeper motive, a grudge held until it took on a life of its own.

There are too many pieces missing from this puzzle, Dan told himself. *I need to step back, see the bigger picture.*

"This way," Alan called out, pushing his way through a gap in the foliage.

Following on his heels, Dan stepped out of the coppice. Then he stood still, holding his breath as he took in the view.

Below them, the field seemed vast, the land stretching down in a gentle, unbroken slope. The hedge that marked the field's lower boundary was only visible as a dark smudge in the distance. Dan scrapped his estimate of the land's value, revising it upwards. There was space here for a large housing development, almost a village in its own right. "All this is Craig's," he said, and Alan nodded.

"The main valley road is just the other side of that hedge, so with the right access…"

"It becomes a very valuable field indeed."

"They'd need to get planning permission," Alan said. "There'd be opposition from the locals. Noise, overcrowding, traffic jams on the narrow roads."

"There are always ways to get these things done. Build a bypass, promise a few low-cost starter homes, and throw in a nice little park with a play area for the kids. When people see a few benefits, they soon come around."

"What you lose on the ring road roundabouts, you gain on the swings," Alan muttered darkly, his expression so dour that Dan didn't dare to smile at his friend's play on words.

"It might not be so bad," Dan said. "These things can be done tastefully, to blend in with the countryside."

Alan stared at him. "This field has been here for hundreds of years, but they'd have to rip it up. It's not just the building sites and roads, it's all the infrastructure they'd need: pylons for power, posts for the phone lines, tunnels dug for cables, pipes laid for water. And don't get me started on the sewers. You know, there are still plenty of houses in the village that aren't connected to the main sewer; they have to maintain their own septic tanks. So you're talking about major excavation for miles around. All this disruption for what? A little slice of the countryside? Don't make me laugh. Houses jammed next to each other, little patches of grass in place of proper gardens, people packed in like sardines: they'd be better off staying in the towns. At least there'd be something for them to do."

Dan didn't reply. He was tempted to point out that this was the way of the world. When you have something people want, they'll buy it from you in a heartbeat. You sold the sizzle, not the steak, and there was no finer sizzle than the promise of a better life, a more fulfilling future, a new horizon. *That's the thing about horizons*, Dan thought. *They're always ahead of you, always out of reach.*

"You probably think I'm one of those awful NIMBY types," Alan said.

"No, not at all. You have a way of life that you value, and you want to protect it. Nothing wrong with that." Dan let his gaze wander across the gently rolling landscape, feeling the sun on his face. A gentle breeze whisked away the smell of damp and decay that had haunted their progress since they'd passed the spoil heaps, and he detected the sweet scent of summer blossoms. In the coppice behind them, the birds sang, and Dan couldn't hear a single car. Not one. He took a deep breath. "It would be a shame to turn this place into a housing estate. Even a city rat like me can see that." He shared a look with Alan. "Now we know exactly why Mortimer was attacked."

"This land could be worth a fortune," Alan said.

"But it goes further than that. This would be more than a property deal; it's about the future of the village. I'm sure Mortimer would've seen any major developments as a threat to Embervale. But for someone, this scheme was a golden opportunity, and it was too good to miss."

"Is that enough to drive someone to kill?"

"Definitely."

"In that case, we're looking at Craig as the one behind the attack."

"Let's take that as a starting point," Dan replied. "Craig hungers for the life of a country gentleman: shooting, fishing and sailing his boat at the weekends. He knew Mortimer was sitting on all this land, and he saw a chance to become a property developer and cash in."

"It seems to go against the grain," Alan said. "Craig is always saying that Mortimer was right to preserve the village, and everyone else seems to think that he has one foot in the past."

"Perhaps Kristen showed him the money. She worked with her uncle for years, and Mortimer trusted her, so she would've understood the land's potential. Once she'd told Craig the good news, all that stood in his way was an elderly man who lived alone. A *frail* old man. A man who could easily be lured into a trap."

"You paint a compelling picture," Alan admitted. "But you saw Craig's phone, and he *was* stuck in traffic. He has an alibi."

"Well, his phone was stuck in traffic. If he was clever, he could've left his phone in someone else's car."

"You're clutching at straws," Alan said. "He couldn't have known there'd be an accident on the road. As far as Friday night is concerned, Craig is in the clear. Even if he was involved in some kind of property scheme behind Mortimer's back, he couldn't have struck the final blow. So who did?" Alan clicked his fingers. "What about Jay? When we were at the Dower House, Craig said something about Jay doing a good job if you paid him in cash."

"I don't think so. If Jay hadn't come forward, we wouldn't even have known what Martin and Jess were up to."

"Perhaps he's working an angle, playing one side against the other."

"Jay isn't quite as shady as he makes out," Dan said. "As a matter of fact, he's going to be doing some decorating for me."

Alan blinked. "Really?"

"Sure. I don't see why not. He needs the work, and I need to get the job done. The sooner I can get the place fixed up, the sooner I can go back to London."

"Right. I see."

Dan turned away from Alan. "I think we've seen what we came to see. But where's the reservoir? I was expecting some kind of lake."

"Judging by that bank of reeds, I'd say that it's just over there. Do you want to take a look?"

"It can't be very big. But since we're here, we may as well."

"Come on then." Alan strode across the field, his path parallel to the coppice, and a moment later, the water's surface came into view. The reservoir was rectangular, its edges bordered with a low wall of concrete blocks, and it was perhaps ten metres long and five metres across. But as Dan approached the edge, he saw that it was much deeper than he'd expected, the vertical sides disappearing into a dizzying darkness. Despite the warmth of the sun on his back, a chill ran through him. There was something unsettling in the water's eerie stillness, and although it looked perfectly clear, he had no temptation to dip his hand below the surface.

"It's unnatural," Alan said. "Not a single speck of pondweed in the whole place."

"Yes. That's it. I knew there was something strange about it. It's completely lifeless." He scanned the reservoir's edge. "Where does it come from?"

"There must be a spring somewhere." Alan pointed to a clump of tall reeds growing just above the reservoir. "That's the most likely place."

"Yes. Let's take a peek."

Stepping carefully over the marshy ground, they pushed the reeds aside and peered down into a rectangular concrete pit: a much smaller version of the reservoir. But this pit was almost completely full of black silt, leaving room for only a thin layer of water. Above it, a concrete-lined channel dispensed a steady trickle, and at each side, the reeds had crept over the low wall to plant their roots firmly in the dark mud.

"It looks like a settlement tank," Alan said. "The sediment settles out here to prevent it flowing into the reservoir. With no one to maintain it…"

"It filled up with sludge." Dan looked up, and an odd shape caught his eye: a bundle of rags, perhaps. No. It was the body of an animal, its dark fur sodden and streaked with dirt. "Oh no," he whispered. "What's that?"

Alan followed his gaze and let out a groan. "Poor creature. Looks like a cat."

"Out here?"

"Yes." Alan skirted the pit, making for the stricken animal. "Most of the cats around here roam far and wide, especially the farm cats. They can fend for themselves, but this one must've met with an accident. Perhaps it was hit by a car, then it dragged itself here." He stood over the cat, bending to examine it. "That's strange. There's not a mark on it. It can't have been here long, or the rats would've been at it."

Reluctantly, Dan went to Alan's side and looked down on the bedraggled creature. And a memory surfaced. "Marjorie has a cat like this; I saw it in her yard. Her house is probably the nearest."

"Oh dear, she'll be upset. We should take it up to her."

"Agreed. Do you have anything we could carry it in?"

Alan slipped his daypack from his shoulders. "I've got a waterproof jacket. We can wrap it in that."

It was a grisly business to extricate the cat from the tangled reeds, but they managed it easily enough between them. As they wrapped it in the lightweight coat, Dan saw that Alan had been right: the cat appeared to be completely uninjured.

"Perhaps it just died of old age," Alan suggested. "You hear of them taking themselves off to quiet places before they die."

"Maybe, but if this is Marjorie's cat, it was in good health when I saw it the other day."

"We'll find out soon." Alan picked up the sad little bundle. "I'll carry it. It weighs nothing." He sighed. "I know it must've belonged to someone, but I hope it wasn't Marjorie's. I expect her cat is the only company she sees for days on end."

The journey back across the fields didn't take long, but both men slowed their pace as they neared Marjorie's cottage. Dan pushed open the garden gate, and as Alan made his way toward the house, the front door swung open, Marjorie standing on the threshold. Her eyes went straight to the bundle in Alan's arms. "What's that you've got there?"

Alan stood still. "I'm sorry, Marjorie, but we found a cat. It's dead, I'm afraid, and we thought it might be yours."

Marjorie lifted her chin. "Give it here then. Let's see."

Slowly, Alan held the bundle forward, opening the coat to show the cat's head.

"That's my Jemima," Marjorie stated. "Hand her over."

Alan opened his arms, and Marjorie took the cat quickly, cradling it in her arms. "Poor little bugger. Where'd you find her?"

"Down by the reservoir," Dan replied. He wanted to say more, but Marjorie wasn't about to let him.

"And what were you doing tramping about down there,

trespassing on my property? You've no business being there at all."

"We were just taking a walk," Alan said. "I've been showing Dan around, and I wanted to look for the old reservoir. That's where we found her." He paused respectfully. "I'm sorry to be the bearer of such bad news."

Marjorie scowled, but her first flush of anger had abated. "Ah well. It was good of you to bring her back, I suppose. You didn't have to do that. I appreciate it."

"We wondered whether she might have been hit by a car," Alan said gently. "Perhaps she was stunned and trying to make her way home."

"Not my Jemima," Marjorie said firmly. "She'd never have let herself get knocked down. She's been roaming these lanes for years and never had so much as a close scrape." She tutted under her breath. "No, it was that bloody water. She must have been drinking it. I've a good mind to drain the damned thing dry. Now that it's mine, no one can stop me."

"Is the water really that toxic?" Dan asked. "Surely, if it's a reservoir—"

"*Was* a reservoir," Marjorie interrupted. "Why do you think nobody uses it anymore? With the price of water rates, people would be falling over each other for free water if the damned thing was safe, but it isn't. It's poison. Pure poison."

"I had no idea," Alan murmured. "Something ought to be done."

"Oh, they know about it," Marjorie said. "It's full of arsenic on account of the old mine workings. I warned Morty about it. I've been telling him to get rid of those spoil heaps for years, but he wouldn't listen. Now look what's happened." Her voice cracked with emotion, and she bent her head over her beloved cat. "Poor little Jemima. It's not fair. First, there's vandals breaking the bloody fence in the middle of the night, and now this."

"Someone broke your fence?" Dan said.

But Marjorie wasn't listening. "It's just not bloody well fair. It's enough to make you sick."

Dan watched her for a moment, his mind teeming with questions, but this was not the right time to ask them.

"Is there anything we can do?" Alan said. "Would you like us to call anyone?"

Marjorie looked up. "No. You've done plenty. I'll take care of her now." She turned away and stepped back inside, her feet shuffling across the quarry-tiled floor as she made her way into the cool sanctuary of her cottage. She left the door wide open.

They watched her for a moment, then Dan said, "Do you think we should go after her? Maybe we should make her a cup of tea or something."

"Leave her be. She needs to be on her own for a bit." Alan inclined his head toward the gate. "Time to head for home."

"Yes." Dan followed Alan back into the lane. But as Dan closed the garden gate, he stopped to look along the wooden fence that bordered Marjorie's yard. "Look at that. What a mess."

"For God's sake," Alan muttered. "Poor Marjorie. It's been smashed to pieces. Who'd do a thing like that?"

"Good question. That's more than casual vandalism. It could be something worse."

"Are you saying this is some kind of deliberate attack?"

"Could be." Dan looked around, then he stepped over to the damaged fence. The horizontal rails of half-round timber were as wide as his fist, but they'd been hacked apart in three separate places, the cuts jagged and splintered. Alongside each break, deep grooves and notches scarred the wood. Dan followed the line of a cut with his fingers, picturing the frenzied blows that must've rained down on the fence. "Someone's taken an axe to this."

Alan joined him. "Yes, it looks like it. But there are plenty of them lying around. Most houses in the village have a wood burner, so an awful lot of us have axes big enough to do this kind of damage. There's a chap on Fore Street who keeps a huge axe propped up against the wall by his front door. It's clearly visible from the street."

"That's a bit reckless, isn't it?"

Alan shrugged. "I always think someone's going to steal the damned thing, but it's been there for years. There's not much petty crime in the village. Not usually, anyway."

"That makes this even more suspicious." Dan walked alongside the fence, scanning the lane, the ground. He stopped to study the overgrown ditch that ran parallel to the fence. There, on the soft ground at the very edge of the lane, a series of square indentations formed a thin line. "What do you make of this?"

Alan came to his side and kneeled down. "The edge of a boot print? A walking boot maybe?"

"No." Dan pointed, tracing an imaginary path from the bank to the lane. "The shape's completely wrong for a footprint. I'd say it was made by a tyre of some kind."

"Oh yes. A motorbike perhaps. Some of them have knobbly tyres that might leave a print like that."

Dan shook his head slowly. "I think a motorbike, even a small one, would've left a distinct track, especially since the ground is so soft from all the rain. But this print is isolated. It's as if someone placed something here, perhaps a bike. They might've rested it against the fence, and then lifted it up again and rode away when they'd done this damage."

"Assuming the print belongs to the guilty party," Alan said. "We get crowds of cyclists on the lanes in summer. Although, that pattern looks too big for a bike."

"True. But it's something to think about." Dan looked back to Marjorie's house. "Do you think we ought to go back and talk to her? She might've seen or heard something."

"No. She needs to be alone for a while. Anyway, I suspect

this was done under cover of the storm. If she'd heard anything, she'd have done something about it."

"Exactly what I was thinking," Dan said. "Using the storm was clever. This could be linked to the attack on Mortimer. It could be the same person."

"And equally, it could be a completely unrelated bit of mindless vandalism, carried out by a kid on a bike." Alan turned away and began walking toward the public footpath. "Come on. We've done enough for one morning, and I don't know about you, but I'm ready for a cold drink and something to eat."

What's new? Dan thought, but he followed Alan through the gate, and they strode along the path at a brisk pace. Alan whistled quietly as he walked, while Dan remained silent, his gaze unfocused. *There has to be a logical order to all these events*, Dan told himself. *There has to be a scenario that makes sense.*

When they passed the spoil heaps, Dan said, "Do you think she's right about the reservoir? Could it really be contaminated by arsenic from those heaps?"

"It certainly sounds plausible," Alan replied. "I can do some research when we get back. I'll let you know."

"Thanks. That would be great. It might be important. If we're right about Craig wanting to build on that land…"

"I'll see what I can find."

Dan detected an edge of weariness in Alan's voice, and they spoke little for the rest of the journey home, each alone with their own thoughts.

Back in the village, they parted company, and Dan went home to see what he could rustle up for lunch. Hurrying across the kitchen and tossing his phone onto the table, he made for the fridge, plucking a tub of Moroccan houmous from the shelf. But the tub was almost empty, and after the morning's walk, he needed something more substantial.

Checking the freezer, he found a pack of veggie burgers, but they'd take almost half an hour to cook from frozen. He threw them back into their frosty tomb, and turned instead to the cupboards, rifling through the packets and tins.

His phone buzzed, and he snatched it from the kitchen table. The notification showed that he'd missed a call from Kristen, and he smiled. But not for long.

If Kristen's brother really was intent on carrying out an underhand property deal, then he was probably involved in the attack on Mortimer. One way or another, Kristen was close to the case, and surely that put her out of reach, didn't it? *She can't be blamed for her brother*, Dan told himself. But even so, the idea of asking her out had lost its shine.

Maybe I'll call her back later, he decided. *Probably.*

A surge of frustration stirred in his stomach. Checking he had his wallet, he headed outside and started walking through the village. Hopefully, he'd find something he could eat at the village shop. If it was still open.

He marched along Fore Street, and he was halfway to the shop before he remembered that his jeans and trainers were still caked in mud. He really ought to have changed before leaving the house. *But it really doesn't matter*, he thought. *Not one little bit.*

CHAPTER 21

D AN'S TOUR OF the shop's eclectic aisles didn't take long. He'd hoped to find something inspiring to cook, but settled for a red pepper, a bag of carrots and some broccoli that had seen better days. Adding a tub of button mushrooms, he presented his meagre selection to Sam's baleful scrutiny.

"Been paddling?" she asked, eyeing the state of his jeans. "Nice day for it, I suppose."

"I've been out for a walk, and after the rain…" He smiled, but Sam had already lost interest, turning her attention to unloading his basket and ringing up each item on the till.

Dan cleared his throat. "Do you happen to know where I can find the soy sauce? I was planning to make a stir fry and—"

"Behind you, second shelf from the bottom," Sam said without looking up. "Next to the mustard."

"Ah, of course." Dan stepped over to the shelf, spotting the soy sauce instantly and choosing the bottle that seemed the least dusty. He scanned the colourful rows of jars and bottles. "I was here just a minute ago, but I didn't see it. I

242

wonder if there's anything else I missed. I could use some more Dijon mustard."

"Sold out," Sam stated. "We've got English or coarse grain."

"Okay. Right, so there are five different kinds of coarse grain mustard to choose from. That's... surprising."

Sam folded her arms. "Gary does the ordering. I'd guess he likes mustard. Do you want some or not?"

"Yes, this one will do." Dan selected a jar of organic coarse grain mustard and added it to his shopping along with the soy sauce.

"Contactless?" Sam pushed the card reader toward him.

"Thanks." Dan checked the amount and paid, but as he started to gather up his shopping, he paused. *I didn't see the soy sauce because I wasn't expecting it to be there*, he thought. *It was a relatively logical place for it to be, but the rest of the shop is so muddled, it threw me off.* He frowned. Perception was everything: the crucial difference between what was observed and what was not. The expected and the unexpected clashed in the viewer's mind, the commonplace becoming invisible, the exceptions drawing attention, the obvious hiding in plain sight. On the previous Friday, Sam had been in the pub, but he hadn't even seen her; she'd slipped beneath his radar.

Suddenly, in the case of Mortimer's death, Dan knew what he'd missed. "It doesn't add up," he said.

Sam looked from her till to the items still lying on the counter. "I was very careful."

"No, I don't mean my shopping. That's all fine. I'm talking about Friday night. Specifically the end of the night, the time when Mortimer was attacked."

She stared at him, her gaze guarded. "Are you all right? Were you out in the sun too long or something?"

"I'm fine. But I need you to do something for me. I need you to go over the exact sequence of events as you saw them on Friday night, from about eleven o'clock onwards."

"Why?"

"I'll explain in a minute, but please, just talk through it with me. It won't take long."

"No." Sam lifted her chin. "You can't come in here making demands. You've got no right."

"I'm sorry if I'm being heavy handed," Dan said. "But this is important. I'm sure you know that Alan's stick was taken from the bar, and it may have been used by whoever killed Mortimer. I'm trying to prove that Alan had nothing to do with the attack, so I need to know exactly what happened in the pub at around that time. I've just realised that there's a discrepancy in the different accounts that people have given me so far. They don't tie in."

"How do you mean?"

"If I tell you that, it'll influence you," Dan said. "Memories are malleable things. It's much better if you just talk through the events, and if you don't mind, I might ask you a few follow-up questions. Okay?"

Sam looked unconvinced.

"How about we just give it a try?" Dan went on. "The pub had been busy, but as it emptied, you started to tidy up. Is that right?"

Sam shrugged. "That's right. I told you this before, didn't I?"

"You mentioned it, but I want to know *exactly* what you did that night."

"Are you being funny?"

"No. Please, tell me everything, every little detail you can remember. What was the first thing you did?"

"I went into the back room and collected the empty glasses."

"How many?"

Sam grimaced. "How the hell would I know? I don't get paid by the dirty glass."

"Sorry. I know it sounds silly, but focusing on the details

can trigger other memories: things you didn't even know that you'd noticed at the time."

"Ah, like when they reconstruct a crime on the telly. Why didn't you just say so?" She rolled her eyes. "I'm not thick, you know."

"I know that," Dan said. "And I didn't mean to imply anything, but please, let's carry on." He sent her an encouraging smile. "Would you say there were a handful of glasses to collect or was it a lot more than that? How many trips did it take to collect them all?"

"There were loads. A few on every table, plus all the empty bottles. But I only made about… three trips. I can stack the pint glasses in the plastic holder, but there were quite a few wine glasses that night. They don't stack."

There was a hint of resentment in her tone, and something in her expression made Dan want to know more. "Do you sell much wine at The Boar?"

"Quite a bit. You know: dry white. It's nothing fancy. Not what you're used to, I expect."

"Perhaps not. But go on. There was something out of the ordinary, wasn't there. I can tell you're holding something back."

Sam started to shake her head, but then she seemed to change her mind. "Nothing really. It was just that I had to collect the champagne flutes. They'd only been drinking Prosecco, but Kev made me hunt out the glasses. They were so dusty, I had to wash them up. Anyway, they shared the bottle and then she left without a word. I mean, it wouldn't have hurt her to say thank you, would it?"

The hairs on the back of Dan's neck prickled. "Who?"

"Kristen. She was knocking back the wine with couple who sat looking miserable, and—" She broke off abruptly. "No, wait a minute. There were four glasses, but only three people at the table. I remember that because I thought it was a waste, washing up a glass nobody had used."

Craig didn't make it to the meeting, Dan thought. *But why didn't Kristen tell me she'd been in the pub?*

"Anyway," Sam went on, "after I'd got all the glasses, I went around and picked up all the rubbish and shoved it in a bin bag."

"And you were working on your own?"

Sam nodded. "Same as always. Kev had buggered off for a smoke."

"Right. Now we're getting to the point. This is what doesn't add up. Kevin told me that *he* was the one who cleared the tables at the end of the night."

"As if," Sam said. "He was outside. I did the whole place on my own."

"And did you see him out there? Presumably you took the rubbish outside."

"What else would I do with it? I'm not saving it up for a rainy day. I'm not going to make a collage out of empty crisp packets."

Dan suppressed a smile. "Have you ever been to Camden Market?"

"Once. I went with my mates. They reckoned we could pick up some bargains, but it was a waste of time. London prices." She grunted in disapproval. "Why do you ask?"

"Never mind. Tell me exactly what happened while you were outside."

"I threw the bags in the wheelie bins. I don't see what's so important about a load of rubbish, so that's enough chit-chat for one day. Some of us have work to do."

She made to turn away, but Dan leaned over the counter and said, "Please. Give me a few more minutes. I'll make it worth your while. I'll buy something from the shop. Anything you want. What's the most expensive thing you've got?"

Sam pursed her lips. "I reckon it's time you left."

"Listen, Sam, I didn't mean to upset or annoy you in any way, really, I didn't. But remember, I'm trying to prove Alan's innocence. Your information could play a very important part in piecing together exactly what happened that Friday night."

Sam stared at him, her expression stony, but just when he thought he'd lost her, she said, "All right then. I don't know where you're going with all this, but Alan's always been decent to me. So go on, ask your questions, and I'll try to help."

"Thank you. I'm sure Alan will appreciate your help." Dan paused. "The wheelie bins are in the far corner of the car park, yes?"

She nodded. "Is that it? Is that your big question?"

"That's only the opener. The next thing I need to check is that you went out of the back door and crossed the top of the garden to get to the bins and back."

"That's right. It took me a couple of minutes, that's all."

"Good. Now, the really important question is, who did you see while you were out there?"

"Nobody. Nobody at all."

"You're sure about that?" Dan asked, and when she nodded, he said, "So while you were walking from the back door to the bins and back, you didn't see or hear a single person."

"That's right."

"In that case, we can safely say that there was no one in the garden. Is that right?"

Sam's expression clouded, and a tiny muscle twitched her lower lip. "Kevin. He was having a smoke in the garden. He has those e-cigarettes."

"Sam, I hate to tell you this, but you're a terrible liar. Really hopeless. You'd be much better off telling the truth."

She lifted her chin. "I am telling the truth."

"No. You're not. Let's go back to that night. Tell me what

really happened. I think you saw something important. Maybe somebody arrived or somebody was behaving in a suspicious way. But let's start with Kevin. Did you see him in the garden or not?"

Sam nodded firmly, but she kept her lips tight shut.

"Did Kevin tell you to say that you saw him there?" Dan asked. "Did he tell you to lie?"

"No. You've got it all wrong."

"Then help me out," Dan said. "Explain the situation. I'll listen."

"But you don't understand," Sam blurted. "I *need* that job. I know it's not much, but that money makes the world of difference to me. It's the only way I can put a bit by. It's the only way I'm ever going to get out of this place."

"Don't worry about that. Whatever the problem is, I'll straighten it out with Kristen. I know her personally."

Sam's eyes went wide. "For God's sake, don't do that. Don't go sticking your oar in with her."

"But she owns the pub now, and—"

"She's the problem," Sam snapped. "It was her who said she'd give me the sack."

"Why would she do that?"

"On account of Steve." Sam's defiant expression crumpled. "It's so unfair."

Dan took a moment to collect his thoughts. He was finally getting somewhere. On Friday, Sam had been the one to clear the back room. Kevin hadn't wanted to admit that he'd taken a break for a smoke, so there were gaps in his version of events. Perhaps Sam could fill in the missing pieces. *She must've seen the person who took Alan's stick*, Dan thought. *Could it really have been Steven Holder?*

But Sam's eyes were growing moist. He had to be careful not to push her too far. "It's all right," he said. "You can tell me all about it. I promise to be discreet."

"It's all Steve's fault. He's always had this idea about me. I

248

used to go out with him when we were at school, but that was nothing really. Kids' stuff. Holding hands and a snog behind the sports hall. You know what I mean."

"And now?" Dan asked. "Does Steve… bother you?"

"He doesn't do anything bad, not really. He just comes and hangs around. He's always getting into trouble on my account. He's got such a temper."

"I see. What does he do when he loses his temper? Does he lash out?"

Sam's eyes flashed in alarm. "No! He's not violent. Oh my God, did you think…?" She drew a breath. "Listen, Steve's not like that. It's all talk with him."

"Can we be sure of that? He'd been drinking on Friday night, and when I last saw him, his temper was already getting frayed around the edges."

"Stop that. Stop putting two and two together and making five." Sam bridled. "I know what he did in the pub, and it was all just a load of hot air. The problem is, he reckons he's got to stand up for me. I don't encourage him, honestly I don't." She looked down at her hands. "That's what all that nonsense with Morty was about on Friday."

Dan's mouth was suddenly dry. "Tell me what you know."

"In the pub, Morty made some remark about me. I won't repeat it, but it was bloody rude. Anyway, Steve heard him, and that's why he squared up to the old bugger."

"Are you sure that's what they were arguing about?" Dan asked.

"Definitely."

"They didn't say anything about the land or the spoil heaps?"

Sam stared at him. "What are you on about? I told you what happened. Don't you believe me?"

"I believe you, but did you actually hear what they said to each other?"

250

"No. But Steve told me afterwards. And some of my mates were talking about it the next day, and they all said the same thing, so it must be right." Sam scowled. "Too many gossips in this village. By the next morning, everybody knew what had happened. That's the whole problem."

Dan pursed his lips. For a moment, he'd been on the trail of something significant, an important revelation within his grasp. But the truth was determined to escape his clutches; he could almost feel it slipping between his fingers. "You'll have to explain what you mean, Sam. When you say *the whole problem*, what are you talking about? Is there something you're not telling me?"

"I'll tell you what the problem is. It's Kristen high-and-mighty Ellington. She got to hear about Steve having a go at her uncle, and she knew the whole story, apparently. So she called me up on Saturday and blamed me for the whole thing. *Watch your step*, she told me. *Watch it, or you'll be out of a job.*"

"But, it wasn't *your* fault," Dan said. "Perhaps Kristen was upset after what had just happened to her uncle. But there's no connection, is there? Unless…"

"Unless what?"

"Sam, you didn't tell Steven to do something to Mortimer, did you?"

"No! That's what I've been trying to tell you." Sam's hands went to her head, her fingers pressing hard against her temples. "Bloody hell! You're as bad as her! This is ridiculous. I've done nothing wrong. Nothing!"

"I know that," Dan said, keeping his tone soft. "It's okay, Sam. I'm not accusing you of anything."

But it seemed as though Sam hadn't heard him. She bowed her head and pressed the heels of her hands against her eyes, still murmuring, her words coming thick and fast: "I tried to tell her, I really did, but she didn't want to know. She was awful to me. Awful. She just wouldn't listen, and she kept saying I must've egged Steve on, like I would ever do anything so stupid. But she didn't listen to a word I said. That's why... I didn't want to tell you." She sniffed. "But it wasn't my fault. I didn't know he was going to come back."

Dan's heart missed a beat. "Who came back, Sam? It can't have been Mortimer, so—"

"It was Steve," she blurted, lowering her hands and looking up at Dan, her eyes filling with tears. "He came back. When I was clearing up."

"What happened?" Dan leaned closer, his hands pressing hard on the counter. "Tell me everything."

"There isn't much to tell, not really. When I went to take the rubbish out, Steve was waiting for me. He was crowing about how he'd stood up for me, the daft sod. He thought I'd be grateful or something."

"And were you?" Dan detected a subtle reddening of Sam's cheeks. "A young man fighting for your honour; that doesn't happen every day. Then later, when he abandoned his friends and made a special effort to come back and see you, you enjoyed the attention."

For a second, Sam didn't respond, but then she nodded slowly. "I told him he was being stupid, but it had been a long day, and I don't know what I was thinking, but... well, you know."

"You shared a moment," Dan suggested.

"Just a kiss and a cuddle. Only for a few minutes. Nothing wrong with that."

"Of course not. But that means you were outside for quite a while, so the bar was left unattended. I suppose you didn't happen to notice anyone acting suspiciously while you were out there."

Sam shrugged. "Sorry. I didn't see anybody, but then again, I was kind of distracted."

"You didn't see anyone slipping into the pub by the back door? Or perhaps someone arrived and left again soon afterwards. Or maybe there was someone in the garden after all."

"No, I don't think so. I mean, Kev was probably lurking around somewhere. He's usually in the garden after work. But it was dark, and he goes off and sits in the gazebo, keeping out the way until all the work's been done."

"I didn't notice a gazebo. Whereabouts in the garden is it?"

"It's right down the bottom end, in the corner. It's only small, and it's in a bit of a state. Half of it's rotten and there's ivy growing all over it, so you'd hardly know it was there. But it's still standing, just about. People aren't meant to smoke in the garden, but if they tuck themselves in the old gazebo, Kev turns a blind eye. At least, that's what used to happen. Now Kristen's in charge, I expect it'll all change. She might've turned the damned thing into kindling by now."

"So someone could've been in this gazebo, and we'd never have known about it."

"I suppose so." Sam wiped her eyes with the backs of her hands, then she straightened her posture. "Well, I probably shouldn't have told you all that, but what's done is done. I suppose I'll get the sack from the pub, so I'd better get back to work before I get into trouble with Gary as well. I can't lose both jobs in one day, that would be too much."

"You won't get sacked from the pub," Dan said quickly. "There's no need for me to tell Kristen about you and Steve. In fact, maybe I could have a quiet word with her, smooth things over. I could tell her what a great job you're doing."

Sam searched his expression. "You'd do that?"

"Definitely. No question."

"Mind what you say, though. She doesn't take kindly to people interfering."

"I can handle Kristen," Dan replied. "Don't worry about it. Sam, thank you for being so honest. It all helps me to build up a picture of what really happened."

"I didn't really tell you anything. I'm sorry for making such a fuss. I didn't mean to get upset."

"But you *did* help," Dan said. "Really, you were great. But I'd better let you get back to work." He gathered his shopping in his arms. "I should've brought a bag."

Sam held up a carrier bag. "I can sell you one."

"That's fine. I've only got a few things. I haven't got far to go." He headed for the door, and as he struggled to let himself out with his hands full, he flashed Sam a smile. "Thanks again. See you soon."

"Bye." Sam raised her hand in a tiny wave as she tried to return his smile.

She has a good heart, Dan told himself as he headed for home, his groceries clutched tight to his chest. *She's wasted on the likes of Steven Holder.*

Occupied by his thoughts, Dan barely noticed the Land Rover trundling past; not until it ground to a halt just ahead. The Land Rover's windows were down, and as Dan approached, an unmistakable voice boomed from within: "Dan! Just the fellow I've been looking for."

Dan stepped up to the vehicle, dragging his feet. "Craig. How are things going?"

"Not bad, old boy. Not bad." Craig leaned sideways, lowering his voice to a conspiratorial whisper. "The thing is, I could do with your help. Bit of advice needed."

"I'm not sure I'm the right person," Dan started to say, but Craig beckoned him closer.

"Hop in, there's a good chap. I'll give you a lift home, and we'll talk on the way."

"There's no need. I can practically see my house from here," Dan said. "You're welcome to drop in. I was about to make lunch."

Craig shook his head. "Busy schedule today. I've got somewhere to be."

"Why don't you give me a call later?"

"No, that's no good." Craig smiled. "I just need a quick word. It won't take you a minute, but we can't talk in the street. Hop in."

Dan wavered. He wasn't at all sure about Craig; the man put on such a show that it was hard to see what made him tick. Was Craig a ruthless businessman, a wolf in casual clothing? Was his jovial demeanour carefully contrived to conceal his true aims? *He served in the army*, Dan reminded himself. *He must be tougher than he looks*.

"Sorry," Dan said. "I really have to get home."

Craig's smile vanished. "That's no good, Dan. You need to get in. Now. It's important." He paused. "I need your help, and I wasn't going to say this, but it affects Kristen. You wouldn't want to see her upset, would you?"

"No, of course not. But—"

"Get in," Craig interrupted. "This won't take up much of your time. You wouldn't begrudge a friend a couple of minutes, I'm sure."

Dan glanced back along the street, but it was empty. If he went with Craig now, no one would know where he'd gone. But it might be worth the risk. Craig clearly had something he needed to get off his chest, and who knew what secrets he might divulge while he was off guard? *If I'm going to solve Mortimer's murder, I need a break*, Dan thought. *Either Craig is involved, or he knows who was, and this might be my only chance to puncture his self-assured armour*.

He locked eyes with Craig. "All right. Just for a minute."

"Good man. Jump in."

Dan shifted his groceries, freeing his hand just enough to work the unfamiliar latch and haul the Land Rover's door open, then he climbed inside. He laid his shopping in the footwell, then he grabbed the seatbelt, but before he could fasten it, Craig revved the engine and the Land Rover lurched forward. The motion pressed Dan back in his seat and made the door swing shut. "Craig, what the hell are you doing?"

"Sorry. No time." Craig grinned. "Still, you'd better pop your belt on."

"I know," Dan said pointedly. He buckled his belt, although, with the way Craig was driving, they'd reach his house in seconds. "So, what was it you wanted to talk to me about?"

"I'll tell you in a bit. I want to get clear of the village."

"But my house is just there. You said you'd give me a lift."

"Change of plan. Sorry to spring it on you like this, but you know how it is."

The Land Rover accelerated, and Dan gripped the edges of his seat. "No. I don't know what you're talking about, Craig. But whatever you want, this isn't the way to go about it."

"Maybe not. We'll see."

Outside, houses whipped past, faster and faster. But the quaint cottages and sunlit gardens belonged to another world: a tranquil place that had so easily been whisked away.

"Stop the car," Dan said. "I'm serious, Craig. Stop it right now."

Craig tutted. "No can do, old boy. I need to have a word with you, and it has to be in private. I need to make sure you aren't going to go blabbing my business to every Tom, Dick and Harry."

"This is ridiculous." Dan took hold of the door handle, but Craig reached across and grabbed Dan's upper arm, squeezing tight.

"Don't do that, old man. Not a good idea. You never know who might be around the corner. If you open the door, you might knock some poor bugger's head off."

"Then stop the car," Dan shot back. "This is just—" He broke off, his gaze fixed dead ahead. They were speeding out of the village now, tall hedgerows rising up on both sides, stray branches rattling against the Land Rover's windows. "Look out!"

The lane curved hard to the left, and though it widened a little, the bend was blind, and Craig was taking it far too fast.

"Don't worry." Chuckling, Craig threw the Land Rover into the curve, hitting the brakes just enough to keep control. The Land Rover skidded over a patch of loose gravel, and Dan was thrown hard against the door. But they stayed on the road, and Craig accelerated once again. "Almost there."

"Where? Where the hell are we going?"

"You'll see. This is our turn." The lane curved to the right, but a dirt track led straight ahead, and Craig headed directly for it, sending the Land Rover bumping over the hard-packed earth. "I'll stop in a minute."

"You'd better," Dan growled. "You're in enough trouble as it is."

"I don't know what you mean. We're just a couple of chaps having a chat, that's all."

They drove over the track for a little longer, climbing the side of the valley, and leaving the road and the village far behind. Staring straight ahead, Dan saw where their route would take them, and his blood ran cold.

CHAPTER 22

S ITTING IN HIS armchair to eat his lunch in the cool of his lounge, Alan paused with his sandwich halfway to his mouth. His laptop was balanced on his lap, and he needed to concentrate while he tweaked his search query, honing it to perfection. He typed with his right hand, while with his left he held the sandwich quivering in mid-air.

Satisfied, he hit the return key and took a bite of sandwich as the results of his search flashed onto the laptop's screen. *This looks good.* Hardly tasting his food, Alan selected the most promising link and opened it in a new tab.

The article was one long block of densely packed text, but he skimmed and scanned each paragraph as fast as he could.

"Lead sulphide," he mumbled through his half-chewed mouthful. "Commonly found in mining spoil heaps with sulphides of zinc and copper." He swallowed, his throat tight. Without taking his eyes from the screen, he placed his sandwich on the plate that sat on the small table beside his chair. "Arsenic sulphide may also be present and is extremely toxic."

Marjorie was right about the arsenic, he thought. *No wonder Craig was having the soil tested.*

But one source wasn't enough; he had to find more.

Returning to his search, he chose a link that led to a PDF document: an abstract of an academic study. The level of detail forced him to read every paragraph twice, and there were a few terms he didn't understand, but even so, he could glean enough information to make the effort worthwhile. Within a few minutes, he'd learned that some forms of arsenic were more soluble than others, and that the amount in circulation might be linked to the pH of the soil. But what did that mean for the local spoil heaps? *The soil must be acidic*, he thought. *There are rhododendrons, and they like acid soil.* He read on, but the report delved into advanced methods of chemical analysis and electron microscopy. *This is no use*, he told himself. *It's over my head.* And then he saw it:

Arsenic concentrations in the samples from the areas around the abandoned mines exceeded the guideline safe values by between one and five orders of magnitude.

He read it again. "Five times the safe level," he whispered. "Five."

Alan scanned the report again, grasping at fragments of meaning. The study was based on the neighbouring county of Cornwall, but the principles would surely be the same. The parallels were all too clear. On his own doorstep, an environmental tragedy had unfolded in slow motion. Aided by a natural spring and the acidic soil, arsenic compounds had leached out from the spoil heaps, little by little, contaminating the ground and the water that ran through it. Then the site had been left undisturbed for decades; plenty of time for the contaminated groundwater to carry its deadly cargo of toxins through the gently sloping fields along the valley. Arsenic, and who knew what else, had accumulated in the old reservoir, rendering it lifeless. Only a few sturdy reeds had been tough enough to creep into the sludge in the settlement tank, but the water itself might well have been toxic enough to poison Marjorie's cat.

But how far had the contamination spread? Had it already seeped across the entire stretch of land that Craig had earmarked for development? And did Craig know about the potential glitch in his plans *before* Mortimer was attacked?

He must've had some idea about it, Alan decided. *He'd already arranged for Martin and Jess to carry out the survey.*

A hard ball of anxiety formed in Alan's stomach, and he almost set his laptop aside. But he needed to know more. Working quickly, he found the Ordnance Survey website and located an online map of the local area. It took only a minute to find the spoil heaps, and trailing his finger across the screen, he traced a path over the contours.

The land Marjorie inherited will definitely be contaminated, he thought. *Does she know?*

Alan sat back. Marjorie had known about the contamination of the water; she claimed that she'd discussed it with Mortimer. But what did that mean?

He recalled how angry Craig had been when he'd found out that Mortimer had remembered Marjorie in his will. *But it wasn't the cottage itself that infuriated him,* Alan remembered. *It was the land.*

That had to be important. Perhaps Marjorie's inheritance was larger than he'd assumed. She owned the land between her cottage and the reservoir, but how far did her newly acquired domain stretch out on either side? *I should've asked her,* Alan told himself. *It's damned frustrating not to have all the facts.* He chewed at the inside of his cheek. He'd uncovered a significant clue, but he wasn't sure how the contaminated land could be tied to the attack on Mortimer. It wasn't as if the problem could be solved by taking the old man out of the picture. Surely, a clean-up operation would take months, years. So how did this new information fit in with what they'd already found out?

I have to tell Dan, he thought. *He'll want to know straight away*. Alan hurried to his landline and called Dan's mobile, but it went straight to voicemail. "Damn."

Alan hung up without leaving a message, then he headed for the door. A handful of seconds later, he hammered on Dan's front door, but there was no reply.

Typical, Alan thought. *Never around when you need him*. Alan cast a final glance at The Old Shop, then he headed for home. He'd call later. But first, he'd make a mug of tea, and have another stab at researching the toxins left behind by abandoned mines. Something told him that there'd be a great deal of material to wade through.

CHAPTER 23

D AN STARED OUT through the Land Rover's windscreen, his gaze fixed on the dense forest that loomed ahead. The closely planted fir trees seemed to form an impenetrable palisade, but Craig drove on, heedless. Soon, the woodland's brooding shadows reached out to swallow them, and inside the forbidding forest, the afternoon's sunlight was blotted out, smothered by the oppressive canopy of overarching branches. The air grew colder, chilling the sweat on Dan's skin. He blinked, peering into the gloom, but all he could see was the rough track stretching into the distance between uniform rows of towering trees.

"Where are we?" Dan asked, keeping his voice steady.

"It doesn't really have a name. It's a fir plantation, that's all. Nothing special."

"Why are we here?"

"Privacy." Craig sent him a meaningful look. "No phone signal up here. Nothing. Just you and me."

"All right. So let's talk. What do you want?"

Craig grunted, turning his attention back to the track. "We'll get to that. Hold on tight." Slowing down, he twisted the wheel, steering the Land Rover away from the track and onto a patch of bare earth. The brakes squealed, and the Land Rover halted beside a tall stack of felled timber, the vehicle so close to the piled wood that Dan doubted whether he could open the door enough to squeeze out.

"This ought to do," Craig said, and he killed the engine, turning in his seat to face Dan. "Now we can talk in peace."

Dan squared his shoulders. "You've made a mistake, Craig. It doesn't matter what you want. There's no way I'll cooperate with you now."

"I wouldn't be too sure about that if I were you." Craig paused, studying Dan as if he belonged to a rare and exotic species. "You've taken a shine to my sister, haven't you? Unless I'm much mistaken, you've got quite a soft spot for dear old Kris."

Dan almost laughed. "Is that what all this about, all this drama? What are you trying to do, warn me off?"

"Hardly. That wouldn't be right. Not the decent thing at all."

"Seriously? You're talking about decency, but you've just snatched me off the street. Where's the sense in that?"

"No need to exaggerate, old boy. Nobody's getting abducted. Like I said, we're just going to talk over some business."

"Unbelievable." Dan leaned closer to Craig, ready to let fly with a few home truths, but as he moved, he caught sight of a long, dark shape lying on the rear seat. He pulled back. "What's in that bag? Is it a gun?"

"Ah, so even a townie knows a shotgun case when he sees it. But you're quite safe, Dan. If I'd wanted to *snatch* you, as you put it, I'd have used the old Purdey. Nothing makes a chap think twice like a shotgun pointing at his chest." Craig chortled, raising his eyebrows expectantly as if he thought Dan might share the joke.

"Why have you brought a shotgun with you?" Dan asked slowly. "What are you intending to do with it?"

"Taking it into Exeter. It needs a service, and there's a place I use. I wouldn't let just anyone get their hands on the Purdey—it was my grandfather's—but this chap knows his stuff."

Dan waited, but Craig added no further explanation. "So you're saying that it's a coincidence. The gun just happened to be in your Land Rover when you came looking for me."

"That's right. Why, what did you think? Did you imagine I'd brought you out here to bump you off?"

"The thought had crossed my mind."

"Why on earth would I want to do that?"

"Because I've got too close to the truth," Dan said. "Because I've found out too much about your plans for the estate."

"I don't know what you think you've found out, but it *is* the estate that I want to talk to you about." Craig took a breath. "Listen, let's start again. I've probably gone about this the wrong way, but that's me; I'm like a bull at a gate. I've always been the same. Head down, charge ahead, and bugger the consequences. Not subtle, I grant you, but when the chips are down, it's the only way to get through. It's a damned sight better than throwing your hands up in despair, I can tell you."

Dan looked at Craig carefully, taking in the rim of red around his eyes, the film of sweat on his brow, and the telltale twitch of a muscle in his cheek. And there was something else, something in his gaze: the way his eyes darted erratically as he spoke. Craig was stressed, anxious, running on adrenaline. He covered it pretty well, his outward display of bluster wrapped tightly around him like a comfortable coat, but the signs were there. Deep down, Craig was unravelling. However he tried to dress it up, he *had* grabbed Dan from the street. The man's self-control was dwindling, his impulses taking over as his sense of right and wrong buckled under an unknown pressure. *Guilt can do that to a person*, Dan thought. *Especially when it's repressed.*

Craig was in this thing up to his neck. He'd been clever, covering his tracks and giving himself an alibi, but he must've been the one to attack his uncle. Now that the old man was dead, Craig couldn't live with what he'd done. But what would he do now? Would his tortured conscience drive him to commit more violence to conceal his crime? Craig wouldn't be the first murderer to find himself drawn into a spiral of bloodshed.

Stay calm, Dan told himself. *I can still stop this from happening. It's not too late.* Dan kept his expression neutral, and when he spoke, his voice remained level. "Craig, it's all right. I think I know what you've done, but we can resolve the problem. We're both intelligent people. We can discuss this calmly."

Craig nodded vigorously. "Absolutely. That's the idea. That's the whole point."

"Good." Dan let out a slow breath. "Now, shall we drive back to the village? I can drive if you—"

"No! Don't be daft. We haven't talked about anything yet. Nothing at all."

"Okay. In that case, why don't we step outside?"

"No. Stay put." Craig pinched the bridge of his nose. "Bloody headache. Haven't been sleeping. Not for days." He whispered something under his breath, then he said, "Look, this doesn't come easy to me, but I'm just going to come out with it."

"That's good." Dan pressed his lips tight shut, waiting. *This is it*, he thought. *I'm going to get the whole story.*

"But this is just between us, right? It doesn't go further. Not one word."

Lie, Dan told himself. *Keep him calm*. But his tongue wouldn't form the words. Instead, he said, "I'm sorry, Craig, but I can't promise that. I've no idea what you're going to tell me, so there's no way I can commit to keeping it secret. You must understand that."

Dan expected an argument, but Craig hung his head and stared into space as if the fight had gone out of him. Dan waited. And waited. Finally, Craig broke the silence. "Fair enough. You play with a straight bat; I can respect that." He looked up sharply. "It's like this, Dan. I'm screwed. Totally, royally, every which way you can think of, screwed."

"You'll have to explain that."

"I don't know if I can. I was greedy, I suppose. And stupid. That's a bad combination, but I was all right for a while. I earned enough to keep the show on the road. You know how it is: loans, car payments, mortgage, credit cards. So long as the salary comes in at the end of each month, you can keep it all under control. But then... all this bloody business happened with the old man's will. That's when the wheels really started to come off the wagon."

"I thought you were the main beneficiary."

"Ha! So did I, Dan. So did I." Craig shook his head, a strange smile fluttering on his lips. "Since Morty died, I've done some pretty stupid things. I've overextended myself. I took out loans, made some investments, splashed out on the plastic. Somewhere along the line, I put my own home up as collateral. I don't know what possessed me, but I did it. I must've been mad."

"There are ways through these things," Dan said. "But what did you mean about Morty's will? Are you saying that you didn't inherit as much as you expected?"

"My inheritance is almost worthless. The shares the old man left me aren't worth the paper they're written on."

"I don't understand. How is that possible?"

"It's very complicated," Craig said. "I don't understand it myself, not really. To be honest, my solicitor was in over his head; he admitted as much. But the short version is, the old man couldn't leave me the estate because he didn't really own it anymore."

"What?"

"It's true. The whole thing was dealt with years ago, parcelled off into offshore companies. Mertonic Holdings: that's the first one we came up against. But they're owned by someone else, and so it goes on. Layer upon layer of corporate ownership. It's impossible to untangle."

"Are you sure it was all done legally?" Dan asked. "You might have grounds to challenge the will."

Craig's expression brightened a little. "You see, that's why I need your help."

"I'm not a lawyer, Craig."

"No, but you must know someone who can handle this for me. I need someone really top notch. A specialist. But the whole thing has to be handled on the quiet. I need you to act as a sort of go-between. You see, if anyone finds out about this, if even one of my creditors gets the slightest hint that I'm in dire straits, they'll all want their money back. Before you know it, I'll be bankrupt. I'll lose everything. I don't care about the cars and the boat, but what about when my home gets repossessed? Do you think my wife will stay with me while we weather the storm?" He let out a bark of joyless laughter. "She'll be gone about three seconds after I give her the bad news. I'll have nothing. Nothing."

"You're right about a couple of things," Dan said. "You do need to take legal advice, and I have contacts who could recommend some good law firms, so I could make an introduction. But I'm not sure why you're so worried about your privacy. Lawyers have to treat everything you say as confidential."

"You don't understand." Craig gripped the steering wheel tight, his knuckles white. Then, through clenched teeth, he said, "Not all of my investments were strictly legal. I know a few people who like to do business in their own way. They prefer to keep the taxman at arm's length, you might say."

"Tax avoidance or tax evasion?"

"A bit of both, I think. To be honest, I've never had dealings with these people before. But I was introduced to them, and I thought all this money would be rolling in from the estate, so we got talking about it. They made it all sound perfectly logical. They said, 'Craig, old chap, why should you hand over so much of your inheritance to the government?' Naturally, I said there was no way around it. And they laughed. They laughed as if I'd just told them the funniest story they'd ever heard. They said, 'There's always a way around it. Always.' And I believed them." He let go of the steering wheel and sat back, slumped in his seat. "Who's got the last laugh now, eh? Not me, that's for sure."

"You've certainly put yourself in a difficult position," Dan said. "But there's just one thing. If you don't own the estate, who does? Kristen?"

Craig shrugged. "Buggered if I know. Everything's tied in knots. She's been let down just as much as I have. She's heartbroken. I told her earlier today. I've known it was all looking doubtful for quite a while, but I've been hoping for a reprieve. No such luck, though. My lawyer rang this morning and officially jumped ship. After that, I had to tell Kristen, and she hasn't been out of her room since."

"I'm sorry to hear that." Dan thought for a moment. "What about Marjorie's cottage? Is that tied up too?"

"No. She's safe. Morty took care of her, apparently. It's a damned shame he didn't think quite so much about his own flesh and blood."

"Had you fallen out with your uncle?"

Craig shook his head. "Never. We got on so well."

"Are you sure? Only, you can never quite tell with families. Old resentments can fester for years. If he was bearing a grudge, he might've kept it to himself. These things can remain buried for a long time."

"You met Morty. He wasn't like that. If he didn't agree with you, he'd tell you to your face." Craig smiled sadly as if recalling a memory. "If he was here now, he'd tell me to pull myself together. He had no patience for fools. Fortunately, we saw eye to eye on most things."

"Most, but not all," Dan said. "Was there something specific, some disagreement that he might've held against you?"

"Not really. Apart from all that nonsense about opening up the old mines. I teased him about it every now and then, like a running joke between us, but I'm pretty sure he knew the whole scheme was a non-starter. He just didn't want to admit it. He hated to back down."

"Perhaps he had an ulterior motive: a reason to cling to the idea of opening the mines."

"Like what?"

"Perhaps he knew that you had plans to build on that stretch of land."

Craig looked as though he'd been slapped. "Build? I don't want to build a damned thing."

"But I thought you were going to develop the land along the valley."

"Then you thought wrong. All I've ever wanted was to keep the estate just as it is. Morty felt the same way, and that was why he was going to favour me in his will. At least, that's what I always thought, anyway. What a joke that turned out to be."

"Mortimer let you think that, right up until the end?"

"Yes. He even knew about the survey. He thought it was a good idea."

"And did he know they were taking samples to analyse the soil?" Dan asked. "Because if you didn't want to build on the land, it doesn't make much sense."

"What are you talking about? Martin and Jess were drawing up a map of the estate. I'm sure I told you that already."

"Wait a minute," Dan said. "Whose idea was it to hire Martin and Jess?"

"Mine."

"Are you sure about that? Only, it seems to me that there must be plenty of local companies who could've done that job. But Martin and Jess had to come all the way from Chester, and you even had to put them up in a holiday cottage. That seems strange to me."

Craig pursed his lips. "Well, er, now that I think about it, Kristen actually did the deal with them. They were her friends, so I just let her get on with it."

"Just like Mortimer let her run most of his business affairs," Dan said. "And now you've been frozen out of your inheritance. Doesn't that strike you as an odd coincidence?"

"No. She hasn't got anything to do with it. Kristen would never cheat anybody. She's as honest as the day is long."

"Mm. Craig, these people who got you involved in their tax avoidance schemes; you said you hadn't dealt with them before. So who introduced them to you? Was it Kristen, by any chance?"

"Well, I... I don't think so. Not directly, anyway." The skin around Craig's eyes tightened as though he was in deep pain but didn't want to admit it. "Sometimes Kristen handles my appointments for me, you see. She looks after the diary. She's a damned sight better at it than I am. She has this way of getting things done, you know?"

"Oh yes," Dan said. "I know exactly what you mean."

CHAPTER 24

ALAN TURNED WITH a start, watching the window. He'd been intent on his laptop's screen, his fingers busy on the keyboard for the last hour. He hadn't moved from his armchair in the lounge, his research absorbing him completely. But unless he was mistaken, someone had just approached his house; someone moving quickly and very close to the window, a shadowy figure flitting across the dusty pane.

His house was set back from the road, and there was no reason for anyone to walk so close unless they intended to visit him. *Probably Dan*, he told himself. *It's about time he turned up.*

The front doorbell chimed twice in rapid succession. *Definitely not Dan*, Alan decided. *It must be a cold caller.*

Setting his laptop aside and pushing himself to his feet, Alan strode toward the door, making his face a mask of polite indifference. He had research to complete, and he wasn't about to be derailed by this month's special offers on uPVC fascias or double-glazed conservatories.

But when he swung open the door, his unfriendly

expression slipped away. "Oh, Kristen. I wasn't expecting you."

"No, of course not. Why would you?" Kristen's smile was warm, and her eyes sparkled as though Alan had just made an incredibly witty remark. "You really are a tease, Alan."

Alan's mouth was dry, but he managed to say, "Am I?"

"Yes." She peered past him. "I hope I'm not distracting you from anything important."

"No, not really. I was just… working."

"Good. In that case, would you mind if I popped in for a while? It's hot, and I forgot to apply sunscreen. I'm getting horribly burned. Look." Her fingers went to her collarbone, tugging aside the thin cotton of her white blouse.

"I don't think you've caught the sun too much," Alan said, although he was trying very hard not to look. "But please, do come in." He stepped back, and she breezed inside, almost brushing against him, the delicate scent of her perfume filling the narrow hallway. "Would you like to come through to the lounge?" he said, but his gaze went to the open laptop. His findings meant trouble for her brother, so she mustn't see what he'd been working on. "On second thoughts," he said quickly, "let's go into the kitchen, and I'll fix us a drink." Pulling the lounge door shut, he ushered Kristen along the hall, and she strolled into the kitchen, casting her eye over the furnishings like a prospective buyer.

"What a lovely room," she said. "It suits you; it's very *manly*."

Alan summoned a hesitant smile. "What can I offer you? Tea or coffee? Or would you prefer something cold?"

"What I would prefer is a gin and tonic, but it's a bit early for that." She pouted. "Mind you, if you have a cold beer, I wouldn't say no."

"Yes, I think I've got a couple of pale ales in the fridge. Have a seat, and I'll see what I can find."

Kristen sat at the table, watching Alan as he bustled around the room to fetch the beers, a couple of glasses and a bottle opener.

"There we are." He opened the bottles and placed one down on a coaster in front of her. "I normally stick to tea while I'm working, but you're right: on a day like this, an ice-cold beer really hits the spot."

Kristen picked up the bottle. *"Powderkeg Speak Easy.* According to the label, it's gluten free and vegan. How intriguing. You were influenced by your neighbour, perhaps."

"I don't think so. I just liked the look of it. It's made in Devon."

"So I see." Kristen tipped the bottle to her lips and sipped. "Oh yes. That's good. And how clever of you to keep it in the fridge. Kevin makes a fuss if you tell him to put anything other than lager in the chiller. But it's summer, for God's sake. People want something cold, and you have to give them what they want."

"Ah yes, I heard that you're running the pub now." Following her example, Alan ignored his empty glass and drank from the bottle. "How's it all going?"

"It's all right, I suppose. The whole place needs a thorough remodelling to drag it into the twenty-first century."

Alan chuckled. "The locals won't take to that."

"The locals don't spend enough to keep the place open, so they'll just have to adapt." Kristen looked away, signalling the end of that particular conversation. "Do you see much of your new neighbour? I had the impression you two were as thick as thieves."

"We get along. It's nice to have some male company once in a while."

"As opposed to all your female company?" Her lips curled in a suggestive smile. "Sorry, Alan, I didn't mean to embarrass you. But I hear on the grapevine that you're flavour of the month with the yummy mummy brigade."

"I don't know about that." Alan's cheeks coloured, and he took a quick sip of beer.

"Come on. I mentioned to a few people at work that I'd met you, and they were very interested. They wanted to know all about you."

"I expect their kids like my books, that's all."

"There's more to it than that. An eligible man with a wholesome image and a certain rugged charm is rare enough, but throw in the fact that you're a hit with the kids, and frankly, what's not to like?" She leaned forward a little, lowering her voice. "Naturally, I told them that your author photo doesn't do you justice. *He's much more handsome in real life*, I said."

She looked him in the eye, and Alan found himself returning her frank gaze. "You're too kind, but I have to warn you that I'm highly susceptible to flattery."

"I'm glad to hear it."

They shared a smile, sitting in silence, sipping their drinks.

"Normally, I like to keep a clear head while I'm working," Alan said. "Hemingway wouldn't approve. *Write drunk* was his advice."

"I can't stand Hemingway. Craig likes that kind of thing. He laps it up, but then he has no taste whatsoever."

"Sometimes it takes an effort to appreciate an author's style," Alan said. "Hemingway's work has a certain visceral quality, and there's much to admire in that. After all, he does have an army of dedicated followers. Hemingway, I mean, not your brother."

Kristen's smile slipped. "In that case, we must agree to disagree."

"I'm afraid so." Alan sent her a sympathetic smile. "How is Craig? He must be very worried about the contamination."

"Whatever can you mean?" Kristen said, her tone polite but decidedly frosty. "What contamination is that?"

Alan sat up suddenly as though ice water had been poured down his back. *Why did I say that? Why did I blurt out the one thing I'd wanted to keep under wraps?* He stared at Kristen, his lips moving soundlessly.

"I think you'd better explain," Kristen said.

"I'm sorry, I spoke out of turn. Please, forget I mentioned it. It's between you and your brother. It's none of my business."

"You disappoint me, Alan. I thought you were the kind of man who believed in straight talking. But here you are with something to say, and you're backing away from it. I think it would be better for both of us if you went ahead and said what you have to say."

"All right. In that case, I have to tell you that we know all about the contaminated land. We didn't set out to find it. We weren't trying to poke our noses into your family's affairs, but—"

"We? I presume you mean that Dan is involved."

"Yes. He's helping me to find out what happened to your uncle," Alan said. "As far as the police are concerned, I'm still under suspicion, and if I'm honest, it weighs on my mind."

Kristen's expression softened. "And that does you credit, Alan. I'm sure the police will realise that you're innocent, but you really need to stop and think for a minute. If you go tramping around the spoil heaps, you might jeopardise the investigation. The guilty person might get away with it. Did you think of that?"

"That's exactly what I said to Dan, but he made me see things differently," Alan said. "You see, I really don't think the police are taking the case seriously. They've packed up and gone. You know what it's like; everything's driven by targets. So if it looks as though they aren't going to get a conviction, they focus elsewhere. Mortimer will become just another unexplained death. Would you be happy with that?"

"No, but so long as you aren't implicated, you'd be better off leaving it well alone. If you listen to Dan, you're only going to get yourself into trouble, and I don't want to see that happen."

Alan dropped his gaze. Kristen was probably right. He'd let himself be led on a wild goose chase. It was all right for Dan; he could afford to stir up trouble and then swan off home to London. *He's got nothing to lose*, Alan thought. *But I have to stay here and face the music.*

In a flash of clarity, Alan saw that he'd been fooling himself. It was as if Kristen had woken him from a bad dream. Dan had dragged him into a doomed venture, caring nothing for the consequences. But Kristen was so sympathetic and utterly sincere. He really ought to listen to her. She only wanted what was best for him.

But something nagged at Alan: a stray thought that he'd almost missed. And then he knew.

Alan looked up. "Just now, you said something about me tramping around on the spoil heaps. But I hadn't mentioned them. I'm sure of it."

"You must've done." Kristen favoured him with a generous smile, but when he didn't respond, she added, "Or maybe you didn't say it explicitly, but you were definitely talking about the so-called contamination. I put two and two together."

"All right, but why do you say *so-called?* Is the land contaminated or not?"

"It's only a minor problem. It's nothing that can't be sorted out."

"Really? From what I've found out, I'd guess that the toxic metals have spread right down the side of the valley."

"We can't rely on guesswork," Kristen said. "We're not experts, you and I. There are specialists who deal with this sort of thing. I'm sure Craig will sort it all out. After all, it's his land, not mine."

"But how can he sort it out while Marjorie owns the spoil heaps? As long as they're still there, the metals will leach into the surrounding area."

"Oh, they'll come to an arrangement. Marjorie's a stubborn old thing, but Craig will make her see sense."

Alan thought of Marjorie's demeanour the last time he'd seen her. After losing her precious cat and having her fence vandalised, she was in no mood to cooperate with anyone, least of all with someone who wanted to tear apart the landscape she loved.

Alan opened his mouth to explain this to Kristen, but suddenly she stood, stepping closer to him and laying her hand on his arm. "Your heart's in the right place, Alan, I can see that. You want justice for Mortimer, and I'm grateful for that, I really am. I'm touched."

She was so close that he had to lean back to gaze up at her. "I just want the truth to be found out."

"I know. That's perfectly natural and very noble. But I think the time has come to let the police investigation run its course, don't you? If you interfere, you risk making yourself look suspicious. Do you see what I'm saying?"

"Yes," Alan admitted, his voice heavy. "I'm sure you're right."

Kristen patted him gently on the arm then withdrew her hand. "You're a good man, Alan. I'm sure your honesty and your integrity will shine through. You did your best to help Uncle Morty, and that means a great deal. You're a knight in shining armour."

"No, that's not true," Alan said, but he smiled just the same.

Kristen said nothing for a moment, her gaze lingering on Alan, and a dizzying rush of blood made him suddenly light headed. "Let's change the subject," he began. "Let's talk about something else."

"That would be nice, but I really must be going. I have things to do."

"Oh. Won't you at least finish your drink?"

"I'd better not. It's stronger than I thought." She grinned. "If I didn't know better, I'd say you were trying to get me tipsy in the afternoon."

Alan stood. "I wouldn't dream of it."

"I know," Kristen said. "Before I go, could I use your bathroom?"

"Certainly." He gestured toward the hallway. "It's upstairs. You can't miss it. When you get to the top, go straight ahead. It's the door at the end of the landing."

"I won't be a moment." Kristen strode from the room, and Alan was left staring at his faint reflection in the windowpane. *You're making a fool of yourself,* he thought. *She wouldn't be interested in me—not in that way.* But when he recalled the way she'd smiled at him, a faint hope stirred in his heart, and he crept through to the mirror in the hallway, smoothing down his hair and checking his teeth for stray fragments of food.

Above him, the floorboards creaked, and Alan tilted his head, listening. The old house had a broad repertoire of mysterious sounds that could be conjured up at all hours of the day and night. But this sounded like footsteps, as if Kristen was walking across his bedroom. That couldn't be right. But there it was again. Then he heard the faint squeak of the hinge on his bedroom door. She'd definitely been in his room, but now the footsteps approached the stairs. *She's coming down.* He stepped back from the foot of the stairs, folding his arms and leaning his back against the wall.

Kristen raised her eyebrows just a little when she found him waiting, but her surprise was short lived. "Well, thank you for the drink. It was very kind of you to take so much time, especially when you were hard at work."

"No problem." Alan paused. "Did you find the bathroom okay, or was there some difficulty?"

"Yes. Sorry, but I was admiring the original beams, and I completely forgot what you'd said about the doors. I'm afraid I opened the wrong one by mistake. I think the beer must've gone to my head."

"No harm done," Alan said. "You know, you never said why you came. Was there something specific?"

"No. It was just a social call. I was out for a walk, and I thought I'd pop in and say hello." She lowered her chin, looking up at him through her long lashes. "You don't mind, do you?"

Alan pursed his lips, but his suspicions were already melting away. Kristen had made a simple mistake in an unfamiliar house, that was all; it would be churlish to hold it against her. *Am I being taken for a fool?* he thought, but when she looked at him like that, he pushed his doubts aside. "No, it's fine," he said. "I didn't mean to make you feel uncomfortable. When I'm working, I spend a lot of time on my own. Perhaps it's turning me into a prickly bachelor."

"There's no danger of that. You're a charming host, Alan. A true gentleman."

"Thank you. It was lovely to see you."

Kristen smiled, her perfect teeth nipping the corner of her lower lip. "I was thinking, maybe we could meet up again sometime. I know lots of nice places where we could go for dinner."

"Yes, that would be very nice. But I thought you were interested in... someone else."

"Who?" Kristen laughed. "Ah, you thought I was keen on Dan. He's a nice boy, but I prefer a man with his feet on the ground. These city types think they're better than us, don't they? They just don't get it."

Before Alan could reply, she took his hand in hers and pressed a business card into his palm. "Call me. Soon. We'll go out for dinner, yes?"

"Yes. I will. I'll look forward to it."

Kristen turned away, and in a daze, Alan escorted her to the door. Then she was gone, and the house was suddenly far too quiet. *Did that really just happen?* Alan asked himself. *Did I just get asked out on a date?*

With his mind reeling, he went back to the kitchen. He probably shouldn't, but he was going to finish that beer.

CHAPTER 25

D AN DROPPED HIS shopping on the kitchen counter, then he grabbed the jug of water from the fridge. He poured a large glass and gulped it down, closing his eyes to savour the sensation. It had taken him some time to make Craig see sense, but he'd got there in the end. Now he needed time to think.

Out of habit, Dan took out his phone and checked the screen. There were four missed calls, three of them from Kristen, and a twinge of anxiety pinched at his gut. *A few hours ago, I'd have been thrilled at the prospect of talking to her*, he thought. *But now?* He placed his phone face down on the counter and refilled his glass with water, then he wandered through to the front room.

Gazing out through the window, a sudden sadness came over him. The village seemed so peaceful, but beneath the air of gentle respectability, the tides of drive and desire flowed as powerfully as those that coursed through any city street; the undercurrents of emotion just as deep and just as dark. *All human life is here*, he thought. *Why did I ever think otherwise?*

He thought back to the angst he'd seen in Craig's eyes, the sheer desperation. The man had been driven to the edge of reason, and though some of his troubles were his own fault, caused purely by his greed, someone else had set him on the wrong path and given him a hearty shove in the right direction. Could it have been Kristen? And was he seriously considering the idea that she could've killed Mortimer? That was ridiculous, wasn't it?

How could he know, one way or the other? He had no proof, nothing concrete to rely on, but his intuition latched onto the notion that Kristen had something to hide, and he held it tight.

Outside, as if summoned by his imagination, Kristen appeared in the street. As Dan watched, she half turned to deliver a friendly wave to someone out of sight then, smiling, she strolled away without a care in the world.

"My God," he whispered. "She's been to Alan's house."

Dan froze for a moment, wrestling with the implications of the scene he'd just witnessed, then he headed outside.

I need to go gently, Dan thought as he stalked toward Alan's front door. Alan was a good man, but he could be naïve, and he'd been knocked off balance by the accusations hanging over his head. *Be polite*, Dan told himself. *Don't go charging in.*

But when Alan answered the door with a benign grin on his face, Dan said, "Well, are you going to invite me in or what?"

"Not if you're going to scowl and carry on like a spoilt brat, no."

"I have to come in," Dan insisted. "We need to talk. It's important."

"Oh well, in that case, you'd better come in."

Dan followed Alan through to the kitchen, then they stood, facing each other.

"Right. What's so *important*?" Alan asked.

"I saw Kristen leave. What did she want?"

Alan nodded slowly. "I see. Like that, is it?"

"Like what?"

"You don't like the fact that Kristen called on me, when you so obviously thought you stood a chance with her."

Dan almost laughed. "Do me a favour. I'm not thirteen."

"Then stop being so childish. Honestly, if you could see yourself now: the image of a spurned suitor."

"That's nonsense," Dan insisted. "This has got nothing to do with me. The point is—"

"That a woman like Kristen could never be interested in a man like me, especially not when you're the alternative," Alan interrupted. "You don't have to spell it out; it's written all over your face."

"You're way off beam, Alan. You really are." Dan took a steadying breath. "Look, Kristen is not the person we thought."

"In what way?"

"Craig came to find me earlier. He took me up to some godforsaken forest in his Land Rover, and we had a very strange conversation. It turns out that he didn't inherit Mortimer's land after all."

"So who did?"

"I'm not sure, but I do know that the whole estate is tied up in offshore companies," Dan said. "It seems likely that Kristen has known this fact all along, but she let Craig believe that he'd inherit."

"No, that can't be right," Alan protested. "I did some research, and it seems likely that the land below the spoil heaps *is* contaminated. But when I mentioned it to Kristen, she said it was Craig's problem because it was his land."

"She was putting up a front. I'm sorry to say this, but she's pulled the wool over our eyes all along. She ran Mortimer's business affairs, remember. She knows a lot more than she's letting on. Craig wasn't spinning me a line. The man is in pieces. He's been left with nothing."

Alan pressed his lips together tight. He looked down for a

moment, and when he lifted his head, the animation had gone from his expression. "She lied to me."

"It certainly looks that way. But don't blame yourself. She took us all in." Dan wasn't sure whether he should pat Alan on the arm, so he settled for a reassuring smile. "At least we know the score now. We know that she can't be trusted. And there's something else we have to talk about."

"You think she had something to do with what happened to Mortimer?"

"Yes. We have to consider that possibility."

Alan nodded, but his eyes had lost focus, and he stared into the middle distance, lost.

Someone hammered on the front door.

"I'll get that for you," Dan said. "Whoever it is, I'll get rid of them. Sit down. We'll figure this out."

Dan hurried to the door, but when he opened it, he stared at the two men waiting patiently outside. "DS Spiller. What's going on? What's happened?"

"Afternoon," Spiller said. "Is Mr Hargreaves at home?"

"Yes. Why?"

Spiller gestured toward the hallway. "Mind if we step inside, sir?"

"I'm not sure. Who's your friend?"

"This is DC Collins. We have business with Mr Hargreaves, and we can only discuss it with him personally. So if you wouldn't mind…"

Dan had an urge to send them packing, but the policemen fixed their stares on him, and he could think of no valid excuse. "I suppose you'd better come in," he said. "This way." Dan led the policemen through to the kitchen. "Alan, it's DS Spiller and his colleague."

Alan had taken a seat at the table, but he stood, his eyes pinched with worry. "Hello. What can I do for you?"

"We won't take much of your time, Mr Hargreaves, but would you mind if we take a little look around the place?"

"Why?" Dan asked. "What's this about?"

"We're acting on information received," Spiller replied, keeping his attention on Alan. "As part of our investigation into Mr Gamble's unexplained death, we'd like to take a look around the house if that's all right."

"I'm not sure," Alan said. "Are you talking about a search? Don't you need a warrant or something?"

Spiller looked thoughtful as though giving the matter careful consideration. "Not necessarily. But let's not get bogged down in the technicalities. We're asking for a little cooperation, and that always makes things go so much easier."

"But what are you looking for?" Dan said. "This is outrageous."

Spiller turned on him. "This is a matter for Mr Hargreaves, sir. I'd be grateful if you'd let us do our job. I'm sure you wouldn't want to hinder a police inquiry." He paused. "Is that what you're trying to do, Mr Corrigan? Are we going to have words, you and I?"

"There's no need for arguments," Alan said. "Just tell me what you're looking for, and I'll try to help."

Spiller sent Dan a superior smile, then he turned his gaze on Alan. "As I said, we're acting on information received, and we have reasonable grounds to suspect that there's material in this house that could be pertinent to our inquiry. Now, it could be nothing. A quick look around the house might tie the whole thing up, and then we can all go about our business. But if you really object, I have to warn you that I can search without a warrant if you've been arrested. It's a question of protecting evidence, you see. So if you want to go down that route, that's fine with me. On the other hand, if our information proves to be false, there'll be no evidence to retrieve and no need for an arrest. Do you follow?"

Alan heaved a sigh. "All right. You can have a look around. I can't see the harm."

"Not a good idea," Dan said. "I don't like this, Alan. I don't like it at all."

"I know," Alan replied. "But I've got nothing to hide. Go ahead, DS Spiller. What do you want to see?"

Spiller smiled. "Thank you, sir." He nodded to his colleague. "We'll start upstairs."

"Upstairs?" Alan's face fell. "Why would you want to go upstairs?"

"It's just routine, sir." Spiller led the way, Collins hard on his heels.

"We'd better go with them," Dan said. "We need to keep an eye on them."

"Right."

They hurried up the stairs and found the policemen in Alan's bedroom.

"Very neat," Spiller said. "Very tidy. Everything in its place." He pointed to a pine chest of drawers. "What's in here, sir?"

"Clothes," Alan replied. "Socks, T-shirts. Nothing out of the ordinary."

Strolling across the room, Spiller pulled open the top drawer. "As you say, socks." He paused. "And also, something else. DC Collins, can you come over here and confirm this?"

Collins joined Spiller in peering into the drawer. "Shall I bag it, Sarge?"

"Oh yes," Spiller replied. "Bag it very carefully, Collins."

Alan started forward, but Spiller raised his hand to halt him. "Mr Hargreaves, do you own a gold watch?"

"No."

"Then can you explain how this item came to be in your possession?" Spiller gestured toward the drawer, and Collins held up a plastic evidence bag containing a gold wristwatch.

"I've never seen that before in my life," Alan spluttered. "Never!"

"I'm afraid that's not the most original response," Spiller intoned. "But you have just seen me discover it in your drawer. It looks like quite a valuable watch, and I have reason to believe that it belonged to the late Mr Gamble. So I ask again: can you explain how it came to be in your possession?"

"Kristen," Alan said. "Mortimer's niece. She was in here just a little while ago. She must've put it there."

Dan stared at him. "She was in your bedroom?"

"She dropped in, and we had a drink, then she asked to use the bathroom. I stayed downstairs, but I heard her come in here. The floorboards creak."

"There you are then," Dan said. "There's your explanation, Spiller. Kristen set him up. I'll bet your informant was a woman, yes?"

Spiller shook his head. "That's DS Spiller to you, sir. I don't have to explain myself to you, but as it happens, our information came from a man: a local, from his accent." He focused on Alan. "Well, Mr Hargreaves, there's nothing for it. I'll have to ask you to come with me for a formal interview under caution."

"But I've already told you how the watch got there," Alan groaned. "I've got nothing more to add."

"Perhaps, but as I've already explained, under the circumstances, I could arrest you," Spiller replied. "It would be a lot better if you'd come along voluntarily. If I have to make an arrest..." He shrugged. "I'll be honest, I'm pretty booked up for the rest of the day, so we might have to hold you overnight and carry out your interview in the morning. Although it is Saturday tomorrow, so things could get held up."

Alan's shoulders slumped. "I really don't have much choice, do I. Okay, I'll come with you, but I'll need to call my solicitor."

"That would be wise," Spiller replied. "Let's go. The sooner we get this resolved, the better for everyone."

They made their way downstairs, and in the hallway, Dan said, "I'll think of something, Alan. There must be some way I can prove that Kristen did this."

"The best way to help your friend is to stay out of trouble," Spiller said. "We may have some questions for you further down the line, Mr Corrigan, so I'd keep my nose clean if I were you."

Dan nodded, but as he followed the others into the street and watched Alan being led to an unmarked car, he made his mind up. He was going to make sure Kristen couldn't get away with this. He was going to make her pay for what she'd done.

CHAPTER 26

B ACK AT HOME, Dan grabbed his phone and paced the kitchen as he made a call to an old friend. Joshua Gifford made it a rule to keep a phone within reach at all times, and he answered immediately: "Dan, what's up?"

"Nothing much, Josh. Just calling to catch up. How are things?"

"Not bad. Not bad at all." A pause. "It's good to hear from you, Dan, but where the hell have you been? I heard you'd dropped off the map."

"Taking a bit of time out. Recharging my batteries."

"Try a triple espresso, that works for me." Josh chuckled. "Seriously though, I called you a couple of times, and you never got back to me. Are you all right?"

"Sorry not to have been in touch sooner. I'm fine. I'm out in the sticks, miles from anywhere. Not much connectivity."

"Sounds dreadful. When are you coming back to civilisation? You owe me a rematch at the squash court."

"I'm not sure. I'm helping my sister with a property she has out here. She's still in the States, so I'm looking after her cottage. Nice little place."

"Okay. Well, I'm guessing you didn't really just call to chat about nothing in particular. What can I do for you?"

Dan took a steadying breath and forced himself to smile. "Rumbled. As it happens, there is something you can help me with, and it's right up your street."

"Ah. A property deal in the offing? Something juicy?"

"Possibly. But it needs someone with an expert eye to look it over."

"And if I help you out, you'll give me a slice of the action?"

"If it pans out, sure," Dan said. "But it's only fair to warn you that this deal needs to be kept under wraps. We need to demonstrate due diligence, but we can't afford to shout about it. If you could make some discreet inquiries, that would be great. But this has to be kept between ourselves."

"Understood," Josh replied. "You know me: discretion guaranteed."

"Thanks, Josh. The company involved is based offshore. It's called Mertonic Holdings."

"Spell that."

"M, E, R, and then tonic as in gin."

"Got it." Josh paused. "I'll get the ball rolling, and I'll email you as soon as I can get the details together. I take it you want the finances breaking down?"

"Yes, but I'd also like some background on the owners, board of directors, senior management. You know the drill."

"Dan, don't take this the wrong way, but is there something you're not telling me?"

"No. It's just a deal that came my way, and I wasn't sure if it was worth pursuing. There may be nothing in it, but if there is…"

"I'm the man to find it. Fair enough. Leave it with me, Dan. I'll get back to you soon."

"Thanks. I appreciate it."

"No problem. Bye."

MICHAEL CAMPLING

Josh hung up, and Dan stared at his phone until the screen darkened, glowering at his reflection on the smoky glass. Josh wasn't a close friend, but they'd known each other for years, and the lies had left a bitter taste in Dan's mouth. *Needs must when the devil drives*, he thought. *If I'd told him the truth, he'd have run a mile.* As it was, there was no guarantee that Josh would uncover a link between Mertonic Holdings and Kristen, but it had to be worth a try.

Time to stir things up a bit, Dan told himself, waking his phone and scrolling through his contacts. He selected Jay's number, and as the call connected, Dan stiffened his resolve. He couldn't entirely trust Jay, but for the plan Dan had in mind, he'd need help. And since Alan was out of action for a while, there wasn't much choice.

Jay answered the call. "Is that Dan?"

"Yes. I need a word."

"If it's about the quote, I've almost got it ready. I've priced all the materials, but I could really do with coming around and measuring up."

"Fine. We'll get to that later. Actually, I called for something else."

"Oh, aye. What's that then?"

"There are a couple of things," Dan replied. "First, I wondered if you could confirm something for me. On the night Mortimer was attacked—"

"Are you still going on about that?" Jay interrupted. "You're like a dog with a bone."

"And that's just as well, especially since the police have just dragged Alan in for questioning again."

"Ah. That's the third time. It sounds serious."

"It is. Someone planted something of Mortimer's in Alan's house, then they called Spiller. He knew exactly where to find it."

Jay cursed under his breath. "All right, you've got my attention. What can we do to help him out?"

"For a start, you can think back to that Friday, and tell me if you saw Kristen Ellington in the pub at any time during that evening."

"Definitely. Let's face it, you can't miss her. She was there early on. In fact, I think she was already there when I arrived, but she left quite soon afterwards."

"And did she come back at all?"

"Nope. I'd have noticed if she'd reappeared. Why do you ask?"

"It could be important," Dan said. "Did you happen to see whether she was carrying anything when she left?"

"Like what?" Jay let out a dry chuckle. "Don't tell me you think it was her that laid Mortimer out. That's just daft."

"Is it? How can you be so sure?"

"A woman like that doesn't get her hands dirty. But if you really want to know, yes, I did see her leave, and no, she wasn't wielding a large stick at the time."

"And she *definitely* didn't come back to the bar?" Dan asked.

"No. I told you. I was there all night. I was the last to leave. It was past midnight by the time they kicked me out."

"I didn't know that." Dan paused, thinking. "How come you left so late? The pub was almost empty when Alan and me headed for home."

"I was chatting to Sam. You know, she works in the kitchen."

"I see. Isn't she a bit young for you?"

Jay grunted. "Behave yourself. It's not like that. We were having a chat, that's all. I've got no reason to rush home, so sometimes she lets me take my time over my last pint, and I keep her company while she finishes up. Truth be told, she puts up with me hanging around because she doesn't like being stuck in the pub on her own. Who would? It's a gloomy old place when the punters have all gone home."

"She told me that Kevin left her to clean up alone. Is that right?"

"It is," Jay said. "Kev had nipped out for a smoke. He's a work-shy sod, plain and simple; too lazy to get out of his own way."

"I got that impression," Dan said. "Listen, can I ask you another question?"

"Go ahead."

"You've got your ear to the ground in this village. Have you heard anything about the vandalism at Marjorie Treave's house?"

"No. What's happened?"

"Somebody smashed up her fence, and they might have killed her cat."

"Bloody hell!" Jay blurted. "Unbelievable. Bastards!"

"Calm down, Jay. It was very upsetting for Marjorie, but I didn't have you down as an animal lover."

"I'm not bothered about her moggy. I suppose it's sad for her, but that's not the point. I spent ages on that bloody fence. And someone's smashed it? Why, for God's sake?"

"I think someone's trying to intimidate her," Dan said. "The more I think about it, the more I'm sure that Mortimer left her that strip of land on purpose. It's a ransom strip. She's in the way, and someone wants her to sell up and move out."

"You've lost me," Jay admitted. "I don't know anything about Marjorie's land, but I've got a feeling you might be right about some sort of intimidation going on. It certainly wouldn't be kids breaking stuff for the hell of it. The youngsters around here wouldn't dare do anything to upset Marge. She knows all their names, and she knows their families. Heck, she's related to half of them."

"I see. Then it's all starting to come together. The pattern is emerging." Dan took a breath. "Okay. Now we come to the important part."

"Go on. Let's hear it."

"I want you to go to the pub this evening and prop up the bar. I'll pay for your drinks all night."

"So far, I'm liking this idea. I ran out of painkillers for my hand this morning, and I've been climbing the walls ever since. Maybe the promise of a few free pints will see me through." Jay chuckled darkly. "What's the catch? And don't tell me there isn't one, or I'll hang up."

"It's nothing much. I just want you to spread a rumour. Nothing too outrageous."

"Go on."

"You can start off by saying that Alan has been taken in for questioning, which is true," Dan said. "But then I want you to tell anyone who'll listen that I've gone down to the spoil heaps. Say that I've found some evidence, and I can prove once and for all who killed Mortimer."

"Sounds a bit far fetched. I don't know if I can say that with a straight face. No one will believe it."

"One person will," Dan said. "We don't know who attacked Mortimer, but whoever it is, they'll have to take this seriously. There's always a chance that they left some clue behind, so if they think I've discovered something vital, they can't afford to ignore it. You can dress it up a bit, make it sound urgent. Tell them the police will be turning up at any moment. I need the killer to be rattled."

A pause. "What if they don't get to hear the story in time?"

"They'll hear about it. Rumours go through this village like wildfire. Don't forget the fact that Alan's hiking stick was planted to leave a false trail; it suggests a strong link between the attacker and the pub. But if my plan doesn't work, all I'll lose is some time. I'll spend an evening hanging around on the spoil heaps for no good reason, but it has to be worth it. If it pays off, I'll know who killed Mortimer for sure."

"Has it occurred to you that when this character shows

up, they might take unkindly to being led up the garden path?"

"Yes, but if it's Kristen, I can handle her."

"And if it isn't? If it's a gang of thugs with baseball bats?"

"Then I'll stay out of sight and take some photos," Dan said. "At the very least, I'll be able to offer the police some alternative suspects."

"Ah well, it's your funeral. And you'll pay for my drinks all night? Are you sure about that?"

"Within reason," Dan replied. "Listen, you mentioned painkillers. Is that an issue? I don't want to—"

"Nothing I can't handle," Jay interrupted. "Anyway, since we lined up that bit of work, I've been doing all right. It's kept my mind busy, given me something to aim for. I feel more like my old self."

"That's good. But maybe you'd better take it easy on the beer."

"You needn't worry about that. I can handle my beer, and I'll do my part. The rumour mill will commence operations straight after opening time. Anything else?"

"No," Dan said. "I think that ought to do it."

"Good luck. Let me know how it turns out, and if it goes south, call me. I can bang a few heads together if necessary."

"Thanks. I'll bear that in mind."

"All right. I'll see you around." Jay hung up, and Dan sat down at the table. *Unless it all goes south*, he thought. *In which case, I'll be stuck in the middle of nowhere, facing a desperate killer.* But he couldn't see another way to uncover the real perpetrator. His plan would have to work.

CHAPTER 27

A T SIX O'CLOCK, Dan called Alan's landline, but there was no reply. *He hasn't come back yet*, Dan decided. But he knew that already; he'd been keeping a careful eye on the road. *Why is Spiller keeping him for so long?* he wondered. But there was something else nagging at Dan's mind. Until that moment, he hadn't realised how much he depended on Alan's steadying presence. Alan had his feet firmly on the ground, and he knew his own mind. He was someone who could be relied upon. Faced with an unknown danger, there was no one Dan would rather have at his back.

But Dan couldn't wait. Soon, Jay would turn up at the pub and begin baiting the trap. Dan had to be in position in plenty of time, so there was only one thing he could do. Dan headed out alone, striding along Fore Street, his mind fixed on the task ahead. But when his phone rang in his pocket, he stopped walking. *It must be Alan*, he thought, fumbling for his phone. But the screen showed Josh's name.

"Josh, how are you?"

A pause, and Dan recognised the hollow symphony of discordant noise that could only come from the London Underground, the sounds strangely unreal when heard from the stillness of the quiet village. When Josh spoke, his voice was strained, hoarse with repressed urgency: "Dan, listen, this is a bit awkward, but if I didn't owe you a favour, I wouldn't even be making this call."

"Why? What's the problem?"

"That company—the one you asked about—you're not already involved with them, are you?"

"No. Like I said, I heard about a deal and wanted to check it out, that's all."

"Thank God for that. But Dan, I'm not going to look into this anymore, and neither should you. Stay well away from this deal and anyone involved in it."

"Okay, but what's wrong? What have you found?" Dan waited, but there was no reply. "Josh, are you still there? I think you're losing signal."

"I'm here," Josh said. "But there are a lot of people around, and…"

"Josh?"

On the phone, the background noise faded, and then Josh said, "I found somewhere quieter, but even so, I don't want to talk about this for long, Dan. After today, I'm never going to discuss it again. All I'll say is this: the company you mentioned is a shell, and beyond that it gets very murky very quickly. I've been around long enough to know the score, so listen up. Whatever this deal is, however good it sounds, walk away from it. Delete any reference to that company from your phone, your computers, everything. And when I say delete, I mean erase it as securely as you can."

"Okay, I'll do that." Dan took a breath. "But what are we talking about? Is this some kind of corporate fraud?"

"No. This is… hang on."

Dan waited, instinctively glancing over his shoulder, a vague sense of unease creeping over him, sweat prickling his scalp. Then Josh spoke again, his voice little more than a murmur. "These people are criminals, and I don't mean the kind that wear white collars, Dan. We're talking about organised crime. You don't want to know about them, and neither do I. So do yourself a favour, and put as much distance between them and you as you can. Got it?"

Dan's mouth was dry, but he managed to say, "Yes. Thanks for the warning. I owe you one."

"Forget it. I know you'd do the same for me." Josh paused. "Call me when you get back to town, but not for a few weeks, yeah? Give my blood pressure a chance to normalise."

"Will do."

"Okay, I've got to dash. But, Dan, watch out for yourself. I don't know what you've been getting yourself into, but this isn't like you. You were always the careful one. What were you thinking?"

"I don't know, Josh. Just a moment of madness. Maybe I'm going stir crazy out here."

"I'm not surprised. You can't run a formula one car on diesel, Dan. You need to be in the city, where you belong, and you'll soon get your edge back. A few days in the Smoke, and you'll never know you've been away."

"Maybe. You're probably right."

"No maybe about it. Okay, bye, Dan."

"Bye," Dan said, but Josh had already ended the call. *Hell's teeth*, Dan thought. *Organised crime! What have I done?* But it was too late to back down. He'd set events in motion, and now he must hold tight as they unfolded. He'd done his best to imagine all the possible scenarios that might play out over the next few hours, but whatever happened, there was a good chance that he'd finally get to confront Mortimer's murderer. Alan would be free, the guilty parties would be brought to book, and justice would be done. *I'll just have to go for it*, he told himself. *The prize is worth the risk.*

Stiffening his spine, Dan resumed his route, not slowing his pace until he turned from the public footpath to head directly for the spoil heaps. Here, the chest-high bracken tugged at his arms and legs as if trying to hold him back. But Dan waded through it, pushing the fibrous fronds aside, lifting his gaze to scan the gravelly grey slopes towering above him.

There was a gruesome architecture to this man-made eyesore. Over time, the rain had worn a network of serpentine channels through the sterile earth, but little else marked the surface of these barren slopes. They were a stark reminder of a harder time: oppressive monuments to humanity's rapacious greed.

Dan clambered onto the crumbling foothills, and he knew that he was exposed, visible to anyone approaching from the path. But that was what he wanted. Dan needed the killer to see him, to feel confident that he was on his own. If it looked like a trap, the murderer would stay hidden, watching from a distance. Dan couldn't afford for that to happen. It was only a matter of time before his flimsy fiction would fall apart. He needed the guilty party to throw caution to the wind, to rush in and face him. Seeing him alone and vulnerable on the spoil heaps, the killer would seize the chance to silence him. But Dan would be ready. The murderer would be off balance and agitated. So long as Dan kept his head, he could control the situation. He was sure of it.

Almost.

Dan took a look back toward the path, then he dug his heels into the yielding earth and set off, trudging diagonally up the slope. His leg muscles were tense, but he held his head high. He was ready.

CHAPTER 28

IN THE WILD Boar, Jay leaned over the bar, searching for someone to serve him. He'd been busy, spreading the rumour that Dan had solved Mortimer's murder, and all that talking had left him with a powerful thirst. Craning his neck to peer into the pub's small kitchen, he caught a glimpse of movement and called out, "Kev, any chance of getting served? I've been waiting for ages."

"Just a minute," someone replied, and though the voice was a woman's, it didn't sound like Sam.

Jay tilted his head to one side. In the kitchen, someone was having an argument. He caught fragments of words, the tone strident, but he couldn't make out what was being said. He watched, waiting, old instincts being rekindled. But he couldn't stand by and do nothing.

Jay strode over to the end of the bar and pushed the hinged section upward, but before he could step through, a figure appeared to face him.

"Can I help you with something?" Kristen asked, her eyes locked on his.

"I was just looking for Kev, trying to get another pint."

Slowly, Jay lowered the bar and stepped back. "Where is he, anyway?"

"He's out the back," Kristen replied. "But I can get you a drink. What would you like?"

"You? Pull a pint?" Jay almost laughed. "That'll be the day."

Kristen's expression showed no flicker of amusement. "Would you like a drink or not?"

"All right then. I'll have a pint of Dartmoor Best."

"Certainly." She snatched a glass from the shelf and hunted for the correct pump.

"It's in that keg behind you," Jay said. "It's the guest ale."

"I know that. I just forgot for a minute." Kristen regarded the keg with suspicion, then she leaned into the kitchen door. "Sam, can you come and deal with this, please?"

"Hang on," Sam called out, then she appeared in the doorway wiping her hands on a towel. "What's up?"

Kristen handed her the glass. "Could you serve this gentleman his pint of Dartmoor Best? I have some figures I want to go over."

"Right. No problem." Sam began pouring the beer, concentrating on the glass.

"So, what's happened to Kevin then?" Jay asked. "Sloped off for a smoke again, has he?"

Without looking up, Sam said, "He's gone out to chop some wood for the fire. On a boiling hot day like this. I reckon he's finally cracked."

Kristen had been on the point of walking away, but she turned on her heel. "Sam, what have I told you about gossiping with the customers? Kevin hasn't gone for firewood. That would be ridiculous. Just give the man his drink and take his money, that's all that's required."

"All right, no need to go through all that again." Sam placed the pint in front of Jay. "Give me a second to figure out this new till. Kev was meant to show me, but he never got around to it, and it's different to the shop."

She studied the till, her eyebrows lowered, then she jabbed at a button. "Oh, that can't be right."

"I can pay Kev when he gets back if you like." Jay took a sip of his drink, and from the corner of his eye, he watched Kristen flounce from the bar. He leaned a little closer to Sam. "What made you think Kev had gone out to get firewood?"

"I didn't say he was going to *get* some wood, I said he was going to chop it." Sam rolled her eyes. "I don't know why Kristen was arguing about it. I mean, what else would he be doing with that bloody great axe?"

Jay put his glass down heavily, beer slopping onto the polished bar. "What?"

"Yeah. Just now, Kev had an awful row with Ms High-and-mighty, then he stomped off with a face like thunder. I saw him outside. I was by the back window, and Kev had an axe over his shoulder. He was marching off down the alley."

"Bloody hell!" Jay fixed Sam with a look. "I want you to call the police. Dial 999. Tell them they need to send someone to the spoil heaps right away. Tell them to pass the message on to a DS Spiller at Exeter HQ."

"Why?"

"Just do it, Sam."

"I can dial 999, but they'll want to know what it's about. What shall I say?"

"Tell them there's a fight going on. Say it's serious. Life or death. Have you got it?"

Sam nodded. "I think so. 999. Fight on the spoil heaps. DS Spiller from Exeter."

"Good. Make the call now, Sam. I've got to go." Jay headed for the door. Outside, he checked the alley down the side of the pub, but there was no sign of Kevin, and the street was empty. How could he have got away so fast?

Jay had no idea whether Kevin owned a car, but he'd

certainly got a head start. *I could go and get my truck,* Jay thought. *Or maybe someone in the pub would give me a lift.* But time was short, and the spoil heaps weren't all that far away. There was nothing for it. Jay took a breath, then he started running along Fore Street. If he was quick, he'd be there in a few minutes. He just had to hope that he'd be in time.

CHAPTER 29

A LAN SHIFTED UNCOMFORTABLY in his seat. It was hot in the windowless interview room, and the stifling air was heavy with stale sweat. Alan needed a break. He needed to stretch his legs and get a cold drink. But DS Spiller was in no hurry to leave. He seemed content to sit opposite Alan, his expression blank, while they went over the same ground again and again.

"Are we nearly done?" Alan asked.

"That depends," Spiller said. "We'll see what DC Collins comes up with. In the meantime, do you need anything? Tea?"

"I've had enough tea to sink a battleship. I just want to get this over with."

Spiller's only reply was a thin and humourless smile.

The minutes ticked by, and Alan stared at the table that sat between them, its surface scuffed and chipped, its edges worn. *How long have I been in here?* he wondered. *Why hasn't a solicitor turned up yet?*

Alan had phoned his solicitor's office earlier, calling from his mobile during the journey from Embervale. But when he'd arrived at the police station, the only thing that had been waiting for him was a message: His solicitor was away for the weekend, and it would be some time before a replacement could be arranged. Alan had waited, but as the long afternoon had slipped into the evening, he'd opted to press ahead with the interview, hoping to clear up the whole business as quickly as possible.

Since then, he'd regretted his rash decision on at least a dozen separate occasions. But every time he'd asked for the interview to be halted, Spiller had somehow talked him into staying put.

Behind Alan, the door opened, and DC Collins bustled into the room, a sheet of paper in his hands. Collins paid no attention to Alan, but as he handed the paper to Spiller, a guarded look passed between the two policemen.

Alan sat up straight, waiting, but while Collins took a seat at his superior's side, Spiller focused his attention on the paper.

"Well?" Alan asked. "Are you going to tell me what's so important?"

Spiller sniffed. "Yes. But first, tell me why you wiped Mr Gamble's watch clean before you hid it in your drawer."

"I've already explained all this," Alan said. "I have never seen that watch before. Kristen Ellington planted it at my house in order to incriminate me."

And for once, Spiller didn't argue. Instead, he nodded slowly. "You see, it's odd for a forensic examination to find absolutely no fingerprints whatsoever on something like this. It's as if the watch has been very carefully cleaned. But in my experience, if somebody takes something as a trophy, it's because they want to treasure it, to own it, to touch it. Yet there it was, pristine."

"Kristen must've wiped it before she left it," Alan said.

"Perhaps," Spiller replied. "That would be one explanation."

"His room was very neat and tidy," Collins chipped in.

"He seems like a very careful man, so he might've cleaned the watch himself."

"Mm. But there's something else that doesn't quite fit." Spiller gazed at Alan. "We've checked the records from the hospital, and when Mr Gamble was brought in, he was wearing a watch. A digital watch. An old Casio with a plastic strap." He paused. "Did you ever know a man to wear two watches, Mr Hargreaves?"

"No," Alan said. "Never."

"Me neither," Spiller said. "So DC Collins rang Mr Gamble's nephew, and made some inquiries."

Alan was on the edge of his seat. "And?"

"You tell him," Spiller said to Collins.

DC Collins took his time, pursing his lips and letting the tension thicken the air. Then finally, he said, "According to Craig Ellington, Mortimer Gamble valued that watch highly. It was a gift, given to Mortimer by his father. A twenty-first birthday present. He wore it as a young man, but in later years, Mortimer feared he might damage it. So he kept the watch in an old cash box in his house. And he kept that box locked."

Alan licked his lips. "So, does that mean..." He couldn't finish the question.

"We'll have to wait and see," Spiller said. "But very few people would've known where that watch was kept, and as far as we can tell, only one person has the key to that cash box."

"Kristen Ellington?" Alan asked.

"Kristen Ellington." Spiller sat back. "Would you like a lift back home, Mr Hargreaves?"

Alan swallowed hard. "Yes. Yes please. That would be very nice."

∽

THEY SPOKE little in the car on the way to Embervale, and Alan was content to look out the window, enjoying the familiar scenery with a fresh eye.

Spiller's phone chirruped into life, and he pressed a button on the car's dashboard to take the call hands free.

Fancy, Alan thought. *I should get one of those*. He grinned to himself. But as he listened to the call, his smile vanished.

"Bloody hell!" Spiller muttered, and gripping the wheel tight, he sent the car racing along the lane.

CHAPTER 30

D AN RAN HIS hand across his brow. The day's heat still lingered, as if the afternoon's sunshine had soaked into the spoil heaps and was only now being released. Pacing back and forth across the sweltering slopes, Dan had worked up a sweat. He gazed back toward the village. But there was no one on the path, no one hurrying through the bracken, and when he strained his ears, he could hear no cars approaching. Even the distant whisper of traffic from the main road had vanished. It felt as though he was the last man on the planet.

What's taking so long? he thought. *Someone ought to have turned up by now.* But perhaps his plan hadn't worked. He'd guessed that the killer was somebody local, somebody affected, directly or indirectly, by Mortimer's will. But he could be completely wrong. And even if he was right, there was no guarantee that the guilty party would be drawn into the open so easily.

The killer had gone to great lengths to incriminate Alan. But Dan had no idea who'd taken Alan's stick, and he couldn't be sure that Kristen had planted the watch. She'd played a part, but perhaps she'd been following instructions. Josh's warning about the involvement of serious criminals had shaken Dan's theories apart. The game had altered. Something bigger than one man's death was at stake, and Dan had rolled the dice without knowing the rules.

I shouldn't have relied on Jay to bait the trap, Dan decided. The man was decidedly unsubtle, and if he'd overplayed his part, even a little, the killer might have seen straight through the subterfuge. Perhaps the murderer had simply decided to make a run for it. Only time would tell.

Dan clenched his jaw. It was beginning to look as if he was in for a long wait.

He looked over at Marjorie's cottage. If she was in, she might let him have a cold drink. He'd come unprepared, and his throat was dry, his lips coated with the spoil heaps' dust. The image of a tall glass of ice-cold water loomed large in his mind; he could almost feel the cool liquid slipping down his throat.

It'll only take me a couple of minutes to go to Marjorie's and back, he told himself. *I can keep an eye on this place from there.* He cast a quick glance along the public footpath, but there was no one in sight, so Dan turned toward Marjorie's house and started walking.

When he reached cottage's front door, he half-expected Marjorie to appear before he could knock, her arms folded and her expression forbidding. But the door remained closed, and his knock brought no answer. While he waited, he checked his watch. Time was ticking away, and if he couldn't get a drink, he ought to head back to his lonely vigil.

He knocked again, then he stepped back to look up at the windows. Perhaps Marjorie was upstairs. If so, it would take her a while to get to the door, even though she was faster on her feet than most people her age.

Fast on her feet. The phrase had a particular resonance, although he couldn't say why. He dropped his gaze. Yes, that was it. Beside the door, a row of shoes and boots had been laid neatly along the wall; no doubt they were for outdoor use only and not allowed onto the pristine tiles of Marjorie's kitchen. Sheltered by the overhanging porch, the footwear would be ready when needed. *You can tell a lot about a person by their shoes*, Dan thought. Marjorie's meagre collection of boots and shoes were sturdy and weatherproof, built to last. They'd been cleaned and polished, the laces replaced, and if he picked them up and examined them more closely, he'd expect to see repairs had been made over the years.

But still, something was bothering Dan; a stray thought tugging at the edges of his consciousness. *Shoes.*

And Dan's eyes opened wide. *Kevin!* He'd noticed the landlord's unusual trainers on the night Mortimer had been killed. He'd known straight away that those shoes weren't made for running. *What brand were they?* He clutched at the memory, but he'd only seen the shoes for a moment when Kevin had stepped out from behind the bar, and by that time Dan had downed several pints. Now, the recollection evaded him, the image blurring, shifting in his mind. *I'd know those shoes if I saw them again*, he thought, and grabbing his phone from his pocket, he opened a browser, his fingers moving fast over the screen. But the search engine refused to load. *No signal!* He wasn't even getting one bar, so there was no hope for any kind of internet access.

But it didn't matter. The memory was crystallising, and Dan recalled with startling clarity the four letters emblazoned on the side of Kevin's shoes. That brand of footwear could only have been made for one purpose.

And he knew exactly what that meant.

Turning on his heel, Dan jogged back to Marjorie's garden gate. He had to get back to the village. He had to find a way to summon help. He knew Kevin was guilty, felt it in his bones, but he was by no means certain that he could tackle him on his own.

The public footpath was just across the road. It would only take him a few minutes to get back to the village. If he met

Kevin on the way, he'd stay out of reach, double back, run like hell. He could make it.

But as Dan raced across the tarmac, he caught a sudden movement from the corner of his eye: a dark shape, taller than a man, hurtling toward him. He half turned, and in that moment, something slammed into him, lifting him from the ground. In slow motion, he saw his feet rise up above him, his legs waving absurdly against the summer evening sky. Somewhere beneath him, metal rattled, scraping across the tarmac with a juddering clatter. Then Dan hit the ground hard, pain arcing from his shoulders to the base of his spine. A flash of white light blazed across Dan's vision, swallowing his senses. He opened his mouth to cry out, but a great weight pressed him down, squeezing the air from his lungs. Someone was on top of him, and Dan lashed out blindly with both fists, his knuckles meeting a mass of muscle and bone. But as his vision cleared, his wrists were grabbed tight, his arms pinned down, pressed hard against the road.

"Stay down," Kevin snarled, his scowling mouth pressed close, and Dan felt the man's hot breath washing over his cheeks. Kevin bared his teeth, his eyes burning with cold fury, and a guttural roar rose from his throat. "You stupid bastard!" he yelled. "This is your own fault. You shouldn't have interfered."

Dan met his wild stare. "I knew it was you. I *knew* it. If I can work it out, so can everybody else. Give it up, Kevin. It's finished."

"You're lying. I'm not stupid. You know nothing."

"Are you sure about that?" Dan demanded. "Because I know you came here last Friday to find Mortimer Gamble. I know you pretended to go out for a smoke, but as soon as you were outside, you used a mountain bike to ride the long way around the lane. You must've been fast, just like today. What is it, electrically assisted?"

"Shut up," Kevin snapped, but Dan took no notice.

"Your shoes gave you away, Kevin. They're *Giro*, aren't they. That marks you out as a serious rider. Then there were the tyre prints where you leaned your bike against Marjorie's fence." Dan turned his head to one side, and there was the mountain bike lying on the road. "I thought so. Fat tyres, twenty-nine-inch wheels." He looked Kevin in the eye. "Why did you do it, Kevin? I know Kristen called the shots, but what did she promise you?"

"Shut your mouth, you cocky bastard, before I shut it for you."

"Was it just a question of money? Or did she come on to you?" A muscle twitched in Kevin's cheek, and Dan knew he'd hit a nerve. "Seriously, Kevin, what did you think? That she was going to ride off into the sunset with you? Or did you picture her pulling pints in the pub?"

"That's enough! You've got no idea what you're talking about. Kristen and me understand each other."

Dan raised his eyebrows. "She understands you, all right. But face it, man, she's out of your league and you know it. She's used you, that's all. You're a means to an end. A hired hand. When she's finished with you, she'll toss you aside."

The punch came out of nowhere, a vicious swipe that connected with Dan's cheekbone and jerked his head back against the road. Pain sizzled through Dan's skull, his ears ringing, but he pushed the sensations aside.

Kevin's weight was suddenly gone, and Dan rolled over, planting his hands on the road and struggling to his feet. Kevin was bent over his bike, his hands moving quickly over the frame. But as Dan stepped back, Kevin turned on him, a long-handled axe clutched in his grip.

"Hold on, Kevin," Dan said. "Don't be stupid. You're not going to do anything with that axe. Put it down."

Kevin advanced on him, brandishing the axe, the blade swinging back and forth in front of Dan's eyes. Closer and closer. "I told you," he muttered. "I told you to stay down."

"Listen," Dan started, but Kevin didn't give him a chance to speak.

"No. I've had it up to here with your smug bullshit. All I want to hear from you is one thing. What did you find?" He raised the axe, his thick fingers twisting tight on its handle. "Talk, Corrigan. Don't try to wriggle your way out of this. Tell me the truth or you'll pay for it."

"There's nothing to tell," Dan said. "I found nothing. It was a trick."

"What?"

"I wanted to force the killer's hand, to flush him out of hiding." Dan tried for a careless shrug. "I guess you could say it worked, but I didn't figure on you turning up. Not until it was too late, anyway."

Kevin shook his head very slowly. "You're lying."

"I'm really not. I made up the story about finding new evidence, and I sent Jay to the pub to spread it around. That's where you heard about my so-called discovery, wasn't it? Jay must've done his job well. I must remember to thank him." Dan smiled. "Admit it, Kevin. You've been played, and you've lost. I fooled you, and Kristen, well, she just used you."

Without warning, Kevin brought the axe down hard, slicing the air. Dan flinched, but the blade skimmed past his face, millimetres from his head. "Bloody hell!" Dan shuffled back, every muscle in his body tensed, ready for action. He had to escape, to get away, even if he was wounded in the process. If he stayed put, Kevin would kill him. It was as simple as that.

Kevin stepped closer to him, levelling the axe. "That's your final warning. Say one more thing against Kristen, and I'll take your head from your shoulders and leave you in the ditch. Got it?"

Dan nodded.

"Now, tell me what you found on the spoil heaps," Kevin

went on. "There must've been something. You wouldn't spread a story like that and then come out here alone. That'd be plain daft. You'd have to be a fool to risk it."

"What can I say?"

Kevin stared at him, then slowly, his face fell. "My God. You really mean it. You're telling the bloody truth. I don't believe it. But that means... that means you never had anything on me. Not a shred of proof. But now..."

"That's right," Dan said. "I'd worked out how you attacked Mortimer without being seen, but it was all circumstantial. Nothing that would've stood up in court if you'd ignored Jay's story and stayed away. But you came along, and that confirms everything."

"Shit!"

"Exactly. I set a trap, and you walked into it. But it wasn't your fault, was it, Kevin? It wasn't your idea to come here. You were sent. That's right, isn't it?"

Kevin didn't respond.

"Naturally, Kristen wouldn't risk confronting me herself," Dan went on. "She was always going to send you in her place. I should've seen it earlier, but once I figured out that you attacked Mortimer, I knew she'd send you to stop me. It's an obvious move on her part, you see, because Kristen really doesn't care whether you're caught or not. You killed Mortimer, and you can go to prison for it. So long as Kristen remains free, you can be sacrificed."

"That's not right," Kevin protested, but his voice had lost its edge of certainty. "You think you're clever, but you've got it all wrong. For one thing, she trusts me. She'd never let me down like that. Never."

"Are you sure about that, Kevin?" Dan made a show of looking around. "I don't see her rushing to help you."

"She had to stay in the pub, to cover for me."

"I see. So, she gets you out of the way, you keep me tied up here for a while, and she makes her escape. Very neat."

"Rubbish. You're whistling in the dark." Kevin chuckled. "Kristen would never run out on me. She knows I could go to the cops. I could tell them everything. It was all her idea. All of it."

"She told you to kill Mortimer?"

Kevin's expression clouded. "We were only trying to frighten him. It wasn't supposed to happen like that."

"But like I said, you'll be the one who gets the blame."

A grunt escaped from Kevin's lips.

"And what about incriminating Alan?" Dan said. "I'm guessing you had Mortimer's blood on your hands, but I suspect it was Kristen who told you to take the stick and wipe the blood on it."

Kevin's glare told Dan he was on the right track.

"I'll bet she told you exactly where to place that stick," Dan went on. "She's good at planting evidence. Did you know that she put Mortimer's watch in Alan's house? She left it in his bedroom. When they were in there this afternoon. Together."

"Bullshit," Kevin muttered. "They weren't together. Not like that."

Dan's cheeks tightened. "Ah! You were the anonymous informant. Spiller said it was a local man. Once again, Kristen made you do her dirty work."

"You just don't get it. We're partners. We're in this together."

"Right," Dan said slowly. "So you know all about the offshore shell companies, the property deals, the tax fraud, the links with organised crime."

"Are you trying to be funny?"

"No, not at all. I've been looking into this for a while, and according to my contact in the City, Kristen has been mixing with some rough characters. I suppose she needed the money to fund her lifestyle. How do you think she got that brand new Jaguar? They don't come cheap."

"Shut up! Kristen wouldn't do anything that stupid. I would've known about it. She tells me everything. We're solid."

"No, Kevin. As far as she's concerned, you're a liability. You've almost outlived your usefulness, but she had one last task for you. She needed you to keep me busy while she makes a run for it. If you don't believe me, call the pub and see if she's still there."

"She'll be there."

Dan looked around for his phone. He'd dropped it when Kevin had collided with him, and now there was no sign of the damned thing. *Pity*, he thought. But maybe he could turn the loss to his advantage. Yes. He glimpsed an opening. "I've lost my phone, but I really think you should call Kristen. Maybe I was wrong about you and her. Either way, you should check in, tell her what's going on." Kevin started to shake his head, so Dan added, "She'll be expecting you to call. You don't want to let her down, Kevin. She'll be waiting to hear from you, and she's probably getting worried, wondering if you're all right."

Kevin hesitated, then he took one hand off the axe and pushed his fingers into a pocket in his jeans. And as he took out his phone, he looked down.

His lapse of concentration lasted only for a moment, but it was enough. Dan launched himself at Kevin, grabbing the hand that held the axe while driving his shoulder into Kevin's chest, pouring the full weight of his body into the impact. Caught off guard, Kevin staggered back, stumbling, struggling to break his arm free from Dan's grip. But Dan held on tight. For a heartbeat, they swayed in an ungainly dance as Kevin fought to regain his balance. Dan's feet slipped on the tarmac. He was being driven back, losing the battle against Kevin's size and strength. But he wasn't beaten yet.

Gritting his teeth and clinging onto Kevin for dear life,

Dan hooked his foot around Kevin's left leg and swept it forward. Kevin went down heavily, Dan on top of him. Metal rang out as the axe's blade hit the road, but Kevin kept hold of his weapon, letting out a roar of frustration.

It would only take a moment for Kevin to recover from his fall, and Dan seized his opportunity. Grabbing Kevin's arm with both hands, he pounded the man's hand against the road as fast and as hard as he could, over and over, until finally, Kevin's bloodied fingers opened, the wooden handle slipping from his grip.

But Kevin was in a rage now, his cheeks livid, his features twisted in a savage snarl. Letting out a guttural yell, he grabbed hold of Dan's shirt with both hands and tossed him aside like a rag doll.

Before he hit the road, Dan lifted his arms to protect his head, but he wasn't quite fast enough. A piercing pain raked across his brow, and hot liquid oozed from his temple to trickle thickly over his eyebrows. He was bleeding, almost numb from the throbbing ache flooding his mind, but he couldn't afford to stay down. Rolling over, he staggered to his feet, facing his opponent.

Kevin stood firm, his fists held at shoulder height, his rage rapidly cooling to cold intent. He was ready for round two.

Dan gestured downward. "Kevin, think about what you're doing. If you fight me, you'll only make things worse for yourself."

"Bollocks to that." Kevin took a staggering step closer. "I'm going to kill you."

"No. You're not going to do that. You're going to calm down, then we're going to sort something out."

For a long second, Kevin stared at Dan. Then in silence, he stalked toward him, breathing hard.

"There you are," someone shouted, and they both turned to see Jay emerging from the public footpath. "All right, Kev?" Jay strode toward them, taking his time. "I've been all over those bloody spoil heaps, running myself ragged to find you two idiots, and meanwhile you're mucking about down here."

"Stay out of this," Kevin said. "This is between him and me."

"Can't do that, lad," Jay replied. "I hate to say it, but I'm on Dan's side in this fight. So if you fancy your chances against the pair of us, go to it."

Kevin sneered. "You haven't got the bottle."

"Oh yeah?" Jay rolled his shoulders as though limbering up, a relaxed smile on his face. "Sure about that, are you?"

Kevin glared, raising an accusing finger to point from Jay to Dan and back again. "I know where you live. Both of you. If you know what's good for you, you'll keep your mouths shut and keep out of my way. Because if I hear so much as a whisper about any of this, I'll know where it came from. Got it?"

Jay looked thoughtful. "Aye, maybe that'd be for the best."

"What the hell are you talking about?" Dan demanded. "We have to go to the police. He killed Mortimer. He admitted it."

But Jay simply nodded toward the lane, and Dan turned to see a Volvo saloon screeching to a halt, its front doors opening as DS Spiller lumbered from the driving seat and Alan leapt out from the other side.

"Looks like the cavalry's arrived," Jay said. "So if I were you, I'd keep quiet about Kev's little confession. Let the boys in blue deal with it. Easier all around."

Dan watched as Spiller advanced on Kevin. The policeman seemed to have shed ten years: there was a determined spring in his stride and a predatory gleam in his eyes. But Kevin wasn't faring quite so well. His shoulders sagged, his jaw went slack, and his livid cheeks were already fading to a sickly shade of ash grey. The man was defeated, and once Spiller got his hooks into him, there was little doubt that he'd confess everything within minutes.

Spiller pursed his lips as he weighed up the situation, taking in the axe lying on the road before letting his gaze linger on the abandoned mountain bike. Finally, he said, "Now then, gentlemen. I think we'd all better have a chat, don't you?" He turned his keen stare on Kevin. "You first, sir. Step into the car if you don't mind."

Kevin hung his head. "I want a solicitor."

"Yes, yes. All in good time." Spiller took Kevin's arm and led him to the car. "Mind your head, sir." He guided Kevin into the back seat and then glanced at the others. "I'll take it from here. You'd all better go home. I know where to find you, and to be honest, I'd rather not have you stomping around on my crime scene. I'll be speaking to each of you in due course. Don't touch anything. Just make your way home and stay put until I call." He nodded to Jay, then he raised an eyebrow in expectation, waiting for them to leave.

"Come on," Jay said. "Let's be good lads and do what we're told." He grinned. "Although, if we're quick, I reckon we might have time to squeeze in a quick pint before DS Spiller comes knocking."

Dan nodded, and as he walked with Alan and Jay toward the public footpath, Spiller took this as a signal to climb into his car.

Dan took hold of the gate, but instead of opening it, he held on to the wooden crosspiece, his arm stiff.

"Are you okay?" Alan asked. "You're still bleeding. Do you need to rest?"

"It's nothing," Dan said. "I'm fine. I was just thinking about Kristen. Will she still be at the pub, do you think?"

Jay chuckled. "Not likely. She'll be halfway to Exeter airport by now."

"There's nothing we can do about that," Alan said. "The police are on their way. I heard Spiller make the call."

"I suppose you're right." Dan let out a long breath, and a wave of exhaustion washed through his muscles. It was over. He could relax, forget about land deals and spoil heaps, arsenic and poisonous honey, and he could try to erase Kristen from his mind. He could put the whole sorry episode behind him. Mortimer was gone, and that was a damned shame, but perhaps now the man could rest in peace.

Even so...

Alan patted him on the arm. "Are you sure you're all right? Do you want to go and have a drink? A stiff brandy might perk you up. Or failing that, I can brew a mug of hot, sweet tea. You need one or the other; you look like hell."

Dan smiled. "Thanks, but there's something I need to do."

"What?"

"I need to stop Kristen, and I've just realised where she'll be." Dan glanced at the mountain bike. "Do you think that still works? Kevin crashed into me pretty hard."

"What on earth are you talking about?" Alan demanded. "You mustn't touch anything. You heard what Spiller said."

But Dan was already bending down to examine the bike. "It looks fine. It's solid as a rock."

"Alan's right," Jay said. "Leave it be, Dan."

Dan looked up. "If I don't press charges against Kevin, this won't be a crime scene, will it? I mean, it was just a scuffle, really. Neither of us was seriously hurt, and anyway, there were no witnesses."

"Hard to say," Jay replied. "The cops like to keep things simple, but they can't let people run amok with axes. It's all a question of intent, and Kev brought that axe with him for one reason only. He meant to do you harm, and that shows premeditation."

"I see." Crossing the road, Dan stepped up to Spiller's car and rapped on the window with his knuckles.

The window wound down with a whir, and Spiller looked up at him, his brow wrinkled in irritation. "Yes?"

Dan sent him a warm smile. "Any chance of a lift?"

"This isn't a taxi, Mr Corrigan. Now, I strongly suggest that you go home. I'll be in touch shortly. I'll make you my special priority."

"I understand. But if you give me a lift, I'll take you to Kristen Ellington. She's behind all this, as I'm sure Kevin has already told you."

"Mr Corrigan, this is a police matter," Spiller said, "and *I'm* sure that you have already done enough. More than enough. So please, step away from my car, and then go straight home. I want you off the street and out of trouble, am I making myself clear?"

"But Kristen—"

"Will be in custody very soon," Spiller interrupted. "We have it in hand, Mr Corrigan. Thank you, but that's an end to the matter."

"She's not where you think she'll be," Dan insisted. "You need me to find her."

Spiller's only response was a cold stare, and a moment later, the car window rolled shut.

"Bloody hell," Dan muttered. "Of all the pig-headed..." He marched away, going straight to the mountain bike.

"Wait," Alan said.

But Dan was already picking the bike up, studying it. "Flat pedals. Good. If it had been clip-ons..."

Jay stepped in front of him. "Steady on, lad. Where do you think you're going with that?"

"To finish this case," Dan said, and then pushing the bike at his side, he set off for the public footpath.

"Come back," Alan called out. "Or at least wait and let me come with you."

But Dan did not reply.

CHAPTER 31

PUSHING THE WOODEN gate open, Dan manoeuvred the mountain bike onto the footpath. Jay called out to him, but he paid no attention. Dan swung his leg over the bike and set off, standing up on the pedals and riding hard, the bike bouncing beneath him as he left the path and headed out over the rough ground. He could see where he'd walked through the bracken just a short while ago, the stems flattened just enough to create a makeshift trail, and he ploughed onward, his progress eased by the gentle downward slope.

Dan shifted his weight, bending his knees to maintain his balance as the bike rolled faster over the uneven terrain. The bracken's fronds whipped against his legs, and Dan's instincts told him to slow down, but there wasn't time. Kristen would get away unless he stopped her; he was sure of it.

The spoil heaps loomed over him, and he steered to their right, emerging from the bracken and picking out a line around the man-made hills. He planted himself on the bike's saddle and pedalled harder, his confidence growing. There was no undergrowth here, and having paced back and forth all evening, he knew the ground well. He felt the bike's electric motor kick in, and now he was racing over the gravelly mounds of bare earth that nestled alongside the spoil heaps. Cresting a low ridge, the bike's broad tyres left the ground, and Dan's heart lurched in his chest. But this was what the bike was made for. He kept his nerve, and when the wheels touched down, the bike's suspension cushioned his landing, and he remained upright.

Dan left the spoil heaps behind him, and the ground grew softer. Gobbets of muddy water flicked upwards from the front wheel to pepper his face, but the tyres' rugged tread held their grip, propelling him forward.

He was nearly at the coppice now, and he should stop before he crashed into a tree. But there were just enough spaces between the spindly trunks, and with a bit of care, he could steer between them. Choosing his path and scarcely slowing, he veered from side to side, dodging one trunk after another. Dan wasn't much of an off-road cyclist, but he'd ridden hire bikes into battle against the London traffic, and his experience stood him in good stead.

The mud grew deeper, but Dan knew he'd be much slower on foot. He stood up on the pedals, shifting his weight by instinct, and he kept pedalling. The bike slipped and slithered through the sodden soil, shimmying, sliding over exposed roots. But Dan's momentum carried him forward, and somehow he made it through to the other side. Pushing through a curtain of thin branches, Dan burst out of the coppice and onto the field beyond. And his heart leapt.

There she was.

Halfway down the slope, Kristen stood alone, staring into space. Her car was parked just inside a gate on the far side of the field. The sleek lines of the Jaguar were oddly incongruous against the tussocks of coarse grass, and the driver's door hung open.

Kristen wore a light summer dress, the creamy folds of fabric fluttering in the breeze, and when she turned to glance in Dan's direction, she bowed her head, and a pang of pity stirred in his stomach. Even now, there was something about Kristen that tugged at his heartstrings. She was driven, ambitious, fiercely independent, but in this moment, she was vulnerable and alone. Could he really condemn her to a long stretch behind locked doors?

Dan brought the bike to a slithering halt, dismounting and walking steadily toward her, making no sudden movements. She might still make a dash for freedom, and if she ran to her car, he'd be powerless to prevent her escape. But Kristen stayed where she was, gazing out over the sunlit valley. When he stood beside her, she didn't even turn to look at him.

They stood in silence for a moment, then she said, "How did you know I'd be here?"

"This place was at the heart of your plans, and you had to see it again. You knew the game was up, and you wanted one last look at what could've been."

She glanced at him, a faint smile on her lips. "Am I that easy to read?"

"No. You did a pretty good job of covering your tracks. But you went too far when you planted that watch on Alan. That was rash. You must've been desperate."

"Yes. I was a fool." Kristen took a breath. "I had such plans for this place. It was going to be amazing."

"Some kind of glorified housing estate? Or were you planning a McMansion for yourself?"

"Neither. This was going to be a retirement complex. Luxury villas, swimming pools, state-of-the-art fitness suites. It was even going to have its own health centre and retail outlets. It would've been wonderful."

Dan nodded, another piece of the puzzle falling into place. "You work in high-end health care, so you must've rubbed shoulders with plenty of wealthy people. Some of them were looking for a place to retire, so you put two and two together. You made a deal with a property developer."

"No. I was going to manage the project myself and run it too. It was my dream."

"But a development like that would've cost millions," Dan said. "How much money did Mortimer leave you?"

"Not nearly enough. Not by a long chalk."

"So you talked to some of your wealthier clients, got them to invest."

"Certainly not," Kristen said.

"Who then?"

"It was the people I work for. They're very big in the world of private health care. They have places all over the world. As luck would have it, some of the directors decided to tour England, checking up on the way we do things over here. They were a charming bunch, and we got talking. They were looking to expand, and I offered them a beautiful site, a stretch of the English countryside. They liked my ideas, and they believed in me. They gave me a chance, and I ran with it. Once we'd agreed on a plan, everything happened very quickly. Suddenly, I was signing contracts, opening bank accounts, registering companies. It was all rather exciting."

"You make it sound very simple."

"It was," Kristen said. "I should've known it was all a pack of lies. My new friends didn't care about me or my plans. They just wanted some way to move huge sums of money from one place to another."

"Perhaps you didn't want to see the truth."

"Who does?" Kristen almost smiled. "I must seem very stupid. But I'd been shown a different world. To some people, when you know what you want, there are always ways to get it."

"Even if it means hurting people?"

"I didn't know it would be like that. Not at the start."

"I'm not sure I believe you," Dan said. "The way you used Kevin was cold and calculated. On the face of it, he had no motive to kill Mortimer, and—"

"I never wanted Morty killed," Kristen interrupted. "I just wanted him to see sense. Morty was stuck in the past, but I wanted to make a new future. My project would've put this place on the map. It would've meant money for the local economy, new opportunities, new jobs. Don't you see?"

"Oh, I understand. I can see it all too clearly. You spent your days pandering to the super-rich, and you wanted to join their cosy little club. So you wormed your way into your uncle's business affairs, taking them over one piece at a time until you thought you were in control. But Mortimer must've figured out what you were up to, and he found a way to stop you. He kept hold of the spoil heaps and that strip of land. Mortimer knew about the contamination. He'd known about it for years, but you hadn't done your homework. You thought it was just a stretch of worthless wasteland, and you didn't suspect the truth until it was too late."

Kristen regarded him coolly. "Nobody wants to retire on a toxic dumping ground, least of all the kind of people I wanted to attract. But that wasn't the point. I couldn't get permission to build a thing until the ground had been cleaned up. It was going to cost a fortune, but there was no point in even trying while the damned spoil heaps were still there. They needed special treatment to stabilise them, to stop all that toxic waste from spreading. But Morty wouldn't even discuss it."

"So you called your uncle and lured him onto the spoil heaps, then you sent Kevin to threaten him."

Kristen pressed her lips tight together.

"But Mortimer didn't want to know," Dan went on. "He stood up for himself, refused to be cowed, and Kevin lashed out."

"The idiot," Kristen muttered. "He ruined everything."

"You used him. Kevin didn't stand a chance against you. You've got him so confused, he hardly knows what he's doing. On that Friday night, when he realised what he'd done, he must've panicked." Dan paused. "Tell me, Kristen, was it his idea to plant Alan's stick where the police would find it, or was that another one of your schemes?"

"I was just trying to throw the police off the scent," Kristen said. "I told Kevin to find some kind of weapon and wipe the blood from his hands on it. I told him it had to be something that couldn't be traced back to him, but I didn't know what he'd choose. I thought he'd employ a bit of common sense and grab a lump of firewood or a random branch. I don't know why he took Alan's stick. He was probably trying to be clever, the poor lamb. Brains were never his strong suit."

Dan stared at her, all trace of pity vanishing in an instant. "For God's sake, Kristen! Kevin hit your uncle on the head, probably with an axe. You must've known Kevin had a temper, but you didn't let that stop you. You sent him to threaten Mortimer anyway."

She looked down, but she didn't reply.

"And you must've told Kevin to intimidate Marjorie, too," Dan went on. "We saw what he did to her fence. What was he going to do next? Was he going to butcher her goats? Or was he going to go straight for the kill and stove her head in?"

"Don't be ridiculous," Kristen said. "Kevin was only trying to shake her up a bit. I was going to make her a generous offer for her house and land. But I've talked to her about this in the past, dozens of times, and I knew she wouldn't sell unless I did something to change her mind."

Dan looked away, focusing on a tree in the distance. He'd met some ruthless people in his old line of work, but Kristen was in a league of her own. *Such callous indifference*, he thought. *I can't believe I was attracted to her.*

But those feelings belonged to the past. He'd let Kristen pull the wool over his eyes for too long, and now it was time to put things right.

He turned to her. "What I said earlier, about you needing to see this place again, I was wrong."

"Oh?"

"Yes. You're here because you have nowhere else to go, and you know you can't run."

She appeared to consider this. "I could try. I know the odds aren't good, but it's incredible what you can do when you put your mind to it."

"You're not that naïve. The police won't have much trouble in finding you, but that's the least of your worries. I know what kind of people you've been dealing with, and your so-called investors won't be too pleased when they discover that you've let them down." Dan studied her reaction, and the tightening of her cheeks told him all he needed to know. "Ah. Suddenly finding that no one returns your calls?"

"Oh, they've talked to me. They've made their position perfectly clear." Kristen met his gaze, and for the first time, Dan saw a hint of fear.

"What did they say?"

It was Kristen's turn to look away. "You don't want to know. Trust me. You really don't want to know." She shook her head as if dismissing an unpleasant image. "The question is, Dan, what are you going to do? I suppose you've been keeping me talking while the police get their act together. But they don't seem to be turning up, so what now? Are you going to grapple me to the ground and then wait for reinforcements?"

Dan smiled. "Tempting though that may be, I'm not expecting anyone to arrive. No one else knows we're here."

"No one?"

"Not even Alan, although he may have worked it out by now. But you're not going to run, Kristen. You're going to turn yourself in. At least the police will give you a chance, unlike your business associates. Then you'll get the best lawyer you can afford, and you'll tough it out until the end. You're a fighter, Kristen. Sure, you won't get away scot-free, but who knows? You might be able to cut a deal. I'm sure the police will be very interested in the names of your investors."

"Maybe. I don't know," Kristen said. "I really don't know what I'm going to do. But Dan, if I go to my car, will you try to stop me?"

"No. I'm sure you're going to do the right thing."

Kristen took one last look across the valley, drawing a deep breath as she let her gaze wander across the sunlit grass. Then without a word, she strode back to her car.

Dan didn't watch her leave. He heard the car door slam, the engine purr, and the gentle whine of gears as the Jaguar reversed from the field. Then all was quiet, and Dan savoured the moment, listening to the delicate strains of birdsong carried on the warm air. *I did it, Morty,* he thought. *I stopped them. Was that what you wanted?*

He tilted his head as if expecting to hear an answer, but of course, none came.

Dan picked up Kevin's bike, and wheeling it at his side, he headed back toward the coppice.

ONE MONTH LATER
THURSDAY

CHAPTER 32

D AN WAS POURING boiling water into a row of mugs when someone knocked on the back door. The team of three scaffolders had been busy outside Dan's house for a couple of hours, assembling their oversized construction kit under Jay's watchful gaze. Jay had insisted that he should start work on the outside of the house while the weather held fine, and Dan had been forced to accept his logic. But he hadn't bargained on Jay being such a stickler for detail. So far, he'd made the workers change the scaffolding three times, and no doubt they were getting impatient for their tea.

"It's open," Dan called out. "Tea's almost ready."

But when the door opened slowly, Dan did a double take. "Craig. Come in, I'm just making some tea if you fancy a cup."

Craig shuffled awkwardly into the kitchen. "Ah, not for me thanks. Just popped in to say thank you for putting me in touch with Fairweather and Hilbert. It was very good of you. Much appreciated."

"Don't mention it. I'm happy to help, and I knew you were looking for a good law firm. I imagine there's a lot to sort out."

"You can say that again. Anyway, they really know their stuff. They're doing a sterling job with the estate, and bit by bit, they're putting things to rights. I expect I'll have to sell off some land to pay all the legal fees, but it's worth it. It'll all work out in the end."

"Good. I hope everything goes all right," Dan said. "And I hope you don't mind me asking, but what about Kristen? How's she doing?"

"Last I heard, she was still helping the police with their inquiries. They say there's a whole web of wrongdoing to untangle. As you probably know, she got herself mixed up with some very unsavoury characters. There's a string of dodgy firms all over the world, apparently. Kristen thinks someone from Interpol is coming over to see her. Between you and me, I think she's secretly rather pleased at the prospect."

"She'll survive," Dan said. "Your sister is a fighter. We all underestimated her."

"Yes. It's all very sad. Morty thought the world of her, you know. She was the apple of his eye." Craig sniffed, then he cleared his throat hurriedly as if anxious to conceal his brief display of emotion. "Ah well, I must get on. Thanks again for all your help. Without your dogged determination, we'd all be up to our necks in it. Alan would be in the clink, I'd be filing for bankruptcy, God knows what would've happened to dear old Marjorie, and the bulldozers would be tearing up half the valley."

"As you say, it was worth it." Dan smiled. "It's funny, but I only came across those lawyers by chance. I was talking to a friend in the City—he's doing a little job for me—and I needed someone to handle the legal side. He put me onto Fairweather and Hilbert, and they seemed great, so I thought they might be able to help you out."

Craig lowered his eyebrows. "They're working for you

too? You're not in any trouble, I hope. I'd hate to think, after everything that's happened…"

"No, it's nothing like that. It's a simple conveyancing job. To be honest, Fairweather and Hilbert are much more high-powered than I really need, but when you want a job doing quickly, sometimes you have to pay through the nose."

"There's no doubt about that. But what are they actually doing for you? You haven't said. Or is it private?"

Dan took a breath, and when he spoke, he found his words coming out awkwardly as if he were making a formal announcement. "I'm selling my flat in London and buying this place. My sister has decided to stay in the States for the foreseeable future, and the timing seemed right, so I made her an offer and she was happy with it. My flat was snapped up very quickly, so it's all going through. I expect to be moving house in a few weeks."

"Well, well, that's a turn up for the books," Craig said. "I thought you were a dyed-in-the-wool city dweller."

"I was. But there's something about this odd little village. It grows on you."

"It certainly does." Craig beamed. "This calls for a celebration. We must give you a proper welcome to the village. Come down to the pub tomorrow night. We're having a grand reopening. Make sure you come in good time, and I'll get you a pint. On the house, obviously."

"Ah, I heard you were going to reopen the pub. Alan will be pleased."

"Yes, it's the one piece of property I've been able to reclaim, so far, anyway. It's all systems go. As of tomorrow, The Boar will be back in business."

"Life returning to normal," Dan said. "I'll drink to that. Will it be your name above the door? I can see you in the role of the genial pub landlord. It would suit you down to the ground."

"No fear. I'm just the owner. I asked young Samantha to run the place."

"Sam Ashford? From the shop?"

"The very same," Craig said. "It turns out she's been keeping the pub going more or less single-handedly for a long time. She's been labouring away behind the scenes, while Kevin divided his time equally between loafing in the garden and chasing after my sister. He's no great loss. But since I put Sam in charge, she's had the bit between her teeth. She's coming up with all kinds of good ideas, and I'm behind her all the way. Give us a month or two, and you'll hardly know the place." Craig was almost bouncing on the balls of his feet. "So what do you say? Shall we see you tomorrow?"

"Sure. I'll be there."

"Excellent. Bring Alan along. I hear he's been a bit subdued these past few weeks. I can't say I blame him, but is he okay, do you think?"

"He's been catching up on his work," Dan said carefully. "He has a deadline to meet, and with one thing and another, he's way behind on his schedule."

"Understood. Ah well, invite him anyway. Tell him there's a pint waiting for him behind the bar. We're getting a couple of special guest ales for the occasion. That ought to tempt him out of his shell."

"Yes. I'm sure he'll be delighted."

"Great. See you then. I'd better get moving." Craig made to leave, but as he headed for the door, he half turned. "By the way, tell Alan to bring his wallet. We're bringing back the old tradition."

"Which one?"

"The most important one," Craig replied. "The meat raffle, of course. It wouldn't be a proper Friday night at The Boar without it."

"Wonderful," Dan said, his voice heavy with irony. But Craig was already bustling through the door.

Am I really moving to a place where they revel in a weekly meat raffle? Dan asked himself. *I wonder if it's too late to change my mind.*

In theory, there was still time to alter his plans. He could cancel the sale of his flat, tell his sister to sell The Old Shop, and then he could head back to London. But Dan smiled to himself and added a splash of oat milk to the rapidly cooling mugs of tea. The scaffolders would complain if they knew they were getting anything other than cow's milk, but as requested, he'd made the tea nice and strong. If he added a bit of extra sugar and pepped the drinks up in the microwave, the workers would be none the wiser.

I'll get them some regular milk for next time, Dan decided. Personal principles were all well and good, but sometimes you had to cut yourself a little slack for the sake of the people around you. *I'll call in at the shop later*, he thought. *If I'm lucky, it might even be open. If I'm really lucky, I can congratulate Sam on her new job.*

He recalled the time he'd first met Sam in the shop, remembering how she'd smiled at him, dimpling her cheeks. He pictured the way the light danced in her warm brown eyes. It would be nice to see that smile again. It would be very nice indeed.

FRIDAY

CHAPTER 33

S TANDING OUTSIDE ALAN'S front door, Dan knocked, then he stood back to wait, his hands behind his back.

It was a fine evening, but even so, a sudden chill prickled the back of his neck. What condition would Alan be in today? Would he even open his door?

Alan had been uncommunicative for days, hardly going out and rarely returning Dan's calls. The last time Dan had seen him, Alan had been almost unrecognisable beneath a five-day growth of beard. His hair, usually neat, had been wild and dishevelled, and his eyes, although bright, had been underlined with deep shadows. But most disturbing of all, Alan's manner had been uncharacteristically taciturn, his sentences clipped and his tone tinged with gloom.

Working to a deadline could be stressful; Dan knew that better than most. But there was more to it than that. *The man's world has been shaken up*, Dan thought. *He's withdrawn to lick his wounds.*

Since Kristen's arrest, the flow of gossip in the village had become a tidal wave. Dan could shrug off the nosiness of his neighbours, but the unwanted attention didn't sit well with Alan, and he'd recoiled from it.

I hate to see him like this, Dan told himself. But what could he do to help? Platitudes and false assurances would be wasted on Alan; he'd see through them immediately and feel insulted. *All I can do is keep showing up*, Dan thought. Sooner or later, Alan would emerge from his self-inflicted exile, and then he'd need to see a friendly face. He'd need to see someone who understood.

And perhaps that moment had arrived. Dan could hear footsteps from beyond the door, and the faint strains of a whistled melody.

He was whistling a tune on the day we met, Dan remembered, allowing himself a hopeful smile. He had a vision of Alan bounding into view, fresh faced and full of the joys of spring. But while Alan was clean shaven when he answered the door, his face was pale, and his gaze darted past Dan to the quiet street beyond, as if fearing what he might find.

"You got my message?" Dan asked cheerfully.

"Yes," Alan said. "Thanks. I was going to come along, but…" He raised his hands and let them fall to his side as if that were explanation enough.

"When was the last time you took a break?" Dan asked. "And I mean a real break, away from the house."

"I don't know. I've been working. Keeping busy. Otherwise, I… I start to think about Mortimer. About the whole thing."

"That's all over," Dan said. "It's in the past."

"Is it? A man died, Dan. There's no getting away from that."

"You're right. I'm not saying we should forget about what happened. But we have to come to terms with it. Remember, we did nothing wrong. We tried to help Mortimer, and then we made sure that the people responsible were brought to justice."

"*We?*" Alan asked.

"Yes. I couldn't have done it without you."

"Yes, you could."

"That's not true," Dan insisted. "And though it shames me to admit it, without your influence, I don't think I'd have tried. I'd have been like everyone else: a spectator. I'd have listened to the news, said how terrible it was, and then I would've gone on with my life as normal."

"Seriously? You wouldn't have investigated on your own?"

Dan shook his head. "Certainly not. You were crucial to the whole thing."

Alan lifted his chin a little. "I'm not sure I believe that, but thank you for saying it, anyway."

"My pleasure. Now, we've got everything straightened out, so I'm going to the pub, and you're coming with me." Dan lowered his voice to a stage whisper. "You wouldn't want me to face the horrors of the meat raffle on my own, would you?"

Alan stared at him.

He's going to refuse, Dan thought. *After all that I've just said, he's actually going to turn me down.*

But the suggestion of a smile twitched the corners of Alan's lips. "I'm tempted to buy a ticket for that damned raffle, just to see your reaction if I win something."

"You'll come then?"

Alan nodded. "Just for a swift pint."

"Excellent. In that case, I have something for you." Dan took his hands from behind his back, and lying flat across his palms was a length of polished wood, one end tipped with a shining ferrule, the other crowned with a heavy knob of polished brass.

"What?" Alan asked, his voice hoarse. He gazed at Dan in bewilderment.

"It's a hiking staff. I assume it will be ages before the police return the one they took, but I saw this one in Exeter, and I knew it was perfect."

"But…" Alan's lips moved soundlessly as he hunted for the right words. "If I walk around with that, it'll draw attention. People already stare at me as if I've grown two heads or something."

"Listen, Alan, I know how tongues wag in this village, and I understand how you feel about it. But here's the thing: you have to show them you don't care about the gossip. If you hide away, people will make up their own stories to fill the void. Then, when you go out, they'll point and stare and say, 'There goes Alan, the man who was accused of murdering poor old Morty.' God knows, some of them will mutter about there being no smoke without fire, and they'll claim they've always had their doubts about you. But that's just people being lazy and careless. It doesn't mean a thing." He paused for breath. "Not unless you *let* it mean something, Alan. If you give in, if you let them get away with their snide remarks, then they'll win. But I won't stand by and let them cast aspersions at you. So we're going to the pub, and you are going to march in proudly, bearing a stick that actually *would* make a decent weapon were you inclined to use it that way. And if anyone so much as sends you a furtive glance, you are going to smile at them until they look away. Got it?"

He thrust the stick forward, and Alan took it, weighing it in his hands. "It's a lovely piece of wood. It looks like chestnut. It's beautifully polished. It must've cost you a fortune."

"The question is, is it the right size? I had to guess."

Wrapping his fingers around the brass knob, Alan planted the stick firmly against the ground. He studied it for a moment, and when he looked up, the gleam had returned to his eyes. "Yes. Yes, it's perfect. Thank you."

"Don't mention it. Now, pub?"

"Pub." Alan stepped out, closing the door behind him, and they set off, heading for Fore Street, Alan's stick tapping on the tarmac in a regular rhythm.

"I've been thinking," Alan began.

"Yes?"

"I was trying to work out whose round it is, and I believe it's yours."

"Okay," Dan said.

"That's it? You're not going to argue?"

"Not today." Dan chortled under his breath. "But listen, whatever else you do tonight, make sure you don't leave that stick behind when we leave, or you never know what might happen."

And after a heartbeat's pause, Alan laughed.

Thank You for reading Valley of Lies. I hope you enjoyed it.
Keep reading for a preview of Dan and Alan's next
adventure, **Murder Between the Tides,**
or dive right in...
Buy the book and get a Free Exclusive Story,
Mystery at the Hall
Murder Between the Tides

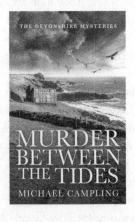

Find it on your favourite store
Murder Between the Tides
Visit: books2read.com / mbtt

PREVIEW - MURDER
BETWEEN THE TIDES

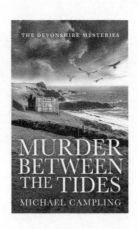

MURDER BETWEEN THE TIDES - PROLOGUE

NEWQUAY

I t's quiet here. But not silent. Never silent.

Far below, the freezing sea hisses, spitting its angry venom against the unforgiving cliff face. It's getting dark now, but the white flecks of spume are starkly visible, spattering over the black rocks.

I take a step closer to the edge, and the rumbling call of the waves grows louder. A sudden sense of emptiness rushes up from the gathering gloom, an icy gust of air swirling around me, tugging at my clothes. I'm light headed, and the stony path that had seemed so solid shifts beneath my feet. My shoes scrape over the damp gravel, but the sound belongs to someone else, someone brave enough to step to the brink.

Specks of sea spray settle on my skin and gather on my eyelashes. I blink, wiping my eyes with the backs of my cold hands, but not all the salt water on my cheeks has come from the sea.

A seabird, a European herring gull, slides into my field of view then glides away, its wings unmoving, the perfect white feathers of its sleek body unruffled. I watch the gull for a moment, following it with my eyes until it dives and disappears beneath the cliff's edge. In the distance, the bright lights of the town twinkle cheerfully, the drab winter streets temporarily brightened by garish strings of Christmas lights.

Even so, I know that the pastel colours of the painted houses are jaded and careworn, the gift shops and cafes empty and desolate. But soon, for one hotel at least, there will be an influx of visitors. I will no longer be alone.

And if everything goes according to plan, I will be avenged.

I take one last look at the hungry sea. *Soon, you will have what you desire*, I tell the churning waves. *You will have your sacrificial offering*.

Then I turn toward the town, and I start walking.

SATURDAY

MURDER BETWEEN THE TIDES - CHAPTER 1

EMBERVALE

I n the front room at The Old Shop, Dan stood back from the window to admire his handiwork. Until a couple of days ago, he'd never owned a single Christmas decoration, but Alan, his neighbour, had assured him that most of the residents of Embervale brightened the village at Christmas by displaying lights on the front of their houses. Sure enough, in recent weeks Fore Street had taken on a cheery glow as more and more houses were adorned with strings of lights.

Eventually Dan had joined in, purchasing a modest set of multicoloured LEDs, and he'd spent the last ten minutes stringing them backward and forward across the inside of his front-room window.

He tested the suction-cup hooks that held the wire to the glass and, satisfied that they were secure, he plugged the lights in. The LEDs sparkled into life, and Dan smiled. Perhaps Christmas in Embervale wouldn't be so bad.

There was to be a Christmas fair in the village hall, a festive-themed quiz evening in the pub, and the local school children were staging a pantomime. Dan had protested that the school event would be for parents only, but Alan had insisted that everyone was welcome, and the matter was settled.

For Dan, a lifelong Londoner, Christmas meant crowded streets, frantic shopping trips and a kind of stifling urgency that crept in at around the twentieth of December. In Embervale, they did things differently. Alan had the bit between his teeth, and it looked as though Dan was to be dragged into the festivities whether he liked it or not.

Time to tackle the tree, Dan thought. The fir tree stood, undecorated, in the corner. It was too big for the room, but he'd bought it on impulse, carried away by the moment.

He'd gone with Alan to buy the tree, but instead of heading into Newton Abbot or Exeter, Alan had driven them along winding lanes until they'd reached a farmyard. There they'd been greeted by a young man in overalls who'd ushered them into a cavernous barn. A row of freshly cut fir trees leaned against the wall, and they'd taken their pick. The price had been ludicrously low, so when Alan handed over his cash, Dan had grabbed a tree for himself.

The deal done, there'd been none of the usual fussing about with nylon nets. As soon as Alan had folded down the rear seat of his car, the young man had simply stuffed their chosen trees into the back. The whole process had taken only a matter of minutes and was entirely painless. And if anyone except Dan noticed the dead leaves and strands of straw dragged into the car by the trees' lower branches, they hadn't mentioned it.

In the past, Dan would've been annoyed if his purchases had come accompanied by debris. But since moving to the countryside, he'd learned that whatever he did and wherever he went, a certain amount of mud and dirt would be inevitable; it was part of life.

It's amazing what you can get used to, he thought. He looked pointedly at the large toolbox that lay open at the side of the room, and at the spirit level propped beside the door.

Although the redecoration of The Old Shop had been nearing completion for some months, Dan's decorator, Jay, always managed to find one more thing that needed doing, and evidence of his activities was everywhere. Once Jay started a job, he was reluctant to let it go, and even though it was a Saturday, he was upstairs, working away.

As if to prove the point, a dull thud boomed from the ceiling. Jay had persuaded Dan that all the carpets should be removed, and the fine old floorboards stripped back and polished. At the time, Dan had been all in favour of the idea, but since then the noise of the floor sander and the inevitable dust and disruption had stretched his patience almost to its limit.

A muffled curse came from the room above, and Dan's heart sank.

Another thud and Jay muttered a few terse sentences, though Dan couldn't make out what was said. Either Jay was making a call, or he was grumbling to himself; both were equally likely.

What's the problem this time? Dan wondered. His money was on something to do with wiring. According to Jay, the fuse box was one short step away from bursting into flames. Dan knew how it felt.

Jay's heavy footsteps thumped on the stairs and, when he appeared in the doorway, his expression said it all.

"Go on," Dan said, "tell me the worst."

Jay winced. "You're not going to like this, but we've hit a snag."

We? Dan thought, but all he said was, "What kind of snag?"

"I'm not going to lie. It's bad. The boards in the main bedroom were okay, but when I got to the landing, it was a different matter. It's riddled with woodworm, and from what I can see it's got into the staircase too. It's a wonder you haven't fallen through it."

Dan scraped his hand down his face. "How much will it cost to put right?"

"We'll have to strip out a lot of the old boards and replace them, but that's not the only problem. The joists are full of holes. You'll need to have the whole place professionally treated, and that's not something I can do. We're going to need a specialist."

"I suppose I'll have to wait until after Christmas, but it can't be helped. It'll have to be done."

"As it happens, I've got a mate in this line of work," Jay said with a wolfish smile. "For him, this'll be a small job. And you're in luck. He can fit you in right away."

"You've called him already?"

Jay nodded. "No point mucking about. He can start the day after next. Monday. That's perfect because I can come in early and rip out the boards. My mate only has a few days free, so he'll have to tackle the bedrooms, the landing and the stairs all at once."

"But I'm supposed to be sleeping in the spare room until—"

"You'll have to move out," Jay interrupted. "He'll be spraying chemicals all over the place. You can't be around when he starts. You'll have to find somewhere to stay for a few days."

Dan shook his head in disbelief.

"Why don't you ask Alan?" Jay said.

"He won't be there. He's going away for some kind of writing event or other."

"There you are then. You can probably stay at his place while he's away."

"Perhaps."

"Right, that's sorted then. I'm glad we've got that fixed up. I may as well leave my tools here." Jay headed for the door. "I'll see you on Monday," he called over his shoulder. "Bright and early."

"Right," Dan said to the empty room. "It looks as though I haven't got much choice."

~

"WOODWORM?" Alan said, ushering Dan into his kitchen. "That's bad news."

"Tell me about it. The thing is…"

"You'll be needing somewhere to stay." Alan nodded as though deep in thought. "Mm. I suppose that might work."

Dan's expression brightened. "Really? I can stay at your place while you're away?"

"No, that wasn't what I was thinking. Don't take this the wrong way, but I'm not keen on people being in the house while I'm not here. Anyway, my idea is better. Much better."

"Oh? Are you going to offer me the use of your shed or something?"

"Of course not. I was thinking you could come with me, to Newquay."

"But I thought you were going on some kind of writing holiday."

"It's a writing retreat, not a holiday," Alan said pointedly. "I'm hoping to get a lot of work done."

"Fine, but I'm not a writer."

"That needn't matter. You'll get a place to stay with bed and breakfast, and you can please yourself during the day. Have you ever been to Newquay?"

"No, and I'm in no great rush to go to the English seaside in the middle of winter."

"There are some lovely coastal walks," Alan said. "And the town is quite nice. I'm reliably informed that there are even some good places for vegans to eat out."

Dan raised an eyebrow. "You were looking for vegan restaurants? Have I tempted you to convert?"

"Certainly not, but since I booked, I've been sent

information on every possible kind of dietary requirement and lifestyle. I happened to notice the vegan options, that's all."

"Fair enough," Dan said. "The point is, I can't invite myself along to your event. Anyway, I expect it's all booked up, isn't it?"

"I know someone who's pulled out at the last minute. He's trying to offload his room, so I'm sure you could get it for a knock-down price."

"I see. I suppose, in the circumstances, I'll have to think about it."

"Well, you'd better be quick," Alan said. "I'm leaving on Monday morning, so if you want that room, you'll need to book it as soon as possible."

Dan hesitated.

"Think of it as a holiday," Alan went on. "I'm happy to give you a lift. I was driving there anyway. All you need to do is sit back and relax. You'll have a few days by the sea, away from all the noise and the dust of Jay's Herculean labours. I mean, you must be getting sick of it. He's taking forever to get the job done."

"Jay is something of a perfectionist." Dan weighed his options for a second, but in all honesty, he had little choice. "All right, I'll come along. If you could tell your friend I'll take the room, that would be great. Just let me know how much and where to send the money, and I'll take it from there."

Alan smiled. "Excellent. We'll go first thing on Monday morning. It won't take long to get there, but I'm meeting the others for lunch and I want to be there in plenty of time. In the afternoon I'll be doing some work, but after that we could meet up for something to eat."

"Won't you be busy discussing the relative merits of the three-act structure or something?"

"This is a hotel in Newquay were talking about, not some

swanky literary reception. I think you'll find that most jobbing writers like a trip to the pub as much as anyone else." Alan chuckled under his breath. "But now that you come to mention it, I might need to escape from the others for a while. They're a nice bunch, but one or two of them like to talk shop all the time, and it can get a bit tiresome."

"Ah, so you have an ulterior motive for inviting me."

Alan shrugged. "I prefer to call it enlightened self-interest. Anyway, you're getting a cheap holiday out of it, so I think you're doing pretty well. It's win-win. A tide in the affairs of men, which taken at the flood, and all that."

"Mm. Julius Caesar. That didn't work out too well for him." Dan stood. "I'd better go and pack. Tell me, what's the dress code for a gathering of writers?"

"Comfortable. And don't forget, bring plenty of warm layers. When the wind comes blasting over the Atlantic, it takes your breath away."

"Now he tells me. I'll be sure to bring a decent coat." Dan crossed to the door, but he paused before opening it. "Thanks for this, Alan. It is a good idea. You're right, I could use a few days away from the house."

"Well, you'll get plenty of peace and quiet at Newquay," Alan said. "I can guarantee it."

SUNDAY

MURDER BETWEEN THE
TIDES - CHAPTER 2

NEWQUAY

E dward Hatcher breezed through the doors of the
Regent Hotel at 9 am precisely, and that was exactly as
it should be. But almost immediately his expression
darkened; there was no one waiting to greet him.

Pulling himself up to his full height and removing his grey
fedora with a flourish, Edward stalked toward the reception
desk and delivered a sharp tap to the gleaming brass bell. *An
unnecessary contrivance,* he thought. *Surely the desk should be
staffed at all times.*

Edward stood motionless, waiting. The bell's chime
echoed through the empty lobby and faded away, but still no
one arrived to welcome him.

Someone barged through the hotel's main door, but it was
only the taxi driver who'd brought him from the station. And
he didn't look happy.

"All right, mate," he said. "Are you going to come and get
these bags or what?"

"In a moment. I have summoned assistance, and I'm sure
that a porter will arrive presently."

The driver rolled his eyes. "I can't wait all day. I've got
another call. Now, you've paid your money, and I've

stopped the meter, so we're done. I'll put your bags outside."

Edward bridled, flaring his nostrils. "You'll do no such thing. You may bring my bags into the hotel, and if you're quick about it, you may get a tip."

"You what? Who the hell do you think you are?" The driver didn't wait for a reply but turned on his heel and marched out.

"Wait," Edward called. But a moment later, he heard the grumbling rattle of a diesel engine as the taxi sped away. "Of all the nerve," Edward muttered. "I should have taken his number."

"What was that, sir?"

Edward turned with a start, staring at the stout, middle-aged man who'd appeared behind the counter. "Where did you spring from? And more importantly, where were you when I arrived?"

The man offered an apologetic smile. "Very sorry about that, sir. I was just in the porter's cubbyhole, answering a call from one of our valued residents." He hooked his thumb over his shoulder, and Edward noticed, for the first time, the small compartment tucked away behind the reception desk. The cubbyhole was separated from the lobby by panels of polished oak, and no doubt it was an original feature of the hotel. Little larger than a broom cupboard, it would have been a place for the night porter to stay warm while keeping an eye on the lobby.

Edward noted the computer screen sitting on a narrow counter inside the cubbyhole, the display filled with the unmistakable image of playing cards. *Online poker*, Edward thought. *Oh well, it could have been so much worse.*

"My name is Matthew," the receptionist went on, "and may I take this opportunity to welcome you to the Regent hotel."

The man's smile was genuine, his tone sincere, and

Edward's mood mellowed. "Very well, Matthew. Perhaps you could start by retrieving my luggage from the pavement outside. My driver was less than helpful."

"Certainly, sir. First, could I just check that you have a reservation?"

"Of course. My name is Edward. Edward Hatcher." He smiled expectantly. His name wasn't always recognised, but it was important to be ready. One never knew when one might run into an avid reader, and it paid to make the right impression.

But Matthew showed no flicker of recognition, and he lowered his head to study yet another computer screen. "Hatcher," he muttered. "Hatcher, Hatcher, no, no." He flicked an anxious glance at Edward. "If you could just bear with me for a moment, sir, I'm sure I'll be able to... Ah! Edward Hatcher. Five nights. You upgraded to the Regency suite."

Edward inclined his head in acknowledgement. "That is correct."

"Of course! You're here for the writers' group."

"Once again, Matthew, you've hit the nail on the head. Now, perhaps you would be kind enough to bring my luggage inside."

"Be right with you. I'm just activating your keycard." Matthew began typing on the computer's keyboard, his fingers jabbing inexpertly at the keys. "Just one minute." Matthew's face fell. "This machine is taking its time, but it won't be long. Probably." He pushed the keyboard aside and smiled at Edward. "So, what kind of books have you written? Anything I might have read?"

Edward's expression froze. "That's hard to say," he began, but before he could explain further, a booming voice rang out across the lobby.

"Max Cardew!"

Edward and Matthew gazed at the man who'd called out:

an imposing figure marching toward them from the entrance, a sense of authority in his every step.

"You're Max Cardew?" Matthew asked, his voice hoarse with suppressed excitement. "I love your books. The wife likes them too. Even my kids read your stuff, and they never pick up a book otherwise. We must have read everything you've ever done. And that series on the telly was fantastic." Matthew licked his lips. "Is it true what they say about *The Seventh Cipher*? Are they going to make it into a film?"

The new arrival let out a bellow of laughter as he joined them at the reception desk, then he gestured toward Edward. "You'll have to ask my friend here. He writes under the name Max Cardew, not I."

Matthew frowned at Edward. "But you don't look anything like him. I mean, I'm sorry, sir, I don't mean any disrespect, but this gentleman is pulling my leg, isn't he? Because, as I say, we've got all the Max Cardew books at home, and the photo on the back—"

"Was taken some time ago," Edward said. "You have to remember that I've been writing for many years, and my publicist insists that I keep the same photograph. It's a question of branding, apparently." Edward recovered his composure. "But thank you for your kind words about my work. If you'd like me to sign any of your books, please do bring them along. I'd be happy to oblige."

"Right," Matthew said. "Thanks. I might do that."

Edward cast a sidelong glance at the man who stood beside him. "Nice to see you again, Brian. I didn't know you were joining us this week."

"Yes, I checked in last night. I wanted to get a feel for the place, get my feet under the table."

"I see. I hope this means that your book sales have taken an upturn. I was sorry to hear that you parted ways with your publisher." Then, to Matthew, Edward said, "I'm sure you've heard of the famous Dr Brian Coyle. His books made

357

quite a splash when they came out. Tell me, Brian, was it three years ago or four?"

"Five," Brian replied from between clenched teeth. "But I've got a whole new series coming out. This one's going to be great. It'll blow the roof off the bestseller charts, you'll see."

"Ah, that is good news. You've found another publisher?"

"Not yet. Actually, I'm thinking of going independent. I can take care of the whole thing myself. It's the way forward."

"Self-publishing. Interesting." Edward favoured him with a benevolent smile. "Good luck with that, Brian. And I mean that sincerely. I hope it works out for you."

Brian watched Edward carefully as though waiting for the other boot to drop, but finally he nodded. "Thanks, Edward. I appreciate it." He hesitated. "And when I came in, I wasn't laughing at you. I didn't mean any disrespect."

"Think nothing of it," Edward said. "I'm very aware that I don't live up to my pen name's glamorous image, but there we are. We work with what we have."

"Very true." Brian chortled quietly. "Still, all those years in intelligence — your old career gives you a certain aura of mystique. That kind of authenticity is gold dust. I can't compete with that."

Edward tapped the side of his nose. "Hush, hush, old chap. You know I never talk about those days."

"And that only adds to your image. The quiet man with a secret past. I've got to hand it to you, you've got it all worked out." Brian gestured at the reception desk. "I'll leave you to get checked in. I've been out for a bracing walk along the clifftops, and I'm ready for a coffee."

Matthew, who'd been turning his head to follow their conversation, was suddenly roused into action. He grabbed his computer's keyboard and typed with renewed vigour. "Right. Before I get your key, Mr Hatcher, I just wanted to check something with your friend if that's all right."

"Be my guest," Edward replied.

"Thank you, sir. *Dr* Coyle, is it? I have you down on my system as *Mr* Coyle. Is that incorrect?"

"Yes. I prefer to go by my proper title. And before you ask, no, I'm not a medical doctor. I have a PhD."

"In that case, I need to update the system." Matthew scowled at the screen. "I'll do it later. Now, Mr Hatcher, you wanted a hand with your bags. I'll fetch them in."

"Oh dear," Brian said. "Edward, I hope those weren't your cases I saw outside."

"Why?" Edward asked.

Brian stifled a smile. "A small dog was passing by, a scruffy little terrier, and I'm afraid he cocked his leg against your suitcase."

Edward's cheeks coloured. "What?"

"Sorry to be the bearer of bad news. I'd have stopped the little brute, but I was too late. There was nothing I could do."

"Oh my God!" Edward pointed at Matthew. "This is your fault, you idiot! If you'd done your job properly, this wouldn't have happened. If anything's been damaged, I'll expect full compensation."

"But—"

"I don't want to hear any excuses," Edward snapped. "Just get out there and fetch my bags then bring them up to my room."

Matthew nodded unhappily. "Certainly, sir. I'll see to it straight away."

Edward held out his hand. "Key."

"Yes. Of course." Flustered, Matthew hunted through the items on his desk, his fingers made clumsy by his haste. At last, he produced a plastic keycard and slid it across the counter toward Edward. "You're on the fifth floor, sir. The views from up there are fantastic. They're our best rooms."

"Is there a lift?"

"I'm afraid not, sir. It's being renovated over the winter.

But we're very proud of our grand staircase. It's an original feature."

"I'm sure it is," Edward said. "And assuming I survive the ascent, where will I find my room?"

"That's easy, sir. Turn right as you leave the stairs, then head to the end of the corridor. You can't miss it."

"Thank you." Edward scooped up the card, then he nodded to Brian. "Nice to see you again. I'm sure we'll have time for a chat later."

"Definitely," Brian said. "I'll look forward to it."

Edward sent a stern glance at the beleaguered receptionist, then he strode toward the stairs. *Not an auspicious start*, he thought. *But surely, things can only get better.*

Read on - get hold of Dan and Alan's next adventure,
Murder Between the Tides,
which includes a Free Exclusive Story,
Mystery at the Hall
Murder Between the Tides

Find it on your favourite store
Murder Between the Tides
Visit: books2read.com/mbtt

GET THE PREQUEL FOR FREE

WHEN YOU JOIN THE AWKWARD SQUAD
- THE HOME OF PICKY READERS

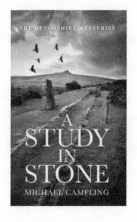

Visit: michaelcampling.com/freebooks

AUTHOR NOTES

IS EMBERVALE BASED ON A REAL PLACE?

The village of Embervale is very much a fictional construct, its locations pilfered from several villages and small towns. There's no single feature of Embervale that I can put my finger on and say where it comes from. The pub, the shop and so on are all amalgams of real places. It's true that I live in a village on the edge of Dartmoor, but there are only sixty houses in my village, and I wanted to create somewhere larger for these stories. I did take the liberty of using the fact that our house was once the village shop. I imagine Dan's house to be older than mine, and again, his house and the other properties, are probably based on the many old cottages I've visited. These little details help me to imagine the fictional setting in a way that I hope is authentic.

I have sketched out a map of Embervale to help me plan the routes that everyone takes. The map is not to scale, and it's rather rough and ready, but perhaps I'll be able to make it good enough to share with you all at a later date. I definitely want to create a digital version as I'm worried I might lose the paper version!

You may be interested to know that Fore Street is a common street name in Devon, so that was an easy choice for the street that takes Dan and Alan to the pub (and back).

OKAY, HOW ABOUT THE LOCALE?

To help me to ground Embervale in reality, I've located it quite near to the small village where I live, which is in the Teign Valley. There is something peculiar to living in a valley, and I say that in the nicest possible way. The sides of the valley and the course of the river define the landscape and affect our lives. There's one main road along the valley, and we rely on it to do our shopping, get to our jobs, go to school and so on. We have been snowed in from time to time, and we have to be prepared for power cuts.

As Alan claims, the valley seems to create a microclimate with a mind of its own. When the mist rises, it's quite spectacular to travel up the slope and look down to see the valley cloaked in a shroud of white. I once had a fantastic geography teacher who told us that on such days, it's possible to imagine the time when glaciers and great lakes were forming the landscape. I know exactly what he meant, and I think he'd be pleased that his lesson has lasted for so many years.

I use real places to surround Embervale, so as Alan says, there is a bridge near the village of Trusham where you can park while you walk along the river Teign (pronounced 'teen'). Exeter and Topsham are real, and sadly, there is a notorious trouble spot on the A38 at a place known locally as the Splatford Split. The road splits into two as it climbs a steep hill, and sometimes people veer from one side to the other with predictable results.

The town of Newton Abbot does have a B&Q (which is a DIY store), but I invented the Paradise Cafe, which is a shame as I'd quite like to visit it.

IS THERE SUCH A THING AS MAD HONEY?

Yes, this topic was all based on research. The rhododendrons that can lead to toxic honey are not common in the UK, but, as Dan and Alan figured out, Marjorie's honey wasn't toxic, she only thought it was.

WHAT ABOUT THE SPOIL HEAPS?

Like the neighbouring county of Cornwall, Devon was once mined for all kinds of metals and compounds, some of them toxic (or with toxic substances in the waste material). There are several spoil heaps in the area where I live, and it's up to the landowner to deal with them. I suppose they're expensive to remove, because these eyesores have been around for a long time. When the heaps contain heavy metals or other contaminants that are toxic to plants, the grey slopes are bare and forbidding.

I'm not claiming that there is a specific spoil heap in Devon that's contaminating the groundwater with arsenic, but I pieced together research from a number of studies to create a fictional scenario that could happen.

A MEAT RAFFLE? SERIOUSLY?

In many pubs, people really buy tickets to win meat. If the meat is from a local farm, it will almost certainly be vacuum-packed in clear plastic. Personally, I think people would rather win something more glamorous than groceries, but some traditions seem to persist beyond their best before date (much like the meat).

ARE YOU LIKE DAN/ALAN IN REAL LIFE?

Like Alan, I used to be a teacher, and like him, I'm a writer, but I see Alan as an entirely independent individual. He's a solid character, and the kind of person we'd all like to have as a friend. If your car broke down, Alan would stop and help you. He'd have all the right tools, and he'd get you back on the road. He's a gentleman.

Alan has always shared the billing. I wanted to make Alan an intelligent character in his own right, rather than a bumbling sidekick. From the beginning, it seemed important to have someone to act as a foil to Dan. At first glance, Dan isn't immediately likeable, but that's what makes their relationship interesting.

Similarly, I'm not Dan. Like him, I have worked in corporate finance, so I can identify with those parts of his life that have brought him to Embervale. But although I enjoy problem-solving, I've never lived in London, and I've never had Dan's restless energy nor his courage. I like to think that I'd get on with Dan – eventually. In his first outing, in *A Study in Stone*, Dan was a little irascible, but he'd just lost everything that had ever been important to him. He was a man who'd had everything and then discovered that it meant nothing. Since arriving in Embervale, he's gradually learning to live in a different way. At first, the rural pace of life drove him mad, but he's ready to reconstruct himself, and I think we have to give him credit for that.

I spend time dreaming up characters, and then I let them loose. Quite quickly, they become very real to me. I borrow some aspects of my life so that I can maintain authenticity. These little snippets of experience make the characters live and breathe, but these things are salt and pepper: added in little pinches to enhance a taste that's already there.

All the characters I write have sprung from imagination. I can't really say where they come from, but those of us who identify as born writers tend to be inveterate hoarders of experience. I listen to people in shops and cafes, I find myself watching people I meet, and it all gets stored away. Later, details emerge in new and unexpected combinations. It's a strange alchemy, but it's an interesting and rewarding form of creativity.

ARE THE POLICE PROCEDURES AUTHENTIC?

I felt very strongly that I wanted to write a murder mystery rather than a police procedural. I enjoy all kinds of crime fiction, but when you're setting out to write several novels, it pays to decide where your passions lie. I kept the police details down to the minimum, but I did research the procedures. In some mysteries, we see the police behaving in ways that would get them kicked off the force, and I wanted to avoid that trap. My aim was to make the police involvement realistic without letting it get in the way. There was some doubt over whether a murder had been committed, and since the police are generally overworked, their response seemed reasonable. I hope I got the balance right.

THERE'S A LOT OF BEER BEING GULPED DOWN – DID YOU INVENT THE BRAND NAMES?

All the beers mentioned are real. I thought it would be nice to lend a little support to local breweries. Part of visiting a place is to sample the local food and beverages, and when yomping around Dartmoor, you need to pop into a few pubs and try an ale or two.

I was introduced to Powderkeg Speak Easy by a nice chap at the vegan food market in Exeter. I knew Dan would like the vegan beer, but to add a twist, it's Alan who drinks it. Is he being influenced by his neighbour? He doesn't think so, but then, we're often reluctant to admit such things.

Kristen drinks gin distilled on Dartmoor, and this is quite a trend at the moment. Gin, vodka and even whisky are being made all over Devon. I hope everyone understands that Alan was joking when he claimed the stuff was made in Her Majesty's Prison Dartmoor.

Jail Ale, Gun Dog, Dartmoor Best – all real and all good stuff, but as with all intoxicating beverages, best drunk in moderation.

I've received nothing in return for mentioning these products and breweries, but if anyone wants to send me a free pint, let me know!

WILL THERE BE ANOTHER DEVONSHIRE MYSTERY?

Yes! The next mystery for Dan and Alan is *Murder Between the Tides*.

If you'd like to encourage me to write more mysteries, please tell your friends about these books. Also, online reviews can be very helpful, and I really appreciate them.

WILL YOU TALK TO MY BOOK GROUP?

Yes. It may even be possible for us to have a live video chat, although bear in mind that I'm on UK time. As a workaround, I can record a video and post it online so that you can all watch it. Please contact me via my website michaelcampling.com

CAN I FIND OUT MORE ABOUT YOUR SOURCES OF INFORMATION?

If you'd like to see some of the sources I used as part of my research, you can see a list of links on my website:
michaelcampling.com/valley-of-lies-sources

THANK YOU VERY MUCH!

If you've read this far, I admire your tenacity. I hope that these notes add something to the experience of reading the book. I really do appreciate your support. If you'd like to keep in touch, the best place is via my readers' group, The Awkward Squad, which you can find at: michaelcampling.com/freebooks

THANK YOU FOR sharing this imaginary world that we've conjured up between us, and I hope we'll visit it again very soon.

Happy reading and best wishes,
Mikey C.
THE OLD SHOP
DEVON
FEBRUARY 2020

ABOUT THE AUTHOR

Michael (Mikey to friends) is a full-time writer living and working on the edge of Dartmoor in Devon. He writes stories with characters you can believe in, and plots you can sink your teeth into. His style is vivid but never flowery; every word packs a punch. His stories are complex, thought-provoking, atmospheric and grounded in real life.

You can start reading his work for free with a complimentary mystery book plus a starter library which you'll receive when you join Michael's readers' group, which is called The Awkward Squad. You'll receive free books and stories, plus a newsletter that's actually worth reading. Learn more and start reading today at: michaelcampling.com/freebooks

ALSO BY MICHAEL CAMPLING

One Link to Rule Them All:

michaelcampling.com/find-my-books

The Devonshire Mysteries

A Study in Stone (an Awkward Squad bonus)

Valley of Lies

Mystery at the Hall (a bonus story)

Murder Between the Tides

Mystery in May

Death at Blackingstone Rock (an Awkward Squad bonus)

Accomplice to Murder

A Must-Have Murder

The Darkeningstone Series:

Breaking Ground - A Darkeningstone Prequel

Trespass: The Darkeningstone Book I

Outcast—The Darkeningstone Book II

Scaderstone—The Darkeningstone Book III

Darkeningstone Trilogy Box Set

ACKNOWLEDGMENTS

With special thanks to these advance readers: Saundra Wright, Janette Mattey, Josie Ingle Vail, Gary Webber, Phil Van Itallie, Rosemary Kenny

The cover was designed by Patrick Knowles. The book was edited by Andrew Chapman

Made in United States
North Haven, CT
16 June 2024

53694802R00232